# THE DESERT KING'S KIDNAPPED VIRGIN

## CAITLIN CREWS

# A SON HIDDEN FROM THE SICILIAN

## LORRAINE HALL

**MILLS & BOON**

First published in Great Britain 2023
by Mills & Boon, an imprint of HarperCollins*Publishers* Ltd,
1 London Bridge Street, London, SE1 9GF

www.harpercollins.co.uk

HarperCollins*Publishers*, Macken House, 39/40 Mayor Street Upper, Dublin 1, D01 C9W8, Ireland

The Desert King's Kidnapped Virgin © 2023 Caitlin Crews

A Son Hidden from the Sicilian © 2023 Lorraine Hall

ISBN: 978-0-263-30689-7

08/23

This ... per

Fo ...

Print ... ity

# THE DESERT KING'S KIDNAPPED VIRGIN

## CAITLIN CREWS

MILLS & BOON

# CHAPTER ONE

HOPE CARTWRIGHT WALKED down the aisle toward her groom, dressed in the requisite white gown and filled with nothing but a sense of relief.

God knew she'd earned it.

*Everything is fine*, she told herself as she walked. *Everything will be perfectly fine.*

Just as soon as she made it to the altar and said her vows. That was all it would take.

She blew out a breath, not surprised to find it was a bit shaky. And she kept her eyes focused up ahead on the man who stood at the head of the shockingly long aisle in this picturesque Italian wedding chapel, looking as grimly impatient as ever. He wanted this done as much as she did, Hope knew. Because this was the business arrangement they'd both wanted, as cold and calculated as it could get.

She could have been walking into something far more unpleasant, given her options and her desperate situation, and well did she know it. She doubted she'd thought of anything else in any serious way for the past two years.

Hope walked alone because her mother had, in her typical fashion, become so overset by the fact that Hope was actually marrying—*because everyone gets a happy ending except me,* she had sobbed in her childish way, quick to forget the last few years when she could nurse her feelings instead—that she'd drunk herself into something close enough to a stupor.

Except Mignon never lapsed off into an *actual* stupor. That was the trouble. Stupors suggested some measure of silence, and that was not her style. She was a storm, always. Sometimes wild with joy, sometimes distraught, but always and ever a storm. Accordingly, there had been scenes all morning as Mignon had turned Hope's preparations for this ceremony into a saga about Mignon's own choices.

This arrangement was as close to happy as either one of them was likely to get, Hope had tried to tell her. First Mignon had been mad with glee. Then the champagne had gone to her head and she'd simply been mad. Then had come the tears, the French love songs all sung off-key in honor of Hope's late father—Mignon's one true love—and last Hope had looked, Mignon had been passed out in a pile of butter-yellow chiffon, snoring off the bubbly.

Maybe that was as much of a happy ending as Hope could wish for.

She tried to remember what her severe groom had told her the night before when they'd indulged in a rehearsal right here in this ancient chapel that sat up above the sparkling waters of the famed Lake Como in Italy.

*It will not do to race down the aisle in an unseemly haste,* he had said in his usual repressive tones after she'd sprinted toward him from the antechamber.

*Even if I feel an unseemly haste?* she had asked, smiling.

Her husband-to-be was no love match for Hope. *Love* had not entered into the discussions. As such, he was not particularly interested in her smiles. He did not find her amusing, either, as he had made clear on numerous occasions already. Hope was a means to an end for him, that was all.

This was a good thing. Hope liked the fact that he required a service of her. So that she was not the only one selling herself here.

It also helped that he was not repulsive, like so many of the men who had auditioned for this particular role. Hope had wanted an honorable benefactor in the classic style. Someone she could rely upon and even feel safe with. Maybe there would even be some affection, in time.

Maybe it wasn't the charming fairy-tale prince she'd dreamed of when she was small, but if she'd learned anything since her father died, it was that life was not kind to childish dreams. Looking for a more businesslike arrangement that benefited her as well as the man in question seemed a practical and even lovely alternative, in its way.

Instead she had discovered that entirely too many men out there were nothing short of horrible.

Like the one who had called what she was doing a *virginity auction*. She had been at some pains to tell him that there was no *auction*, thank you. That such a notion was unpleasant and, anyway, not true.

What *was* true was that Hope was, indeed, a virgin. That, like so many things in her life, had been an accident, not any sort of morality crusade on her part. It was a twist of fate, nothing more. If her father had not died when Hope was barely turned fourteen, she imagined she would have had the same kind of adolescence her old friends at school had enjoyed. Silly parties and boys to giggle over instead of having to act as the adult she wasn't. Because Mignon, as delightful as she was most of the time, was sadly incapable of behaving like the adult she actually was with any regularity.

It had been down to Hope to sort out the funeral, then all the bills that followed. To do the best she could with the money her father had left and her mother's seeming determination to blow through it all at an alarming rate as she dealt with her terrible grief. Hope had been the one who'd sold off the family estate, sorrowfully parting with her father's staff, who had all been there longer than her, because she could not afford to keep them on. It had been Hope who had found the two of them a flat in London that Mignon wailed about on some maudlin evenings, because the neighborhood was questionable—Hope liked to think of it as *up-and-coming*—and what would people *think*, and what was next, the *poorhouse*?

Mignon kept clinging to the hope that even one of the men who partied with her, took advantage of her, or used her as they wished might love her if she let them do as they pleased.

They never did.

And so it was Hope who had to save them.

That was how she'd come to the attention of far too many obnoxiously wealthy and self-involved men since she'd turned eighteen. Her birthday present to herself, such as it was, had been leaving Mignon singing into her wine to meet her first potential contender. Hope had used her father's connections to put herself forward, but only to a very specific sort of individual. He needed to be rich, first and foremost, because while she felt that she might quite like to make her own way in the world, what mattered was that Mignon would want for nothing.

That was what Hope's dad would have wanted. No matter what flights of fancy her mother might commit herself to. No matter what Hope did or didn't do.

That was what Hope wanted too, because she loved her mother. And she understood, somewhere deep inside, that she had a certain grit her mother lacked. She had a fortitude while Mignon was made of pretty smiles and too much air. She had no head for reality.

Reality had been Hope's father's job.

Mignon needed looking after, that was the beginning and end of it. In return, Hope was prepared to sign anything. Any prenuptial agreement, any contract, anything at all. After two years out there on what only an optimist like her mother would call "a dating scene," Hope had *almost* convinced herself that she was well and truly prepared to be the virgin sacrifice she had learned a certain kind of man dreamed of finding.

After all, she had but two things that she could use to her advantage, according to far too many of the unpleasant men she'd encountered, having had to forgo any A levels to leave school at sixteen to take care of her mother as best she could: her father's august pedigree and the fact that Hope herself was entirely untouched.

Sometimes she almost thought it was funny, that the thing her friends had teased her about in the years since her father's death had become the only weapon Hope had, it seemed. The only possible way she could get *both* herself and her mother out of this mess.

Though she had taken her time coming to that conclusion, because it was so medieval.

Because she could always get a job, she'd told herself at first, the way normal people did. She sometimes thought about a glorious *career* the way she imagined some people dreamed of beach vacations in the Spanish sun. But the trouble was, Mignon could not do the same. Several attempts on her part had proved that, until Mignon had been forced to confess that she thought she was, perhaps, an idiot missing its village. Which had broken Hope's heart.

*In my dreams I am a fierce warrior for you,* Mignon had

whispered, working hard to keep a tremulous smile on her lovely, tearstained face. *While in reality I am a mess. Beyond redemption, I fear.*

*No.* Hope had been certain. Fierce. *Never that.*

That had left Hope to set aside any lingering Prince Charming fantasies—as well as any notions of a career, for that matter—and attempt to find a decent job that could support her *and* her mother when Hope had no work experience as well as no advanced education. But that was fine. She was scrappy. And while she had feelings, she was not buffeted this way and that by them, like Mignon.

She viewed this as a superpower, really.

But regardless of her feelings, and whether or not they ruled her, it had been a grueling two years of "dating" the sort of men who she found increasingly and almost unbearably unpleasant as time went on. Which was deeply unfortunate, as her dwindling funds made her more and more desperate to find someone—anyone—to help them, and running out of money meant she was running out of options.

Because one after another, the terrible men who took her out to such seemingly elegant dinners confessed their darkest and most furtive fantasies to her as if she'd *asked* for such intimate details, making it impossible for Hope to agree to any terms they might put to her.

One after the next, they made it impossible to do the thing she knew she had to do to save her mother.

And when she refused them, they took great pleasure in making it clear that her virginity was her only currency, and her pedigree a mere gloss to go with it.

She began to fear that sooner or later, she would have to marry one of them and do whatever their vile imaginations conjured up, somehow.

Two years ago, Hope had foolishly believed that she

would find the perfect solution to all her problems, and quickly.

After all, she'd started her search for the proper benefactor by aiming straight for men her father's age, many of whom she'd met when she'd been a little girl. The men who she'd known had precious little in the way of scruples. Because she knew precisely which ones had taken it upon themselves to offer her mother what they called *comfort*, while drooling, after the funeral.

Instead, she'd had two years of exploring precisely how twisted and appalling some men really were.

A lesson she would have preferred not to learn at all, though she supposed it was good she had. Since there were *so many* of them.

Lionel Asensio had been a breath of fresh air, she thought now, because it was good to remind herself of reality. And the fact she'd survived those two years without succumbing to those revolting suggestions she had found so impossible to imagine, much less imagine *doing*. She kept her eyes trained on him as she continued down the aisle, reminding herself further that this was an escape today. A victory. Because his notice of her had been a solution.

Finally, the kind—if cold—benefactor she'd been seeking all along.

Lionel Asensio had his own reasons for marrying in cold blood and in such haste. Hope did not care what those reasons were—she was merely delighted that he had them. She'd felt nothing but relief when he had actually wanted the gilt and gloss of her father's spotless pedigree. That the fact that the Cartwrights stretched back through the ages ever since the original cart-making owner of the name had been elevated from his humble origins by a long-dead queen had intrigued him the most. Even her mother had helped in that respect, for Mignon had been raised in a family that seemed unaware that there was no longer the sort of French aristocracy that had once led to any number of revolutions. She had been made to shine brightly, that was all, and that was what she did. From her still-pretty face straight down into her thoroughbred bones.

All of this had impressed Lionel Asensio.

Her innocence had not been part of the initial discussions at all.

And none of that mattered today. Today was a day to walk very, very slowly down this aisle and congratulate herself on her own grit, not worry overmuch about terrible men or once noble blood. Mignon was even now sleeping off the morning's excesses and would no doubt rise to dance again later this afternoon, flushed and happy that her daughter had wrangled the only thing Mignon had ever wanted in life—a husband.

As she walked without any undue haste, Hope was actually entertaining the notion of getting some kind of job after all. The wife of a billionaire like Lionel Asensio could create charities with a wave of her hand. She wouldn't have to worry about not having the proper qualifications to work in the nearest chip shop.

Hope could hardly wait to see what she was *actually* good at. Not what she was *forced* to do instead.

All it would take were a few vows. A few signatures on the contracts she'd already read over and agreed to verbally. So little, in the end, to be free at last. Really, her stone-faced husband-to-be was lucky she hadn't sprinted down the narrow stone aisle to get on with things more quickly, which she suspected he would find unseemly in every regard.

There weren't many people here today, which Hope was happy about, because this wasn't exactly an all-out celebration of whatever a wedding usually celebrated. *Fairy tales*, she thought, but not *wistfully*. She'd learned her lesson there. *Wistfulness* was about as useful as childhood fantasies about far-off princes and castles made of stone. She thought the entirety of the congregation, sparse as it was, were members of Lionel's staff—with the exception of one woman in the back, who was scowling from behind big glasses and looked like a library was missing its fearless leader. She entertained herself for a few slow steps by imagining that was a special guest of the groom, who might very well have hidden bookish depths that required a personal librarian on call, for all Hope knew.

What she did know for certain was that Lionel himself was a man of some renown, as most people in his tax bracket were. Wealth created its own legends, she had discovered over the past two years. She had been subjected to a great number of meetings with his PR team once she and Lionel had come to an agreement. They had decided how to fashion this strange wedding into a palatable romantic tale that could sell newspapers, appease the ever-nosy public, and serve Lionel's own ulterior motives.

Hope didn't care about any of that.

All she wanted was to get this over with, so that she could move at last into the next phase of her life. Maybe let herself grieve the loss of her father at last, now that she wasn't forced to deal with the fallout of losing him.

While she was at it, she planned to pay off the last of her mother's creditors and set up pensions for the loyal staff she had been forced to let go when she'd sold the family estate. She had promised them that if it was ever within her power, she would do exactly that. She'd been flattered back then that they'd pretended to believe she might when she hadn't believed it herself.

Now she could prove, at last, that she was more her father's daughter than her mother's. She loved them both, she truly did, but she did not want to think of how scared her mother had been these past few years. She did not like remembering how Mignon had sobbed and sobbed, too aware that her attempts to help only made things worse.

Hope had no intention of letting circumstances wreck her like that. Ever.

And she was imagining how good it would feel, to take care of the people who had always taken care of her—and walking slower than a snail, God help her, because it made political sense to obey her almost-husband's instructions as soon as she could—when there was a sudden great noise from the back.

Hope froze, her eyes closing of their own accord.

That would be her mother, no doubt. And there was no way Mignon could have slept off all that champagne and sobbing, so she would be wilder than usual—

Up at the head of the aisle, she saw the way her groom's jaw tensed, and she couldn't have that. Not until they were well and truly married, and all of this was done.

Never had she wanted to break into an impolite sprint for the altar more than she did just then, but Hope turned instead. She expected to find Mignon staggering toward her in some or other questionable state. Or dancing down the aisle, singing French lullabies.

She opened her mouth as she turned, prepared to try to redirect her mother, but Hope found herself unable to speak at all because it wasn't her mother who strode toward her.

It was a vision.

Her first impression was of light and heat. A kind of mad explosion that seemed to take place entirely within her.

It took her long, jarring moments while her heart clawed

its way out of her chest to understand that what she was looking at was a man.

But he was like no man she had ever beheld.

And she had spent these past two years becoming something of a reluctant expert on the species. This man was… not like the others.

This man walked as if his footsteps upon the ground were a favor he was doing for the stone floor beneath him and, perhaps, the earth itself. He was very tall, and though he was dressed in the sort of exquisite suit that could have made any form look perfect, she had an immediate and innate understanding that there was no sleight of hand here. His shoulders were truly that wide. He was *actually* made of all that muscle, lean and hard, and every step he took made it clear that unlike the sorts of men that Hope was used to, he used his body for hard, physical things.

*Hard, physical things*, she whispered to herself, a hot little echo that seemed to send a kind of too-bright, glittering burst straight through her.

But more than all of that—though *all of that* was a lot— he was dangerous.

She could feel that danger like a new, intense heat, like flames breaking out from the nave and taking over the whole of the church. And the strangest sensation swept over her, like her own skin had simply burst out all over into that same kind of fire. She would not have been at all surprised to find flames dancing up and down her arms, part of that fire that climbed and climbed, hotter and higher, the longer she looked at him.

Hope had some odd thought that perhaps he was a guest who had merely come late, that perhaps he knew Lionel somehow—

But even as she thought it, she realized that he was focused on her.

Only on her.

That meant she could do nothing at all but stare at him in return.

This was not a hardship, but her body reacted as if it was a *hard, physical thing* all its own. He had eyes of an unholy midnight in a face sculpted from bronze. He had a blade of a nose, dark brows, and a mouth so stark it made something inside her feel hollow, as if overwhelmed with the austerity she saw there.

So overwhelmed it made her shiver, and not because she was cold.

He bore down upon her and Hope knew on some level that it could only have taken a few seconds. His strides were so long, so deliberate. It could only have been one breath, maybe two, but it felt like an eternity.

An eternity of gazing at this man, this apparition, and all of that light and heat. An eternity of a kind of wonder as one explosion fed into the next inside her, making new and strange sensations burst into life all over her skin and then reach deep in her core.

An eternity that felt like fate.

Like a deep recognition when she was more certain than she had ever been of anything that she had never laid eyes on this man before.

An eternity—

But then he was *right there* before her.

And the whole world seemed to tilt and whirl, knocking her so far off its axis she felt as if she was spinning off into space—

It took her far too long to understand that he had lifted her up, tossing her over his shoulder as he spun around to march right back up that aisle again.

It took her too long because once again, all of that impossible sensation seemed to detonate inside of her.

That hard, muscled shoulder was making itself known against her belly with every step. Worse—*better?*—his hand was on her bottom, holding her fast.

She was reduced to a shiver with head dangling down against the hard stretch of his muscled back.

Surely she ought to…fight this, or something, she thought, but she felt no particular *urge* to do anything of the kind.

And she couldn't tell if anyone else was protesting—not when there was far too much ringing in her ears and a mad noise in her head. But by the time the thought landed in her, fully formed, they were already outside. She could feel the sweet Lake Como breeze that seemed to press against her face, making it clear to her that she was already far too hot for anything like comfort.

The man kept going, stalking away from the chapel and down the narrow old road—really more a path—that she'd walked up not long ago.

Hope felt dizzy and outside herself—yet no matter how she tried to lecture herself, she couldn't quite bring herself to cause a scene. To shout, make demands, or attract attention.

Everything shifted again, a rush and tumble. And she could hardly make sense of that, either, until he slid into the back of the vehicle where he'd tossed her, slammed the door behind him, and said something in a foreign language to another man at the steering wheel in front.

A foreign language that was neither the Italian a person would expect to hear while in Italy nor even the Spanish that was her almost-groom's first language.

She should have been terrified. Yet as the vehicle lurched away, Hope found herself blinking back the strangest rush of an emotion that certainly wasn't fear.

*Relief,* something in her pronounced, and though she told herself it was an accusation, it didn't feel like one.

Because if she was being spirited away, against her own wishes and without her own advanced knowledge or direction, she couldn't be expected to go through with her wedding, could she?

Deep down, she could admit that delighted her, because she didn't really want to marry Lionel.

Or anyone else.

And, sure, this felt a great deal like a frying pan into the fire moment, but if she had learned anything in these last, difficult years, it was that she should always take time to mark the little victories. No matter what.

Because they were few and far between, and needed celebrating when they came.

Mignon had taught her that.

"Do not attempt to escape," the man beside her told her as if she'd lunged for the door. It made her think she should have tried, at the very least, for appearances' sake. Especially because she couldn't quite *look* at him. Not directly. He was too…. beautiful, yes, in a harsh kind of way that made her think of a storm. As implacable as he was stunning, and she found she had no place to put that.

"We will be in the air within the hour," the man continued in that same forbidding way that she really shouldn't have found so…*compelling.* "Nothing and no one will stop us. And anything but the strictest obedience on your part will be met with consequences I doubt very much you will like."

"Well," Hope said, mildly enough, looking down at her hands. She thought her hands ought to have been shaking, though they weren't, and moved them against the skirt of her gown to feel its smoothness against her palms. She had gone for very little adornment because even the faintest embellishment had felt romantic and this wedding had been a business arrangement, nothing more. "That's me told, then."

Beside her, she could feel the man shift, and was aware of his affront even before she glanced over to confirm it.

"This is who you are," he said in a low voice that was rich with a kind of betrayal that made her stomach flip, even though she couldn't understand it. Not from a stranger. "You do not even care what man claims you, do you? You flit from one to the next as if it is nothing."

"This was a bit less of a flit," she pointed out, trying to focus slightly to one side of his outrageously handsome face because all of that hard bronze was too distracting. "And a bit more of a kidnap, really. So it's not exactly sporting to hold me responsible for it, is it?"

And it was only as she said that out loud that the truth of what was happening really rushed through her, like some floodgates had opened deep within. When Hope hadn't even known that she *had* floodgates. She would have said that all such emotion had been carved out of her years ago.

*That's just what happens when you're desperate*, she told herself tartly.

In her desperation, Lionel had seemed like a savior. He was not unpleasant. He was not even unkind. He was businesslike all the way through and his wanting to marry her saved her from far worse fates. Hope knew that well enough, though she hadn't wept with joy when she'd agreed to marry him the way her mother had. But she could admit that she'd felt some measure of peace, and even happiness that she'd managed it. That she'd saved Mignon.

And herself in ways she hadn't imagined she'd need to when she'd started this journey two years ago.

But at least she'd *agreed* to her deal with Lionel. She hadn't agreed to *this*.

"You are mine," the man beside her told her then. "You will spend what remains of your life in the palm of my hand. And your behavior alone will dictate whether my hand remains open or closed up tight, like a fist. But hear me now that this will be the only choice remaining to you."

Hope nodded along, the way she'd learned to do when powerful men spoke, only realizing when he frowned at her that this was probably not the correct response. Not when he was very clearly issuing a threat.

Because it was most certainly a threat, she had no doubt about that.

What this man did not seem to understand was that she had creditors whose threats were far more concrete.

"I can see that I'm supposed to cower," she said then, helpfully. "But if I can be honest here, is there any way we could just skip this part and get to what you actually want from me? It's only that I had a very dramatic morning. And as much as I appreciate being carried off from a wedding I wasn't exactly thrilled with in the first place, I really am going to have to go back. There is my mother to consider."

The frown on the man's beautiful, arrogant face had turned into an open scowl that deepened with every word. "You are never going back. Was I unclear?"

"You were perfectly clear. It's just that it won't work," Hope told him, matter-of-factly. "It's not you. This is really a wonderful kidnap. Very overwhelming, I promise you. It's only that I'm pretty much dead inside, so I'm afraid that mustering up tears and caterwauling and whatever else you might have been expecting is beyond me. And again, there is my mother to consider. There is always my mother, you see. I love her. And I promised."

She thought of the fond way her father had gazed at Mignon and how he'd said, his voice so affectionate, that one day he hoped that Hope would love her and care for her when he couldn't. *I always will,* Hope had assured him, because she had always wanted to do anything and everything her father wanted. And because she'd loved her delightful, always happy and usually silly mother beyond reason.

Beside her, the man was silent for a moment—but in a way that she could only think of as *thunderstruck.* And not in a good way.

"Do you know who I am?" he asked, his voice a bare ribbon of sound.

"I don't think anyone asks that question and expects the answer to be no," Hope said apologetically, "but no. I don't know who you are. Should I?"

"My name should ring inside you like a bell," he told her, his voice seeming to fill the whole car. "I should be the only thing you see when you close your own eyes. The barest hint of my approval should be the sun your whole earth moves around."

Hope blinked at that. "Goodness. That's…specific indeed." She tilted her head to one side. "I didn't even think to ask. Were you just wandering around local chapels today or did you specifically come for me? I'm Hope Cartwright, if that helps. And I don't want to be rude, but I think you have me confused for someone else."

He lounged in the seat beside her and she had the stray thought that no man she'd ever met could have seemed as brutally elegant as this one did. He was dressed like any of them, so it wasn't his clothes. It was something about him. He was wrapped up in a kind of ferocity that made all of her nerve endings seem to *sing out.*

And keep right on singing.

"You are Hope Cartwright," he said, not as if he was sounding out the name. But as if he was confirming her identity. *As if,* something in her thought then, *he is speaking me into existence.* When it was her mother who lived by the Lewis Carroll rule to think of at least six impossible things before breakfast, not Hope. "The woman who was promised to me at her birth and who has instead spent these last years making a mockery of that promise."

She could not seem to breathe. He only shook his head. "Did you really believe that I would allow you to marry another? I am Cyrus Ashkan, Lord of the Aminabad Desert, and what I have claimed will never belong to another. This I promise you."

And despite herself, Hope felt those words inside her.

Very much like a single bell ringing, low and deep.

But she shoved that aside, because there was nothing in her life that left any space for *bells.* Or this man with eyes like midnight and the way he looked at her, as if he had yanked her out of the life she knew and into some solar system where there was only him.

What did it say about her that she found the notion… oddly comforting?

Hope didn't know, because everything always came back to the same place. Some people got to spend their twenties wafting about in search of various identities to try on and discard. They got to take the geographic tour, moving from one place to another, one job to another, one party to the next. Always betting that by process of elimination alone, they might figure out what to *do* with their lives.

Yet Hope had never had that option.

So she smiled at the impossible blade of a man beside her as if nothing could touch her or bother her—not even her own abduction.

"You can claim me all you like," she told him calmly enough, even as the car raced away from Lake Como. "That sounds great, actually. But I will require that we carve out certain concessions in any contracts we sign. That's as a baseline." He seemed to stare at her without comprehension, and somehow, it seemed perilous to keep going. But she did. "Mostly it involves allowances for my mother. Nothing too onerous, I assure you."

The car had been careening through the narrow roads of the Italian countryside, but it stopped now, in the middle of a field where a huge helicopter sat. Hope didn't have to ask if it was his. She knew it was.

She waved a hand at the sleek machine as if she didn't know or care that it would fly her away from Italy and there was precious little she could do about it. Part of her was glad of it, if she was honest. She even smiled a bit wider. "Especially not for man who has one of these on call."

And Hope wasn't at all prepared for what happened inside her when all Cyrus Ashkan, Lord of some desert, did was laugh.

As if she belonged to him after all.

# CHAPTER TWO

SHE WAS MORE compelling than he'd expected and Cyrus Ashkan did not care for surprises.

He arranged his entire life to make certain there were precious few.

In the case of Hope Cartwright, the insult had already been delivered. Accordingly, he had already decided exactly who and what this woman was to him.

He did not like the part of him that wondered if there might be another path, despite everything, now that he had finally met her.

Cyrus had not expected to find so much mystery in her gaze. He had not expected that lifting her into his arms to toss her over his shoulder would *grip* him the way it did. So much so that he could still feel his sex responding to her as if she were his lover instead of merely his possession— not even a prisoner.

For how could he imprison what was already his?

He had expected the gleaming blonde hair, like strands of competing gold in sunlight. He had expected her general comeliness, for he had studied it in too many photographs to count—but in person, she was…something else.

Something unexpected, damn her.

There was a surprising hint of steel about her, as if beneath the pretty picture she made and her sort of English rose loveliness—exactly what he had taught himself to hate, as it reminded him of his own mother's softness and the childhood he had long ago disavowed—her architecture was as unyielding as his.

He dismissed that immediately, of course.

But no matter what it was, or wasn't, she surprised him.

As did her curious defiance. He had expected wailing, temper tantrums, tears.

He had not expected…this quiet negotiation. This total lack of fear. The notable absence of any apparent guilt that she had turned her back on the promises her father had made and the deal he had made with Cyrus's grandmother, for the Kings of the Aminabad Desert had always wedded in this way.

If he didn't know it to be impossible, Cyrus would be tempted to imagine she truly did not know who he was to her.

But that was absurd.

He reached over and wrapped his hand around one slender wrist, disliking intensely the way so simple a touch exploded within him. Her skin was too soft. And there was the sense of some kind of innocence about her that he knew was a lie, no matter how he might wish it otherwise.

"Come," he growled at her.

She only smiled. That did not help.

Because his sex did not seem to know the truth of her when he was afraid he knew it all too well. But then, Cyrus was King of a harsh and unforgiving land. He was not ruled by any man alive and he did not take direction from his sex, either.

He was still laughing at the very idea as he tugged her from the car. He marched her over to the black helicopter that waited there for his next command, then led her inside. They would fly north to Germany where one of his jets waited, and only then would they fly out to the deserts he called his own.

Leaving enough international smoke and mirrors behind them that her would-be husband, a man of no small wealth in his own right, could not hope to find them.

He expected her to pitch a fight as he ushered her into her seat as the rotors began to spin, but she didn't. Instead, Hope came along in a manner he could only describe as *happy*.

As if she could think of nothing better to do on her wedding day then participate in her own abduction.

That, too, was not what he'd expected.

Cyrus told himself that this meant only that she was far more treacherous than he'd imagined. For surely she was recalibrating, that was all, and intended to try her hand at negotiating with him further. As if contracts had not been signed years ago.

But as the helicopter took off, shooting up from Lake Como and carrying her away from the site of her latest bit of perfidy, she didn't seem the slightest bit concerned. She didn't look back at the scene of what would have been the ultimate betrayal—longingly or otherwise. She didn't even fire questions at him.

Hope simply sat in her seat, folded her hands in her lap, and then closed her eyes.

Very much as if she was taking a nap.

Cyrus sat beside her and seethed.

But then, he had been seething for two years now, because he held the vows he made as sacred. If he did not, he would have married long ago instead of waiting for the bride he had been promised. He was owed this debt.

Though she had not been meant to come to him until she was either of age or out of university, he had imagined that once her father died she would reach out to the man she been given to and ask for his aid. She had not.

And then, when she had finally turned eighteen, she had

embarked on an enterprise he could only assume had been directed right at him.

She had delivered insult upon insult. A lesser man might very well have taken personally the stain upon his name, but Cyrus was a benevolent lord. That didn't mean this woman who had been promised to him might not wish for a great many different avenues of deliverance all the same.

Because he was owed a debt and he was calling it in.

Her eyes remained closed beside him, but Cyrus stared down at the land below him as the helicopter flew north, low over the mountains and across parts of Switzerland and Liechtenstein before making its way into Germany.

He wanted no part of this place.

He preferred the stark honesty of the desert sands, as he had been well taught. The simplicity of the life that could, at any moment, be snatched back by the elements. A life where softness was nothing short of deadly. His father had hammered this point into him, again and again.

A place where kings had always ruled and always would.

Cyrus had taken the sins of his mother, each and every one trotted out before him by his father who claimed she had betrayed him, and used them as a cautionary tale. He had allowed the tumult of his early life to teach him and he never took the lessons he had learned at his ruthless father's side for granted.

Indeed, those lessons had always been and would always be his guide in all things.

To this day, he counted himself grateful that he had been saved. That his had not been a destiny of betrayal and boredom like the too-soft woman who had dared attempt to steal him from his father when he was still a boy.

Even if it astonished him that the woman beside him now, the Englishwoman he would never have looked at twice had it not been tradition that he honor his grandmother's promises, did not seem to know that vows in his part of the world were like iron. They did not, could not bend.

But he would show her.

Whether she liked it or not, she would learn.

Just as he had, long ago.

In Germany, the weather was wet and much colder than in Italy. He spoke to his men in a low voice as he climbed out onto the tarmac and ushered his stolen bride toward the jet that waited for him there.

"Gassed and ready to take you home, sire," his man told him in their language.

"Not soon enough," Cyrus growled in reply.

Once again, he expected her to cry foul. To put up some kind of fight or offer some measure of defiance. But she didn't.

Hope simply let him tug her along, almost as if she didn't care where she was going or with whom.

He laughed at that, too, though it was a sound devoid of amusement—because she would learn. There were any number of so-called men littering the cobblestone streets of these European cities. There were men everywhere, all of them making their claims to some power or another, as men always did.

But there was only one Lord of the Aminabad Desert. There was only one Cyrus Ashkan.

And well would this woman come to know what it cost to defy him.

He had not expected to want her at all, though he'd intended to do his duty, as always. He'd expected that her offenses would mark her unattractive in his eyes no matter how pretty she was, but that did not appear to be the case.

It was not that she didn't offend him, of course. She did. She wore a wedding gown, had been walking down an aisle in a chapel to marry another man. How could he be anything but offended?

The trial was that he still wanted a taste. And the fact that she was not behaving the way he'd expected she would only made it worse.

"Sit and prepare yourself for takeoff," he ordered her curtly once they boarded. "We will not stop until we reach the desert."

He did not specify *which* desert as, to him, there was only and ever one.

"How delightful," she chirped as she swept to the seat he indicated. "I've only ever been to Marrakesh, where one is always going on about the desert without ever actually sticking a toe in the sand."

And if she noticed his scowl at her temerity, she ignored it.

Cyrus settled himself and then watched her closely as the plane taxied down the runway, then made its smooth jump into German airspace. He studied her for clues as the plane made a slow, lazy turn to head south. Hope sat in the seat opposite him, her hair clipped back by some or other set of quietly elegant jewelry and that white dress gleaming.

Like a reminder. Like another insult.

Not that he needed his memory jogged on that score.

He waved a hand when the plane steadied on its course, and his attendants hurried to set out the in-flight meal he normally preferred. A selection of meats and hard cheeses, the fragrant flatbread his people made in the heat, and the filo dough tarts stuffed with something sweet. He indicated the plate before her when all Hope did was stare down at it.

A lot like she'd never seen a meal before.

"Let me guess," he said, and he did not try particularly hard to keep the censure from his voice. "Like so many women, you prefer to starve yourself for attention."

"Oh, I would love to starve myself," the impossible woman replied. And she seemed to mean it, it had to be said. "I've tried and tried. It turns out that I don't really have the knack. I've always preferred to eat my feelings whenever possible."

Then, as he watched in no little astonishment, she dipped the flat, dull knife the attendants had provided her into the pots of butter and jam, slathering both all over the flatbread before her. And then, holding his gaze with an insolence that left him rigid in astonishment, she took an enormous bite.

More, she then seemed wholly unfazed as they both sat there while she chewed and chewed, even having press her fingers over her lips to keep the enormous portion of bread and butter and jam within.

Like a child, Cyrus thought.

But the true outrage was that his body did not consider her any kind of child. Not in any respect.

He thought that would be the end of her games. He assumed that at any moment she would show some sign that she understood the precariousness of her position here, but glare at her though he might, she continued to eat her fill.

With what looked a great deal like pure, unselfconscious delight.

And only when she cleared the plate before her, filled it again, and then picked her way through the better part of the tray besides did Hope sigh happily and sit back in her seat. Fell back, more like, he thought darkly as she sighed again.

With every appearance of deep and total contentment, one hand slung over her middle.

"I can't remember the last time I really ate anything," she confided, as if he had inquired. "Left to my own devices I would make sure to keep my stomach full at all times, because I do tend to act out when I'm hungry, but my mother wouldn't hear of it when there were dress fittings to consider. I feel as if I've been fasting for weeks."

"Nerves?" But unlike every last one of his men and most of his subjects, Hope did not react to the ice in his voice with instant obedience and respect. "I hear they are common in brides."

That languid hand made a line through the air between them. "Hardly. Or not the way you mean, I think. It's just that managing my mother takes a good bit of effort and it can sometimes be difficult to slot in meals around her."

And Cyrus was hailed far and wide for his ability to see the truth of a man at a glance. To know the truth of whoever dared face him, no matter how unpleasant or hidden. Because of this, he had maintained a constant peace with his neighbors no matter how many new rulers rose and fell in those lands. Aminabad ever remained.

This was one of his great talents in this life, this discernment that had served him so well while he ruled. But he could not, for the life of him, make any sense at all of the girl before him.

Instead he found himself noticing tiny, unimportant details that he should have considered beneath him. Meaningless details, like the fact that her eyes seemed laced with gold and seemed far more intriguing than the more prosaic shade of muddy hazel he had expected. It was the way they shone, perhaps. As if she carried untold treasures inside of her.

He was, equally, not best pleased with the curve of her cheek or the way her lips tipped upward, making it look as if she was smiling all the while. No doubt smug and happy in her many betrayals.

And then there was that curvy figure of hers. She was not one of those lean, willowy tree trunks—much like his reedy mother, betrayer though she was, and that whole side of his family, though he did not like to think of his child-hood years at her side—that some men found so attractive. Hope was a lush little creature with the kind of hips real men appreciated. Not only because they suggested a woman would bear children well.

She possessed the wide hips and ripe breasts that en-hanced pleasure, and childbearing was secondary to such pursuits. His own palms itched to test the weight of the breasts she wore strapped into the bright white bodice of her gown. And though her waist nipped in, it only made him want to span the width of it with his hands, then see how the flare of her hips felt in his grip.

He had not expected this overwhelming *need* for her. He was having some trouble accepting that he could not brush it aside as he did so many of the things he desired in this life, second always to the demands of his people, his position.

For no reason he could fathom, he remembered how he had once yearned for his mother when he had been taken from her so suddenly, and the way she had always sung to him, crooning and nonsensical songs she made up as she went—

But over time he had turned his back on nonsense and found reason instead.

He no longer permitted himself childish things, and yearning was one of them.

"Have you no questions?" he demanded when he de-cided he had glared at her long enough, the ferocity his voice a shock to his own ears. The fact that Hope did not seem to notice only kept him on edge. "Do you accept, so easily, simply being removed from your life? On such a day as this?"

"What would you have me do?" And though her tone was easy, there was that hint of something flinty in her golden gaze. It reminded him that she was not so easygoing as she pretended. "Should I have wrestled with you, a man who must outweigh me by some hundred pounds? There in your vehicle, or here, surrounded by your men? Have would that go for me, do you think?"

He didn't like how rational that was. "And so instead you simply…accept your lot? I had no idea you were so meek, Hope. I find myself even more deeply amazed that you took it upon yourself to break the contract between your family and mine."

She took a moment to study him then, and he should have found that satisfying. Surely, at any moment, he would see a dawning awareness break over her features. Then it would begin, he told himself. She would beg him for mercy. He would give it, though he did not intend to forgive her.

*"Forgiveness is for the weak,"* his father had thundered at him, again and again.

Which was not to say Cyrus did not wish to hear her excuses, for he did.

But instead she only lifted a shoulder, a gesture so disrespectful that she was lucky that his men were not here to see it.

"I know of no contract between your family and mine," she told him. Dismissively, if his ears did not deceive him. "But then again, I don't know who your family is. Still, if there were contracts lying about, I would have seen them. Assuming when you say *my family* you mean my father." Then she laughed. "What I'm certain of is that no one attempted to make a contract with my mother. For anything. Might as well throw stones at the moon, and between you and me, you'd getter better results that way."

Though she sounded almost…indulgent, to his ears.

"I have told you who I am." And there was something in Cyrus then, far more wintry and frozen than a man of the desert should have been capable of. "My father was Lord of the Aminabad Desert before me, though I believe he was more commonly known as King Hades in your gutter press."

"King Hades." She repeated the name, then blinked. And then, as he had known she would, she sat up straighter, her head cocking to one side. "You don't mean that you...? That you are...?"

"The one and only," Cyrus replied coldly, though he could admit there was a certain satisfaction that, at last, she knew him.

"But you had a different name. You were not called *Cyrus Ashkan*. You were known instead as—"

"I am, according to some, Justin Arthur Cyrus George. Then a viscount. Now an earl, or so I am told."

She was already nodding along, looking more animated than she had since he'd stormed down that aisle in an Italian church and removed her from that wedding that should never have taken place.

"Viscount Highborough," Hope breathed. "Earl Alcott. I know that story. Everyone knows that story." But she seemed to think she should tell it to the person who knew it best, sitting up and leaning forward. "Your mother was one of the great supermodels of her time and also happened to be from the British aristocracy. Her face was everywhere—until she met your father at some event and they fell madly and instantly in love. He swept her off into his desert kingdom, and everyone expected them to live happily ever after. But they didn't. She only stayed there for a little while. A year? Two?"

"Five," Cyrus corrected her softly.

"And then, when they were back in England visiting her family, she ran off with the King's baby." Hope blinked, presumably because she recalled who she was speaking to. "You."

"Me," he agreed.

"I don't really know what happened then. But it was years, wasn't it?"

"I was four," Cyrus told her, his voice as even as he could make it, though he could not imagine why revisiting these memories should affect him. Why those old songs should move in him again, when he would have told himself he'd long since forgot the melodies. "For the first year after my mother left him, running off under cover of night, my father attempted to fight her out in the open. But she came from a very old family. She was the only child of the old Earl and thanks to him, there was no relief to be found in an English court."

"What did he do?"

"He waited. Because what my mother did not understand is that the people of the desert do not recognize time. There is only sand. Sun. And stone that is slowly and inexorably washed away by the exposure. I was twelve when my father and his men liberated me from captivity."

"That's not quite how I heard the story told," she said, and Cyrus could not place her tone. It sounded almost… But no. Who would pity a king? "They kidnapped you. It became an international incident."

"There were those who wished for to become such a thing, yes," Cyrus agreed. "But it is one thing to sit in the concrete streets of London and declare this or that to stir up the British populace. It is something else again to find one's way through the treacherous Aminabad sands. No one managed to do so. My father kept me hidden for six more years so that my mother could enjoy being without her child the way that he had been forced to do."

"That sounds difficult." But there was something about

the way she said that, as if her sympathies were not where they should have been.

"It was just," he told her. "And when I was of age, I could do as I pleased without worrying about being kidnapped by my mother. I returned to that cold island so that I too could enjoy this education that men must have to convince other, lesser men that they are equals."

"I saw a documentary about it," she said quietly. "Your mother's position is that your father poisoned you against her."

"She is the poison," Cyrus retorted, mildly enough. "As I told her myself before I started university in England, the better to disabuse her of any fantasies that we might enjoy some sort of reunion. But as long as she poisons only herself with it, what should I care? I know the truth of things. But my mother's deficiencies are not the point of telling this tale, Hope. I require neither your sympathy nor your concern."

"Noted," she said, but her expression was nothing but smooth when he frowned at her.

He pushed on. "While I was at Oxford, my father and I agreed that it would be a work of strategic importance to put to rest, once and for all, the notion that my father's quarrel with my mother was my country's quarrel with England."

"That makes sense." She shrugged, and he thought her deeply unserious, which he would have told her if he'd imagined she'd take it as the insult it was. But she was too languid, waving that hand as she did. "Nobody likes a quarrel."

He should not have found her fascinating, quite against his will. It would have been easier to shrug off the promises he had made. He had considered doing it many times in the years since her father had died, given her seeming disinterest in the promises that bound them together.

But breaking promises was something soft, weak, poisonous creatures like his mother did, claiming it was a virtue. Claiming she was saving them both, Cyrus and her, long ago.

Cyrus had made himself a man who did not make promises he did not keep.

No matter what.

"I could see the wisdom in the strategy," Cyrus said reprovingly now. "Given the legal skirmishes my parents had engaged in when I was younger. And so my father's mother—also an Englishwoman, as is tradition—approached your father and the two of them came to an agreement. This has always been our way."

"This promise you say he made." Hope shook her head. "I told you, I don't know anything about it. And even if I did, he's gone. I wish he wasn't, but one thing I've learned is that wishes do not come true."

"We are not speaking of wishes," Cyrus told her with a certain quiet ruthlessness.

If his tone troubled her, she did not show it. "And I know they don't come true, because I've tried. Again and again and again."

There was something in the way she said that. It made its way beneath his skin when he should have been immune.

Perhaps that was why he sounded so severe when he continued. "It is not a wish, but a fact, that your father promised your hand to me on your eighteenth birthday. Or, if you took it upon yourself to go to university to educate yourself, upon your graduation."

She made a soft little sound. "He didn't. He wouldn't. Would he?"

"He did. And yet you were walking down that aisle to marry another man." He found he was leaning forward himself now, his gaze so intent on hers it almost felt as if this was a kiss. *Almost.* "Quite as if no promises had ever been made at all."

# CHAPTER THREE

THIS WAS BEGINNING to feel like a bit of a roller coaster and Hope had never been any kind of fan of amusement park rides. She didn't even like a too-fast car, much less the games some liked to play on small watercraft.

No, thank you. She liked her stomach to stay put.

But that didn't appear to be an option available to her today.

Not when the most beautiful man she'd ever encountered had not only snatched her out of the jaws of her own wedding, but claimed she'd been promised to him, too. Wholly unbeknownst to her.

"That seems a bit harsh," she pointed out, while her stomach put on a little bit of a show inside her. She would have told herself she was hungry, that was all, had she not stuffed herself. This was...a different sort of hunger.

"Does it?" Cyrus sounded wholly unrepentant, his midnight eyes dark. "I would have said that the breaking of promises was far harsher than any discussion of them. But I am an elemental creature, as you will soon discover."

Hope thought she was doing pretty well, trying her best to make sense of what was meant to be her step forward into the role of wife to a stranger that had taken a dramatic left turn into the clutches of Cyrus Ashkan, a man who had been his own soap opera, back in the day. Who hadn't pored over every article? Every picture? Every questionable tell-all from supposed staff?

Her own story paled in comparison to his. First she'd been frog-marched from car to helicopter, helicopter to plane. Then she'd been…fed, which did not seem to fit with the frog-marching. Then he'd told her the story of his own infamous kidnapping, though he didn't seem to view it the way the rest of the world did. *He* did not seem to mind that no one had laid eyes on the boy Cyrus had been for all of those years. *He* appeared to be under the impression that his mother was the villain.

His mother, who had never modeled again, had been seen in public only when petitioning various members of the government to take up her cause, and who had been considered a study in parental grief ever after.

Especially once Cyrus had reappeared and had been nothing short of scathing toward her and about her.

But all of that, as sensational as it was, paled in comparison to the notion that her beloved father had married her off to some stranger long ago, then had never mentioned it again… Though, of course, he had intended to live.

He would have thought he had time.

Oh, how she wished he'd had time—

Hope decided she couldn't possibly think too much about that part of it. Not now. Not yet. Not until she knew what she was in for.

Hope was inclined to wonder if this was all some kind of pre-wedding dream she was having, trying to save herself at the last minute from a marriage that was certainly better than the kinds she'd assumed she'd likely have to suffer. But still wasn't exactly what she would call *desirable*.

After all, while Lionel Asensio had many fine qualities— mostly that he wished for her to play a very specific marital role for his family with very clear requirements, none of which were icky—it was not as if, deep down, Hope had *wanted* to marry him.

She wasn't thrilled about *this* turn of events either, no matter how good the food was. What didn't track was the way this man was looking at her as if she, personally, had made him promises. And then had recklessly and thoughtlessly and deliberately broken them.

It was almost funny. Truly, she almost laughed, because if she'd had the faintest notion that there was someone she could have run to she would have done it ages ago.

But Cyrus Ashkan was far too *elemental* to appreciate a bit of helpless laughter, she was betting. Particularly if it was at his own expense.

"If you believe that I betrayed you, then I don't understand why you would go to the trouble of ruining my wedding today," she pointed out. Very reasonably, to her mind. "You're well shot of me, I would have thought."

"This is your response?" He looked relaxed in the seat across from her, though that fire in his dark gaze told a different tale. "This is another inappropriate attempt at humor, I can only assume. Do you believe that this kind of defiance will be tolerated?"

"Until about ten minutes ago, I didn't even know who you were," she reminded him, gently enough. "I haven't given a lot of thought to what it is you will or won't tolerate." She shrugged—partially because the last time she had done it, his eyes had widened. As if he'd never seen such a thing in all his days. "Anyway, I can't be responsible for a promise or a contract or a handshake I didn't know anything about. My father never mentioned it or you. So, I'm sorry? I guess?"

And there was something about the way he stared at her then. Some level of unholy fury though he sat perfectly still.

Too still, something in her whispered.

As if his was the stillness of a great predator, a scant moment before it attacked. All that focus. All that *intensity*. And the scope of what was about to happen already visible in that dark gaze, if she dared look close enough—

Hope found herself holding her breath, wanting things she could not name, but he did not come for her.

Not then.

She told herself she was relieved, not disappointed, when instead he rose from his seat. Then stepped away, moving toward the back of the plane to speak in a language she didn't understand with his ever-watchful men.

The men she could admit she'd forgotten were even here.

Hope assured herself that her stomach was *fine*, not madly flipping this way or that *at all*, and settled further into her seat. Because she still couldn't think what, exactly, she should do otherwise. Despite the amount of action films she'd watched in her time, she doubted very much that a person who didn't have the slightest idea how a plane worked could land one.

And Hope needed to make sure she did not crash, nor get too caught up in the palm of Cyrus's hand or whatever he'd been going on about, because she still needed to save her mother.

As always, there was that…grief and helpless adoration inside her every time she thought about Mignon. Every time she thought about the past few years and how she'd been so sure her wedding would make it so they were both happy again—

But then, maybe that was why she wasn't reacting to this abduction the way she should have been. The way anyone else would have been, surely. This was the first time since her father had died that Hope could say, with complete honesty, that there was absolutely nothing she could do to solve this or fix this or make it better.

She couldn't *work harder* and come up with any sort of solution here. She couldn't *think out of the box* and make something happen. There was nothing to *do*. Sooner or later the plane would land. And maybe then she would feel slightly less relieved than she did now. Maybe she would feel fear. Or the stirrings of temper to paper it over. Maybe then she would once again take up the great worry she always usually felt about Mignon.

Maybe then she would ask herself how, precisely, this controlling man would let her care for her mother when he famously liked his own so little.

But her stomach was pleasantly full, no matter how he might have looked at her like a great big *thing* about to pounce. And the drone of the plane's engines was like white noise, lulling her as she sat there, letting the adrenaline drain right out of her.

And for once, there was literally nothing she could do for her mother except love her as she always did.

She would have to come up with something a bit more concrete once they landed.

Her eyelids grew heavier and heavier, or maybe it was that she could hear Cyrus's raspy growl of a voice from the back of the plane, so commanding, so intense, even using words she couldn't comprehend.

Either way, before she knew it, she had fallen asleep.

And then came awake again in a jolting hurry some time later—

Only to realize that it wasn't really *jolting*, it was the plane bumping along a deserted runway as it came in for a landing. Controlled jolting, anyway.

Hope was aware of too many things at once. The light,

pouring in through the plane's windows, so much brighter and hotter than anything she'd ever seen. She squinted out the windows to get a sense of where she was, but there was…nothing.

At first she thought it was an optical illusion, but then she realized. This was the desert. The blue sky above, the endless, undulating sand like some kind of sea, and nothing else.

In all directions, that same *nothing*.

And then there was Cyrus besides, standing in the aisle above her seat and looking at her with an expression she could not pretend to read.

"Oh," Hope murmured, scrubbing at her face with the heels of her hands. "I guess I fell asleep. That tracks. I haven't been doing much of that lately either."

"None of that matters," he intoned from on high.

Hope found herself sitting up a bit straighter, though she couldn't have said why she thought *her posture* would help here. It was something about the way he looked down the length of his body at her, as if looking down from some immense altar. Or mountaintop.

Or some impossible desert sky.

"It matters to me," she pointed out, because she couldn't seem to help herself. "The importance of good sleep habits can't be exaggerated, Cyrus."

"We have landed on Aminabad soil," he told her, and again, there was a certain cadence to the way he spoke. As if he was issuing proclamations. It was notably different from the way he had been speaking to her before. This was not…*speaking*. This was not *a conversation*. She understood that instinctively. "Allow me to welcome you to your new life, Hope Cartwright. *Hayati. Rohi. Omri.*" He intoned those words in such a way that she knew at once that they were endearments—and more, that he was making certain she heard the ironic way he was saying them. "You have been honored immeasurably, little though you deserve it, and are become my wife."

She wanted to laugh. But she couldn't, quite.

Not quite.

It all felt too fraught, somehow.

There was something in the way he studied her, with a suppressed sort of intensity—though she could see the gleam of it clearly enough, there in his dark gaze. She could see the way he held himself too still once more. She could feel the difference in the air between them. And there was something, too, in the way her body responded to that difference. It was as if she'd been plunged into a cold pool and was even now standing at the edge, shivering.

God—was she actually *shivering*?

Hope made herself stand up, though that put her perilously close to him. Too close, by far, to this intense and compelling stranger who spoke of promises broken. Of her as his wife, of all things.

Now that the plane had landed and there was nothing outside that she could see in any direction, save an endless expanse of waiting desert, she found she possessed far less equanimity than she'd felt in the air. When all she'd been able to concentrate on was the fact that she was not even now married to Lionel Asensio.

She couldn't really access the wild relief she'd felt then any longer. Mostly because, if she wasn't married to Lionel, that meant she still needed to sort out a way to take care of her mother. And herself.

At the same time, she didn't want Cyrus to know that. Not really. She didn't want him to guess that she didn't feel the same way she had since he'd swooped in and rescued her—and who cared how or why he'd come to do that? He'd done it all the same.

She would prefer it if he continued to think she was relatively unaffected by all of this.

Hope opted not to question herself on that.

"Did I sleep through our wedding?" she asked instead, aiming for the dry, amused tone that had come so naturally to her before. "I feel certain I would have woken up for a whole wedding ceremony. Given I'm already dressed for it."

Something she would not call a smile moved over his hard face and echoed inside her like a tuning fork. "There is no need for a wedding ceremony, *omri*. My word is law."

He stepped back then, and curtly indicated that she should step past him to walk toward the blazing light that it took her long, stupid moments to realize was the door to the outside. Hope cleared her throat and told herself it was the desert air that was even now drying out sinuses that had been born and bred in England's greenest, most humid hills.

It didn't occur to her not to obey him. She had not the faintest shred of a defiant thought. And when she realized that, she rationalized it away. Because what did she plan to do instead? Stage a sit-in on the plane? She'd bet that would end pretty quickly once they turned off the air-conditioning and she began to broil.

There was nothing for it but to march outside into all that blinding light, so that was what Hope did.

Because that was what she always did.

No matter how overwhelming a thing looked, she charged straight for it, because the only thing worse than an overwhelming thing was dreading it.

She made her way down the jet's stairs, finding her darling wedding slippers a rather poor match for the tarmac. And the whole *desert* situation. There was sand swirling this way and that every time the faint and inconstant breeze felt like moving it along. The heat was oppressive. It seemed to *glow* into her. It wasn't like a face full of sunshine. It was like the heat started *within her* and was setting her alight from the inside out.

Hope felt as if she was burning alive already and she hadn't even had time to sweat.

She felt Cyrus come down the stairs behind her, then stop—close enough that she had the panicked notion that she could actually differentiate desert heat all around her from the heat he gave off, and both heat sources were far too much for her—

Though thinking things like that could not possibly help her here.

The plane's door folded back in on itself and the plane began to move again, bumping slowly along the tarmac at first, then picking up speed. Then, too quickly for Hope's taste, hurtling itself off into the cloudless sky that seemed to press down upon them like a great blue fist.

She watched the plane fly away until it was a small dot on the horizon and her eyes hurt from the glare.

Or possibly also because she was trying her very best to keep tears at bay. When she never cried. Not since the night her father had died—because what was the point? It didn't bring him back. It didn't change a thing.

Still, that felt a lot like the wrong question to ask herself just now. Here on a rapidly disappearing tarmac, surrounded by shifting sand on all sides.

And the man who called himself *lord* of this alien place.

She didn't look at him. Not yet. She scoured the horizon instead, desperate to find something that whispered of civilization *somewhere*.

But there was nothing.

The endless, pitiless blue sky above. White sands in every direction, rising and falling like hills. Like waves.

Like the end of her, something in her whispered.

Yet that whisper didn't feel *too much*. It felt something much more like *right*.

Which might have been the most frightening thing of all, had she allowed herself to focus on it.

"Beautiful, is it not?" Cyrus intoned in that way of his, as if he was proclaiming it to the skies and sand. Imprinting them with his will.

"I can see how someone might find it beautiful," Hope hedged. Her lips were already dry and she truly couldn't tell if that was the desert air or her own mounting panic. "It's not what I'm used to, I can tell you that. So much sky. And all that *sand*. One expects a desert to be *sandy*, of course, but I still feel entirely unprepared for the *immensity*—"

She realized she was babbling and stopped herself in the next moment.

Even though it made her throat hurt.

She pressed her tongue against the roof of her mouth, hard, and made herself turn to face Cyrus. To squint at him through all this *light*. So much light that the glare of it felt like another source of heat, all on its own and apart from the temperature, scalding her eyes in their sockets.

That seemed as good a reason to feel faintly teary as any.

And looking at the man before her was not *soothing*, exactly. Nothing about him was *soothing*. He was his own immensity. He stood there, a dark slash of color against all that blue and white. His gaze was near black. His face seemed even more bronze, set against the landscape that pressed in on all sides.

He merely regarded her as if she was the curiosity here. As if she didn't fit, and she believed it. Because even though he wore a suit, she could tell that he belonged right here in this overwhelming place. That the desert had made him, no matter how many years he'd spent in England.

That he was made of the lonely sands, rolling on forever. That he was too expansive to fit beneath the gray clouds of England, the manicured fields, the old stone walls cutting the land into digestible parcels for too many centuries to count.

He looked like the desert, she thought, and then felt herself flush. Because she was being fanciful and that wasn't like her at all.

"I think I'm dehydrating as we speak," she told him, attempting to sound something close enough to cheerful. "In another moment I'll be a crumbling husk and the breeze will scatter me all over this tarmac until I'm indistinguishable from the sand."

For a moment Cyrus did not respond, and she thought he wouldn't. That he would stand here and watch as she blew away before him like dust.

"I do not expect you to appreciate the desert," he told her, and though his tone was bland enough she could see the faint disapproval all over him. A different sort of disapproval than the kind he'd been aiming at her since they'd met. This was less about vague promises he'd claimed had been made and more about *her*. What he clearly saw as the deficiencies in her character, immediately evident in the fact that she was not *instantly in love* with this stark, terrifyingly empty place. "I expected nothing else."

"Did you love it at first sight?" she dared to toss right back at him. Maybe it really was the dehydration setting in and collapse was imminent. "When you found yourself here again as a twelve-year-old, was your first reaction *joy*?"

His face seemed to harden, becoming more a part of that

glare. "My first and only reaction was gratitude that my father saw fit to return me to myself."

"Really. Not even the briefest moment—"

"But you will have ample time to get used to the sky and the sand," he continued, something cutting and ruthless in the way he said it. "As you will never leave this desert again."

That was clearly meant to land like a blow. And maybe it would have, if Hope had been anyone else.

But she had taken far too many blows in her time. Too many to even bother counting. This one didn't even feel like a blow. It was more like a kiss—

Not that she wanted to think about *kissing* when this close to him. In all his...*state*.

She didn't *quite* laugh, squinting off toward one or other impossible horizon. "*Never* is a long time."

"I told you. You are become my wife, Hope."

Hope opened her mouth to argue that point, but stopped herself. Because the *way* he kept saying that finally registered. It was...almost archaic, really.

Like another proclamation.

Like a law might sound in a place like this.

She was too hot to *shiver*, surely. "You keep saying that."

"I am anxious for you to hear me, Hope."

Yet she could not make herself believe, for so much as an instant, that this man was anxious about anything, nor ever had been. "I hear you. But I don't understand."

"This is the Aminabad Desert and I am its lord," he told her, a certain satisfaction in his tone. In his gaze. All over him, in fact. "What I declare becomes fact, and then is made law. That is the way of things here." When she only squinted back at him, he relented. Slightly. "If I say you are my wife, we are married. It is done."

Hope still thought she might topple over—and would have, probably, if she didn't think she'd sizzle like a proper English fry-up right there on the tarmac, and her here without a hangover that needed that kind of indulgent mopping up—but sighed instead.

"Felicitations to us both, then. I guess?" She found her hands on her hips, somehow. "I think you'd better tell me what that means to you, Cyrus."

Was that the first time she'd said his actual name? It felt illicit. Like stolen chocolate, melting on her tongue. She was sure she could feel the way his eyes blazed. As sure as she was that he felt it too, that melting.

Heatstroke, she told herself. That was all.

His dark brows arched high, command and condemnation at once, and no sign whatever of any reaction to the heat. "I don't actually know you. I don't know what you want in a wife. I don't know your feelings about marriage at all, much less what it means in a cultural sense in a country I've never visited before."

Hope really did laugh then, because it was that or give herself over to the heat. Her dry lips. That urge to cry, collapse, or both. That terrifying *melting* that felt worse than all of those combined.

She hurried on. "This might come as a shock to you, but I am something of an expert when it comes to various takes on the institution of marriage. I've discussed it at length, with all manner of people, and I can tell you that none of them agree. On anything, really. So when you tell me, in all your state, that I am *become your wife*—you're going to have to tell me what you mean by that. In detail, so there can be no mistake."

"You have already made the last mistake you will make," Cyrus told her, his voice a low and dangerous thread that she could hear all too well above the breeze. Above the sound of her own heart, pounding much too hard. "Your indifference to the promises made in your name has showed me your character, but I have chosen to marry you anyway. In time, I am certain you will thank me for this gift."

"Why would you *gift* someone you hated on sight?" Hope asked, and that was when the laughter she'd been holding at bay—possibly because it was a touch hysterical—bubbled up. "Surely it would have been easier to leave me to it. I certainly wouldn't have known any different."

"But I would have. And regardless of what you do or do not do, *I* keep my promises."

"That doesn't sound like much of a foundation for a marriage," she managed to say, not laughing any longer.

"And what was the foundation for the marriage you intended to embark upon today?" he asked, his brows high and his dark gaze intent on hers. "You could not wait to tell me it was no love match. That you were as happy to marry him, or me, as any other. By your own rationale, why should you care why I have chosen to elevate you in this manner?"

She wanted to tell him she didn't care. She wanted to sweep everything he'd said aside and focus on the things she did care about, like making sure her mother was cared for. She wanted to defend herself, though she wasn't even sure what accusations he was making—because he was right. Wasn't he? Why should she care who she married?

The again, she'd never encountered a man who got beneath her skin like this.

And maybe it was the heat. Maybe it was sunstroke. But she had the strangest, fairy-tale-like notion that it was possible she did the same to him.

That maybe, just maybe, she wasn't the only one feeling

all this. That if she dared reach over and put her hand on his chest, his heart would roar as hers did.

"Fair enough," she whispered.

He nodded, as if it was done. As if they were set in stone now, her and him. That, too, should have terrified her. "There is nothing left to you now but a life of quiet obedience, locked away from the world as if you were never here at all."

"You say that like it's a punishment," she managed to say, even producing a slightly less hysterical little laugh. "But it sounds like a holiday."

"It will be no holiday." There, before her, he seemed to grow in size. He was an immensity on par with the desert that surrounded them. His dark eyes flashed, the darkest midnight she had ever beheld. "It will be an exercise in humility."

"Cyrus…" she murmured, not certain what she wished to say to him. What she *could* say.

"I kept waiting for you to remember yourself," he told her. "To remember that you were promised to one who waited for you to come to him, but this never occurred. Right up to this farce of a wedding, which you should have known I would never allow to take place."

Hope could only listen to this in a kind of awe. Aware, on some level, that deep inside there was a trembling. Maybe even a yearning—to imagine that someone, anyone, had looked out for her these last years.

Though perhaps that was temper, not longing, that he had watched her over these past years and failed to intervene. Either way, she was completely unable to tear her gaze from his.

"It is lucky for you that you appeal to me, *omri*," he told her, and the strangest thing was that she really did feel lucky for a long, dizzying sort of moment. Then he kept talking. "I did not expect that you would, but I am happy to accept the gift of your body in return for the mercy I have shown you already, and the incalculable honor I bestow upon you by marrying you."

"Will my body truly be a gift in this marriage of yours?" She made herself ask the question, somehow not giving in to the trembling thing deep inside her that she was terribly afraid was not fear at all, but desire. Another thing she had never felt before. "Will it be mine to give—or not give? Notably unlike this kidnap?"

"You will beg to bestow this gift of yours upon me," he assured her, as if he knew. As if he could see the future. And the look on his face was so intense that she thought for a moment that she could see it too. Because the mad whirl deep inside her was unlike anything she had ever felt before in her life. Almost as if it really was a gift, these things he thundered at her so sternly in all this wild heat. "But you may be certain that I will never give you the gift of my sons."

Hope blinked at that, and maybe it was a welcome break from all those vast things inside her, changing her where she stood. "No gifts in the form of sons I didn't ask for. Got it."

Cyrus took a step closer, making her catch her breath. Then he reached out and took her chin between his fingers.

That was all. A minor touch, really. Nothing at all in the grand scheme of things.

But she could feel the strength of him, the heat. She knew without having to ask that he was a man who took pride in the fact he used his own hands. There was nothing soft on him. The was not so much as the faintest hint.

"I will enslave you with passion," he informed her, and even though the way he said that was almost remote, the look in his gaze was nothing short of a forest fire. And here in a place where there were no trees, the only thing that could burn was her. "There are few women on this earth who can resist the Supreme Ruler of the Great Sands, and I doubt very much you are one of them."

"Thanks for that," Hope managed to reply, though she felt dizzy again. And *on fire*. "That's something to look forward to, then. Supreme and sandy passion on command."

"I will use you and then cast you aside," he told her, almost tenderly. A new promise. "I will sentence you to a life of fruitless yearning in my harem, a drudge of a wife with no standing while the other wives I will marry give me many, many sons. This is the life you have earned, and you will thank me for it."

She heard him. On some level, she even understood what he was saying. Drudgery, yearning, unlikely expressions of gratitude on her end. But his hand was on her chin, his fingers pressing into her flesh. And all she could seem to do was tip her head back and gaze up at him, as if he really was as powerful as the desert sun.

Maybe more.

"R-right," she managed to stammer out. "Used and cast aside, no standing. With the passion."

It was the passion as punishment part she couldn't really get past.

The part that made something deeply feminine and knowing, tucked away in a place she'd never encountered within herself before, turn over and stretch. Like it was waking up after a long sleep.

Like it had been waiting there, just beyond desire, all the while.

But there was no time to worry about such things, *knowing* or passion or the kind of punishment that Cyrus still seemed to think sounded like something other than a luxury retreat. There was no time left.

He dropped his fingers from her chin. He raised his arm, up over his head in a grand sort of slashing motion, as if he meant to slice the sky above in two.

Bringing with it a pack of horses from behind the hills, descending upon them like riders on a storm.

Like fate.

And there was a part of her that was rightly overwhelmed. More than overwhelmed, as Cyrus swung her up into the saddle of a horse, then held her up in front of him, like the spoils of war.

But inside, in that part of her that was newly awake, she was smiling.

# CHAPTER FOUR

CYRUS RODE AT the head of the pack of fine Aminabad horses, as befit him as the Lord and King.

And he was not certain he had ever felt more like a desert king of yore than he did now. The merciless sun above, the sand below. His men at his back and a woman caught up before him, in that great white dress that billowed around them as his cavalry galloped with him over the dunes.

It was almost enough to make him wish his father was still alive, that the old man might see that he had achieved what he had always set out to achieve. He had made his only son over into an appropriate heir to this ancient, dusty kingdom, despite the best attempts of the mother who had stolen Cyrus away.

Yet as he rode, he found that he thought less of what he must do as King and more of the needs that rose in him—as a man. Because he had claimed this woman as his wife. Not merely some bit of sweet flesh for an evening's entertainment. And she sat before him, as wives and captives alike had done for centuries on horses like his, the lush curves of her bottom nestled up tight against his sex.

Making sure that ache in him only grew as the miles passed.

An ache he intended that she would soothe, though he had not lied to her. He wanted her, yes. That wanting had astonished and outraged him—that was also true.

But he wanted her to give herself to him, this woman who would marry another so cold-bloodedly.

He wanted her wild with wanting him.

She was fair, which would do her no good in the desert heat. And so he had taken the time to wrap scarves around her as they'd started their ride, covering her hair and the skin that already looked flushed from the sun's merciless rays.

But even though he knew those scarves protected her, he resented them.

For he could not see that delectable curve of her chin. Or the way she held her mouth, giving herself away in a thousand different small expressions he was not certain she even knew she made.

Yet he did. He knew far too much after an afternoon's observation of her. In person.

He could have headed to the south, where the heart of his country's wealth was arrayed around the oil fields that brought in the Western businessmen to try their wheeling and dealing and imagine they were cannier than the tribe who had been living off the bounty of this desert forever. There in the southern oases lay the commercial center of his country. The marketplaces, the businesses, and the many dwellings of those in his tribe who did not wish to follow the seasons north and south the way their ancestors had. He supposed they were cities, in truth, though he did not like that word.

But in any case, that was not where he was headed. He turned to the north instead, and made haste across the shifting sands for the fortress that had once been all that protected his people from their enemies.

He meant for it to do so again.

They rode hard, for the sands seemed restless today, and wise men never tested the will of the sands. They knew too well that if they did, they would lose—and usually more than any one man could bear.

It was a solid hour's ride, flat out, from the northern tarmac they only used regularly. For it was too easily swallowed whole by the dunes and was often lost, no matter how many men were dispatched to keep it clear.

The sands did ever as they wished.

That was one of the first things Cyrus had learned when his father's men had brought him here.

Today, like then, he saw the fortress first. He only rode faster at the sight, but he still knew the very moment that the woman in his arms saw it too. He felt something like an electric shock go through her body and he thought she might say something, but she did not.

And he wondered if she was having the same experience that he'd had as that twelve-year-old boy who had barely remembered the desert from his youth. His father had expected that. He had anticipated and had brought Cyrus here for the same reasons that Cyrus was bringing Hope here today.

Because there was nothing like a medieval fortress, plunked down in the middle of an inhospitable desert stretching out to the horizon on all sides, to encourage a person to get right with themselves. And the desert itself.

Though as a child, what he had felt was…overwhelmed.

His father had seemed cruel to him then, overbearing and ferocious, and he missed the mother he'd loved, then.

These things seemed impossible to him now, but riding up to the fortress again, like this, brought it all back.

First, Cyrus remembered, he hadn't believed what he saw before him. He'd been certain that he'd gotten something in his eyes at first—presumably sand. That would explain the smudge he saw, off the distance.

The closer they got, the more he had blinked and blinked,

because there was nothing. There was nothing but the dance of the sand, the whisper of the wind, the movement of the horse beneath him. And only the endless, cloudless sky above.

As a twelve-year-old boy, he hadn't known how to explain to himself what was happening. Why his mind kept filling in the vast expanses when there was only desert—until he'd realized that he couldn't blink what he was seeing away. That it was a great wall rising from the desert floor—and they were riding straight for it.

That the cruel man who had taken him from his home and hauled him here intended to keep him in what had looked, to him, like a prison.

*When you found yourself here again as a twelve-year-old, was your first reaction joy?* Hope had asked him.

Inexplicably, he heard his mother's singing in his head once more.

And before him, he could feel the way Hope shook his grip, and more, how she fought to repress it.

He knew exactly what battle she was fighting.

And he told himself that he was glad. That he should congratulate himself, for this was all going precisely as planned. She was his now, as had been promised long ago. He had kept his vows.

Now all that remained was making sure she regretted what she'd done while he'd been waiting for her to take her place at his side.

The pack of horses, Cyrus at the front and twelve of his men arrayed around him, rode toward the steep, forbidding walls of the fortress and did not slow their steeds as they approached.

He felt the woman—his wife, he reminded himself again, for so had he decreed—brace herself as it seemed they might dash themselves against the very rocks that rose before them.

Instead, at the last moment, his men let out a cry. It was answered high up on the battlements and thus the great gate was raised.

They thundered straight through, coming to a stop in the grand court.

Cyrus took a moment to remind himself that he, too, had once looked around this place with awe and wonder, so different was it from the ruins of English castles and the like that he had known while in his mother's possession.

Different, though its tactical uses were much the same. Like any fortress, it was built as much to keep people within as to keep marauders without.

He rather thought that was the part Hope was wrestling with as she looked around, golden eyes wide from behind her scarves. For all the ornate scrollwork, tile and mosaic and flourishes, fountains and hints of greenery on the other side of the archways, this was to be her prison, just as it had once been his.

Perhaps she was perceptive enough to know it.

And perhaps it would even be the making of her, as it had once been for him.

He slung his leg over and dismounted his favorite horse, then took his woman down after him, letting her body brush against his as he lowered her feet to the earth.

His woman. His earth.

And once again, he could feel that blazing thing between them, as much an insult as it was intriguing.

Cyrus had not anticipated that he would want her like this.

That he could *make* her want him, he had not doubted at all. Feminine eyes followed him wherever he went, whether here in the desert or out there in the wider world. They did not even need to know who he was to gaze hungrily at him wherever he went.

He had seen a similar hunger in her gaze, too, and had every intention of using it against her—of doing exactly what he'd told her he would, making her into nothing more than a mindless, careless slave to sensation. His to command.

Cyrus would build that fire in her, then let her burn out the rest of her days.

This had always been his intention, because it would keep the promise he had made but also incorporate the punishment he felt she deserved for ignoring her part of the bargain struck for her. But it was not until now, surrounded by his men on all sides, the thick walls of the grand fortress rising all around them, that he fully understood that he would enjoy it too.

Far more than he had anticipated he might when he had only watched her from afar.

He sensed more than heard her sharp intake of breath, but even as he did he stepped back to put space between them. Because he did not enjoy parading his private life about in front of the world. He'd had his fill of such things when he was a child.

Instead, Cyrus glanced to one side, where his man of arms waited and raised his brow. His man nodded, and that was all the communication necessary. Cyrus knew that everything was as he had asked. That while he had flown off to Italy to handle this situation before it got even worse, his people had handled things here in this usually abandoned place in accordance with his wishes.

"I would not have you in this gown," he told Hope then, looking back at her with some small measure of pity as he imagined, in detail, what awaited her. What he would demand of her. "This gown you wore when you imagined you would marry another man."

"It's less comfortable than you might imagine," she said

in that way she had, as if she imagined she was being helpful in some way. Because apparently, she did not have it within her to feel even the slightest hint of the shame she ought to have felt at her own behavior. She even smiled, confounding him. "But, fun fact about being carried off from your own wedding ceremony—I don't have anything else to wear."

"That will not be an issue," he told her. In repressive tones that, as usual, appeared to have no effect on this woman.

It made him wonder what would.

He raised a hand then, and the women came. They spilled out from inside the fortress's mosaiced walls and came hurrying toward him. Once there, they fanned out around Hope, sneaking glances her way while they kept their gazes lowered before their king.

"The women will ready you," he told his wife.

*His wife.*

Grandly, he could admit.

But she did not look cowed like the rest. Though she did not look quite as relaxed as she had on the plane, either. He chose to take that as some kind of victory.

"Dare I ask what I am to be ready for?" she asked.

"I'm sure they will prepare you sufficiently." He waved his hand at the women around her. "I believe they have perhaps seven English words between them, should you imagine you can sway them to your side. Their job is to make you acceptable. To make certain that their king is not offended by you in any way."

"Too late," Hope murmured.

He ignored that. "Your job is to submit to their ministrations, no matter how odd they may seem to you."

"Thank you." Her voice was dry, her golden gaze sharp. "That's very comforting."

"Did I not make myself clear? It is not my aim to make you comfortable, Hope, *omri*. That will never be a goal of mine."

He thought she might wilt at that. Anyone would. But instead, *this* woman smiled at him. A great, big, brilliant sort of smile that made him grind his teeth together. Because she shouldn't flash that around. It should come with a warning, that smile. Particularly in a place like this, where it could only reflect the sky and the sun, and she risked blinding the whole kingdom.

But he did not wish to tell her such things, so he settled for a scowl instead.

And then made himself turn away and stride off when what he wanted was to watch her go—an urge he could make no sense of.

But as the afternoon wore on, he found it was far more difficult to lose himself in the usual matters of state than expected. This fortress was set up to withstand modern as well as medieval attacks, and thus had been renovated in his father's time so that it could function as a reasonable office if necessary.

*It is necessary,* his father had told him years ago, when he was at the end of his reign. Cyrus had come back from his years in England by then, filled with sheer delight to be out of all that rain. *You and I might wish that this place could remain untouched by the march of time, but wishes only highlight our weaknesses, my son. We must use them only as guides toward what we should eradicate.*

Cyrus found himself repeating those words again and again as the day wore on.

Because he knew exactly what the female attendants were doing with Hope. They knew nothing of any rumors about her. What should they care about what happened in far-off lands? They knew her only as their king's new bride. As the Lord's first wife.

First they would have swept her off into the old harem that he'd ordered aired out and redone to his specifications. These days, the Lord of the Aminabad Desert did not live in a palace that was easily discoverable from above in a time of satellite imagery. He did not gather all his people's valuables into one place, inviting attack.

Cyrus preferred to make himself more difficult to be found.

He had turned the country's ancient Royal Palace into a set of museums, so that his people could enjoy the spoils of their own wealth as they pleased. He himself split his time between different compounds, not because he was paranoid like his father, but because his tribe had always been nomadic.

And Cyrus found his people loved him all the more when he made himself accessible to them in the old ways, moving from place to place and speaking with those he asked to follow him. So that every citizen and every region might consider themselves as royal as the next.

But this fortress was something else again. It had been built in a different time. When the King was a warlord and one of the greatest sources of his wealth and consequence was the women he collected and the sons they gave him.

As a child, he had explored the old harem himself. He'd wandered in and out of the alcove rooms gathered around the central courtyard, with its grand fountain in the middle, pools for all, trees and flowers and every detail carefully thought out to proclaim the glory of the desert Lord. So that even when the women were not tending to their master's needs in the royal bed, they might think of him. Long for him.

Vie for his favor.

It was there, in the baths that were fed by the warm spring

deep beneath the fortress, that the women would be tending to the undeserving woman he had elevated to the coveted position as his first wife, because that was the promise he had made long ago. They would take that wedding dress, meant for another man, and burn it. They would cover Hope in oil, massaging it into her skin. They would make certain that all blemishes and unsightly hairs were covered or removed, according to his preferences and the custom of the land.

And they would tell her that was what they were doing, whether they used English words for that or not, so that she would know at every moment that everything that was happening to her was to make her his.

Entirely his.

Only once they had tended to the standards of beauty that he required would they bathe her, washing every part of her and allowing no modesty. They would lather her once with handcrafted soaps, then again with sweet sand, then a third time with scented lotions, moving her from pool to pool until she was clean. Ready. Only then would they anoint her.

This time, when they applied oils, it would be to make her glow. To make her hair gleam. To make her skin soft and supple.

They would bedeck her in jewels as befitted the wife of their lord. Then they would drape her in silks and perfume her all over before, at last, they brought her to him.

He knew this was a process. That it would take the time it took.

And still Cyrus found himself counting the minutes. As if he were little more than the adolescent he had been when he had first discovered the joys that could be found with a woman. She had been older than him, a great catch in his eyes, and she had taken her duties as his bedmate seriously.

She had helped him make certain that the next Lord of the

Aminabad Desert was as formidable in bed as he was anywhere else, a man of myth and legend wherever he roamed. She had done her job well.

So too would these women, he knew.

He only wished he could give his the same attention.

By the time the sun set, leaving trails of bright lights in the sky behind it as it went, Cyrus had given up pretending to tend his responsibilities. Instead he waited in the King's traditional chambers, connected to the harem by one hall that had no other entry or exit. Back in antiquity, blind guards had lined this hall as the King sampled his wares, making certain that no one else dared look upon the royal bounty.

He felt the weight of all that history work within him like heat as he stood in the ancient rooms, staring at the same statues and mosaics that a long line of his ancestors must have gazed upon just as he did now. All of his windows along one wall were archways that led onto a balcony that looked down into the harem courtyard, where kings of old had stood in their time and selected which women they wished might join them of an evening. Some even made them fight for the honor. They had also watched their children run and play here, protected from any who might rise against them, for the fortress boasted the most impregnable walls in the whole of the kingdom.

No one had ever breached the fortress. No one ever would.

By the same token, of course, no one ever got out, either.

As his father had reminded him when he'd brought Cyrus here.

In many ways, Cyrus knew that he was a modern man. He had his Western education. He had his Western blood, for that matter. He liked books from all corners of the globe and was not opposed to Western entertainment—for if his time at university had taught him anything, it was that one should not critique things blindly. For that could only and ever lead to knee-jerk reactions and such responses were beneath him. Far better to understand why people enjoyed such things, so that any critique would necessarily be of what any given thing *actually was*. Not what he feared it might be.

And so, though he had learned right here that women like the mother he had adored could hide betrayal behind their smiles, he had not rushed to judge Hope after her father died and she hadn't come to him. He had watched. He had waited.

He had learned today that she truly intended to walk to that altar and marry another. Only when she had gone to such lengths to show him who she was had he acted upon that information. And yet even then, had honored the promises that had been made to her father and married her, though it could have been argued she deserved no such consideration.

In truth, what happened between them now was justice.

The sort women who hid behind their softness, their prettiness, could not deserve.

But Cyrus did not seek justice because it was or was not deserved, he told himself then, but because it was no more and no less than *just* and therefore *right*.

And he could think of no reason at all that he should see Hope wave that languid hand of hers in his head then, as if laughing at him once again. When no one else had dared, not since he was small.

He heard the sound of the harem doors opening then, but he did not turn, because there were old songs in his head once more. He waited them out, taking notes of the sounds he actually heard here and now, keenly aware that it must have sounded just like this centuries before. Her bare feet against the cool tile. The swish of her silks against her skin.

The scent of her reached him first, that hint of spice and

a warm, heady fragrance that made him think of flowers that bloomed only in the dark.

"Sire, all is as you wish it," his man told him with the usual deference.

Cyrus turned then and felt himself go still.

For Hope Cartwright had been dangerous enough when she had existed only in photographs. She had been astonishingly perilous when he'd put his hands upon her, tossing her over his shoulder and carrying her away from the scene of her perfidy. Dressed in a wedding gown meant to be removed by another man, she had been something like a siren—even to him, who should have been immune.

But all of that faded to insignificance next to *this*.

Hope Cartwright, dressed in the King's silks with jewels gleaming in her navel and at her throat. She wore a pair of loose, billowing trousers that he knew only suggested the shape of pants and were mostly there to protect a woman's most secret places from any stray glances of anyone who was not him. Her golden hair tumbled down all around her, brighter and more lustrous that he could possibly have imagined. Her breasts were caught in a kind of bodice that held them aloft, the same rich color as the pants, and everything else was bare.

Bared to his gaze. Bared *for* his gaze.

These truths were like a roaring within him.

He was filled with the sudden, primitive fury that his man had gazed upon her like this. He understood at last the distasteful old practice of blinding the harem guards. But he shuttered these strange furies even as they beset him. He nodded at the loyal retainer who had served him so well and stayed where he was, still and in control of himself, as the other man quit the room.

At last.

"I didn't realize when you said *harem* that you intended to go full tilt at it." Her voice was bright. As if this was that holiday she'd mentioned. She even flashed that outrageous, heedless smile at him. "Complete with outfits."

Because, of course, she would treat even this as something deserving of that jocularity she prized so much. Clearly she did not understand the significance of where she was. Much less what she wore.

He studied her, ordering his flesh to obey him. Ordering his sex to behave. He folded his arms, not at all certain he liked the creature this woman made him.

As if she was the one in control here, not him.

But his father had taught him the futility of wishes and the scourge of weakness, beating his own out of him in the years he stayed here, and he had not survived all of that to bend now. He no longer regarded those years as a cruelty. They had been a kindness. They had taught him, and well. He would not repeat the mistakes of the past. He would not allow a woman to get between him and his kingdom.

His children would not cry their unworthy mothers, burying their faces in their pillows in the dark of night.

He had married this woman, but he would not let her ruin him.

Cyrus watched as she took her time looking away from him, and catalogued—distantly, he told himself—the flush that appeared on her cheeks, telling him that despite the effect she had on him, she was truly only a woman, in the end.

As susceptible as any other woman was to him, and always had been.

He would do well to remember that.

She was staring at the great bed that stood at the far end of the room, in its own kind of alcove so massive that the posters that surrounded it seemed to go nearly up to the ceiling itself.

"Will we get right to it, then, after all?" she asked the same bright voice. "Is this more of an immediate total immersion situation or is it better to ease our way in and see what the water's like…?"

He raised a brow, finding himself perhaps too pleased when she flushed again. "If that is your wish. I assumed that perhaps we might share a meal, *omri*. But by all means, if you would prefer to begin offering me the gifts we discussed before…?"

She laughed, but this time the sound seemed tinged with the faintest hint of hysteria. Something he found he also liked, because unlike the dryness and the arch amusement, a touch of hysteria in these circumstances seemed appropriate. For her.

"As a matter fact, I find I'm starving." Her gaze found his, again. "I am slightly concerned that this is part of your plan. Making me hungry to the death."

Cyrus could have told her that was, indeed, part of his plan. But he did not mean to ignite the hunger she was talking about.

"I am delighted to offer you a stay of execution," he told her instead, though he wasn't sure why he was bothering. Not when, clearly, the notion of rolling about on his bed was all she could think about. But then, he could use that to his advantage.

He could use all of this to advantage. And wasn't that the point?

Cyrus led her out from the bedchamber into the rest of his apartments, leading her up the small stone stairway that climbed a wall on the far exterior side, then wound its way out onto the fortress's roof.

On either side of the fortress, the battlements stood and were manned by his guards. But this was the King's personal watchtower. Too many of his ancestors had stood here before him, gazing out at the mighty desert that provided the Aminabad people with their wealth and staved off their challengers in turn. His own father had viewed this tower as a retreat. The one place he could come and get himself right with the desert that made them all.

Tonight Cyrus had ordered his people to prepare the very top of the tower, surrounded by its thick walls that allowed a man to keep safe while he viewed the onslaught of attacking armies, for an intimate dinner.

He saw at once that they had outdone themselves. It was an Arabian Nights fantasy come true, as ordered. There were rugs on the floor, colorful pillows tossed this way and that, and too many candles to count. In the center, on low, round tables, a feast to feed an army had been laid out on gleaming platters.

And despite what she'd said below in the bedchamber, Cyrus had watched this woman stuff herself on the plane. He had spent his formative years with a woman who had professed herself full to the gills if she ate an entire salad, and he half expected Hope to do the same sort of thing now. To take one look at the platters piled high with roasted meats, cheese and honey, dishes containing savory and sweet pastries alike, and confess that she was not quite so hungry after all.

But that was not Hope.

Because unlike his mother, who had viewed all food with suspicion and particularly tempting food with outright horror, Hope made a small sound that sounded a great deal like a squeal at the sight of the feast awaiting them. Then she flung herself down on one of the cushions and did not wait for him to join her as she dug in.

This was a good thing, because he found he needed a moment to compose himself. For there was something wildly erotic about watching a woman indulge her appetite so thoroughly. So recklessly. And with such merry abandonment.

What would it be like, he found himself wondering, to take a woman with an appetite such as this to his bed? Was this the reason why she had found herself incapable of keeping her promises to him? Was she so voracious, so carefree and enthusiastic in all things, that she could not be contained by a vow to a single man?

Even though the very idea was anathema to Cyrus in practice, there was something about the notion that got to him anyway. A woman whose art was sensuality itself, in whatever form it took. A woman who deserved appreciation, for such an art was a gift in truth.

A woman who it would be some kind of sin to lock away forever, starving her of all the materials she needed to create her masterpieces—

But he shook that off. Cyrus was not a man who could allow himself to indulge even the faintest hint of weakness. Not even if it first came to him in the guise of something else entirely—and maybe especially not then.

He ordered himself to eat sparingly, and with no particular *sensuality.*

And it was only when she was finished, when she sat back and made a lusty sort of sound that set everything in him alight, that he decided it was time to remind them both why they were here.

That her appetites were to be used against her, not indulged.

Not even by him.

"I regret to inform you," he told her coldly, the better to keep the bulk of his fury hidden because a leader did not lower himself to *displays,* "that the man you wished to marry today did not tear apart the Italian countryside in pursuit of you when you were taken. He did not even follow you out of the chapel. I am to understand that what he did instead was gaze about the assembled witnesses until he could choose a different woman to wed in your stead. They were married within the hour."

Across the low table, gleaming in the golden candlelight, Hope paused in the act of licking honey from her fingers. Yet Cyrus could not read the expression in her gaze. He only noted some emotion or other before she looked back down again.

He did not like that much at all.

"Have you nothing to say?" he growled at her. "Or is it that you do not wish to show me, the man you have betrayed so terribly, what it feels like to be betrayed again in turn?"

He saw her shoulders shake slightly and felt a stab of something that very nearly felt like guilt—but could not be, for what had he to feel the least bit guilty about? He was not the one who had broken promises. That she was here at all indicated that he alone had kept them.

Still, something in him turned over too quickly, because he hadn't imagined she *could* weep, this shockingly unbothered girl who did not seem to apprehend her own peril—

And when she raised her face toward his again, he could see that her eyes were bright, indeed.

But not with tears.

With laughter.

She was *laughing*.

"The thing is, you actually did me a great favor, Cyrus," she told him. And laughed more at his expression. Then harder when he began to scowl. "I'm sorry if you thought I might throw a fit of some kind. I won't. All I *can* do is thank you."

# CHAPTER FIVE

EVEN IF SHE hadn't meant what she said, Hope probably would have found a way to say it anyway if she'd known that doing so would leave that stunned expression on Cyrus's absurdly handsome face.

She was only human, after all. And she hadn't had anything much in the way of fun since before her father died. This was the closest she was likely to get.

The upside was, it really did feel like fun just now—though she supposed that could be all the sweets she'd inhaled.

"I beg your pardon?" Cyrus asked, his voice still in that growly register that seemed to burrow deep into her veins, crawling all over her from the inside out.

Speaking of things that were also fun, in one way or another.

"Lionel and I had an arrangement," she told him when his scowl began to tip over into fully thunderous. "It was business, not pleasure."

Hope could admit that she was enjoying herself, even if what she should have been doing was worrying about her poor mother, on her own for the first time. Maybe it was just that her belly was full again. That she'd lost herself in tasting the sweetest honey she'd ever encountered, and it was impossible not to feel delighted by even the memory of that. Not to mention the sheer number of happy little candles flickering in the desert night atop this little tower, as if doing their best to hold on to that faint hint of remaining sunlight out there on the distant horizon like a few inside out smudges, quiet suggestions of the day that would not dawn for hours.

Or maybe it was as simple as the dark, consuming way that this man who claimed she was his wife looked at her, as if he intended to eat her whole. Possibly tonight.

That was enough to make anyone giddy.

"He had no interest in sharing a life with me." Hope waved a hand in Cyrus's general direction, which felt unwise. Perhaps that was why she did it. Twice. "Or even a bed. He comes from a very old family in Spain, you see, and his grandmother has a lot of opinions about what he should do and how he should present her with grandchildren at the first opportunity. He does not wish to do this. And as she is quite old, he intended to present me as his bride instead and tell her we planned to try to come up with a few grandchildren. In five years, if his grandmother was still with us, we agreed that we would address ourselves to the issue of creating an heir, likely still not in a bed. But it was his fervent hope—and mine—that none of that would ever come to pass."

"You cannot possibly expect me to believe this…fiction." Cyrus's voice was the barest scrape of sound and yet still it seemed to scrape like a knife's sharp edge against her nerves.

And other parts of her.

"Why would it be fiction?" She was still replete from all the food she'd eaten and the honey still in her tongue. She was still tempting fate by lying there dressed in very little silk, waving her hand *languidly* as if she imagined she might be safe. "Why would I bother to tell stories in the first place?"

"Why does anyone lie?" He made one of those faces that he was so good at, she knew already. It managed to suggest that he *could have* delivered a dissertation on *her* lies, but was holding himself back by sheer force of will. "I cannot answer this for you, because I have always prided myself on telling the truth, no matter how unpalatable."

And she was already living dangerously. There seemed to be no particular reason to stop now.

"Have you ever noticed that the people who say things like that *mostly* just want an excuse to be rude?" She smiled when he flashed that particular affronted look at her, as if no one dared say such things to him. Why did she think that meant she ought to be the one who did? When it wasn't clear that she wouldn't spend the rest of her life in some kind of prison? "I'll take that to mean you hadn't noticed. But I'm betting you will now."

"I'm glad that you find this as amusing as you do everything else." Cyrus neither looked nor sounded the slightest bit *glad*. Much less amused. "I hope you may always find it so. But I doubt very much that it will be possible."

"Yes, because of harems and not being allowed to have your sons, and all the rest of it." She almost laughed again, but checked herself when his dark eyes gleamed in a manner that felt a good deal like retribution. Hope made herself frown instead. "That all sounds terrible. But really, what I'm most worried about is my mother."

That part was not only not really a laughing matter, it was true. The fact that she had no idea what messes Mignon was making *even now* could, if she let it, become like a kind of rash that would sweep over her and make her start…prickling.

She did not need to start *prickling* in front of this man.

What she needed was Mignon safe.

And Hope knew that Cyrus knew all about her mother by the way he sighed. He reached over to pick up his drink, then took a moment to swirl the liquid around in its glass. Juice, not alcohol—and that made perfect sense to her.

Cyrus Ashkan did not strike her as a man who wished to soften his senses. For any reason. Because he was clearly a man who gloried in his control over himself and everything around him.

Not because he feared that others might use his dulled senses to take advantage—which was why Hope never touched alcohol. She couldn't imagine what might have become of her over the past few years if she'd indulged.

Cyrus did not look at her when he spoke. "I cannot think why you would trouble yourself with fruitless worries about your mother. I'm not certain that she has ever thought of anyone but herself in the whole of her life."

And Hope was still living her way through a very long, very strange day. It was hard to fathom that just this morning, she'd been close to tearing out her hair over her mother in a villa in Lake Como, as ever.

But she had spent hours upon hours since in the most outrageously decadent spa of all time. If this was what harems were like, she kept thinking as she was handed from one marvelous treatment to the next, then it was clear that she'd been sold a pack of lies her entire life. Because this harem was delightful.

She'd been massaged until her muscles felt like butter. She been fussed over at every turn. The little sting of this or that treatment had been quickly soothed away. She been bathed and then oiled, her hair brushed and styled, and when all that was finished they'd topped off the experience by wrapping her in the finest silk she'd ever felt against her skin.

Hope had never felt so nurtured in her life.

And maybe that was why she found herself thinking about her mother with all her usual sympathy, but now mixed in with an instant desire to defend her. Because *she* might think any number of things about her mother's failings. *She* might spend all the time she liked totting up Mignon's shortcomings, because she did all of that with love.

Hope really didn't want to hear these things from anyone else.

Especially not a kidnapper.

"My mother was raised to be a trinket," she told him, feeling less languid. More serious. Maybe even something like vulnerable, though she was sure that wasn't wise. "My grandparents were very old-school, by all accounts, and they taught her that her job, her single purpose on this earth, was to be pretty. To make everyone around her gaze upon her like she was a lovely piece of art and expect nothing of her except that she should sit on her shelf and be looked upon. So that was what she did."

She felt as if her voice filled the night around them, calling down the tangle of stars above. Making the desert night feel like an embrace shot through with just enough starlight, like inverted candles, so everything was a part of that same fire.

And Cyrus was looking at her intently—maybe too intently—so she continued. "My father adored her. He loved her at first sight and every time he looked at her thereafter, he loved her more. Or so he told everyone he encountered." She swallowed then, because this part was harder. More complicated. "And when he died, she didn't know what to do. On an epic scale. She has spent the years since trying to find someone else who understands her particular provenance. And who will want to treat her as my father did. But the trouble is, she can't tell the difference between a man who only wants to look at a pretty thing for an evening or two and the kind of man who will make her the centerpiece of his world. His first, best collection, if you will. So it's been one heartbreak after the next."

"Heartbreak is one word for it, yes," he said, his voice colder than should have been possible for any number of reasons, starting with the fact that they were in the desert. "I know a little something about women who are considered nothing more than adornments. I cannot say that there is much to them behind the scenes. My own mother was hardly an exemplary human, so determined was she to keep me away from my birthright. She would have done better to pay more attention to the sort of trinket she was meant to be, I think."

Hope did not follow that up the way she wanted to, by pointing out that he had an entire other birthright he chose to ignore, back there in England with that mother he seemed to loathe so much. Somehow she understood that he would not be open to the subject.

"You can call it whatever you want. Heartbreak or otherwise, it doesn't change anything. She is who she is. But she still isn't any good on her own, you see, and she needs me to take care of her. That's the only promise I made my father before he died. It was part of my agreement with Lionel." She looked for some softening on Cyrus's face of sheer, impassive bronze, but there was nothing. She might as well have turned her face the other way entirely, so she could stare out into the desert. It was about as soft and inviting. "I was prepared to act the part of his wife to cater to his grandmother's wishes if he made sure that my mother was taken care of for the rest of her life. It was an easy exchange."

And it seemed easier now, so far away from having to enact it. So far away from that little chapel and the man who had glowered with annoyance as she'd drawn near. And who had still been the best of all the options available to her.

She'd considered that wedding, that man, her *triumph*.

And Hope wasn't sure that she would call this any sort of victory, this odd so-called wedding she'd had on a sandy tarmac today. But at least the way Cyrus looked at her did not suggest that he was *annoyed*. "That is not what I will require from you, *omri*," he said.

Again, there was that sardonic inflection when he said that word. *Omri*. She had said it herself in the baths earlier and one of the women had sighed as if it was romantic, then whispered, *my life*.

Hope had not had the heart to tell her that she thought the King meant it a bit more like a life sentence.

"I cannot abide acting," he was saying. "Or falsehoods of any kind."

"And according to you, you've already announced that I am your wife and that makes it as legal as any contract I could sign."

He looked as close to amused as she'd seen him so far. "More legal than any such document, for I am certainly considered a far more trustworthy source than your average barrister."

But marrying a man had always been her leverage. The worry for Mignon that had been kicking around inside her—if tamped down by an unexpected spa afternoon—seemed to intensify, then. It bloomed throughout her like a new rash altogether.

"Tell me what I need to do to make sure that my mother

has what she needs," she said, and tried to force a smile. Not well, if his expression was any guide. "You've already gone ahead and kidnapped me. You've already carried me off to your lair, conveniently located in the middle of a desert. Tell me what it is I can give you. What it is that you *want* from me."

And for what seemed like a small eternity, there was only the starlight. The matching intensity in his midnight gaze.

The *gifts* he'd mentioned earlier seeming to simmer there between them.

"You must realize that I can take anything and everything I want, if I so wish," he said, very quietly.

But she didn't tense up at that, or get scared. Mostly because she *wasn't* scared, she realized in the next moment, the way she would have been upon hearing similar statements from other men—and it was because he wasn't other men.

He was Cyrus Ashkan and he was not threatening her. He was making a statement of fact.

A simple statement of undeniable fact that was, in its starkness and his quiet restraint, a demonstration of the power she'd felt emanate from him even down the length of that long chapel aisle.

A power he could have used against her already, but hadn't. Oddly enough, that made her feel as close to safe as she had since her father died.

It hummed in her like a new heat all its own.

Cyrus inclined his head slightly, as if he could read in her precisely what he wished to see there. She didn't know why she hoped he could. "Yet all I want from you is a kiss, Hope. Just one kiss."

"A kiss?" She couldn't breathe, suddenly. She told herself it was the dry air. "But…why?"

It was as if he knew she would ask that. His harsh face

altered as his stern mouth…curved. Just slightly. "To see the truth of who we are, you and me. That's why."

Hope was not at all certain she wanted to know who she was, just then. Not when it felt like this—like a sudden rush of heat inside of her, so overwhelming that she wasn't sure if she would actually manage to remain sitting up straight. Or as close to straight as she was managing, propped up on all these pillows.

She had been so busy gorging herself, again, that she'd been able to tell herself she'd missed the sensuality that seemed to hang in the air between them. That desire she hadn't known was in her until today that she'd managed, somehow, to tuck back in its place again while she was buffed to a shine. And though she knew that there were guards and staff spread out all over this fortress, up here on the top of this tower it was only them. The nearest other people were the lone guards who walked the segments of the battlements down below.

Otherwise it was only the two of them, alone in the silken night. The two of them, cast in the light of so many flickering candles. The two of them splayed out on the floor beneath a ceiling of careless stars, no matter how many bright pillows were festooned about here and there.

No matter if Hope could breathe or not.

"I make it a personal policy not to kiss men who dislike me," she told him, trying to summon some kind of authority as she spoke. But she didn't think she got there. Not in the face of all the power he managed to generate simply by… staying where he was, seemingly at his ease as he lounged there opposite her.

Though that hard gleam in his dark eyes and that sense of hovering danger all around him suggested otherwise.

"Do you indeed?" he asked her, without the slightest indication that he was even attempting to conceal the fact he was challenging her.

*This is who you are,* he had said to her in a different country today, as if she had betrayed him when she still hadn't known his name. And he hadn't stopped there. *You do not even care what man claims you, do you? You flit from one to the next as if it is nothing.*

And she couldn't understand why she didn't feel more offended. Why she hadn't then. Why she didn't now. Surely it said something about her that his accusations didn't seem to land like the blow she knew they should be.

Then again, maybe she was more like her mother that she'd ever imagined possible.

Hope couldn't say she particularly liked *that* line of thought. Had she really gone through all of this—all the struggle of the past years—to be no more than a man's bauble, in the end? Perhaps loved in her time, but in the end, as disposable as any other bit of tat a man collected over the course of his life and left behind when he was gone?

To be tossed out or packed away as it suited whoever came next?

Imagining such a future made her feel cold.

Hope made herself sit up straighter, as if that could somehow draw attention away from the pillows strewn about. Suggesting that in this place, the lines between things were blurred in advance. No need to worry about how a person got from point A to point B when all the points were mashed together like this. If there was no differentiation between eating dinner and rolling on the floor, it was all part and parcel of the same sensuous experience—

But she didn't like the way her body was responding to that line of thought. She didn't care for the way a sweet sort of shiver, like its own sort of honey, snaked along her arms. Or the way her nipples seemed to join in, hardening against the silk that barely covered them and making that, too, feel like a caress.

She *really* didn't like the fact that all of that melting heat that she could feel inside her wound its way down the length of her, spiraling around and around until it became a bright, hot problem between her legs.

And Hope knew a whole lot about men. More than anyone should know, to her mind. All of her interactions with men had been inside out—she understood that now. There was her father, who she had loved beyond reason, and on the other side there were... all the other men. All the ones Mignon had brought home, who had leered at Hope when she should have been too young for them to notice her. All the men she had taken it upon herself to interview over the past few years, who had shown not the slightest shame in sharing with her every last bit of the depravity that animated them. They had all been so *proud*, in fact.

All of them.

She understood now, when it already felt too late, that she was missing a crucial bit of her education.

Because never before had a man looked at her and made her feel like *this*.

Her father had looked at her with fondness and adoration, and she had bloomed in his regard. Then missed him when he was gone. Other men looked at her and she cringed. She had flushed with disgust on more occasions than she could count. Her heartbeat had always kicked into high gear, usually because she was worried for her safety in one way or another.

She had thought of Lionel Asensio as a savior because he had looked at her as if he was examining produce at a market. That had felt much colder and therefore safer than anything she'd experienced before him.

*Cold* was not how she would describe the way this man looked at her.

"I think you're trying to intimidate me," she said quietly.

"*Omri*, please. Do not mistake the matter. I do not need to try." That should have been even more intimidating, and yet somehow, it was the opposite. Because she knew by now that the bullies didn't sit around playing games or *talking* about these things. They bullied. That was exactly what they did, always. "We are here, in a fortress so impregnable that its very name makes my enemies weep. For they know that whatever it is that waits here, they can do nothing. And have you not been treated well, Hope?" Was it her imagination that he seemed suddenly...closer than before? "Why is it that you imagine I would go to the trouble of tending to you if I planned now to tear you apart?"

She did not think he intended to do that. Exactly. But she was caught up in the way the light danced over his bronze features and she could not begin to explain why it was that *looking* at him made her ache. In ways she couldn't make sense of, even to herself.

"Is that not what men do?" she asked softly. "I thought the purpose of all of this was to punish me. To make me pay for breaking a promise I can't even remember."

"Can't you?"

She laughed at that, though she felt significantly less amusement than before. "You have no idea what I've been through these past years. If I'd had the slightest idea that there was some Prince Charming hanging around, waiting to rescue me—"

But she stopped, suddenly.

Maybe it was the *Prince Charming* bit, reminding her

of all the daydreams she'd been thrusting aside on her way down the aisle today in Italy. Maybe it was because her full stomach and the soft light had lulled her into sense of security, the first she'd felt in a long, long while.

Hope couldn't tell what it was, but all of a sudden, memories of her father swept through her. When she'd been a little girl and would find him in the evenings after her bath in that cozy study of his, lined with books, smelling of cigars he loved, and, in her memories at least, always sporting a happy fire in the grate. He had always welcomed her with that jolly laugh of his, opening up his arms so she could run into them.

Then she snuggled against him, sitting there in that cozy armchair before the fire.

When she was older and thought of herself as far too old for sitting in laps she would tuck herself into the chair across from his, so he could look at her with his kind, wise eyes as he listened to her prattle on about her prosaic days as if worlds hung in the balance.

Sometimes, even now, she would think of that study and his obvious, open love for her as she drifted off to sleep. Sometimes she thought she could almost catch his scent, or feel his arms around her, or hear his laughter in her ears again.

But tonight she found herself remembering the stories he would tell her when she complained that her life was boring or sad, for reasons she couldn't fathom now. The stories were bright and happy, about the life she would lead, joyful and sweet.

They were usually some or other take on how she might not have been a princess herself in the eyes of the world, but was her papa's princess, all the same.

*And a princess like my Hope deserves to have a fine*

*prince of her own.* She could hear her father's voice so clearly now, so distinctly. *Wouldn't that be nice?*

After he died, she had remembered those stories, but had thought nothing of them. They were just stories, after all. Just fairy tales a lovely man had told his daughter. There was no harm in them—and no truth, either.

For she had learned quickly enough that there was no point believing in fairy tales. Not the kind that people told these days, anyway. Real fairy tales were different, of course. They were dark and grim, and there was nothing cozy or safe about them at all.

Hope had learned that the hard way.

It had never occurred to her, until this moment, that there could possibly be a kernel of truth in those stories her father had told her.

That there could possibly be a prince after all.

She pushed back from the low table, then onto her feet, before she realized that she meant to move. Hope looked wildly around as if she might find an explanation for this in the candlelight, on the table itself, or even on the uncompromising face of the man who only watched her, his gaze hooded.

But with an unmistakable satisfaction stamped all over him.

"Perhaps your memory is not so faulty after all?" he asked softly.

Dangerously.

As if he could read her so easily when he remained a mystery to her.

And as she watched—not sure if she was taken aback or something far more complicated—he unfolded himself from that lounging position and rose to his feet with a breathtaking grace, fluid and athletic at once.

"My father used to tell me stories," she said, maybe too quickly, though without any real idea why she should find herself confessing anything. "But I never thought…"

"There are contracts, Hope."

"There were no contracts in his office." She shook her head, thinking of all the papers she'd gone through, the folders upon folders she'd thrown away. Could she have missed something? After all, it was unlikely to have been marked *Prince Charming Is Not a Fairy Tale*. Had her escape been in her reach from the start? Hope could barely cope with that idea. "Who could possibly think that princes in foreign lands and kingdoms I'd never heard of were anything but stories?"

He studied her for what felt, to her, like a lifetime.

"Perhaps what you say is true. That you did not know you were mine. For I am many things." His voice was like the night. Like the desert all around. It was within her as well as without. It was taking her apart without him having to so much as lift a finger. "And many stories have been told about me. But the only tale you need tell yourself is this: that whatever you knew or did not know, you are here now. Where you belong. And you are my wife, as was promised long ago. A prince now a king in a place that is very real, who wants only a kiss. Is that story enough for you?"

And she could see that he meant that as another challenge. Maybe even a warning a wise woman would heed. But Hope felt the strangest sensation wash over her, then. So strange that she knew it was mad even as she thought it.

But…if all those fairy tales her father had told her were true, then why not all fairy tales?

Maybe she really should kiss him, here and now, because wasn't that how spells were broken? Maybe if she kissed him, everything would go back to the way it was.

Maybe if she kissed him, with all these feelings she'd shoved down deep inside her, she could turn back time.

So she would never have to find her father unresponsive in that study that had always been about their coziest family moments. Her mother dancing to the music her father played for her. Her parents sometimes dancing with Hope held between them, as if that kind of joy could last forever if they all sang along.

Maybe all of this was a dream. A terrible dream, nothing more.

Maybe if she kissed an impossible man on top of a magical tower, surrounded by candles and beneath the stars, she could wake up at last.

So Hope didn't think.

She closed the distance between them, and she didn't stop at that. She threw herself at Cyrus, knowing on some instinctive level that he would catch her—

And he did.

Hope was aware of the strength in his arms, and how that chest of his felt even more like a stone wall now than it had earlier today, when he had carried her so easily away from the cold life she'd seen as a reprieve.

Bracing herself against the hard ridges of his abdomen, she tipped back her head as she surged up onto her toes.

And she thought, *If this is a fairy tale, the spell should be broken.*

So Hope leaned up as best she could and kissed the Prince who had become a king, just like her father had told her she would long ago.

# CHAPTER SIX

HOPE KNEW TWO things immediately.

One, that this was not the spell she had imagined it was, because his mouth was both harder and softer than she ever could have conceived when she pressed her lips to his.

And two, that this was magic all the same.

It was true that the world didn't explode into a shower of stars that turned into small dancing creatures. There was no magic wand or sudden swell of music.

But there was heat. Almost too much heat to bear.

When she made as if to step back, his arm went around her and hauled her even closer against him. And then she stopped worrying about what was happening, or what was magic and what wasn't, because his mouth opened against hers and it was so *good* and everything seemed to slide into that same spiral of sensation that was winding tighter and tighter within her.

Cyrus licked his way along the seam of her lips, silently commanding her to open for him. And she shivered, but she did. And though she felt hesitant, maybe, and yet wild at the same time—everything seemed to feel *right* when his tongue stroked hers.

She hadn't understood, before, how a kiss could involve *a whole body.*

Hope was *aware* of him in a thousand different ways.

There was the spicy scent of him, all around her, like the candlelight flickering over them both. And more, the profound and alien *maleness* of him—of his body, of the way he held her, of the differences between his mouth and hers.

That he felt so hard when she felt soft, and softer by the second.

She was aware of herself, too, in whole new ways. There was a driving need between her legs, but that was only part of it. Her breasts felt rounder and softer even as her nipples hardened against his chest. And her body seemed to make up its own mind about what it should do, because she found herself pressing against him, rubbing herself into him, so caught up in the way all these different sensations made her feel—the mad storm of it all—that she found herself making greedy little noises in the back of her throat.

And all the while, his mouth moved over hers, with hers.

Hope didn't have to have had sex herself to understand that the way he thrust his tongue into her mouth, over and over again, mimicked that action.

So well and with such delirious heat that she could feel a kind of throbbing in the core of her, as if her body was readying itself for that most intimate invasion.

And perhaps the true magic was, after failing to understand why her mother let all those men get close enough to break her heart, Hope finally got it.

She finally understood completely.

Because she thought in these wildly hot moments, with all the careening sensations setting her alight, that she had never wanted anything more than to tear off her clothes and his and do whatever was necessary to wrap herself all over him, take him inside her, and follow the sweet hunger wherever it led.

And it took her too long to understand that he was laughing, a dark and rude and yet stirring sound, when he set her away from him.

"I don't..." she began, shaking her head, though that failed to clear it. There was too much sensation still kicking around inside her, and for some reason she wanted to cry, and yet all the while there was an ache that only seem to grow and grow—

But then there was the way he was looking at her. That made her want to curl up into a ball. And cry for different reasons altogether.

"Cyrus?" she whispered.

He moved past her, still laughing in that way that made the back of her neck prickle.

"I will give you this, *omri*," he said, his voice much too dark and that word like a gut punch. "I can certainly see why you are so popular."

And then, without a backward glance, he left her there.

There on top of that tower, alone in the desert night—and it took Hope far too long to understand what had happened.

First she stayed where she was, her breath coming so fast and so hard that it made the silks she wore move against her, which didn't help her oversensitized skin.

She thought he would return, but instead the women came, murmuring things in low voices she found she was happy she didn't understand. They led her back down into the fortress, down the stone stairs that wound away from the seductive night, the watching stars.

They took the same route through Cyrus's bedchamber, though he was nowhere to be found. And they did not stop at his towering bed, leading her instead into the harem, lit up with soft lanterns and the sound of tumbling water.

It was there, tucked up in the little alcove of a room they'd told her was hers in her soft and welcoming bed, that she pulled the airy blankets over her and let herself understand at last what that look Cyrus had given her meant.

Because it had been so scathing. Almost disgusted.

"He thinks that's how I am with every man," Hope whispered out loud, into the feathers of her pillow.

And there was still that part of her that wanted to curl up into the fetal position, rock herself the way she always did when her heart felt bruised, and soothe herself to sleep.

But she didn't.

Instead, Hope laughed.

And she kept on laughing for a long while, her whole body shaking with it and the faintest hint of moisture appearing in the corners of her eyes.

She laughed and she laughed, until the laughter turned into all that heat and aching that coursed through her body and she couldn't seem to keep herself from running her hands over her own desperate skin. She found the hard pebbles her nipples had become and imagined her hands were Cyrus's, testing the weight of her against his palms and then slowly making their way over her ribs, her belly, until he reached that heat between her legs. She thought of the way his tongue had thrust between her lips, and even thinking about it made her shiver all over.

Hope followed that delicious shivering, dipping her own hands into the heat of her core and imagining that things had ended in a different way entirely up there in that tower. That Cyrus had taken her down into all those pillows, pushed her silks aside, and kept right on kissing her like that even as he thundered between her legs.

For surely he was a man who would always feel like thunder.

She was still laughing as the glory of it took her over,

there alone in her harem bed, so she pressed her face into her own pillow and kept what magic there was to herself.

The next day, she woke to find the light streaming into the courtyard, making everything gleam like new. And she hadn't bothered to change out of the silks they'd given her when she'd fallen into bed, so she wore them as she padded out of her room to find herself alone with the great fountain as it babbled and burbled, making its own song into the morning. The courtyard was filled with trees that shouldn't grow in a place like this, ripe with fruit and covered in green, and there were even songbirds in their branches.

Hope supposed she should have felt scared, but she didn't. Instead, it was the first morning in a long, long while that she didn't feel the usual grinding panic of what she would do, how she would do it, *if* she *could* do what she must to keep herself and her mother safe.

Because there was nothing she could do here but…be here.

And there was a liberty in having no choices. Even if, deep down, she knew that eventually the panic would return to her—because Mignon was still out there, doing God only knew what in Hope's absence.

But if she thought about her mother, she would fall apart, and that wouldn't help her at all.

So she didn't.

She breathed in and out, again and again, and she didn't. She couldn't.

Mignon was a grown woman and Hope had to believe that she would find her way.

Because she couldn't allow herself to think anything else.

Her attendants found her there some while later, sitting beneath one of the trees while the fountain laughed, the birds sang, and the desert sun warmed her. They brought her rich coffee and decadent pastries, and so she had chocolate on her tongue and music in her ears when she looked up—caught by more of that magic, maybe—to find Cyrus standing in those arched windows in the King's bedchamber, looking down.

For what seemed like an eternity, Hope held his eyes with hers. She felt filled with his midnight gaze.

Captured as surely as she was in this harem.

He looked down at her, his face a study of ruthlessness, his gaze stern.

And that, too, felt like glory.

When he turned and walked away from his windows, Hope thought that despite everything, or maybe because of it, she was going to be far happier here than he might imagine. Because whatever else she might feel, she wasn't *afraid*.

And that felt more like freedom than it should.

As her days in the desert bled one into the next, that was exactly what happened.

Hope thought at first that Cyrus, having discovered what he clearly thought was proof of her promiscuity, would avoid her. But he did not.

Later that same day she was once again buffed to a gleam and brought before him. This time there was no tower beneath the stars, no pillows on the floor.

Instead, she joined him out on the battlements in the bright heat of the afternoon, and walked with him.

"I thought you had guards for this," she said as she walked beside him, grateful that she was not dressed only in those harem silks that bared most of her body. They had draped her in different garments, more enveloping, so that she might walk in the sun without burning to a crisp.

Though there was something electric about concealing so

much of herself. It made Hope only too aware that she still wore that same silken harem outfit beneath it all.

Judging by the light in his gaze every time he looked down at her, she thought Cyrus felt that same electricity too.

"I ask nothing of the men who serve me that I'm not willing to do myself," Cyrus told her, sounding as forbidding as if she had suggested he lay about on couches, demanding peeled grapes, while his underlings fussed over him.

"I'm sure that that wins their loyalty," she murmured. Thinking that was an uncontroversial statement.

He stopped, and frowned down at her. "I do not attempt to *win* their loyalty." As if the very notion was outlandish. "They're loyal to me because I am the Lord of the desert. Because Aminabad rests between my hands and will do so for as many days as I draw breath. That is what wins their loyalty, *omri*. They would be loyal to me even if they hated me, because that is the way of my people. It is my role that matters."

"It was meant to be a compliment," Hope said mildly.

"You cannot understand." And his voice was clipped enough that it made her think that he was speaking to someone else. Not her. There was too much bleakness and outrage in his gaze for that. "My people do not put their loyalty up for grabs, or sell it to the highest bidder." He stood with his back to the great desert, scowling down at her. "I am the Lord of this desert not only because my father was, but because I earned it in sacrifice and struggle. I gave up more than you can imagine. All the softness within me, like songs. I tore them out and made myself what was required. These are the things that matter, Hope. Not *compliments*."

"I'll make a note to keep them to myself, then," she shot back, without thinking.

And then nearly jumped out of her skin when Cyrus

moved toward her, backing her across the width of the battlements so that her own spine came into contact with stone. Still he kept coming, until he held her there.

Then he reached over to put his hand against her cheek. "I would work more with honey than vinegar, if I were you."

"You can't mean more kissing, surely." She made herself laugh as if he hadn't gone dark on her last night. As if he hadn't made more of his ridiculous accusations. "Though I don't know why you think I would bother to try when all it does is make you think the worst of me."

"I already think the worst of you. I married you anyway."

"Why? When you don't even believe me when I tell you the truth?" She was breathing too hard and she didn't like that he could see it.

"I believe that you didn't know," he said, as if the words cost him something—but not enough, Hope thought. Not quite enough. "What's done is done, *omri*. The choice you need to make is what kind of marriage this will be now we are in it."

She went as if to knock his hand away from her face, but something in the way his eyes glittered kept her from it. "I'm not sure what my impetus for that is, either. Didn't you tell me that the goal of all of this is to make me yearn endlessly for you while you parade about, impregnating other woman? Not exactly the lure you seem to think it is, Cyrus."

"And yet you yearn for me already," he said quietly. "Do you not?"

It was not a question. He knew.

She could see it all over him.

And it was not until she was back in the harem courtyard that Hope understood that it had been deliberate, on his part, to keep from kissing her then. He had gone out of his way to avoid it, in fact.

Because he *wanted* her to spend the rest of that afternoon and evening *lit up* with yearning for him.

He wanted her to lie in her bed just as she did that night, unable to sleep and thinking that there was nothing he did that didn't have a good reason—and that reason wasn't only making her *yearn*. The battlements themselves, for example. He had wanted her to see exactly how remote their location was. How there was nothing in any direction but sand and space, just as she'd feared when they'd first landed. She was well and truly trapped here, locked up tight until and unless he relented and let her go. Or didn't.

What he didn't understand was that Hope was resourceful. Maybe she couldn't extinguish that burning flame that flickered only for him, but she could play with it.

Especially if it helped her sleep.

"I don't think you really understand what's happening here," she told him a day or two later, sitting across from him at yet another low table. This one was in one of the numerous rooms that made up his expansive apartments. "England can rain on forever without me. I don't care if I ever go back. I certainly don't care that my wedding carried on with a different bride. It wasn't the groom or the ceremony I cared about. But I do need to know how my mother is faring. If I wasn't worried about her, I wouldn't mind in the least how long you plan to keep me here."

"You expend a great deal of energy on her," Cyrus observed, leaning back against another set of bright pillows, propping himself up on one elbow and looking like some kind of avenging angel.

Hope told herself that shouldn't make her feel like squirming where she sat. "She's my mother."

He only shrugged. "Everyone has a mother, Hope. Not

his chest, all muscle and heat, that put the bat-
hame.

leaned in even more and pressed her lips to his.
efore, there was that wild, spinning dizziness,
simple press of her mouth to his.

a song.

, after a moment or two of that alone, Cyrus
all over again.

her deeper this time, Wilder. He hauled her up
and then turned, rolling her down into the pil-
the weight of him was pressing into her.

...exulted.

moved the way she'd imagined they might—
making it to her breasts or the greedy center of
finding all the places that were exposed when
away.

fires wherever he touched.

he kissed her again and again—tutoring her,
, tearing her apart.

er hips rising up as if they were trying to find
ked her arms around his neck, hauling herself
trying to press every square inch of her body

s no surprise, really, when he eventually set
in.

me, he was breathing just as hard as she was.
as a certain fierceness in his gaze that would
er shiver anew—

ld tell the difference between one sort of shiver

take it that this is you showing who you re-
" Hope asked, because she couldn't seem to

everyone ties themselves into unnecessary tangles in service
of their mothers. Quite the opposite, I would say."

"You say that as if it's perfectly normal to treat a mother
the way you treat yours," she said, careful to keep her voice
even. So he could not possibly take what she was saying as
some kind of attack.

But she should have known better. When it came to the
topic of his mother, he viewed everything as an attack. If
she so much as mentioned his father, on the other hand, he
was prepared to wax rhapsodic about the man's greatness
ad nauseam. As if it was not possible to elevate one in his
esteem without crushing the other.

Someday, she thought she might ask him why that was.

"I treat my mother as she deserves, no more and no less,"
he told her in that dark way that suggested she should not
pursue the issue further. "And far better than some would
do."

"It has always sounded to me as if she loves you beyond
reason," Hope dared say, and then held her breath.

Because he looked at her as if she'd picked up the nearest statue and bashed him over the head with it. As if she'd
said something horrid and vicious, and her heart thumped
painfully in her chest as he stared back at her, letting her
know that her emotions were far more engaged here than
they should have been.

"That," Cyrus said when the silence between them grew
so loud that Hope worried she might choke on it, "is not a
word I would use when discussing my mother."

"You mean your father," Hope said, though she knew better, truly she did. "He was all harsh edges and ranting on
about property rights, wasn't he? While your mother was
wracked with anguish and only wondered how you were.
It was in the documentary—"

And if he had been anyone else, she would have said that the look in his dark eyes then was something like fear.

But that was impossible. This was Cyrus Ashkan, Lord of the Aminabad Desert and all he surveyed besides.

"You are mistaking the matter," he told her, flatly. "My mother has always played well to a camera. And I think a great many people on this planet feel exactly about their mothers as I do about mine. I wouldn't be surprised if you did, too. The only difference is that I am not afraid to say so."

"I love my mother," Hope said quietly. "Neither one of us is to blame for who we became because we lost my dad."

She thought that might shake something loose in Cyrus, remembering how shaken he'd looked for a swift moment there. Just that moment. As if he might open up about what had actually happened to him here. And for a beat, then another, of her heart, she thought he might.

Or better still, kiss her again in that stern and stirring way of his, all confidence and certainty and enough fire to set the world alight—

But he only lifted a hand and crooked her finger in her direction.

"I will let you call her, if you truly wish it," he told her, with great magnanimity. "But there is a price."

She told herself that she didn't know what she would do. She told herself that she took her time mulling it over.

But that was a lie.

She moved almost without thinking at all.

And it felt unseemly, the way she sighed in such a long-suffering fashion and then crawled her way around the low table. It felt significantly more dangerous than what had happened on the top of that tower.

Because they weren't standing. They were already

---

lounging there, on the gro
she imagined all the things
like this—

And how much she want

Hope could have pretend
she didn't. All she'd wanted
she'd wanted moments ago

She thought he might sit
didn't. He merely waited fo
challenge when she reached
still, angling herself very ne

But though she held herse
effort of suspending herself
position, he didn't pull her

"You must kiss me, Hop
was bored. She might have
not for that dark glittering

"Then it isn't a kiss free
If she thought that might
taken.

"What makes you ima
"What you are is mine."

And then all he did was
bright, that curve of his mo

She sat back and consid
nothing for it, because he
new storm that danced ov
prophecy. She tipped herse
his chest, making no secre
breath as the sensation ro

Hope leaned all the w
lowered herself so she was

---

The wall
tlements
Then s
Just lik
all from
It felt l
And th
took chan
He kis
against h
lows so t
And H
His ha
never qu
her need,
the silks
Buildir
All wh
teaching
She fel
him. She
even close
into his—
And it
her aside
But this
And there
have made
If she cc
and anothe
"Should
ally are to
stop hersel

And on some level she was aware that she clearly felt safe enough with this man that she thought she could be so reckless. That she could say such things without worrying about reprisals.

Cyrus bared his teeth into something she would never call a smile. It was too fierce. Too elemental. Then he rolled away from her and up onto his feet in a single swift move.

Once again displaying that particular grace that made him more dangerous and more sensual than any man should be all at once.

And as he stalked toward the door, she laughed dark and low, the way he had before. Hope pushed herself up onto her elbow, and watched him as he paused in the archway that led deeper into his chambers.

She decided to take it as evidence that he was as wrecked as she was that he had to reach out a hand to steady himself. Hope decided to view that as nothing short of a victory.

"Did you lie about giving me my one phone call from prison?" she asked, sounding far more bitter than she felt.

Because it was that or melt all over him, and even though she wanted to do nothing but, there was Mignon to think about.

Cyrus looked back at her, his eyes so dark they might as well have been black. Hope held her breath.

He said no other word, he simply walked from the room.

But before she could think to get back up onto her feet, to try to chase him down or argue the point, his man came and found her. He waited as she scrambled to her feet and then he led her into yet another room in these endless chambers. There was an armchair inside and a table with a phone on it.

The man dialed out, then handed her the receiver.

Hope took it numbly, staring at the old rotary phone as if she had never seen one before.

"One call is all you are permitted, by the grace of our lord and king," the man told her matter-of-factly. "I will be waiting just outside."

And Hope didn't know how she was supposed to process that Cyrus was the first man she'd met since her father had died who had actually kept his promises to her. Or the fact that there was still that same overwhelming storm stampeding about inside of her.

But the phone was ringing.

And there was a part of her, little though she might wish to admit it, that almost wanted to cry with the rush of joy and love and daughterly obligation when she heard her mother answer.

"It's me, *Maman*," she made herself say instead. "Don't worry, *Maman*. It's me."

And she closed her eyes, wrapped her free arm around her middle, and braced herself as her mother began to wail.

# CHAPTER SEVEN

SOME WEEKS LATER, Cyrus returned to the fortress from a necessary overnight trip down south to tend to the business of running his kingdom. He accepted the cold drink his staff pressed upon him upon his arrival, took his time showering as if he had felt no pressing need to rush back here, and then stood in the windows that overlooked the courtyard of his harem.

His harem with its single occupant.

He told himself that the project was an unqualified success.

Surely the fruit of this particular labor was ripe and sweet, no matter the uncomfortable questions she dared ask him on occasion. He had only to gaze down into the courtyard to assure himself of that.

The women danced below, all of them draped in flowing silks, but he knew precisely which one was Hope. He could see hints of that gleaming gold that drove him to distraction. Her hair. Her eyes.

All the other women danced well, as it was customary in Aminabad to learn these dances at their mothers' knees. It was a matter of hips and sweet elegance, finding the melody within them as they moved.

His wife—a word he still found sharp and strange, even in his own thoughts—was still learning. That was obvious even from a distance. And there was no denying that she did not possess the natural talents some of the others did.

Yet she was the one who mesmerized him.

Cyrus found himself transfixed. He could not look away.

But as soon as he realized how intently he stood there, how little it seemed possible he might ever drag his attention away, he forced himself to do exactly that. He tossed back the rest of his drink, the sweet cold juice he liked best, and hated that he found himself making pointless comparisons between the sugary hit of a mango and the taste of Hope's lovely mouth.

Of her kisses, greedy and demanding, that stole his sleep from him on too many nights to count.

The project might have been a success, by Cyrus's estimation, but Hope herself remained a puzzle. She was not afraid to negotiate with him, about anything and everything. Sometimes he thought she argued with him simply because she enjoyed it—when no one else would dare behave in such a manner. It was how he had agreed to allow her to call her mother each day, though he was not sure he liked it.

It was good that the older woman was doing better than Hope had imagined she would. Cyrus was pleased this was so, as it made Hope visibly happier and he found he was far more interested in her happiness than he should have been.

He had accepted that she hadn't known that she was promised to him. That her father had not told her directly and she had found no papers in his things—or, as she had confessed one night, perhaps she had but had not known what they were.

*I was fourteen,* she had said softly. *And I had to take on so many things.*

When Cyrus was fourteen, his father had decided it was a kindness to teach him how to survive sandstorms in the desert with nothing but a horse and a tarp. They had ridden toward the sand, not away, and Cyrus had spent long nights in between these sessions waking up in the night from dreams of sand filling his mouth, his nose, his eyes—

Or sometimes with tears on his face and his mother's songs in his head, something he had not admitted then and could not admit now, either.

That was the part of her keeping in touch with her mother that seemed to lead to more of those questions from Hope that he did not wish to answer.

Or maybe the deeper truth was that he did not know how to answer her, and he liked that even less.

*You do not seem to have much use for mothers in general,* she had said one night, walking with him in one of the gardens that were the pride and joy of the courtyards in this place. Gardeners from all over the kingdom competed for the chance to come here and make the fortress green in some small way as a way of celebrating and yet shifting the kingdom's past when this place really had been a military outpost.

Yet that night, the only bloom he had seemed able to focus on was Hope.

*Don't be ridiculous,* he had replied. *I hold mothers in general in the highest regard. Motherhood is a sacred state. Some claim it is the apotheosis of a woman's life.*

*According to...women? Or according to the men who wish to lock them away to breed?*

*I do not wish to lock* women *away.* He had frowned down at her. *You are the wife of the King, Hope. You could be taken and used against me by any enemies who might happen upon you. More than that, were I to allow such a thing to occur, it would paint me as a small, weak man, unworthy of the crown.*

As was typical with her, she had only smiled. *So it's only mothers, then. Only mothers who you can't abide.*

*The only mothers I have paid the slightest bit of attention to in this life are yours and mine,* he had told her shortly. *And it is not the fact they are mothers which offends me. It is that they are both dreadful at the only important jobs they have ever had.*

Hope had only looked at him in that way she did sometimes. As if he broke her heart.

*My mother loves me unconditionally,* she had told him. *What she might do or not do doesn't change that. You don't have to be a perfect person to love someone, Cyrus.*

And despite himself, he had been hit with another memory he went out of his way to lock down, far out of sight. He had been sixteen. It had been a long time since he'd woken in the night for any reason at all. But one night he and his father had journeyed to one of his father's minister's homes in the southern city, and Cyrus had been relegated to a guest room while the older men talked privately.

He'd seen the interview by accident. He'd been flipping through the channels, telling himself that he was merely cataloguing the sorts of things that rotted the minds of Aminabad subjects, and then there she was.

Until he saw her, he hadn't remembered it was his birthday.

*I don't need it to be his birthday to remember him,* she'd said, and though she hadn't been singing, her voice had gone through him all the same. Into him, like bone finding bone. *He's with me always. I hope he knows that.*

He'd felt as if someone had taken an axe to his head. He'd stood there, frozen in the guest room of a stranger's house, unable to move. He'd drunk her in on the screen before him. Her face, just as he recalled it. The anguish in her eyes.

The way she put her hands to her heart. *I love you, Justin,* she'd whispered, looking directly into the camera, her eyes filled with tears. *No matter where you are. No matter what. I will always love you.*

It had taken him so long to remember himself, to move from where he stood after the new program moved on, that his feet had fallen asleep beneath him. And it wasn't until weeks later that it occurred to him that she'd used the name he was meant to hate and reject.

What had shamed him since was that he'd never admitted what had happened to his father. And he'd played her words over and over in his head during the military exercises his father made him practice, to harden him, and the nights his father made him sleep alone on the bare floor of the fortress's dungeons, so he might understand that even that was a measure of his benevolence.

That his life was the gift his father had given him, and everything else was up to him to make his own.

He had told himself then, and since, that he was grateful for the lesson.

What he had never told a soul was that he had heard his own, lost name like a song all the while. As if it alone had sustained him. His mother's voice in his ear, his heart, his bones.

How he had always despised himself for the weakness.

Back then and that night with Hope in the garden, too. In the garden, he had stared at her until she looked away. Then he had told her that there would be a price if she wished to have closer contact with her own mother, and a greater one still if she insisted on mentioning his.

Cyrus could not pretend, now, he had not greatly enjoyed collecting on these prices she paid, but he had not expected that Hope would enjoy it so much too.

Oh, he had known that in the heat of things, she would

want nothing more. That she would beg him to continue. He had never had any doubt on that score with any woman, not that he could seem to remember any others of late, and certainly not one who looked as if she was as fascinated with him as Hope always did.

But he had expected that when faced with the fact that she wanted this man who she had been promised to and had therefore wronged, however unknowingly, she would shrink into herself and at least *pretend* she could not feel the heat between them.

Perhaps he would not even have blamed her.

Blame or not, he had expected her to feel shame.

Instead, she danced in the courtyard with the other women. Last he had heard, she had made friends of them all, and half the rest of the staff as well. Her laughter could always be heard in the halls and in the baths, until he began to wonder if he'd heard it on the wind down south, too.

Until he woke, craving the sound.

Cyrus had started to wonder why it was she never gave him what it was she'd given other men—and why it was he wanted her anyway. Had he been wrong about her dating life these past two years?

But no. He'd had the men she'd had all those dinners with extensively researched. He could not imagine any one of them would have let her slip between their fingers. Yet still he wanted her—and more by the day.

He had imagined that fulfilling his part of the promises made would be a coldhearted exercise, something he could compartmentalize as easily as he did everything else. With a swift and calculated seduction that would leave them both in precisely the places they belonged, as he'd explained to her at the start. He'd intended to give her the position her father had wished her to have, but nothing else.

None of it had gone as expected.

Because he'd met her, touched her, carried her from that chapel. He'd tucked a scarf around her face to protect her from the desert sun. He had watched her laugh at him, more than once.

And there was nothing cold or calculated in the way they kissed.

He was quickly realizing that he wanted this wife of his far more than he should. Far more than was wise, as he had always been taught, for wanting was itself a weakness.

Something he was forced to reflect upon even more intently once he tore himself away from the dancing in the harem, settled himself in the office he used here, and tried to convince himself that he was neither besotted nor obsessed.

Which was hard to do when his man had asked him the very question he wished to answer least of all.

That of phase two of that original plan of his.

"I have assembled a slate of candidates, sire," his man told him, with obvious pride. "I have personally located the finest daughters of the finest men in the land. I have vetted the families myself, and I can tell you that not only are these women beautiful enough to be worthy of your notice, they are all eager for the opportunity to take their place in your harem and provide you with fine sons, so that the choice of the next Lord and King need not be made for them."

His own father had not been lucky in sons, something he and the whole of the country blamed on the woman who had stolen his firstborn from him. Whether that made sense or not had never mattered. Historically, the Lord of the desert tried to have as many sons as possible so he could, if necessary, make them into their own army. So had it been throughout the ages.

Cyrus did not feel he required an army. He tried to tell

himself that was why he was not moving to fill his harem the way he'd planned to have done already.

"You have done fine work and I am pleased," he told his man.

The man placed a tablet before him. He indicated that all Cyrus needed to do was swipe this way or that to view pictures of the women on offer along with dossiers outlining precisely who they were and the benefits they would provide the kingdom if elevated to one of the Lord's wives.

Cyrus nodded along.

And later, after he had taken several phone calls and video conferenced with a number of advisors, he found himself flipping listlessly through the pictures. All the women ran together. They were beautiful, each and every one of them. But instead of congratulating himself that he had such loveliness to choose from, he found himself instead entirely too preoccupied with Hope.

As if he was the one imprisoned, songs in his head once more.

It was unsupportable.

It had to stop.

"It is time," he muttered to himself, staring out his window and seeing her face in place of the endless sand.

He had the staff prepare the usual dinner he would share with her, but this time, in his actual bedchamber. They arranged it in front of the grand fireplace, there to make tolerable and comfortable the winter nights that could made this old place of stone intolerably frigid.

As he had discovered by living without a fire on the nights his father wished to teach him that lesson, too.

Then Cyrus found himself waiting for her arrival like some kind of moonfaced swain. A notion that made him so tense, his jaw hurt.

*This must end*, he growled at himself.

And there was only one way he could think to make that happen. An exorcism of sorts, though he intended for it to be far more pleasurable.

He turned when he heard a faint sound behind him and nodded curtly at the guards who bowed to him from the antechamber.

But his eyes were on the woman who came in when they stepped aside.

Hope looked far less anxious than he thought she should. Not a hint of worry marred her brow. If anything, she looked happier every time he saw her.

Happy, healthy and sporting a sort of glow he found enraging, because he liked it.

She looked far more beautiful than she had when he'd taken her from that chapel. As if she was blooming here in his desert, and more by the day.

"You look even more ferocious than usual," she told him as she moved toward him, her hips a mesmerizing roll. One more thing she had learned down in the harem, he knew. And this thing, she was good at. Too good, perhaps. "A bit too grizzly for your own good, I'd say."

"It occurs to me that you're entirely too happy." He sounded dark and mean to his own ears. Worse, he sounded perilously close to out of control. "This is meant to be punishment, Hope. Not summer camp."

If he needed any further indication that things had gone astray, she didn't cower at that. She didn't seem to hear what he did in his voice. She didn't fling herself prostrate before him so that she might press her lips to the toe of his shoe, as he had seen his father's other wives do on many occasions. Not Hope.

Hope laughed.

And kept walking toward him, so that he almost thought she meant to do something—

But instead she passed him entirely, then flung herself down onto the pillows as if this was her chamber and he the interloper.

As if she had been the one to summon him here tonight.

As if the Lord of the desert could be *summoned.*

"The time has come to begin selecting other wives," he told her, realizing as he did that there was a part of him that wanted that information to…wound her, somehow.

In case he needed an unwelcome reminder that he was not as free in his ideas as he liked to think. Because if he had been raised here the way his father had intended and without the corrosive influence of his mother and his formative years abroad, surely such a notion would never have occurred to him.

Men in his position took as many wives as they pleased and women vied for the honor. When she expressed her hurt, he would view it as an outrage, because it was.

"Wonderful!" Hope cried instead. "Do I get to help you choose?"

And Cyrus found that this was the greater outrage by far.

Because she was not a woman of the Aminabad Desert. She should have reacted the way he'd expected her to react. With tears, at the very least. His memory of his mother's reaction to each new wife his father took had been smashed crockery, anguished wailing and screaming threats—even years after she had left him and taken Cyrus with her.

Until this moment, he had not understood that he wanted that from Hope. And that what he wanted from this woman was some kind of indication that she—

But he stopped himself. That she…what?

Cared about him?

When he knew very well she did not. When he should not want her to in the first place. Nothing about this had anything to do with *caring*.

One of the things Cyrus had long enjoyed about his life and his position was the clarity of purpose it provided. He knew what his job was. He knew how he was meant to rule.

Cyrus had known exactly who he was since he was an adolescent.

His father had made sure that the things that were expected of Cyrus were etched deep into his bones.

He did not like this murkiness. He despised the way it sat upon him, a mess of something too dark and far too edgy for comfort.

And this woman dared to sit there *beaming* at him, as if he had offered her gifts instead of the kind of marriage she was supposed to find horrible.

"You wish to choose your own rivals?" He made himself laugh. "Let me guess. You think you can rule over them that way."

It was proper protocol to wait for the monarch to take his seat and taste his food before anyone else dared, but naturally Hope did as she liked. She broke off a piece of flatbread from one of the platters arrayed before her, then dipped it into a bowl of hummus flavored with garlic and tahini. She popped the bite into her mouth and closed her eyes for a moment, another example of that sensuality of hers and the way it infused everything.

The way it infused *him*.

It made his entire body clench tight.

And he wanted to believe that she did this deliberately to toy with him—but he could not quite make himself accept that. Hope seemed too unselfconscious. As if she didn't much care if he stood before her, watching her, or not.

He could not understand why that made his hunger for her all the more intense.

When she opened her eyes again, her golden gaze looked merry. "I don't believe that these women would be rivals at all." His disbelief must have showed on his face because she smiled. "It sounds like fun. Built-in friends and no one has to feel as if they do too much of anything. All of the labor is shared. Isn't that the point?"

"That is not the point." He folded his arms over his chest. "A man shows his wealth and might to the kingdom by the number of wives he is able to support. And then again, by the number of sons he has."

"So a mighty fortress and calling yourself King of this and Lord of that doesn't do the trick, then?"

"I tire of these games of yours," he gritted out.

But he was not tired. And she did not look at all chastened.

So Cyrus lowered himself to the cushions, and lay back. Then he waved a peremptory hand before him. "I think it is time you dance for me, wife. As is only fitting."

She went still, her hand hovering over the flatbread. For moment, he thought she might balk.

Did he want her to? Was that the point of this?

But in the next moment, she smiled. "I would love to, but I'm terrible. The women have been wonderful teachers and everyone agrees that while I'll never be up to the standard of a girl who's been doing these dances since birth, I should be competent enough in time, and potentially less embarrassing, too."

"Dance," he told her, gruffly. "Do not speak."

He knew as the words left his mouth that he wanted her to argue. Because he already regretted asking for this. Because when she moved, the silk moved with her, like a man's caress.

And when she got all the way to her feet and stood before him, there was no pretending that his hunger for her wasn't taking him over. It was.

There was no pretending that there was anything cold or calculating about this.

He was so hungry for her it nearly hurt.

"I still think it's weird that there's no music for this," she told him, when he could hear nothing but music in his own head.

He shook his head, but the music kept on. "Dance anyway."

She laughed a little, under her breath. But then she began.

And perhaps Cyrus had intended for this to snap him out of the spell he seemed to be under where she was concerned.

Perhaps he had thought that alone, without the other women to surround her and encourage her, she would be nothing but awkward and lose some of that brashness he found so baffling.

Perhaps that was what he wanted.

But instead, this woman he had taken to wife and had only kissed the slightest bit for his trouble, closed her eyes.

The way she did when she intended to enjoy something to the full, God help him.

And slowly, she began to roll her hips this way and that, making the silk dance around her.

That age-old song of his people. That call to lust and longing.

With that same sensuality that he saw in everything she did, Hope danced like fire, like flame.

Her feet were bare against the floor. He could see the enticing length of her legs nearly all the way up to her thighs, depending on how the silks moved. He could see most of her belly, jewels winking in her navel. And the top she wore looked soft and gleamed as she swayed, picking up the light in the room.

As she danced, she tipped her head back, a smile on her lips as if she was as lost in the pleasure of this as much as he was.

Maybe more.

It was too much.

"Open your eyes," he ordered her, in a gravelly voice he could not seem to control. "Dance for your king." She lowered her head, still moving, and opened up her eyes as he'd commanded. But that meant he was caught by all that gold. And revealed by it in turn, for he could not keep himself from gritting out what he shouldn't. "Dance for your husband, Hope."

And then everything was flame.

Everything was the roll of her hips, the fire in her molten gold eyes.

She danced and she danced, until they were both breathing too quickly. Still she kept on, whirling around and around the room, until Cyrus couldn't tell if she was claiming it, or him.

Or if she already had.

Maybe that was what pushed him to stand and go to her, sweeping her up into his arms, then carrying her across the vast chamber to his bed.

*At last.*

"I want your kisses," he told her, feeling rough and outside himself and as if he might perish if he did not do something about this madness clamoring inside him, this abominable need he could neither quit nor ignore. "But tonight, *omri*, I do not want you to stop."

She looked too beautiful there, finally lying in his arms. Her cheeks were flushed and her eyes were bright. Her golden hair fell all around her.

And she could not seem to lie still, as if the dance claimed her still.

As if she wanted to test out that same age-old rhythm with him, in the time-honored fashion.

Hope took a steadying sort of breath, and when she smiled he was sure he saw a wickedness there. It called to things in him he would have said could not possibly exist.

For Cyrus had been raised hard. His duties and responsibilities had been hammered into him again and again and again. He was the Lord of the desert and he did not bend, he did not break. He did not deviate from his path, and woe betide any who dared stand against him.

Even in song inside his own head.

But they were not standing, Hope and him.

And her smile made him wonder if he knew himself at all.

"I won't stop if you won't," she said, and it was a challenge. A dare.

And then she pressed her lips to his, rocked her hips against him, and Cyrus forgot he was anything but this.

Flesh and blood and a man.

And hers, whether he liked it or not.

# CHAPTER EIGHT

SENSATION WAS LIKE the music for dancing that Hope quickly found she didn't miss.

This melody was heat and flame.

It was the way Cyrus used his hands, his palms creating their own symphony against her skin.

And now they were wrapped around each other on this bed that had loomed so large in her imagination since the day she'd arrived in this fortress of stone, a monument against the sand.

How many times had she dreamed about the things they might do here? How many nights had she lain in her bed in the harem, pretending her own hands belonged to him instead? Now she wasn't pretending. Now it was finally happening.

And it put all her dreams to shame.

Cyrus was made of that same perfect bronze, everywhere. And as he held himself above her, the harsh lines of his face did not soften, precisely, but there was something about the intense way he gazed down at her that made her feel as if she did the softening for him.

Especially when his mouth was a stark line that carved out a hollow space within her, a cavern of fire and longing.

She was not at all surprised at the way she ached for him even now, with that melting heat everywhere. That ache was inside her, an overwhelming wildness that felt not unlike the desert outside. Shifting, voracious. An expanse with no end. Beautiful and terrible and all-consuming.

But then, he was the same.

Cyrus took her wrists in his hand, hauling her arms up over her head so that her breasts jutted up against him.

She had spent too long his harem, perhaps. Because she liked the way her breasts performed for him. For that look on his harshly beautiful face. For the way his dark eyes gleamed as he looked down upon her, freeing her quickly from the silk that barely contained the bounty that was his.

Only his.

The way her nipples were bold and needy and jutted toward him pleased her. Just as dancing for him had pleased her.

Because kissing this man had not broken any spells. If anything, kissing him had cast new ones, spinning her out and into the endless enchantment of need and desire, so she felt lost somewhere in the magic.

But the kind of lost that felt a whole lot like finding herself at last.

Especially when Cyrus made a low, deep noise of purely male approval at the sight of her breasts unbound for him.

He bent, one hand flat on the mattress beside her and the other stretched high to hold her hands where he wanted them, and he took one nipple deep into his mouth.

And as far as Hope could tell, tossed her straight into that molten flame.

Especially when Cyrus settled in as if he planned to be there some while.

Then he set himself to the task of driving her mad.

First he used his tongue and the suction of his devilish mouth. Then he used the edge of his teeth. As she arched against him, desperate to give him more—and more still—

he slid his hands down to span her ribs so he might hold her up to him like an offering.

His mouth was a glorious delirium, and then he would use one hand to make the sensation that much more intense. That much better.

Over and over again, and all Hope could do was surrender.

To the crash of lightning, one strike after the next. To the wild storm of passion that taught her things about herself she hadn't known before. Like the way everything was connected. That there was a straight line from each breast down into her core, and he knew precisely how to play it to make her moan.

He knew exactly how to make her little more than his instrument. How to play her body expertly until she was sobbing and shaking.

And then, even better, hurtled straight off the side of the cliff he'd made and broke apart entirely in midair.

For a while, then—perhaps an eternity—she drifted off somewhere. Into the starry night itself.

But she floated her way back down to earth, and she found that Cyrus had gone to the trouble of removing his clothes and was even now dispensing with what remained of hers.

And when he slid back into place beside her, the feel of his naked skin against hers was sweet and hot and so perfect she thought she might cry.

Everything inside her was humming and yielding, like she was made of honey, and she wanted nothing more than to sink into it. To *become* it.

Meanwhile, everything about Cyrus seemed heavy and taut and almost too hot, and that felt like more evidence that all of this was *right*.

That despite the distraction of harem dances and her daily

calls to a surprisingly not distraught Mignon, *this* was the point. That it didn't matter how she'd gotten here or what had come before. That she could have conducted a thousand not-quite dates with appalling men, and none of them mattered at all, because her whole life had been leading to this.

To him.

To *now*.

"Cyrus..." she began, in a voice that sounded both like her and not like her at all.

As if she was already changed forever.

"Quiet, *omri*," he murmured. His gaze was a glittering thing and she wasn't sure what left more fire in its wake—the places where his eyes traveled or the work of his hands. Either way, she could feel that softness in her shifting already, heating up, becoming its own bright heat. "The time for words has passed."

And that seemed more than fine to Hope, because words took effort and all she wanted to do was throw herself headfirst—again—into the abandonment he promised with every touch, every look.

A promise he had already more than kept.

But first Cyrus took it upon himself to explore every bit of her body.

He flipped her so that she was facedown on the bed and she found herself laughing with the sheer joy of it as he began at her feet, then took his time, seeming to learn every bit of her while she pressed herself into the caress of the sheets beneath her and felt her own temperature skyrocket.

And by the time he made it to her neck, she wasn't laughing any longer.

He pressed hot, stirring kisses to her nape. And his hands were like angels and demons at once, making her writhe and moan.

Cyrus held her to him, palming the side of her face and turning her head so that his mouth could find hers.

His kiss was bold and deep, demanding and stirring, and she could do nothing but give herself over to it—to him—completely.

Especially when he took his other hand and stroked his way over one breast, down to her navel, and then, at last, found her soft, swollen folds.

He played there for a moment, then delved within.

It was almost too much, Hope thought, but she could barely form the ghost of that thought in her own head.

Because he drew figure eights in her softness, learning the honeyed contours of her most secret place. And even as she moaned into his mouth, his tongue stroked her there, too.

And when she shuddered at the dual assault, his fingers reached deeper and he found her entrance.

Then, with an inexorable twist of his wrist, he thrust a long, hard finger in deep.

Making everything seemed to throb and glow.

He kissed her and kissed her, still holding her splayed out between his mouth and his hand.

At her core, he played her expertly, that impossibly hard finger inside her while his thumb found her proud center, making her buck against him, moving her hips in an inexpert haze of joy and need—

Until she broke apart all over again.

And this time, Cyrus didn't let her drift off.

He rolled her over to her back, and found his way between her legs, drawing them open and settling himself between them.

Hope was still sobbing wildly, still shaking.

And that hard jut of his manhood that she had felt against the small of her back became something else again as he ran the length of it through her folds, making the storm that gripped her go on and on and on.

Making her shake even more at the size of him.

And the sure knowledge that he intended to replace his finger with…*that*.

Hope might have been a virgin, but there was nothing shy about her.

Quite the opposite. She'd researched. Extensively.

From films so explicit she'd had to watch them from between her fingers to breathtaking erotic writing that had made her a little too susceptible to unfortunate fantasies that she knew better than to hope the sort of man she was set to marry might fulfill in some way. Much less exceed.

She knew where all the parts went and how they fit together. She had done her level best to get ready so that nothing would faze her too badly no matter who she ended up marrying.

But nothing could have prepared her for Cyrus. Or how this *felt*.

When Cyrus lowered his hard, beautiful chest to hers. When he wrapped his arms around her, holding her so much closer, so much tighter than she had imagined—because, something in her understood belatedly, all the films she'd watched had been staged for a viewer.

Here, now, there were only the two of them.

The two of them and this magic conflagration between them.

The two of them and too much sensation to bear in one body. Maybe that was why it took two in the first place, to share the glory between them, because surely it would otherwise be too much.

Especially because he knew how to wield that great, hard, and hot part of him that he rubbed and rubbed through her softness, driving her mad.

Making her feel turned inside out.

And all of that was nothing—a clamoring whirlwind of a glorious nothing—next to how it felt when he reached down between them, wrapped his fist around his thickness, and guided himself to her molten channel at last.

His finger had felt too big, a decidedly male intrusion, but this was something else again.

This was an undoing.

Cyrus pressed his way in, but only slightly, stopping when both of them felt him catch on the flesh that his finger had eased past, but the enormity of his manhood could not.

His midnight gaze found hers, and she could not tell which one of them was breathing heavier just then. Nor which one of them was making that sound, so raw, so needy, that seemed to fill her from within.

He did not speak. She could not have answered.

And still, it was as if a whole conversation happened there in that lightning hit of his gaze to hers.

Some understanding. Some knowledge, primitive though it might have been.

A kind of anguish on his face that even here, even now, she had succeeded in surprising him.

Something entirely feminine and deeply held within her seemed to nod, as if she'd known how this would be all along.

As if she'd known it would be him, and now, and *this* since before she'd known her own name.

"Forgive me, *omri*," Cyrus murmured, and his voice was like a dark ribbon of sound that tied itself around her. And with her thighs wide open to hold him and all of him pressed between them, he had finally said those words as if he meant them.

*My life. Forgive me.*

It didn't occur to her to ask him why he needed her for-giveness, or to tell him it was already freely given, or to wonder why this moment felt like an intense *recognition*—

Instead he thrust home.

And everything went dark.

Then burst into light, so bright and so hot that Hope wasn't sure she could tell the difference between a marvel-ous pain and a maddening pleasure.

It was so *intense*. It was too much, of everything. He was too big, and she *couldn't*, and she could hear, far off in the distance, sounds she knew were her own odd little pants—

But Hope couldn't possibly care about that, because he pulled back out a little, then thrust deep again.

Making room.

Making a kind of symphony tear through her, like a new kind of storm.

And then, stroke by stroke, Cyrus taught her how to sing.

With every part of her body.

He taught her what it was to be a song. How the two of them fit together, wrapped tight around each other, melody and descant at once.

He taught her how to climb straight up to a high note so pure, so good, it felt like flying.

And how to fall, brought back to earth with each ruth-less thrust of him inside her.

Again and again and again, they sang this song. They learned the words. She tasted them on his tongue. She dug her fingers into his wide back, and learned a far better dance with her hips against his.

Until, at last, she felt apart so hard it made her voice shake.

Cyrus followed her, shouting out his pleasure.

Then he wrapped her in his arms, murmuring words in

his language that made her shiver all the more, and let them both go still.

Hope thought lifetimes might have passed. He rolled over, taking his weight from her and pulling her with him. She lay splayed out over his chest, her ear over his heart, and found she could hardly remember a *before* or think about an *after*.

There was only that drumbeat beneath her. The heat of his skin. Cyrus, all around her, and his hair-roughened thighs against hers to remind her even now of their differences. Of his delicious maleness that she wanted to explore all over again.

Just as soon as she caught her breath.

She thought he would hate it if he knew that she could hear his heartbeat. If he knew how deeply that pleased her. How she wanted to dance to the beat of that low thunder beneath her head.

Eventually she felt his hand as he moved it up and down the length of her spine, easily. Lazily.

Spinning out a new, sweet flame as it went.

And when she shifted to look up at him, his midnight gaze seemed brighter than usual, almost as if—

But he was moving before she could complete that thought, bringing her with him. He swept her up into his arms and this time, did not toss her over his shoulder as he had in that chapel she could barely recall.

This time he held her before him, so she could have laid her head on his shoulder if she wished. He carried her through the mazelike rooms of his apartments, down yet another stone stair, until they ended up in a place she knew well. The baths.

Except these were not the harem baths, tucked away where the hot springs bubbled from below, hidden away in the belly of the fortress. He walked her past a long pool with windows than arched up over the central courtyard that would have let the light in, if it were day. He carried her up a set of wide, mosaic-laid stairs, and then into what seemed like its own oasis.

There were smaller pools gathered here and there beneath clusters of trees, and up above, when she tipped her head back, she realized she could see the stars.

Cyrus took her over to the furthest pool that bubbled and murmured into the night. He did not release his hold on her as he stepped in, then settled them both on the bench beneath the water.

Hope sighed a little as the warm water enveloped her, assuming he would let go of her. Set her aside now that they were both wet.

But instead he shifted how he held her, and kept her in his lap, her back to his chest and his chin resting on the top of her head.

And between the heat of the pool and the hard heat of his body, she felt sleepy. Yet wide awake. Because she felt far more safe and secure than perhaps she should have.

Not like a child. Not like that little girl that she had been in her papa's study, but as if this had been the point all along. To grow up, leave home, and find a place or person that could make her feel as gloriously alive and as much of a woman as he had tonight, but then also give her this besides.

As if, at last, she was protected. The way her father had intended.

Hope felt her heart kick at her, hard, at the thought.

It was like this intimacy with Cyrus bled into everything. As if, even now, sitting in this water, she was changing.

His fingers played idly with her hair, his body was a warm, slick chair, and the water was like a soft prayer all around them. She didn't want to say a word. She didn't want to think.

Hope wanted nothing more than this.

For as long as *this* might last.

And, unbidden, she felt a well of understanding for her sweet, silly mother wash over her then, there in the starlight. Was this what Mignon had always been after? This sense that she was finally complete?

Because Hope was tempted to believe that nothing truly bad could ever happen when there was this connection, this quiet joy.

That this was the beginning and the end of everything.

"You should have told me," Cyrus said some long while later, there in the quiet dark, lit only by the stars far above. "You should have told me from the first."

She didn't pretend not to understand what he meant. "Would you have believed me if I had?"

Hope felt more than heard him sigh at that. And then his hands were on her, shifting her around so that she knelt up over him, there in the thick, soft water.

Hope's eyes had long since adjusted to the dark. And sitting this way was better, because that bronze face of his was covered in stars and it was as if all of that shine blurred the sharp, cruelly beautiful edges.

So that he looked the way he always did when she imagined him, alone in her bed.

She followed an urge she might have restrained in the daytime, tracing the shape of his cheekbones and then that stark, hard line of his mouth.

"You should have told me," he said again, but his voice was darker then.

Hope thought it sounded more like a condemnation of himself than of her.

"If I'm honest," she told him, "I quite preferred the moral high ground."

She'd meant that to lighten the mood, somehow. She even smiled, but he only looked at her as if she was some kind of ghost.

"As well you should," he told her then, in that voice of his that sounded like a proclamation. "But I have always held myself to higher standards of behavior than others. When I am wrong I say it, and I have wronged you, *omri*."

And then there was nothing light in Hope, either. Only the weight of his gaze and the way he looked at her, straight on, so there could be no hiding from this. From the apology he made so fully and matter-of-factly.

"Allow me to compensate you for any suffering I might have caused," he said in a low voice. "An apology, if you will."

"I don't want your apologies," she told him, though she would treasure his all the same. I want—"

"Hope." And she stilled as he held her there, still kneeling over him. "I know what you want, if nothing else."

And she thought she should argue about that, but he was huge and hard between them and she was already shivery with delight.

Then his hands were on her bottom, shifting her up and over him, so he could work his way inside her, slick and hot. Until he was settled in deep, nudging the very depths of her once more.

Where he stayed, his gaze as hard on her as he was deep inside her, watching her work to accommodate him. Because he filled her so completely and slightly more than was comfortable.

And she had never imagined that he could feel like this. It was as if she had never been more herself than when he was deep inside her, connecting them like this. Changing everything.

Changing her most of all.

And Hope didn't need him to tell her what to do, just like she didn't need all of that research she had done before. Her mind was a perfect blank of everything but this.

There was nothing for her but him.

Nothing but Cyrus, forever.

And then her body's insistence that she roll her hips and teach herself how to rock back and forth against that deep shaft of pure male fire deep inside.

She did it again and again.

And it was different like this, kneeling over him and rubbing the greediest part of her against him every time she moved.

It was different this time, because she knew where they were going. Because she had an inkling, now, of the catastrophic joy that awaited them both.

*Because you love him*, came a voice from deep inside her that sounded too much like fate, like another thing she had always known—

But she threw that aside, because what mattered was this, him, now.

This apology of his that felt like grace. Like a new song and the same song, blended into one, into *them*.

What mattered was the sensation, nothing more.

Because he might have made her his wife, but Hope knew full well that she was still his captive.

And love had nothing to do with this.

So she told herself as she rode them both to a shattering finish, and poured herself out into his hands.

Again and again and again.

# CHAPTER NINE

HOPE'S VIRGINITY WAS yet another shock this woman had delivered to him.

It was the biggest yet.

Cyrus could admit, days later, that he still had not fully taken that particular reality on board.

Because he had misjudged her. He had wronged her, as he had said. And he could take all his men to task for failing him—he did—but that didn't change the broader issue. Cyrus, who prided himself on his discernment, had been completely and utterly wrong about the woman he'd married.

In every respect.

He didn't know what to *do* with that. He didn't know what it *meant*.

What else was he wrong about? What else had he missed? These questions haunted him.

And having enjoyed her in full at last, he had spent the whole next day doing nothing but exulting in her, certain he would find himself satiated at any moment. But when that moment never arrived—because, once again, he was entirely wrong—he thought it prudent to institute some rules.

Meaning, it became a necessity.

Because he was the King. He was the Lord of this desert

and he could not lose himself in a woman's bed, no matter how tempting Hope was to him.

So he waited with ill-concealed and somewhat worrying eagerness until nightfall each day, when he could meet with her at last, suffer through a meal, and then gorge himself on what he truly wanted.

Tonight, while Hope licked her fingers and drove him mad with her greedy little noises in appreciation of the sweet pastries she claimed were her favorite, he thought he might as well satisfy his curiosity as well as his other, baser urges.

If gracelessly. "I don't understand why you made it seem as if you had enjoyed the company of so many men when you had not done anything of the kind," he said, as if she was to blame for the reports his men had delivered to him and the conclusions he had reached.

"I don't know what made you think I was enjoying the company of men in the first place," Hope replied in her usual bright and carefree way, here in the privacy of the tower, where their only ceiling was the starry night high above.

She lounged back against the bright pillows, and no longer did the silks she wore seem like a costume. It was clear to him that she inhabited them fully. That somehow, she had become the very height of femininity to him, awash in wiles and without peer.

Or maybe it was simply that he knew too well how happy he was to watch the silk against her skin, caressing her as he knew he would. And soon.

He told himself restraint was a virtue, though at the moment it felt far more like a curse.

And he knew too well now that she was not the brazen, careless, hedonistic socialite he'd imagined her before he'd met her. No morally bankrupt creature like so many he had met while doing his Oxbridge duty and had assumed she emulated.

There was also that part of him that knew too well that he had already felt lost in her long before he knew of her innocence. He had already wanted her too much.

He had already married her and had already been entirely too consumed with kissing her—but he did not choose to focus on those uncomfortable truths. Not now.

He frowned at her instead. "I still cannot understand what you thought you were doing. Surely there were better options available to you than looking for a potential husband in such an unseemly way."

She eyed him lazily, almost insolently, from her pillows. "How did you set about looking for a wife?" she asked. "I was under the impression your grandmother made arrangements and you signed papers, sight unseen. Would that have been better? More *seemly*, somehow, than going out to dinner the way people have been doing for ages?"

He regretted telling her the details of how the contract she'd never seen had come to be, not that he planned to admit such a thing. Because Cyrus had the lowering suspicion that once he started making more admissions, the fortress would crumble all around him like so much dust.

And he wasn't sure if he meant the actual fortress they sat in or...himself.

"Better than letting it look as if you were dating half the men in London? Yes."

"It only looked that way if you were spying on me when you could have helped me," she said reprovingly, though her eyes were gleaming. "But even if I had been dating merrily, so what? That's another thing people do, you know."

And he knew the cheeky look she got about her when she was poking at him, deliberately, because he usually answered in the way that pleased them both the most. Cyrus could not say he minded it.

Still, today, he ignored his body's immediate reaction to that sparkle in her gaze. "People might," he agreed. "But not you. Not an innocent who hardly knew what her body was for when I met her."

He stated that as fact. And knew it was one when she flushed.

"I know what my body is for now," she said, her voice soft.

Cyrus no longer sat across from her, because that was too far away after whole days apart. And because if there was a table between them, he could not do what he did now and simply pull her close so he could get his mouth on her. So he could pull her over him, or beneath him, or like now, simply flush against the side of his body, because he always preferred to feel her.

"Hope." He said her name, there against her mouth. "Why?"

She breathed something that sounded like his name, and then she sat back, pushing her golden hair back as she moved. And there was something almost helpless in her bright gaze when she looked at him. "My mother."

"Your mother made you date these men?" he asked, astonished—and instantly deciding to cut the older woman off entirely.

"Of course not." Hope sat back from him, and frowned down at the place where her hands rested on her own thighs as she knelt there beside him. "She would have loved to save us herself. She tried. Oh, how she tried. But she wasn't made for hard things."

"Softness is an indulgence," Cyrus told her, not sure why

his chest felt tight. "If you do not indulge it, it cannot rule you."

"And a dandelion is unlikely to turn into a loaded gun simply because it stops coddling itself," Hope replied, with a laugh. But the laugh ended quickly, and now she was looking at him with that helpless gaze that made that tightness in his chest…worse. "But I wasn't made to be a pretty flower. It made sense that it was me."

"You were the child." Cyrus scowled at her. "It was her responsibility to care for you, not the other way around."

And he heard himself say that. He heard it, and he felt it, too. The way it made his own bones seem to shift their places inside him.

Worse, he saw that helpless look on Hope's face shift too, into something like compassion. "If she could have, she would have. But I love her too, you see. So I did what needed doing and regretted that I couldn't do more. That there were…limits to what I could stomach doing. She didn't hold that against me. She isn't like that. She's like a hummingbird, dancing from one sweet thing to the next. That's where she's best."

"She should have tried parenting," Cyrus said, because he couldn't seem to stop. Not even when the words made his bones feel as if they were breaking themselves inside him. Not even when he couldn't decide if he was betraying the memory of the man who'd made him or finally speaking the one terrible truth he'd been avoiding since he'd been brought to this place when he was twelve.

But if he chose, if he acknowledged what this was, he didn't know what would happen to him. He didn't know what would become of him.

If so many of the pillars he'd built his life on were wrong, if *he* was wrong, then who was he?

And somehow, Hope seemed to know that, too. Because she leaned in and slid her hand over his jaw. "I don't hold that against her, either. Do you know why?"

Cyrus was terribly afraid he did.

But he couldn't seem to stop her from saying it anyway. He couldn't seem to move.

"Because that's what love is," Hope told him with a quiet certainty and that look in her eyes. "It forgives and loves on, no matter what. There's nothing soft about that."

And Cyrus wanted to shout his own battlements down, but he could not let himself do such things. He was the King.

So instead he hauled her to him. And then he showed her precisely how he felt about the things she'd said to him tonight, right there on the tower floor, bathing them both in starlight, as if that could chase away that ache in his bones.

As if that could hold off the storm Cyrus was terrified was coming for him, no matter how clear the skies looked as the sands shifted all around him. Whispering of a reckoning to come.

Whispering words he had never allowed to be spoken in his hearing.

Singing old songs he kept imagining he could scrub from his mind entirely, only to wake up with those same old melodies on his tongue.

More days passed, turning into weeks. Summer settled in. And even though Cyrus knew it was long past time that he got back to his usual travels, staying in each of the desert's four separate regions for a season so that his people could know him and follow him because they knew he understood them, too—he was loathe to do it.

Just as he found himself curiously uninterested in adding to his harem as originally planned. No matter how many times his man discreetly placed the tablet back in the center of his desk, he set it aside and focused on other matters.

He told himself he was merely indulging this strange desire for Hope that had overtaken him, but that he would soon grow bored. For nothing could last, this he knew. That was one of the desert's finest lessons. Nothing was truly permanent, save change itself.

Certainly nothing this intense, this all-consuming.

Storms were not made for longevity. His father had taught him that long ago, right here in the fortress. They had watched sandstorms—sometimes from the safety of these walls and sometimes out in them with only a makeshift cave for shelter—and no matter how terrifying, they always blew themselves out. And no matter the new formations, the dunes knocked down here and raised again there, it was still the desert.

The desert always remained.

And so too would Cyrus once this particular storm blew itself out.

He held on to that.

He told himself that it was no catastrophe that all he thought about was Hope. It was simply the nature of a storm—who thought of other things while sand whirled about like rain? So too during all of his calls, all of his tedious video conferences, all the short trips that felt like an imposition instead of a part of his sworn duty—he found that he could not give the whole of his attention as he usually did because part of it was always with her.

The summer wore on and he told himself that even though this madness between them seemed to grow in intensity by the day, it would stop. It would end.

As all things ended.

But in the meantime, he was like a man possessed.

It didn't matter how many times he told himself that she was only a woman, and surely no woman was that much different from another.

Because it seemed to him in those hours when he moved inside of her—when they came together again and again so that it seemed there was no end or beginning to the shapes they made or the things they felt—he knew deep inside of him that if asked, he would be unable to remember if he had ever touched another.

He could hardly remember it away from her, either.

One night, while waiting for his guards to bring her to him so they could enact that formal handoff that he knew pleased them both with its archaic formality, he found himself thinking that all his ancestors who'd stood here before him were to be pitied. For surely none of them had found a woman like this. A woman like Hope. If they had, he knew, there would have been no need for a harem in the first place.

But even as he thought such a thing, it infuriated him.

Or rather, what infuriated him was that he thought the notion ought to enrage him—but it didn't.

As if his particular storm was here to stay.

And when he heard her feet behind him, he was scowling as he turned to look at her.

She did not pause. Not Hope. She came straight to him anyway, her fingers finding that furrow between his brows and smoothing it away.

More damning, he let her.

"Do I displease you tonight?" she asked, but not as if she had the slightest worry that she might. "It's my dancing, isn't it? You've finally accepted what I told you all along. I really am utterly dreadful."

Cyrus should have hated that she made him want to laugh. But he didn't hate it. He didn't hate a single thing about her and that was the trouble. He could even feel his mouth betray him with the slightest curve.

It was an outrage.

"You are truly dreadful," he agreed, but he found that outrage couldn't quite take hold. "But I like it."

He could not wait for the ritual of a meal. He took her then in a swift glut of what he told himself was fury, tossing her over the edge of the bed and kicking her legs aside. He tugged her silks out of his way so he could slam himself inside her, lifting her hips up to meet him as he took her in a hurry from behind.

As if he thought that if he gave himself over to the madness of it all, she would not join him in the glorious, plummeting fall from such heights. That if she didn't, that might put him right at last.

But she did. She always did.

Even if, like tonight, she dared to reach down herself and make certain of it.

No other woman would dare, Cyrus knew. No other woman would dream of taking pleasure he didn't give her. It would be seen as an insult.

He did not understand why it was that he loved it when this one did as she pleased.

Cyrus could not even manage to pretend to feel it as some kind of insult, because he liked it when she shattered all around him, her tight sheath gripping him, tugging him, taking him with her when she took flight.

Later, after they'd showered together—and he'd spent some time using her sweetness an appetizer, kneeling before her as the water beat down and licking that sweet honey from between her legs that he found he craved far more than anything served from his kitchens—they settled in for a meal before the windows that let in the desert.

It was starting to get darker sooner. It was full dark now, when, back when he'd first brought her here, they had watched the last of the sunset over their meals.

Cyrus had to acknowledge that the coming change of seasons made him restless. As if the turning of the earth would force him into making the decisions he been putting off, if not facing the storms he knew were coming for him.

"If I am your wife because you said so when we arrived, does that make me your queen as well?" Hope asked, drawing his attention back to her from the great desert outside.

Another woman would have asked that question in a voice filled with court intrigue and politics, but this was Hope. She seemed far more focused on the savory dishes in pots before her. He could not imagine that she was suddenly showing any real interest in the Aminabad throne.

Perhaps that was why it seemed no particular hardship to answer her in a way he would not have done if he'd imagined she was angling for a crown, like too many of the women he'd met in his lifetime—blurry as they all seemed to him now.

"They are not the same," he told her. "In order to be known as my queen, I would need to pronounce you such. My father was renowned for having many queens, one after the next. It was a gift he gave each new wife when he thought they might be the one to give him another son. It was not a gift he ever extended to my mother."

"Because he was punishing her." And it was only when he had been silent some while, glaring at her, that Hope looked up. She blinked, looking baffled. "Did I say something wrong?"

"My mother kidnapped the heir to this kingdom, Hope. You seem to forget that."

"Yes, but he kidnapped you right back. If it was wrong when she did it, why was it right when he did it in return?"

Her eyes were clear gold and there was no reason he should feel as if they pierced him straight through.

"The issue of whether or not she was a queen was before all of that," he heard himself say.

Hope tilted her head to one side, holding a piece of the flatbread she preferred in her fingers. "But she'd already given him a son. You."

And it struck without warning, the storm he'd been hoping he might avoid after all. The last remaining pillar seemed to crumble into dust between them, and without the howl and thunder he had been expecting.

It was such a quiet thing, in the end.

His father had punished his mother after she'd given him a son, but before she'd taken Cyrus away from him. He had refused to make her his queen. The scenes that Cyrus remembered, of shouting and weeping and smashing crockery, must have occurred between those two things, though his father had always made it sound as if his treatment of Cyrus's mother was predicated entirely on her betrayal.

But what if that wasn't the truth? What if the things his father had always told him were as wrong as everything else?

What if it had all been a lie for a cruel man to not only justify his treatment of his wife, but of his son?

What if Cyrus's entire life was the lie?

He felt the floor beneath him seem to buckle. He focused on the frown on Hope's lovely face.

"You are not my queen," he told her, as if it was a confession. His voice felt gritty in his own mouth. "Unless I choose to make you my queen. The kingdom is always mine—you would be Queen only at my pleasure."

And he understood as he said it that this, too, was a cruelty his father had visited first upon his mother, then upon him. He had given every other wife the designation, purely to rub salt in the wound. But then, after beating it into Cyrus that he was to hate the woman who had stolen him from a man Cyrus knew full well was barbaric, he had seen to it that Cyrus would repeat the cycle.

"It is easy to take a wife," he made himself say, because she was still watching him, still frowning at him, as if she sensed the storm yet could not see it. "It is slightly more complicated to make that wife a queen, as it requires more people. So yes, there is a ceremony of sorts. The woman in question does not need to be present, though she can be. It is typically a conversation between a king and his men, asking them to offer fealty to the new Queen."

"Naturally." Hope eyed him. "Why should the woman be involved at all? You might as well make the nearest chair your queen, by that logic."

He was surprised that hadn't been suggested. Instead, his father had seen to it that Cyrus would marry an English-woman because it was tradition and hate her, too, because he'd spent so many years being primed to find her every move suspect. It would not surprise him in the least if the old King was somehow responsible for that missing contract, too.

If he had somehow made certain that Cyrus would come into his marriage filled with exactly the sort of deep, cruel fury his father had claimed was a family trait.

Cyrus had always seen himself as more rational than his father, though he had wisely kept that to himself. He had always assumed that when tested, he would never behave as the old man had.

And yet he had kidnapped this woman with his own two hands. He had thrown her over his shoulder and car-ried her away, and it was only by the greatest luck—luck he did not deserve—that she happened to be *this* woman, who had laughed in his face, danced in his harem, and ruined him completely.

But the nights were growing colder. It was impossible to pretend that summer was not coming to a close. A whole season that he had spent here, with her, instead of doing what he had long held to be the most critical part of his duty.

He knew that was on him.

Just as he knew that he could not be around this woman again until he looked himself full in the mirror and undertook his own reckoning.

Until he found out who he really was, not simply who his father had made him.

"It is unacceptable that the Lord of the Aminabad Desert should be beholden to anyone," he decreed then, making her eyes go wide. "Much less a woman. You must see that this can't go on, Hope. Not like this. It is time to return to reality."

"It was the talk of queens, wasn't it," Hope said, staring back at him. Though she didn't look at all concerned. "It wound you right up."

"I am not *wound up*." But he wasn't going to argue with her. He was going to do what he should have done a long time ago and act like the King he'd been born to be, not the man who had been made in the fire of old cruelties and too many poisons to name. "I will leave you here. You can carry on as you like. You might even get the hang of dancing."

"Dancing," she repeated, as if he'd said something shocking.

"I will return to you next summer," he told her and this time, he meant it as the decree it was. "My men will let me know how you are faring."

"Oh, good," Hope said, though her eyes were dark. "They've always been so good at that."

"We had a summer," he said, though he was afraid he could feel his own body crumbling where he stood. As if he was one more pillar rendered unto dust by these terrible truths he still didn't want to face. But he would. "We will have another one."

It felt like a concession. Yet as his words hung there in the bedchamber between them, Cyrus reflected on the fact that, really, he could have chosen his moment with more care.

This announcement would likely have gone over better if he had not been seized with his usual hunger for her when she'd arrived tonight. If he had not blurted it out like that.

If he could find a way to stop looking at her as if she was the only safety from the storm he'd ever known while she looked at him as if he'd taken leave of his senses.

Still, he had not expected her laughter.

Particularly because it did not sound the way it normally did.

Tonight he thought it seemed tinged with a little bit of that hysteria that he remembered from long ago.

He found he liked it a lot less now.

"That sounds like a great plan." Hope did not sound as if she thought it sounded anything like great. But she was smoothing her silks back into place, so only the way her hair swung indicated that she was more agitated than she wished to show him. "There are only two problems, as far as I can see."

He stepped away from her, because he could not seem to think straight when she was near. "There are no problems. It will go as I have said it will. For so I have decreed it."

"You can decree it all you like," Hope said, her voice more clipped than he was used to hearing it. Even the gold of her gaze looked far darker. "Your first problem, though

I'm sure you'll consider it a minor and inconsequential one, is that I'm in love with you, Cyrus. For my sins."

"That is nothing to do with me," he growled out at her, because it should have been exactly that. Nothing. Air. Forgotten as soon as it was said.

He certainly shouldn't feel a kind of roaring triumph deep within him. This was what he had wanted at the start though he had nearly forgotten it, somehow, over the course of these months. She was *meant* to be in love with him.

This was the whole point. He'd wanted her to feel sick with it. To suffer for it.

He had always assumed that when she told him it had happened, as it inevitably would, he would laugh. Because his revenge would be complete.

Tonight, he did not feel like laughing.

Because if he did, wouldn't that mean it was his father's revenge that had won the day? It would mean he had made Cyrus exactly like him. The kind of man who would take a woman away from everything she knew, love her until she loved him back, then tell her it had all been a bit of seduction and he would never feel the same.

Wasn't that the trajectory of his parents' relationship?

How could he ever have imagined he could behave this way? Cyrus couldn't access the man of fury who had so coldly told this woman that he would hold her life in his hand—when all along, it had been the opposite.

He had been wrong about her in every possible way.

And anyway, she did not appear to have heard him.

"But you have a bigger problem," she was saying instead. "And I'm certain you won't think it inconsequential in the least."

She smiled, and he had an inkling that he was not going to like whatever she had to say at all.

*Or*, something in him whispered, in a voice he told himself he did not recognize as he had not heard it in so long, not unless it was a song, *you might well like it too much, Cyrus. And then what will become of you?*

But he could not entertain his mother now, not even in his own head.

He thought he might explode.

"Hope," he began. *"Omri—"*

But she would not be silenced.

Not even by that endearment that he had not said sardonically in quite some time.

"Congratulations, Cyrus," she said instead, with that steel beneath her soft tone that always told the truth about who she was. How had he let himself forget that, too? "I'm pregnant."

And that was when Cyrus understood that Hope had been the real storm all along, delivering him straight into his doom.

# CHAPTER TEN

HOPE DIDN'T EXPECT Cyrus to throw her a baby shower. She wasn't *completely* delusional.

But she also hadn't expected that she would end the night in the dungeons.

Or that she would be the one to march down into the bowels of the fortress and lock herself in.

It had seemed liked a good idea at the time.

"You can come out of there any time you like," Cyrus growled from the other side of the bars. "This stunt of yours has gone far enough."

"When you say you're going to throw someone in your dungeons, I bet you mean it," she observed, then beamed a smile in Cyrus's direction. "So do I."

"You cannot throw yourself in a dungeon, Hope."

"I just did."

And there were other things she could have said to him then. Like the things she'd said a little too hotly upstairs, thinking she could poke at him the way she always did and he would explode the way *he* always did, and everything would end the way it normally did—with him so deep inside her there would be no telling who was who.

But Cyrus had not imploded.

If anything he had looked as close to defeated as she'd ever seen him, and that had made her want to sob as nothing else could have. She'd felt her eyes well with tears, when she hadn't cried since her father died.

*I would have locked myself away in the fortress dungeons if I had ever imagined these things could be possibilities,* he had told her.

That was the first she'd heard of dungeons.

But she'd been focused on the rest of it. *Love isn't a disease, Cyrus. And I was the virgin when we met, yet even I knew that since we weren't particularly responsible about protection, a baby was always a possibility.*

That wasn't strictly true. She'd known, yes. But after a lifetime of not understanding why any woman would have sex with a man if she couldn't talk to him about protection, she'd found that she always had better things to talk to Cyrus about.

Somehow, the subject never came up.

*I thought this was what you wanted,* she'd said to him, all the while thinking that maybe it was what she'd wanted, actually. Way down deep where even she didn't know, maybe she'd longed for happy families all along.

And wasn't that a shock? When she'd long since thought herself far too worldly and sophisticated to believe in such fairy tales.

*No,* Cyrus had said in that gruff, low voice that hurt her to hear, his dark eyes so grim, so lost. *This was not at all what I wanted.*

Hope would have taken a moment to take stock of her new surroundings now, but it didn't require a moment. There was nothing here but bars on the door in front of her, a slightly raised hole in the floor she didn't care to consider too closely, and the cold stone floor.

This was well and truly an underground cell, as promised, with only the faintest sliver of a tiny window that she imagined might let in the sun in the morning.

If the sand didn't cover it first.

"At least the cell is dry," she said, cheerfully enough. Because she'd chosen this, after all. "It doesn't feel too warm or too cold, which is lovely. Honestly, Cyrus, if I hadn't spent the summer being fussed over in the harem, I might not have noted much of a change between my old flat in London and this. I'm happy to stay here for some time."

"Happy," he echoed. "And do you know, *omri*—? I believe you mean that."

Cyrus stared back at her as if he was looking for some kind of answer on her face. Hope kept her smile welded into place. Then he made a low sort of noise, wheeled around, and walked off down the hall. Back the way he'd come.

That was just as well, Hope told herself. Because she had been the one falling apart upstairs. She was the one who had come perilously close to an implosion.

Demanding the keys to his dungeons when he'd been implacable about leaving her here had felt like the only thing she could do.

Now, alone in her cell, Hope wondered for the first time in her whole life if she was more like her mother than she'd ever believed possible.

Because if she wasn't mistaken, she'd just pitched what could only be called a scene. Though if ever there was a time to do it, she had to think being rejected by the man she loved after telling him she was pregnant with his child had to rank pretty high on the list.

She was sure that Mignon would approve.

*Good job I'm not afraid of the dark*, she told herself stoutly, now she was alone and there was only a bit of insipid light from out in the otherwise empty dungeon hall.

Then she took herself off to the furthest corner of the cell, which was to say, she took three steps, turned her back to the stone wall, and slid down onto the floor.

She listened to his footsteps disappear down that long stone walkway that she'd charged down as if she'd known where she was going. And when the last sounds of him faded and she heard that old iron door slam shut, Hope let herself breathe.

It had only been the other day when she'd realized that one of the reasons her time here had been so blissful was because there had been no monthly interruptions of that moody gargoyle that overcame her for a handful of days at a time.

And once she started thinking about that, she'd known.

She'd *known*, as if the knowing had always been there just beneath the surface, waiting for her to acknowledge it.

Hope had been lying in her alcove with one hand pressed to the belly that still felt like hers when Yara, her favorite of all her attendants, had appeared in the archway, looked directly at the place where her hand rested, and lifted dark eyes filled with speculative wonder to meet Hope's own.

*I d-don't know,* Hope had stammered. *I only think maybe I might...*

The girl had whirled around and disappeared, but had come back swiftly. Hope had been standing by then, filled with a strange energy and a kind of indecision, too.

*I don't want to tell him anything unless I know,* she'd told the girl, maybe with too much of the things she felt in her voice, whatever those were. *I assume you must have your ways here. Ancient ways. Tea leaves, or some sort of magic drink, or...?*

The girl had held out a perfectly modern pregnancy test. *Or...* she'd agreed, with a smile.

They had known the truth within moments. It had been undeniable. Right there on the little stick.

*You will tell our king tonight,* the girl had said matter-of-factly, with more confident English than she'd exhibited all summer. Despite the lessons Hope had given all the women in the harem when they'd asked, then taught her a little of their language, too.

And perhaps there had been a different sort of knowledge in her gaze, too.

*I will,* Hope had agreed.

Though she was testing how that agreement tasted on her mouth. She didn't intend to share that with her attendant.

*Our great lord will be the happiest of men,* the girl had said, though she and Hope had continued to gaze at each other, engaged in a different sort of conversation altogether.

*I'm sure he will be transported,* Hope had replied.

And then had found herself wishing both that she'd taught the girl no English at all, or that she'd taught her a good deal more. Because she thought it would be better if she hadn't spoken up at all. Or, having done so, it would have felt much nicer if she could have gone down the list of pros and cons with the girl, as if she was any one of those old friends Hope had once had, long ago.

Instead, she'd ended up taking herself off to the dungeons.

She nodded off, there on the floor of the cell, which was significantly less comfortable than it looked. Which was saying something.

And then she woke up in a rush to a commotion out in the hall. She blinked in confusion at first, scrubbing her hands over her face and wondering if she would ever regain feeling in her bottom, then looked up. She expected to see Cyrus.

But instead, it was the women who attended her in the

harem. And a selection of the guards. They all carried piles of things in their arms.

One of the older women barked at the guard outside the cell, the door was flung open, and in they streamed. Two of them came to Hope and clucked over her as if they'd found her in a garbage heap. The rest bustled this way and that until the cell better resembled the harem alcove room Hope had left up above. The cell was draped in luxury and not to be outdone, they had tucked Hope into the bed they'd made out of a pile of soft mattresses.

She almost sent them away, because she knew who must have ordered this.

But there was such a thing as cutting off her nose to spite her face.

"This is some kind of miracle," Hope breathed.

One of the older women said something in reply, and everyone—or rather, every woman—burst into laughter. Yara laughed too. But she sobered, patting Hope's hand. "She says that the curse of the King is that he must also be a man, and therefore given to foolishness like any other. So it is with our lord."

"Such a pity," Hope murmured, without as much guilt as she should have felt for not making sure they knew he hadn't put her here. "That even kings must be men in the end."

The women all laughed again. And only when they were all satisfied that their charge would sleep as comfortable a night as possible did they leave her to it.

And the next time Hope woke, the Lord and King of Aminabad was watching her from the other side of the bars.

Hope stretched as she sat up. "You're the one who encouraged me to believe in fairy tales, and look at what happened in the night! Don't you know? Anything is possible if you make a wish, Cyrus."

"It looks comfortable enough," Cyrus said quietly. "But there is a whole world out there, and I suspect you will grow tired of this cell soon enough."

And every time he came to visit her after that, the cell was even more pleasant. First there were thick rugs on the floor so her foot need not touch the cold stone. The women had erected something far more pleasant and civilized over that hole in the ground, then moved screens around it for privacy. On the walls, they hung priceless tapestries, and a series of tables to hold lanterns and the books they knew she liked to read.

One time he came she was eating a meal they'd brought her that was most decidedly not prison rations. Like gruel, she imagined, whatever *that* was.

She waved a roast chicken leg at him as she sat cross-legged on the comfortable floor that easily rivaled the luxurious space they'd used many times on the top of his tower. "Some people are queasy when they're pregnant," she told him, as if he'd asked. And it was easy to smile cheerfully when he looked so…glowering. "But not me. If anything, I'm that much more ravenous."

"Tell me how this happened," Cyrus said, his voice low and intense. Though she did not think he sounded *betrayed.* It seemed a crucial distinction.

"I think you know," she said. She patted her belly. "At least, I hope you know, with all your fancy education. Because I know, and I left school at sixteen."

"I don't mean the child."

And Hope studied his face, there on the other side of the bars that separated them. And she thought the bars made it all too clear what else separated them, that she had not paid enough attention to these last months.

"You don't want me to love you," she said softly.

"How could you?" he asked, sounding eminently reasonable when the question was anything but. "We met when I kidnapped you."

"From a wedding I am just as happy to have missed. Let's not forget that part. Surely I should be the one who gets to decide if I feel traumatized by my own rescue."

But he only shook his head, looking at her as if despaired of her.

"This should not have happened," he said, in that same low voice that sounded like grief.

"You don't like that I'm in love with you," she said then, holding his gaze. "I understand that. But Cyrus. Have you asked yourself why?"

"This is the desert." He sounded almost astonished that she would question that. "It erodes everything it touches, especially love."

"Is that what you feel?" she asked him, too aware that the key to the cell was tucked under her pillow and she could go to him. Right now. She could let herself out and touch him, hold him, kiss that broken expression off his face. "Or what you were told?"

Cyrus did not reply. But he did not have to. She could see the truth all over his face, making that deep bronze face of his seem something like pale around the edges.

"Or is it worse than that?" she asked, almost too softly to hear. "Is that what he did to you here?"

"Enough," he muttered.

She didn't see him for two days after that. But that was good, in a way. It meant she had time to think.

Her life in the harem not only meant toiletries were provided—and usually applied by someone else—it meant that she was rarely on her own at all. Only when they left her to sleep for the night did she have a measure of solitude, though there was no door on her alcove. If she wasn't under her covers, there were always eyes on her.

The women and the guards were always, always watching, and even if she accepted that the watching was mostly benevolent—as her current situation suggested, since they'd outdone themselves making the cell into a luxurious retreat—it was still a lot for someone who'd spent most of her life feeling entirely alone.

Feeling it and usually actually experiencing it, too.

Now it all snuck up on her at once.

She'd found that she was pregnant, and instead of feeling terrified and overwhelmed, she'd been very much afraid that the overwhelming feeling that had raced around inside of her and threatened to swell up and burst free...was joy.

As foolish as that seemed, even then, when she hadn't known what Cyrus's reaction would be. Because she already knew she loved him. It had been a gradual dawning of awareness, and the way they made each other come apart only added it to it.

At first she'd thought she was simply addled by endorphins.

But she *liked* him. She liked how seriously he took his role here, so unlike so many of the men she'd met, who shrugged off responsibilities because theirs were inherited fortunes and needed no input from them. She liked how kind he was to his staff, always, no matter what they might have found him doing.

She liked the man his people thought he was, the man she learned about every day in the stories the women told her. About the time he had strode into an accident scene and took a child out of the line of danger. About how scared he had clearly been as a young boy, brought back here by his remote and rather terrifying-sounding father, but had shown such courage and bravery every day.

And if the women had sometimes heard the sound of muffled sobs at night, a lost boy missing his mother, they had never told the old King.

When the women had come to take her through her usual preparations for an evening with Cyrus that night, Hope had been happy to let them talk all around her, their voices rising and falling, as she considered the fact that she was carrying *life* inside her.

She had felt that only hours after taking that test, she was changed. Something in her had opened wide. No matter what happened, she knew what this felt like, now. She understood an entire new world of *possibilities.*

It had been easy to talk about things like this in an academic sense with men she was delighted she hadn't had to marry.

But now there was *a life* inside her, and Cyrus was the father. She had made love to him so many times that even thinking about him made her body warm. They had loved each other and the result was a life inside her, changing her even then. Changing her already.

She'd thought she'd understood a bit more about her own mother then, in a way she never had before. Not her fragility, her hummingbird flits and fancies, but those odd moments of power.

*Like a mother tiger lives in her too*, she'd thought that night. *Somewhere.*

Now, lying in her cell after having not seen Cyrus in two days, Hope found she understood Mignon even more.

Because her mother was not resilient. Not the way that Hope had been forced to become. Mignon's father had taken care of her. Then Hope's father had done the same and Mignon might have drowned her sorrows in too much wine and too many pills that were supposed to make her happy, or supposed to make her sleep, but in the end she had been loved.

She had been so loved. And she had been in love. Was it so terrible that she wanted to be loved again?

Hope had already been pretty certain that she was falling in love with Cyrus. How else could she explain how greedy she was for him? What else would make sense of the way she could not get enough, ever?

Knowing that she carried his child, and that she was fairly certain that he would not take kindly to that fact— but she was happy all the same—let her know there was no *falling* involved.

She had already fallen. And hard.

It was possible she had been half in love with him ever since he'd carted her out of that wedding chapel.

And the next time he turned up on the other side of her cell's bars, she regarded him solemnly.

From the freestanding copper bath where she had been soaking for some while, with bubbles in a foamy riot all around her and a bit of music playing in the background, too. For texture.

"How long do you plan to stay down here?" Cyrus asked. More stiffly than the bars that stood between them.

"As long as it takes," she said. And when he only sighed, and did not ask to explain what she meant, she didn't know if she should be pleased. Or worried.

"I did not intend to get you pregnant, Hope," he told her, his voice still gruff—but laced through with that formality that never heralded anything she wanted to hear. She braced herself where she sat. "I understand I did not prevent it. I cannot account for my lapse. But you must see that this ruins everything."

She supposed he meant his plans. Her life in his palm and all the rest of it. The mighty desert and sand in all directions. The other women he told he would marry, though he had brought no others here.

Maybe all men were fools, as the old woman had said.

Or maybe it was that he thought love was a ruin all its own.

"That sounds like a you problem, Cyrus," she replied. She considered him and how he stood straighter at her tone. At, no doubt, the disrespect in her words—but she knew him. She knew he liked it when she talked like that. So maybe everything wasn't quite as ruined as he pretended. "And while we're talking about these things, I want my mother."

"Your mother?"

He sounded as if she'd requested a pit of poisonous snakes be thrown into her bathwater.

"My mother," she repeated, enunciating each syllable. "I'm pregnant. I'm going to become a mother myself and I'd like to take what solace I can in mine. And honestly? That you don't understand why that might be the case is everything that's wrong with you."

Something sparked in his dark gaze. "There is nothing wrong with me. As a matter of law. I am the Lord and—"

She waved a hand, dismissing him from behind iron bars in her cozy cell. "I'm a prisoner, Cyrus. You might not have put me in this cell, but you had every intention of jailing me in this fortress. Not only this summer, but for the next *year*. A prison is a prison no matter how big it is. All I did was make it obvious."

Then she tipped her head back, closed her eyes, and pretended to be asleep.

When she opened up her eyes again, he was gone.

Another few days passed. Hope assumed that he was off having a very kinglike temper tantrum somewhere else. Though usually when he took his trips, someone told her so. As if his staff was invested in her thinking well of him.

When what she'd thought was that their investment was what spoke highly of him.

Whatever he'd been off doing, he appeared in the dungeon on the fifth day, ordered the cell door flung open, and then bore her with great ceremony back up out of the dungeons and into the harem again.

"What's going on?" she asked him as the doors were opened and Cyrus himself actually walked her into the harem courtyard.

He didn't answer. He merely extended out his arm toward the center of the of the pretty square. And took her some moments to stop blinking in all the bright and dazzling light that poured down from above. From the glare of the blue sky and the scent of all the flowers.

It took her a moment to accept that she had missed this place.

And another moment to make sense of the figure that stood there next to the fountain, not dressed like the other women at all.

Mignon. It was Mignon, who was already crying—leaving Hope to work very hard not to do the same.

They threw themselves into each other's arms, murmuring in a long stream about the time they'd spent apart, and so many apologies, and any other number of inanities that all meant the same thing.

*I love you.*

*I missed you.*

*I love you.*

Later that night when the guards came for her they found her sitting in the room in the harem that had been made up for Mignon. Hope rose from her chair, leaving her mother sleeping soundly. Still not quite believing that Cyrus had actually let her come here.

That he had gone and fetched her, according to her mother.

"It's amazing what good it does my soul to see her happy," she said when she'd been led up the stairs and out into a terraces of his bedchamber, with heat lamps blazing all around to keep the cold desert air at bay. "It's been a long while since I've seen her sleep without chemical help. And I owe that to you."

It felt strange to be with him again like this, but also familiar. Deliciously, marvelously familiar.

"I am sorry," Cyrus told her from where he stood near the rail, so stiffly she understood that he had not come to her on purpose. That he was even, perhaps, unsure of his welcome.

As if he was unused to the very words he used, come to that. If she thought back, had he actually said he was sorry the last time he had admitted he was wrong? All she remembered was losing herself in his arms.

She knew she should be mad about that. And yet she smiled at him, because she couldn't seem to help it. "You mean…because your pregnant wife felt she had no choice but to lock herself in your dungeon?"

"That," he said, inclining his head. His midnight eyes seemed to gleam in the dark. "Among a great many other things. Too many things to name, though I will if you wish it."

And once she would have laughed at that. She would have teased him into saying something or other that sounded like a list of wrongs, though it would never be finished. He would end up thrusting into her. She would end up forgetting.

They would do this again and again.

There was a part of her that was perfectly fine with that.

But things had shifted now. She was in love with him. She was going to be the mother of his child. And love Mignon though she might, she did not intend to end up like her mother. So destroyed by love that she'd been rendered weak because of it.

Hope was prepared to be many things, but she'd never been weak. She did not intend to start now.

There was the baby to think of.

"You have dungeons and palaces to match," she agreed, "though I've only heard tell of your palaces. I suspect you think that's the sort of thing you should apologize for, but it doesn't matter. If I were you, Cyrus, I would be far more worried about the little jail cell you keep right here."

His gaze was on her, as intently as ever, as she drew a little circle on her chest. Directly over her heart. "Because there's only one person who has that key, Cyrus. Only one."

He muttered something she didn't quite hear and then he closed the space between them, dragging her across the cushions and bearing her down into their soft embrace.

And there was some part of her that wanted to fight him. That wanted—

But even as she thought that, she also thought that she'd be punishing herself that way. He might deserve it, but Hope knew she certainly didn't.

And so she exulted in him instead.

In every stroke of his wicked tongue. In every glorious touch of his skin next to hers.

This had been the longest she'd gone without him since she'd met him and Hope felt as if she had a lifetime of pent-up hunger inside her.

They took each other in a blaze of passion, right there.

They ate, not bothering to put clothing back on, and then he carried her to the bed, where they feasted on each other all over again. As if they were touching each other for the first time.

And that whole night, hour after hour, it was as if they bathed themselves in each other, in this passion that was only and ever theirs.

That was another thing Hope knew, without needing context or conversation. What they had between them mattered. It was special. If it was only sex, she would not be the only wife he kept in his harem.

If it was only sex, it wouldn't wreck them both like this.

It was near morning when she woke one more time to find his hands on her. Hope blinked as she looked around the bedchamber she knew as well as her own, now. And then to Cyrus, who had his hands on her belly.

Not attempting to stir her up into another display of that endless fire between them.

But for another, more intimate reason.

Because their baby curled up right there, inside of her. The baby they had made in love, though he might call it something else.

She knew better.

He glanced up, his midnight gaze finding hers and holding with such intensity that she caught her breath. Her stomach flipped over. Butterflies when they'd had each other already, too many times to count.

"I think this can work," he told her, his voice almost excruciatingly solemn. It made her ache. "You will have my child."

"I will," she agreed.

Because she might have locked herself in that cell, but he hadn't only sent furnishings and feasts. He had also sent in his doctors. She knew that everything was moving along as it should. As she was certain he did, too.

"You will have my sons, if the fates permit," Cyrus intoned, the way he did when what he was saying was *important*. In case she hadn't already been hanging on his every word. "I will make you my queen, Hope. There is no denying this passion between us and I have decided that I do not wish to deny it." He nodded then, though his gaze never shifted from hers. "I will allow it, Hope. And in so doing, it will perhaps become like any other duty."

And then he waited, as if he had offered her the world on a platter.

Or even a few sweet words.

"This is not the most romantic thing I've ever heard, Cyrus." Hope considered. "Then again, maybe it is. You haven't mentioned any dreary contracts yet. Or questionable activities. I'll give you points for that."

He frowned at her, then he withdrew his hand from her belly. He rolled up, moving so he could sit with his back to her and his legs over the side of the bed.

And that did not bode well.

Hope wanted to reach for him, but something about how straight he held his spine, then, made her think better of it. She crawled to the far edge of the bed, then stood. Then she went around to the foot of the bed to see if she could find her clothes.

And she had only just finished smoothing her silks back into place when he spoke again.

"All of these things are possible between us," he told her, his voice dark. Foreboding, she could not help but think. If not actively forbidding, too. He turned to look at her then, and there was something about those midnight eyes, so dark across the stirrings of the brand-new dawn outside the windows. It was suddenly difficult to breathe and it was nothing like butterflies at all. "But for this to work, Hope, you must never mention love again."

And Hope had really never felt more like her mother than she did at that moment.

Because everything in her wanted to say yes. *Needed* to say yes. She wanted to scream it out loud, because surely if he gave her all these things she wanted, himself most of all, love would come.

That was what she believed, in truth. That love made its own rules. That Cyrus did not need to believe in it. He did not need to feel it, though she didn't believe he didn't. That was the thing—love didn't require belief.

There was already a softening deep inside of her and a little voice—her mother's, she knew that, but then again, it was hers too—whispered, *Tell him whatever he needs to hear. Then love him enough for the both of you.*

And maybe she would have done exactly that, in a different life. If her father had lived long enough to tell her about the marriage he'd arranged for her and she had met Cyrus the way, perhaps, she'd been meant to all along. If all she'd known was that boundless love that had filled up and patched over every hole, and made certain each night that the day would come.

But she had lived through those other years, too. She had watched as her mother had tried her best to make men love her when they did not. She had watched her mother dash herself against those rocks again and again and again.

Still, everything inside her told her that this would be different. That *she* was different. That he was certainly like no other man she'd ever met, and surely all of that had to count for something.

She almost said yes.

God, how she wanted to say yes.

But instead she shook her head. "No."

His head tilted slightly to one side, as if he could not understand the syllable he had just heard. "What did you just say to me?"

"No, Cyrus."

Hope made herself breathe, then she made herself stand tall. She had been looking for a job her whole life, hadn't she? And now she had one. She would be a mother to this child inside her. She would be a daughter to the mother she had.

And she would be a queen to this man, but only if he was the King she needed.

Hope had taken on the wisdom of the desert in the course of her summer here, because the desert was everywhere. Its lessons were unavoidable.

And the real fairy tale, the one that mattered, was that a princess could become a queen with or without a man who was too foolish to know what was right in front of him. The desert was eternal. So too was love.

She wanted a man who could appreciate both.

"I have never been any man's whore," she told him, though the words hurt more than they should. "You know this. Why should I be yours?"

"Hope—" Cyrus began.

But she lifted a hand and silenced him, that easily. He did not need to tell her that she was the only one who would dare such a thing, because she knew it.

The same way she knew that this man, the King of the Aminabad Desert, was the love of her life.

Yet this was not a stunt. This was *life*. Her life, her child's life. And his life too, little though he might realize it.

"I won't," she told him, as regally as she could manage. "I would rather be back in the dungeon."

Then she made for the doors, throwing them open, and stalking through—paying no attention to the startled guards.

Hope did not go back to the harem. She walked herself straight back down to the cell she had left behind earlier, closed the door behind her with her own hands, and locked it tight.

Letting her silks fall where they liked.

Because she was perfectly prepared to stay where she was.

For as long as it took.

# CHAPTER ELEVEN

Cyrus had tried reason.

He had tried thundering his commands through the bars of the dungeon cell in the hope that might cow her.

He had tried rash promises. That he would take no other wives. That he would make a formal proclamation, not only declaring her Queen, but making it clear to the whole of the kingdom that this Lord of the desert would keep her even if she never gave him a son at all.

But for reasons that escaped him, she remained wholly unmoved by his every attempt.

*Are you truly determined to give birth to our child in a jail cell?* he had demanded at last.

All Hope had done in return was invite her mother into the cell with her, so that Cyrus had two pairs of reproachful golden eyes glaring back at him as if he had somehow disappointed them both.

When he should not have cared either way.

Her mother had dared to mutter something in French that she clearly thought he could not understand. He wished he had not.

*Mother, that is not helpful,* Hope had murmured calmly. Also in French. Too calmly, to his mind. *I think you know perfectly well that he is in no way impotent, or we would not be in this position, would we?*

Cyrus had ground his teeth together, his jaw so tight that

it hurt. He had clenched his fists, but he'd stayed on his side of the bars.

*What I really think,* Hope had said after a moment of studying him in a way he found disrespectful and outrageous in the extreme, *is that if you want something to happen with me and with our baby, you had better start with your own mother.*

He had refused, of course. What use had he for that accursed woman?

But whether he flatly refused or shouted his reasons why, his wife would not be moved.

So he stopped.

It took perhaps an hour before he found himself growling out orders to ready his plane and fly him north once again.

And that was how he found himself standing at the end of a winding, rainy lane, on a typically vile autumnal English afternoon.

Being England, it wasn't even a proper storm. It was just rain.

And it tore into him all the same.

He'd had his driver drop him a good mile or so down the drive, because he needed to clear his head. He needed to make sense of what was happening.

He needed to do this without all those *songs* in his head.

Because he, Cyrus Ashkan, Lord of the Aminabad Desert, had returned to this benighted country to see the one woman he despised above all others because his wife—who he should also despise, but did not—had demanded it.

Even though he was still sorting through all those revelations he'd had about his father. Even though he was still reeling.

Hope had told him to come here and so he had, to this house where he had been held prisoner for so many years.

*Although*, a voice inside him whispered as he walked along the lane that became more familiar with each step, *how much of a prisoner were you really?*

Because he remembered his time here all too well, now he was here again. He had learned to say otherwise. And he had eventually said it so many times that he had come to believe it was true, in its way. That those dreams he sometimes had—of swimming in these ponds and rowing boats across the lake, running along the wooded paths and climbing the trees, as free as he liked—were just silly fantasies out of storybooks.

Instead of real memories of the way he had spent the bulk of his days here.

Not that any of that mattered now, he told himself grimly, and marched on.

The house sat on the little knoll it always had. But he was bigger now, and could only look at the small incline and remember how he thrown himself down it so he could roll and roll, laughing riotously because his mother had always joined him.

He had not thought of that in years.

He did not *want* to think of any of this, just as he had not *wanted* to face the terrible truths he'd finally understood about his father.

Because it was one thing to acknowledge that, secretly, he had always known that she was not quite the horror his father had claimed she was while he was still far away. It was one thing to accept all the ways his father had been cruel to her as well as to Cyrus himself.

He had found that contract, tucked away in the office here, like a final taunt.

While Hope conducted her dungeon sit-in, Cyrus had stood with his feet in the sand, allowing himself his own reckoning with a man who had been dead for years.

A man who had never deserved Cyrus's obedience, much less his respect and admiration. He'd won those one beating at a time.

He sighed as he walked, climbing up the old stone steps. He remembered that his mother might have worried about the state of her figure, as many women did and as she personally had to do for her job, but he had never seen her abuse herself as his father had claimed. Nor had he ever seen her use any substances harder than the same alcohol he knew his father had liked to drink, though his father liked to tell a different tale, making her out to be a monster.

Cyrus had never considered her a monster. Not while he'd lived here, and not after, when he visited her for the express purpose of breaking her heart.

It was that visit that sat heavily on him as he walked up to the great front door, feeling cold and damp and furious straight through.

But this time, not at his mother. He wanted to say that he was mad at a golden-eyed woman who was even now eating her way through his kitchens while reclining at her leisure in an overly luxurious dungeon but he knew better.

The person he was angry at, always and forever, was himself.

Cyrus took his time at the door before he reminded himself that he was a king, not a boy, and rang the bell.

He had loved ringing it as a child. And it was funny, the things a man could carry around inside himself without knowing. The exact sound of that bell. The way it echoed through the grand old house. The sound of footsteps in the hall and the way the great old door opened with a stout, deep sound.

He remembered all of that. It sounded inside him, like words to those melodies he'd tried so hard to make himself forget.

And then he found himself staring at the same butler who had been here when he was a child. The old man had to be halfway to the crypt, but he still managed to give the impression that he was looking down at Cyrus from a great height.

Even though he had shrunk to half his size.

"Master Justin," he said, which was not the impeccable courtesy Cyrus recalled. But then, why bother with the faultless address he surely knew when he could remind them both that he had known the boy Cyrus had once been. "I must tell you, sir, that no one in this house will take kindly to it if you are here to further abuse your mother's kindness."

"If you could take me to her, please," Cyrus replied.

From between his teeth.

The old man glared at him for a moment so long that Cyrus wondered if he was going to have to take matters into his own hands—but then, at the last, turned on his heel with a hauteur that was meant to land like a slap, and did.

Cyrus found himself feeling more shame that he could remember ever experiencing before in all his days.

*"You had better start with your own mother,"* Hope had said.

Had he known all this time that if he dared, this would be the reception he'd get? Or worse, that he would deserve it?

But he'd come all this way. And he was not a coward, despite all evidence to the contrary, so he continued.

He followed the old man deeper into the house and pretended he didn't recognize the place with every step he took. The rooms he had treated as his personal playground. The banister he had treated as his own, particular slide. The games of tag in and around precious artifacts, heedless of the fact that lords of the desert were not meant to enjoy themselves like grubby peasants, according to his father.

They were meant to conduct themselves with dignity in all things.

That desert he loved now, deeply and fully, had been a hard landing. He had been forced to change his own memories in his head to survive it, or he wouldn't have made it—not with his father so determined to claw out any hint of weakness in his only son.

It had been easier to pretend he'd hated it here. Safer, maybe.

In time he'd believed his own reframing.

Maybe that, too, had been survival.

But he cast the clamor of his memories aside as he was ushered, with freezing cold courtesy, into what he recognized as his mother's favorite drawing room.

He stepped inside, then stopped still.

Because she was there.

His mother stood at a window that looked out over the drive, and Cyrus realized she must have seen him coming.

She looked older too, even from behind. She was tall and willowy, still clearly *her* in every way that mattered, and he wanted to go to her more than he wanted to admit.

The last time he had hated that urge in him. He had wanted to claw it out with his own fingers. This time he did not quite dare approach her.

"Mother," he said, getting the words out even though he wasn't sure what there was to say. "I've come to you because—"

But the woman who had once graced every major magazine on the planet with her face, and who had briefly been one of the richest women in the world entirely because of her commanding presence, turned then and silenced him with a single glance.

From dark blue eyes far too much like his own.

Though hers were haunted.

And he knew without having to ask that any ghosts there were his fault.

"You have said quite enough over the years," she told him, in that quietly cultured voice he remembered so well. "I believe I'd like to take a turn."

"You don't understand," he started. "It isn't—"

"I love you, Justin," she said, stating it baldly. She did not drop her gaze, not even when she shook her head. "To me, you will always be the baby I carried in my body. The baby I made with your father, in love. The word he always hated most because he could not control it and so it made him feel weak."

When he had been eighteen she had tried to say something like this to him. She had called him by that name he had rejected for years then, too. Cyrus had refused to hear it.

He could almost see himself standing here in the corner of this very same room, shouting at her. *My father is the Lord of the Aminabad Desert,* he had thundered at her. *He has never known weakness, nor ever shall.*

But Cyrus wondered now if he had been that angry because she'd called him *Justin.* Because she'd made him remember and he'd been too concerned about chasing his father's approval back then.

About living up to all the harsh expectations his father had made sure he felt as if they were branded into his flesh. As if he could not be whole without them. As if they were as real as the bruises.

As if, he thought now, he'd had no choice but to hate his mother— for if he didn't, he would have to face what his father had done by stealing him away from her.

Cyrus was older now. His father had died a bitter man, with too many daughters for his liking and talk of a curse hanging over him. And he certainly would not have approved of this.

Of Cyrus coming back here of his own volition, a clear sign of weakness so great it might have killed his father if he had not already died.

But what Cyrus had learned from Hope was that he was not afraid of his weaknesses. On the contrary, he liked to indulge in them.

He understood more than he thought his father would like, if he were still here.

No man would react the way his father had unless, at heart, he was more afraid of what love could do to him than he was of what power would.

Because power was easy. It required nothing except greed, if you liked.

But love asked for everything.

Cyrus could not say he liked being asked. He had not reacted well.

Maybe he was more of a coward than he'd imagined.

And in the end, it came down to what he wanted more. The life his father had handed to him, wrapped up in a bow, but with entirely too many strings. Or the life that he saw in Hope's bright gaze.

A life where he was treated like magic and also a man. Where she saw who he was and all his many faults of arrogance and willful blindness, and forgave him anyway. Loved him anyway. Where there was always laughter and never that cringing, terrified awe that women had exhibited around his father. Where she not only made him smile, she made him imagine that he was not the creature of stone and silence he had long imagined he was. That he could make her laugh, too. These small, happy gifts lit up even an austere fortress in the desert. Even him.

And they made the harder parts of life seem brighter.

She did that. Hope did.

"Mother," he started again.

"I loved him," his mother told him in her same deliberate way, as if these were words she'd practiced in the hope of saying them someday. "And I know he told you a thousand stories of how that wasn't true, but I did. I would have loved him forever, but he wouldn't allow it."

Cyrus let out a breath, but he did not try to speak over her. He did not try to take control of this conversation. He let her speak.

And she straightened, there before him, as if she had been prepared to wilt instead.

He didn't like how that sat in him.

"And I might have accepted that, for your sake, but it became clear to me that he could not love anything," his mother told him. "He could not allow even the faintest hint of it into his dreadful little kingdom because I believed you deserved more than sand and stone. I wanted you to have a heart. I wanted you to love something, anything."

He wanted to tell her that he had, that he did, that he wasn't that furious youth who had come back here to denounce her. That he knew, now, that he had done that because it was the only kind of love his father recognized. That twisted inversion of it.

And because he had needed to believe what his father had told him, or he would have had to face what he'd lost.

God, what he'd lost.

And she moved closer, still holding his gaze intently. "And I don't care if you don't love me, Just—*Cyrus*. I don't care if you break my heart in a thousand pieces again and again. I'm your mother. I will love you enough for the both of us. I do."

As Hope would, Cyrus understood then in a rush and he hated it. For Hope. For his mother. For the creature he'd become that both of them thought it necessary.

When he was the one who had something to prove here, not them.

His mother stopped then, her eyes too bright, and seemed to recollect herself. Cyrus found his chest working overtime, as if he had done something more active than simply stand here, listening.

At last.

She inclined her head, looking almost perfectly composed. "I don't know what you have come to bludgeon me with today, my son. But you may go ahead. I only ask that you do so fully aware that I will love you all the same, whatever you say. Whatever your father told you, whatever you believe, I have always loved you. I will always love you. And nothing either he or you did or could do will ever change that."

And there were so many things that Cyrus could have said to that. So many ways he could have responded.

But instead he found himself moving toward her, like the boy he'd once been. And he could see how badly he'd hurt her when he saw the way she stiffened, as if bracing herself for attack.

That was the man he had let himself become. He could see that in her eyes, as she braced herself.

And he vowed that no matter what it took, he would not be that man again.

He would not be that man, that father, to his own child.

His own father was dead. And would stay buried.

When he reached his mother, he took her hands gently in his. He bent his head.

"Teach me how," he said.

And for the first time, he saw a crack in the armor she wore.

"Wh-what?" she stammered out.

"Teach me how you can love like that, Mother. Teach me how you do it."

He felt her tremble. He saw her eyes brighten more, though she did not allow a single tear to fall.

Cyrus wondered why it had never occurred to him that he might not have gotten all of his strength from his father's side after all.

Well. He knew why. But now he saw his mother plain, and he could not unsee it.

"My darling boy," his mother whispered, a joy too intense in her gaze, so sharp it was nearly grief. "I will teach you anything you wish."

And so she did.

He stayed with her that night and through the next day. They walked together on those lands he had told himself he'd forgotten. But he wanted to know her and the life she had crafted here in the wreckage his father—and he—had left behind.

And he could admit that the boy who had always loved her wanted to tell her what he had done and what he had learned, so she might know that what she'd given him might have been hidden—but it had never been truly lost.

Then, on the third day, he promised her that he would never stay away again, and took the lessons his mother had imparted to him home to his desert fortress.

And he ordered his men to bring his wife before him.

But not, this time, into his bedchamber. Not high on top of the tower, or hidden away in the baths.

Not even in the harem, which had been built for the King's eyes only.

This time, he gathered all his men and all the staff of the

fortress, from the women in the harem who tutted at him to Mignon Cartwright herself, who studied him as if looking for a way that she, personally, might take him down. He believed that she might try.

And then, finally, when everyone was assembled, he allowed his men to bring Hope herself before him. In something slightly more modest than her silks, because while he was not his father, he was still a man. And he liked to keep what was his to himself.

Even out here with the sun beating down, making it impossible to hide.

"Oh, dear," said Hope as she walked into the center of the courtyard and stood there before him, looking undiminished and unafraid.

And more beautiful than any woman had the right to be.

She made him feel weak, but he understood that now. She made him feel mortal. As if he was nothing at all but a man.

And that, his mother had assured him, was the point.

*Vulnerability is joy, if you let it hold you,* she had said. *You'll see.*

And he had wanted that to be true, back in England in all of that damp and gray.

But here, in the unforgivingly clear glare of the desert sun, he knew it was. He felt it deep in his bones, that had not crumbled. He heard it like a song that he was no longer afraid to sing.

And more, he reveled in it, because of Hope.

He strode to meet her. And when she was within reach, he stopped. Turning slowly, there before his people, he stretched out his arms, inviting them all to look upon him.

"I stand before you, Lord and King," he said, and all of his people murmured the appropriate words in reply, bowing their heads. Hope stared back at him, her head unbowed.

"But first, I am a man. A husband. And soon enough, I will be a father."

He turned fully, back to Hope.

And then, holding her gaze, he sank to his knees before her, smiling when he heard the mutters that ran through the crowd. "I kneel before you, the mother of my child. I kneel before you because I grant you that power over me that some call weakness, but that you and I know is far stronger than thrones or armies or ancient tales whispered down through the ages."

"Cyrus..." she whispered then, her golden gaze wide. "What are you doing?"

"This is the love of a king, *omri*," he said. And he used that word deliberately now, here in public where it could not be taken back. *Omri. My life.* So that all who heard it would know he meant it. So that she would. "I will always do my duty to my people, to my land. But my life, my heart, my soul—all of these are yours, Hope. There will always be a Lord of the Aminabad Desert, as long as there is sand to dance beneath the desert sun." All his people murmured their *hallelujahs* when he said this, as was tradition—but he kept going. "But as long as that lord is me, I will love you. As long as there is breath in my body and blood in my veins, I am yours."

He waited as she stood there, looking something like stricken as she gazed at him.

So Cyrus let his mouth curve, and did not quite incline his head. "If, that is, you will have me?"

And for a moment, he thought all was lost.

That he had taken this too far, with plots and harems and his regrettable reaction to the news he should have known was coming, that of course she would fall pregnant if he did not one thing to stop it—

*I suspect you wanted not to think about it,* his mother had said, too wisely. *So that you could force the issue. You are an Aminabad king, Cyrus.* And she had smiled. *You like a choice to feel like an inevitability. Preordained, if possible.*

But that didn't mean that Hope had reached the same conclusion. Or would.

She shook her head and stepped back, breaking his heart into pieces.

He thought of his own mother, who had loved long beyond any hope that it would be returned. Who had told him, in all seriousness, that even if he had never come back to her, she would have loved him forever. *Love is not about what does or doesn't happen,* she had said. *Love is about love, and I know you don't understand this, my darling boy, but it is its own reward.*

But here, in this moment, he understood.

Loving Hope had taught him what it was to be alive.

Not simply the brutal creature his father had insisted he become. He was a man grown, and he could make himself in his own image. There were already too many cracks in the stones his father had placed around his heart.

For one thing, Cyrus could not imagine caring at all if the child Hope carried was a daughter or a son, so long as it was healthy.

So long as he and this woman who had given him everything already could care for it together.

Cyrus knew he would still feel these things, because she had taught him how to feel in the first place, no matter what she said next.

He accepted this.

But that didn't mean he couldn't try to sway her.

"I love you," he told her, and he did not care if the whole of his kingdom heard him. "I love you like the sun loves the earth and I will continue to love you, even if you cast me aside. I loved you before I met you, building you up in my head. I loved you when I brought you here, when you defied me at every turn and confounded me because you would not cower and you would not become every wrong thing I imagined you to be. You would not bend, you did not break, and in so doing, you have taught me that there is no shame in either. You have taught me strength and you have taught me hope itself, like the beacon of it you have been and always will be. I was wrong about you in every possible way, and I am so glad you loved me anyway. And all of this will be true, *omri*, no matter what you say next."

And for a moment there was only the sun all around, the sky up above. The desert outside these walls where the sands were always shifting. Always waiting to take back what belonged to them. Filled with the ancient knowledge of the thousands of lives that had come and gone before his. And thousands more that would come after, then blow away again, sand into sand again.

All of those lives meaningless, he thought, without love.

As his father's had been.

Just as his had been without Hope.

"With, of course, some draconian custody arrangements, I assume," she said at last. "Should I decide that I prefer less sand, on balance, than you have shown me thus far."

But she said it all in that dry, amused tone that flooded him with relief.

And joy.

Cyrus let himself smile at her, heedlessly, and then rose to his feet. "But of course," he said. "I am a man of great power and might, lest you are tempted to forget."

And what he wanted most was that smile of hers that

took over her face now, and the way it made the bright desert day seem dim.

He wanted to talk to her forever. He wanted to fence words, and learn how to laugh as she did. He wanted to sink into each and every moment as she liked to do, so that all of it, all of life, was a sensual act.

But first, here and now, he needed more than that.

He moved forward and took her face between his hands.

"Hope," he managed to get out, to the only audience that mattered, "I love you. And I may not know how, but I can tell you this. There is nothing I cannot learn, and nothing I cannot do. My father made me a king. You made me husband. And I will make myself the man you deserve. I will make certain that I am worthy of the love you gave me so openly. When I could not even recognize it for the gift it was."

"And yet it is yours," she said simply. Truly. As openly as she ever had, because this was who she was. "It has always been yours."

"I will never deserve you," he whispered fiercely, bending his face to hers. "But I promise you this, *omri*, my beautiful life and my only Hope. I will never stop trying."

"I won't let you," she whispered back.

"Then it will be so, you and me," he told her, in the way he made all the proclamations in the land. "It will be love, as long as we live."

For he was a man of stone, fashioned by the desert sands and subject only to the whim of the winds that shaped them—and the woman who loved him and made him whole.

# CHAPTER TWELVE

AND SO IT was that the mighty Lord of the Aminabad Desert became a great legend, hailed forever after as the King who changed everything.

For in this modern age, it was not war his people craved. Not the kind of wars he had been trained to fight by a man made of bitterness and bile.

What they wanted was joy, if they dared reach for it across the chasms of tradition and superstition.

Cyrus showed them how.

Hope gave him a daughter. Then a son a year later.

Then one more of each.

"Not an army, I know," Hope liked to say. "Because we wanted a family."

And they raised them together, in ways men and women in Cyrus's country did not often do—especially when they were of royal blood. Cyrus sang them all the songs his mother hand sung to him when he was small. He played with them as his father never had with him.

He loved them, that was the thing, and they did everything together. The King and Queen did not like to be without each other, and so they traveled from region to region as a family. They spent a season in each, so that the whole of the country could know them.

And love them.

And learn from them that it was possible to live the way they did—in a marriage where love came first, vulnerability was championed, and brutality was never tolerated.

Not even when Cyrus turned over a stone and found such things in himself.

The children were raised by the whole of the land, so that there could never be any doubt that the great desert kingdom was ruled first by love, and only then by the power and might of its people, who knew exactly the character of those who would lead them.

Some even began to think that the eldest daughter might be their first ruling queen, in time.

Cyrus's mother came back to Aminabad, hesitant at first. But as she was not there to have her heart broken again and again, she found many things to admire about the kingdom. And, in time, to love.

She and Mignon struck up an unlikely friendship, and it was through her connections that Mignon met her second husband at last. A man who felt strongly that he had married above himself. A man who loved her, not as a trinket, but as a treasure, and cared for her all the rest of their days.

Cyrus's own mother had no wish to remarry. *I loved him,* she said simply, when Cyrus asked.

Instead, she became his children's favorite. She was often the person they loved more than their parents, who did insist on instilling in them rules and boundaries.

But as for Cyrus and his beautiful wife, his marvelous life in all ways, the balance always tilted toward joy.

Sometimes all there was of joy was her hand in his, holding on tight and refusing to let go.

That only made it more precious when it was easier, when both of them laughed themselves silly. When pride in their babies made them swell up as one. When the kingdom lurched its way along toward the kinds of change they'd thought they would only ever get to whisper about in the privacy of the quite modern homes they lived in, one in each region.

And whenever they could sneak away, they went back to that fortress in the desert.

Back to the harem, where the women would prepare her for his pleasure and they were free to feast on each other as they had at the beginning.

Recklessly. Carelessly.

And every year, more bright with love.

So that the legacy they left behind them, and in each and every one of their children, was that same bright joy they found in each other.

Love like the sun. Joy as eternal as the sands.

And knowing how to dance, however badly or without music, wherever the wind took them in between.

\* \* \* \* \*

# A SON HIDDEN
# FROM THE SICILIAN

LORRAINE HALL

MILLS & BOON

# CHAPTER ONE

BRIANNA ANDERSEN WATCHED out the window as her airplane touched down in Palermo, Sicily. Her stomach was tied in a million knots while butterflies danced across each and every said knot.

Most of the nerves were excited ones. She was going to show her pieces at an international art show. She would have the opportunity to explore a new place. She was going to attend fancy cocktail parties and hobnob with artists from all over the world. People with too much money were going to bid on her art and this all had the possibility to set her up for life.

All her dreams coming true...in this place she didn't really want them to come true. Because part of her nerves stemmed from worry. Palermo might be a big city, but she knew the chances of seeing *him* were too high. Anything above *no chance at all* was too high, to be honest.

She put him out of her mind as much she could. *If* she had to run into him, she would pretend she barely remembered the summer they'd spent together two years ago in Florence. She, a young artist soaking up all the art and history Italy had to offer. He—well, the version of *him* he'd shown her—a businessman vacationing after a particularly profitable quarter at his company back in his native city of Palermo.

He hadn't mentioned his business was one of the largest and more profitable in Europe. He hadn't mentioned he was its owner and CEO, which made him a *billionaire*. He certainly hadn't told her anything about the hostile takeover his company had accomplished before his little vacation. And most importantly, he'd never told her why he'd abruptly ended things.

He'd simply been there one day, gone the next.

Brianna had been gutted, she could admit that to herself now, though at the time she'd tried to be so sophisticated and strong. But despite the sadness, she had also been philosophical about the whole thing. What artist didn't want some wild, temporary love affair in Florence before returning home to New Jersey? It was very worldly and European after all, and she might have pined a bit while pretending to laugh to her friends back home about her stormy, Italian love affair, but then something… bigger had come along.

In the way of a positive pregnancy test. Suddenly, her feelings about the man mattered less than what she was going to do about the little parting gift he'd left her.

She'd been so determined to tell him. She wanted to laugh at the memory. Bitter though the laugh might have been. There had been a few moments of dreaming up fairy tales, yes. She wasn't immune to wanting a happy-ever-after for a naive little whim she'd indulged herself in.

But then she'd discovered the truth about Lorenzo Parisi. Not just that he was a billionaire. Not just that he'd built an empire from the ground up. But that he was engaged in some sort of feud that had turned violent. On *his* end.

Article after article had painted Lorenzo Parisi as a dangerous, ruthless businessman and billionaire. The accusations had shocked her. At first, she'd refused to believe them. She'd been with him for almost two months and he'd never so much as raised his voice to her or even *near* her.

Could he be intense? Yes. Exacting? Absolutely. Had she ever been *afraid*? Never once.

But how could so many stories be wrong? She'd pored over every story she could find and it was widely accepted he'd been the driving force behind the attack on his rival's *child*. It was that piece of information that had finally gotten through to Brianna.

At the time, her child hadn't felt real to her. Positive test or not, she'd barely had any symptoms. A little exhaustion, a little soreness. She'd only tested because she'd been so late. So, though she understood she was pregnant, it had still been a kind of fanciful knowledge. A dream of what *could* be when she told Lorenzo.

Oddly enough, it was the details of the violent attack on the teenage son of Lorenzo's rival that had made her put her hand on her stomach and finally fully accept that she would grow, and give birth to a *child,* should she so choose and everything went according to plan. The baby wasn't a dream or a fantasy or some possibility. It was a choice to make.

So, in that full realization, she'd come to the conclusion that she could not tell Lorenzo. If this was the truth of him—violence over something as pointless as a few extra dollars when he already had so much—she could not risk herself *and* her child to a ruthless and violent man.

She wouldn't.

So she'd moved in with her parents, kept a low profile, and been blessed with a healthy pregnancy that resulted in a beautiful, wonderful baby boy.

It was only after Gio was born that she'd gotten back into her art again. Something about the sleepless nights and the 24-7 demands of an infant had opened up a *need* for her former creativity, and she'd been fortunate that her involved and helpful parents had never made her or Gio feel like a burden.

Thinking of her parents and Gio, she turned on her phone as the plane finally came to a stop. While everyone bustled around her, Brianna waited for her texts to come through.

When they finally did, she smiled at her phone. All messages from her mother, all photos of Gio. Food-covered face, pulling his grandpa's hair, cheesing for the camera, and in deep, blissful sleep. She felt a pang at each and every one of them.

And still, she couldn't regret coming or leaving him behind. He was safe and sound under her parents' care and she could focus on why she was here.

Her art. Her career. An opportunity to ensure her parents and Gio never wanted for anything.

And above all else, avoiding Lorenzo Parisi.

Lorenzo Parisi stood in the shadowed corner of the art gallery watching the proceedings with grim amusement. No one approached him. A few looked his way then whispered behind their hands. Most made quite the effort to ignore him.

He let everyone do what they would. He knew there was nothing to be done about public opinion that was already out there. That was why Dante Marino had waged such an impressive media war against him.

Whether Lorenzo denied his involvement in the threats against the Marino family, or got angry about such accu-

sations, or calmly explained how he was not to blame...
it did not matter. Dante had bought public opinion. He
had centuries of family history and respectability at his
fingertips. And he'd used them all to his benefit.

Lorenzo could hardly hold it against the man. If Lorenzo had such things at his disposal, he'd use them, too.

But Lorenzo did not come from a long line of ancestors who'd been paragons of society. He did not have the
luxury of generational wealth or connections across de-
cades. He had grown up poor, in charge of far too many
mouths to feed, and had scrabbled for every last dime
and scrap of power.

Luckily, he was a very good scrabbler, because he had
ended up amassing far more than he'd imagined in even
his exceptional dreams. Perhaps this was why he could
take Dante's lies with a grain of salt. Eventually the man
would show a weakness, and Lorenzo would pounce.

He always knew just when to pounce.

Besides, Lorenzo's business continued to succeed. And
this was the bottom line. Let Dante wage whatever personality wars he wanted. Lorenzo was interested only
in the bottom line.

Of course, tonight his bottom line was a little different than it usually was. He was not here for business. Not
here to thumb his nose at all the screaming tabloids or
even Dante himself. Though he enjoyed both.

No, his attendance at this art show was about one very
specific artist.

And there she was. Not dressed in black like the other
artists present. She had never quite fit the stereotype he
had in his head of artists as moody, strange, dark and
brooding characters.

She was bright. Cheerful. Dreamy. And her art was

all of those things, with touches of a kind of whimsical macabre. She painted beautiful landscapes and portraits, then used some kind of embroidery to hint at darker shadows. Bones beneath a dress, blood spilling out of the beautiful earth.

He was not shocked her art had taken off. She was *unique*, his Brianna, and what did the art world like if not that?

*His* Brianna. He scowled at that. He had broken things off two years ago when she'd started to get *ideas*, and he had not found those ideas as horrible as he should. He'd been fresh off a business success and it had gone to his head. He could admit that now. He'd gone to Florence for a holiday overly confident, careless enough to make him soft.

But then and now, Lorenzo had a clear plan for his life, and while he had to adapt to certain challenges, detours and surprises, women and relationships would *never* be one of those. Marriage to a struggling American artist did not match his life or business plans, so it had needed to be over.

He'd cut her off and continued to focus on what truly mattered.

Building his empire. Protecting his family.

He had no regrets about that, though the vision of her now threatened that belief. It was as if the entire past two years had evaporated, and he was once again an overly confident fool desperate to have her alone.

Because no one had quite compared to Brianna in the time since he'd left her, and *that* was irritating. That two years later she could appear in the same room as him and he could feel exactly as he had when he'd first laid eyes on her.

Then, she'd been in a museum. Painting. She'd been dressed casually. Jeans and some multicolored sweater with her hair piled up on her head. But unlike the rest of the artists in her group, she'd been focused on her work. The students had been chatting, packing up, and she had been lost in what she'd been creating.

He had been rapt. He'd watched her until she'd finished. Then approached her. Coffee had led to dinner, and then in the blink of an eye two months had gone by and he'd extended his holiday long past when he'd meant to leave.

Sometimes he still wondered if those two months had been a dream. A hallucination. He had certainly not been himself. Maybe she'd cast a spell on him. Sometimes he'd rather believe that than the truth.

Brianna Anderson was remarkable.

She was not dressed so casually tonight—she was wearing a white-and-gold gown that exposed triangles and diamonds of skin at different points. Her eyes were smoky, her hair in long, dark waves around her shoulders. Her cheeks were flushed as she spoke animatedly to a woman dressed from head to toe in black in front of a large piece Lorenzo recognized as Brianna's own artwork at once.

But his gaze kept following the artist herself around the room. She was introduced to different people by the woman in black, and engaged in a variety of conversations over the course of an hour. She carried around a flute of champagne but never took a sip, just worried the stem in her fingers.

Never once did she look his way. Never once did she venture too close to where he still stood in the shadowed corner. He might have thought she simply didn't see him.

But it was too convenient—this distance between them at the same party.

So he bided his time. Let some of the people begin to filter out and away. The exhibited pieces were marked as sold—hers more than any other artists. A strange burst of pride settled in his chest that she would be the star tonight.

He supposed it was that pride that had him acting when he'd been determined to just observe this evening. Instead, he approached her. He tried to make some observation about the portrait she was staring so intently at, but he couldn't look away from her. Within reach. He stood there, looking down at her, while she stared resolutely at the painting. As if she didn't sense him here.

He doubted very much that was true.

"Hello, Brianna."

She didn't move. For ticking seconds, she stood perfectly and utterly still. So still it wasn't as if she hadn't heard him. It was as if in fight-or-flight she was stuck at *freeze*.

There should be nothing remarkable about her. She was of average height, size. She had brown hair and blue eyes and a fair complexion. She had the mark of *American* all over her.

And yet...

The fabric of her dress, glittering in gold accents, settled on her curves like poetry. That fair skin seemed imbued with a warmth he'd once felt...and hadn't since, no matter how many women he'd taken to his bed. And the blue of her eyes reminded him of something he could never place but spent far too many hours trying to.

She finally turned her head. She looked up at him, but her expression was politely bland. Her gaze fairly puzzled. "Oh. Hello…" She trailed off purposefully. As if she didn't remember his name.

He laughed. Perhaps it was arrogance. Perhaps it was the fact she was no actress. But he did not for a second believe she'd forgotten him.

"Now, let's not play games, *dusci*. It doesn't suit you."

He'd give her credit. She held his gaze. Didn't cower or even narrow her eyes. She remained looking faintly puzzled. But her cheeks grew darker and darker red. "Lorenzo. It's been a long time," she said after a long, considering moment.

"That it has, Brianna." He smiled at her in the way she had once called *disastrous* to her better judgment.

She did not smile back.

"I… I'm sorry. I have to go." She backed away from him, and he realized she wasn't *really* making eye contact. She was just looking at his forehead as she made a large circle to avoid being with arm's reach. Then she darted for the restrooms.

He watched her go, utterly confused—not a condition he found himself in very often. She looked back at him, once over her shoulder. He did not see any sort of anger in that gaze. This wasn't vitriol in those blue eyes, hatred over the way he'd ended things. It wasn't embarrassment or even some sort of romanticized emotional distress over their long-past breakup.

It was *fear.*

He could understand all the other responses, but even if she'd heard all the rumors about him, fear didn't make sense. All the accusations against him related to the Marino family and business. No woman had ever accused him of violence—though Dante had no doubt tried to pay off a few to. Dante would stop at nothing.

Lorenzo watched the space where Brianna had disappeared. Something was…off. Something was *wrong*. And he wouldn't rest until he knew what.

# CHAPTER TWO

"WELL, THAT WAS very stupid," she muttered to herself as she stared at her reflection in the restroom mirror. Luckily no one else was in here, so she could do things like groan and talk to herself.

Running away was hardly playing it cool. All she'd had to do was stand there and make some small talk, and *then* excuse herself without running.

But coming face-to-face with Lorenzo was like sticking her finger into an electrical socket. No amount of preparation had hardened her against that *zap* of reaction.

She had felt exactly like she had two years ago. Dazzled. Charmed. Tempted. And all he'd done was say hello and accuse her of playing games. What was *wrong* with her?

She sucked in a breath, pulled her phone out of her evening bag and looked at her lock-screen picture. Gio grinning at her from the middle of a clutch of tulips.

She was here for *him*. For everything this show might be able to do for their future. She stared at the picture, usually her guiding star, but in this case all she could see was that he had his father's nose and smile. *Disastrous.*

Yes, Lorenzo was. But she wasn't the same girl she'd been two years ago. She was a mother. She had someone to protect, and she would protect Gio at all costs.

She would *not* feel guilty for keeping Gio from Lorenzo. Not when it could potentially put Gio in danger. Even if it was hard to believe Lorenzo was dangerous, it was clear his business dealings *could* be. And if it could affect his rival's family, why not Lorenzo's own?

She needed to stay away from him. Just by being near him she risked too much, and she was evidently not nearly as clear-sighted as she'd thought she was. So she'd just…go back out and make her excuses to leave. No one needed her here. She'd sold plenty of art so far.

Why was he even here? She didn't allow herself to consider the possibilities because the one she wanted to be true was the one she couldn't want to be true.

*He's here to see you.*

Well, too bad. She was leaving. She wouldn't give him a chance to… Whatever it was he wanted to do. Even if her heart nearly skipped a beat at the thought of him thinking of her all this time later. Thinking of her and wanting to see her and…

*No.* There was no *and.* There was only getting out of here so she didn't make any mistakes that might put Gio at risk.

Determined, she slipped her phone back in her purse and marched back out to the gallery. Chin high, shoulders back, *all* determination.

But when she scanned the crowd…she didn't see him. He was gone. She let out a long breath. She felt relief, really.

*Really.*

It was just it landed strangely like disappointment. And it sat with her. Heavy until she couldn't think past how *exhausted* she was. She found the organizer and said her goodbyes, thanked a few people who complimented her pieces on her way out, and then made her way to the exit, where a car would be waiting to take her back to her hotel.

But before she could get from door to car, there was a slight obstacle.

The man she was trying to avoid.

He stood on the sidewalk, looking up at the beautiful building while Palermo sparkled around them.

She hadn't forgotten the *punch* of him—the figure he cut, all broad-shouldered confidence. Something innate that simply vibrated from him, like a frequency she'd been attuned to since long before she'd met him.

She thought about turning around and running back inside—no matter how stupid that would have been—but his gaze met hers and she found herself frozen—half in the door and half out.

He smiled. *Oh, God.* She was going to end up doing something stupid again. *Think of Gio. Protect your son.*

"Hello again," he offered. "Coming out or scurrying back inside at the sight of me?"

She blinked. She should have a scathing retort. She had known this might happen. She had *prepared* for this. She had even practiced in the mirror all the casual, unbothered, dismissive things she might say to him.

But she had not prepared for everything she'd felt back then to come rushing back. Slithering through all the cracks in her armor so she felt like an exposed wire—sensitive and dangerous. On the verge of something terribly *explosive*.

"Are you afraid of me, *dusci*?" he all but purred. "I must admit, I cannot imagine why," he said with a silky arrogance that helped break through the haze affecting her.

"You can't?" she returned, finally finding her voice in her irritation with him. She forced herself to step outside, though she kept by the door. She would have an escape if she needed one. "When rumors swirl about you the way they do? None of them good?"

There was the *tiniest* flicker of something in his expression. Not aggression, but that intensity she'd once been enthralled by. *You still are.*

"Tell me, Brianna. Do you believe every rumor you hear, or only ones about former lovers?" He asked it casually, *conversationally*, but it had far more of an effect on her than it should.

The word *lovers* in his deep, dark voice seemed to travel down her spine, her body trying to remind her of what her brain was desperately trying to forget. Just how good at *lovers* they were.

*Gio. Think of Gio.* But that wasn't exactly helpful, because as much as she wanted to protect her son—more than *anything*—she couldn't fully absolve herself enough to not feel guilt over the situation.

This man did not know he had a son at all. He'd never been on the receiving end of Gio's smiles or held the boy as he'd grown.

*Because he's a violent criminal, Brianna. Because he deals in dangerous things that could hurt your son. This is not your fault.*

"I haven't seen one article or media story to refute any of these claims against you," Brianna replied, determined to keep her position even as he stepped closer. She would not let him physically intimidate her. "Never saw *you* attempt to refute it, in fact."

He cocked his head, reached out and touched a finger to her cheek. His gaze was focused on that finger, and he slid it down the length of her jaw. The touch arced through her like electricity. She shuddered and knew she shouldn't. She *yearned* and knew she couldn't.

This was no intimidation. It was seduction. She'd been down this road once before. She had to be smarter than she'd been two years ago. Stronger.

"My original statement refuted it," he said, his voice low, serious. His dark gaze matched it.

And it was basically a lie. "That was your publicist." She should move. Step away from his wandering finger. Not let him block out the light. Block out her sanity.

"You are *very* abreast of this. I didn't realize the dealings of a Sicilian businessman would make news in America."

"You're hardly *just* a Sicilian businessman. Which I did not find out until I got home."

*Home. Gio. Get out of here, Brianna.*

She finally got her mind to get through to her body enough to move—sidestep away from his shadow, his finger, his orbit. She began to stride toward the car that would take her to safety.

She had to be safe. For Gio. Safe and smart and... protect Gio at all costs. Which meant protecting herself.

"I thought we could have coffee. Catch up."

She stopped midstride because was he *insane?* But she didn't look back at him, just forced herself to continue walking. "It was never just coffee with us, Lorenzo."

He chuckled as he matched her stride easily, the sound deep and warm as it settled inside of her like a drug. Only a drug could make her want something she knew was far too dangerous. "That would be enjoyable as well."

*Those* words hit a little hard. Not just because they were tempting, and she hated herself that they were, but because she'd been busy preparing for motherhood and then being a single mother for the past two years. She had not *enjoyed* anything remotely sexual in so long she had begun to wonder if she even had those kinds of desires anymore.

Leave it to Sicily and Lorenzo to remind her that she did.

But it was *infuriating*, really, to be tempted by so little. He hadn't apologized for breaking things off with her abruptly. He hadn't even acknowledged that two years had passed. He was just…propositioning her, like that was all he *had* to do.

"I won't be having coffee with you. Or anything else, Lorenzo."

"Why not?"

Why not. *Why not?* She whirled on him, a surprising anger spurting up inside her. Surprising because she'd convinced herself she was over this. That by keeping Gio a secret she had somehow gotten even with him. But the emotion stirred, even years later, from him flirting with her like he'd done nothing wrong, like nothing had changed…

"You lied to me. You deserted me. Abruptly and without explanation. We can chalk that all up to a naive art student on her first international trip being easily charmed by a suave businessman who knows the games people play and plays them oh so well. Fine enough. But I'm not that woman anymore. And I'm not in any position to have random flings with men who have so little depth or human decency."

Lorenzo did not allow his temper to flare, though the shot about his *decency* landed sharp enough to make his control a hard-won thing. But he held on to the shield. He carefully iced the anger and offense away. He even smiled. Because there was something underneath her words he couldn't quite understand or guess at.

She was behaving…strangely. Like she had something to hide. Like he was someone to fear. None of that added up, even if she was angry with him, still, for his…abrupt breakup two years ago. "Why not?"

She blinked, clearly caught off guard. "Why not what?"

"Why are you not in a position to engage in 'random flings' with men you once enjoyed?" *Enjoye*d seemed a dim word for what sparked between them—then, now—but he didn't wish to overplay his hand.

Her mouth opened, but no sound came out. He saw her struggle to come up with an answer.

"Married?"

He watched her carefully. Once again she didn't speak right away. Was she considering lying? And what would be the lie?

More important, what was the truth? Why did it *need* a lie?

Well, he'd find out soon enough. He'd know everything there was to know about Brianna Andersen over the past two years and her strange behavior in the here and now.

She straightened her shoulders, lifted her chin, and met his gaze with direct blue eyes. Not like the sky or the ocean or even a flower. Just a shade that haunted him still.

"Lorenzo, we had a brief affair years ago," she said, and she sounded tired though she didn't look it. "I'm sure you've enjoyed many a model, actress, and who knows what all since then."

"You really *have* been paying attention, Brianna."

Her mouth firmed. "Some drugs are hard to kick, Lorenzo. But I won't be returning to this one. So I'd appreciate it if you leave me alone."

He couldn't quite keep his smile in place at her treating him like he was some kind of drooling stalker. A *drug,* when he knew the utter destruction those could do. "I do not stick around where I'm not wanted."

"You don't even stick around where you *are* wanted," she shot back.

And here was the anger he'd maybe expected. Or thought he deserved for his abrupt goodbye. The scorned woman. Still, no matter if it was deserved or not, he didn't *appreciate* her little barbs. "What is it you want from me, Brianna?"

"An apology would prove to me that you're a better man than I think you are, but the fact of the matter is, it'd have to be genuine. And begged-for apologies don't tend to be genuine. So I don't want anything from you, Lorenzo. Except to be left alone."

"I am not sorry for what I did." It had been necessary. He didn't do things that weren't *essential*.

*Except you're standing here right now having this ridiculous conversation.*

"Fantastic. Regardless, I'm not here for an apology. I'm here to sell my art. In a few days, I'll go home. I had no intention of running into you, asking for apologies, or dealing with you at all. You're a piece of ancient history and I'd like to leave it that way."

She stood there, delivering these statements with an anger and bitterness he never would have guessed existed inside of someone so…warm. But she had not only been warmth and sweetness. Even then. That was the problem with Brianna.

There were so many facets to her. She was an easy woman to read, and yet not an easy woman to get to know. Because she could be strong and she could be vulnerable. Naive and innocent. Cynical and passionate. He could see all these things on her face as easily as the makeup she wore—and yet it did not mean he understood the *whys* behind all her feelings, or that he could predict them. She'd gone from ignoring him, to being skittish, to an exhausted kind of rejection of him in a handful of minutes, and he understood very few of these abrupt changes.

But they were all her. Not acts. Not games. Just…her.

Perhaps that was the secret of why she'd lingered in his mind even after he'd left her. Even after he'd spent considerable time trying to cut her out of his memory.

She was an unfixable problem. A jumbled puzzle that would never have all the pieces. He couldn't herd her into one of his boxes, even though he desperately wanted to.

Needed to.

Otherwise she existed in his brain like some sort of evil spell. Constantly hovering and poking at him. Two years. No one haunted Lorenzo Parisi for *two years* and simply dismissed him with a few harsh words.

No more than he would continue to chase someone who had made it quite clear she wished him to remain history. *He* was in control of himself. In control of everything.

So he didn't follow her as she walked to the car. He didn't demand to know where she was staying. He didn't press his advantage—which he knew he still held, from the way she reacted to him when he'd done little more than touch her with the tip of his finger.

He let her go.

But that didn't mean he was done with Brianna Andersen.

Or she him.

# CHAPTER THREE

BRIANNA HAD BEEN dead set on leaving early. Going home to safety, half a world away from Lorenzo Parisi.

Then she had gotten back to her hotel room and spoken with her parents. The video call with them and Gio calmed her. It eased those jagged edges inside of her. She had all this to go home to. And all this to succeed for.

So she'd gone to bed knowing that going home now would be a failure. There was still one more art showing and a cocktail party that her manager had insisted could be a place to make lasting partnerships. It was a few more days and surely she wasn't so cowardly as to run home after one uncomfortable encounter.

She had woken up the next morning determined she would attend all these events as promised. She'd gone about her day certain she could handle it. If Lorenzo continued to appear...

She closed her eyes now as she sat on her hotel bed, procrastinating getting ready for this evening's party. She needed more time to herself for the memory of her encounter with Lorenzo to fade, but she didn't have that.

She would have to find a way to be stronger in the face of him. It was will power. It was strength. He wasn't threatening her. He didn't pose a *threat* to anything other than her peace of mind and that was *her* problem. Certainly not his.

Besides, if he continued to harass her, she could always call the police. If he was capable of violence against his rival's *child*, then surely the police would listen to her and do…something.

Surely.

She shook her head. This was catastrophic thinking. It wouldn't come to that. Maybe Lorenzo had attended last night's art show because she would be there, but he lived in Palermo. It was likely a lark. To see if she was still so easily beddable.

And she *wasn't*. Maybe she'd *felt* temptation, but she had not given in to it. Gold star for her.

If only she could trust herself to *maintain* such a stance. She closed her eyes, rubbed her temples. She really needed to get ready. She needed to trust herself. She needed to find all that strength she'd honed since Gio had come into her world.

Or perhaps feign illness and make arrangements to go home. Was the potential for a big payout more important than her sanity? She could be back in New Jersey with her son by tomorrow. She'd get a job at the grocery store. At the local school district. She could drive a bus. Or serve sloppy joes to high school kids. She could do *anything* other than…

*Follow your dreams? Give up everything you've worked for because of some man?*

"Ugh," she said. Out loud. Letting the sound echo off the walls. Here she was in Sicily, selling her art, and she couldn't even enjoy herself because she'd had one short-sighted affair two years ago. That was hardly the kind of woman she wanted to be.

But before she could determine exactly *what* kind of woman she wanted to be in this situation, she heard the telltale noise of a door being opened.

*Her* door.

She got up off the bed, more puzzled than leery at first. Until she saw the man enter her room. As though he could. As though he *should*.

For a moment, she only gaped. But that didn't stop his forward movement, even as he closed the door behind him. He came right into the main area of her hotel room, glaring at her the whole way.

"What are you doing here? How did you get in? I…" She backed away as he got closer. Put the expansive bed between them as if that would somehow save her. "I'll… call security," she said, her voice a panicked whisper more than a decisive or threatening shout.

He did not change course. Did not look the least bit concerned. Simply gestured for the phone she now stood close to. "Be my guest."

She stared at him, mouth open, heart pounding. This was threatening behavior, after all, but he didn't *act* like he was threatening her. He took a seat on the armchair in the corner like he was just going to…wait for her to make the call.

She grabbed the phone and punched the number for the front desk. When the cheerful woman answered, Brianna stumbled over her words, but she got them out. "A…a man has barged into my room. I need the police. I need…"

"No worries, Ms. Andersen," the attendant said, none of her cheerful customer service voice changing in concern. "Mr. Parisi has assured me his team can handle any disruption. You're in very good hands."

She looked at the man in question. Who lounged in her hotel room chair like he had every right. But he was a *billionaire*. He'd clearly told the hotel staff some…story. And now what? Who did she call? What did she do?

Well, she wasn't just going to *take* it. Carefully, she replaced the phone in its receiver. "What are you doing?" Brianna demanded, clutching the ends of the robe together as her mind whirled. Was there anything in this room she could use as a weapon? Was she justified in using a weapon when all he'd done so far was sit there?

Well, he *had* broken into her room. That was against the law.

Right?

"We need to have a discussion, Brianna," he said. Like they were sitting in a meeting room talking about a contract or business merger.

But they were in her hotel room. She was barefoot in a robe, with her damp hair piled on the top of her head. Which struck her as an unfair disadvantage when he sat there in a suit looking like he owned the whole world. "Yes, normal discussions happen when people break into other people's hotel rooms." She considered the lamp, but it was still plugged into the wall. There was no way she could unplug it and throw it at him before he did something. Except…he *wasn't* doing anything except sitting there.

There were no smiles like last night, she noted. Everything about him was serious. Businesslike.

"You have a child," he said. Flatly. Without emotion.

But she saw the fury in his gaze. He did not make a move. He sat there as calmly and leisurely as if they were sitting down to tea. But the temper was all there in his dark eyes.

She swallowed. Her gaze darted toward the door. She could crawl over the bed and run for the door, but would she be fast enough?

"You can run, Brianna. I will not hurt you, but I will follow." He stood, slowly and menacingly even though he'd just said he wouldn't hurt her. "You have a child, Brianna."

"So you keep saying." He didn't make a move for her, and something about that very fact kept her from lunging over the bed. No matter how angry he was, he wasn't trying to hurt her.

*That doesn't mean he won't. Don't be an idiot.*

"A son," he continued in that calm, even voice she assumed worked *very* well in whatever fancy boardrooms he frequented. "Born in July of last year."

"I don't know—"

"Think very carefully, *dusci*, before you lie to me." *This* was laced with anger. With a sharp-edged viciousness that had her swallowing and fighting the desire to cower.

And still, he kept his distance. Just stood by the chair, looking at her like she was a trail of slime. Too low to even bother to hurt.

"I haven't lied to you, Lorenzo." She tried to fall back on her own outrage. Her own sense of betrayal, hollow though it was in the moment. "I know the same cannot be said of *you*, but that does not make *me* a liar."

"You have kept something from me, then. You prefer secrets to lies. I prefer the truth. Did you give birth to *my* son on your return to America?"

"I don't know what concern it is of yours."

He was very quiet. The kind of silence that grew heavy as it stretched out. She felt no need to break it. There was nothing to say. *Somehow* he'd found her secret. And she did not know how to change the course of that except curse herself for ever coming here. For thinking she could have success and creative fulfillment *and* be safe from her secret getting out.

This was Lorenzo's fault—for leaving her, for ordering violent attacks, for being here—but it was also her own for putting herself in this foolish situation all for the sense of freedom selling her art had provided her.

She should have known one person didn't get too much of a good thing. She had wonderful parents, a beautiful son. It should have been enough. Shame on her for wanting more.

"Here is how the rest of your time in Palermo will go," Lorenzo said matter-of-factly. Whatever anger had slipped into his voice earlier had now chilled. "You will attend tonight's party, as I am told it is very important for your career. You will attend your final showing in a few days. Then we will fly to New Jersey, together, and you will take me to *my* son, Brianna. As you should have done long before now."

She did not care for his bossy tone. For the formality of it. Like she was an employee or a subordinate. He had never spoken to her like this before, and it was enough to put her back up. No matter how ill-advisedly.

"I have done *everything* to protect my son and I will never, *ever* stop. You are a violent criminal. No doubt if you weren't a billionaire, you'd be in jail."

He laughed then, but not the same chuckle from last night. Nothing that spoke of levity. It was dark and it was bitter.

"I would think this would go without saying, but if it needs to be said, so be it. I have *never* ordered anyone be hurt in my name, Brianna. I am not a coward. If I wished to attack my rival, I would attack him—not a *child*—with my own two bare hands."

She could picture it. Which did not send the sharp bolt of fear through her as it should. "Is that supposed to make me feel better?" she asked instead.

"I do not care how *you* feel. I care that my son breathes, even as we speak, and I have never once laid eyes on him or held him. That every choice about his life has been kept from me. My own flesh and blood. I care that you are the architect of this betrayal."

"Betrayal? Betrayal is being left without a word. Without a second glance. Betrayal is being *abandoned*. You lied to me, time and time again."

"You knew who I was."

"No, I did not, Lorenzo. Not how you mean. Your name, your body, the man you wanted me to think you were, yes, but not the business, the billionaire status, the cruelty in the name of it. I was going to tell you about the pregnancy, but first I had to find out how to reach you— because you'd certainly left me no ability to do so. And all I found was story after story about how the father of my child was a cruel, dangerous man."

"Do you think I would hurt my own flesh and blood? Is this how little you think of the men you invite into your bed?"

"Who was I supposed to believe, Lorenzo? The man who'd left me high and dry after two months of lies, or a series of stories that no one refuted except your publicist, with a tepid statement I knew you had nothing to do with."

"You were supposed to inform me I had a son."

"No. A mother's job is to protect her son. No matter what. *That* is what I did." Even now, hearing him deny the accusations against him and believing him—whether she should or not—she knew she'd done the right thing. Protecting Gio was all that could ever matter.

But guilt settled in her gut like acid at the way he'd said, *"I care that my son breathes, even as we speak, and I have never once laid eyes on him or held him."*

With such barely contained emotion she could only think how *horrible* it would have been to have missed all Gio's firsts. Those sleepless nights, the gurgling smiles, the warmth of a baby's cuddle.

It made her want to soften, apologize, insist they fly home right now so he could meet his son.

But this couldn't happen. She had to protect Gio. And until she knew for certain her child would be safe from the violence surrounding this man, she had to do whatever she could to keep them apart.

Lorenzo did not have a temper. Anger and impetuousness had never served him well, so he'd never allowed himself outbursts. The oldest of ten, he'd had to learn at a very young age—so young he barely remembered—how to be responsible, how to control what he felt, how to put others first when they needed it.

In a house full of hungry mouths, many had needed it.

But his family was no longer destitute. He had more money than a god. He enjoyed his work, his life, and didn't allow himself very often to consider the fear and pain of growing up the way he had.

But ever since his investigator had brought him news of this child this afternoon, he'd been reminded of the darkest times in his life. The anger that threatened to take hold and destroy everything he held dear.

He had a son. The child was over a year old. Walking

and no doubt doing some talking—Lorenzo was well versed in child development. He'd helped raise most of his youngest siblings from diapers to adulthood—and he had not known his own son existed.

Anger, sharp and dark and dangerous, swirled inside of him like its own entity. The only time he could remember feeling this furious before was a time he never let himself consider. Memories too painful to ever address.

How dare this woman bring them up in him.

"You should get dressed or we will be late," he said to her. In cool, calm tones because he was in control. He was in charge of *everything*.

*Except the boy she's kept from you.*

She stared at him, still clutching the edges of her fluffy hotel robe together. As if it were armor that would save her. He could force her to miss the party, the art show in a few days. It would be her just due to miss these opportunities for her career.

But that would be needlessly cruel, and while he might be all for that on a personal level, he also knew what it was to be the child of a parent who grew more and more bitter with the other. Who blamed and manipulated and used and hurt.

He would not give that to his child.

On the other hand, he could leave Brianna here and fly to New Jersey himself and lay claim to the boy.

But he would not put his son through anything that might scar him. Arriving a stranger without the boy's mother would not be what was best for the child. Even if Brianna deserved to miss two years of their son's life in retribution.

Someday, he would find a way to punish her. But it would not be at his child's expense. Never.

He would give Brianna one thing. The vehement way she spoke of protecting her child at any cost was good. He could even admit—at least in the privacy of his thoughts—he imagined she was a good mother. It was that warmth, that nurturing she'd shown him two years ago she no doubt showered on her own child.

But that did not excuse her actions. Protection did not excuse them either. Believing paparazzi fodder and unfounded accusations was...

*Betrayal.*

She stood there, daring to look like *she* had been the one betrayed. Still not making a move to get dressed. Still not offering any groveling apologies. Just standing there, far too tempting with her bare legs and feet and big blue eyes full of conflicting emotions—none of them sharp enough.

Brianna had never been much of a sharp edge. It was one of the things that had drawn him to her. That infinite softness. *A good thing for a mother to have.*

Mother. The mother of his child. A child he did not know. He had his reasons for not rushing off to meet this boy. The one he liked least was the conflicting emotions that threatened to rule him.

He would not meet his son in such a state—no matter how he ached to hold his flesh and blood.

No, he would be in complete control. He would map out every move. By the end of Brianna's time in Palermo, he would be ready. He would have everything under control.

Including Brianna.

Who still had not moved.

"I don't understand what you're doing," she said at last. "Why... Why aren't we going to New Jersey right now?"

He looked down at her, shoving the anger down underneath all the ways he'd learned to control it. "You should understand, recognize it, if you are a good enough mother. That now that I know his existence, every step I take will be in making certain my son has the life he deserves. Which, much as I may despise it, involves a mother who is not miserable. You will have your career highlight, Brianna. *I* certainly won't be the one to stop it." He made a big show of looking at his watch. "Now. Let's not waste any more time. I believe you have patrons to woo."

# CHAPTER FOUR

BRIANNA WAS HARDLY cognizant of getting ready, though that was just what she did. Dressed. Put on makeup and did her hair. On the surface, she looked exactly as she was meant to—the American artist eager to make connections.

But surface hid so much.

She sucked in a slow, long breath, then let it out twice as slowly. Lorenzo sat next to her in the car, a living, breathing rock of absolutely no reaction whatsoever. In the dark of the car, she couldn't see his eyes, but she imagined the anger still lurked there.

He hadn't lost his temper. There'd been no threats, not really. He'd laid down the law—his law—sure, but it wasn't... Maybe he would have become violent if she'd argued, if she'd refused. Maybe he had that in him...

But she was having a harder and harder time believing it. He was a proud man. Sending someone to do his dirty work...it did not fit what she knew of him at all. And even if he was ruthless enough to harm someone else in his business affairs, he would never harm a child.

That much she'd gathered from his choices tonight.

Had she made a mistake two years ago? She closed her eyes. It didn't matter. She'd acted in her son's best interest. If that had been a mistake, so be it. Better safe than sorry and Gio's safety would always trump everything.

She had only a few days to decide what that looked like.

The car rolled up to the beautiful old building the cocktail party would take place in. Beyond it, the sun was setting, lighting up Mount Pellegrino. The city itself beginning to sparkle to life as night began to fall.

Brianna took another deep breath and tried to remind herself that even with this unfortunate turn of events, she should enjoy her time here. Somehow.

She did not look at Lorenzo, knew she would not be able to keep her facade if she did. "I do not think we should enter together," she said as regally and coolly as she could manage.

He said nothing for a long, stretched-out minute. Then he sighed. As if she was very, very dim. "If you think you are leaving my sight before we leave for America, you are sorely mistaken. I will be by your side through every moment of this party. I have a staff member packing your hotel room for you as we speak. You will be staying at my residence until we leave."

She whipped her head to face him now, anger overtaking worry. He'd sent staff to pack *her* things? "It did not occur to you to *ask*?"

"No, it did not. Because there is nothing to *ask* of you, Brianna. You have done everything the way *you* wanted since you learned of *our* son. Now it is my turn to approach things as I want. Luckily, we can both agree to put the child first."

It was a slapdown that landed because it was true. She had, in fact, chosen everything. She would put Gio first, always. But she didn't think he got to claim he would too at this point. "You haven't even asked his name."

Lorenzo's expression was hard as granite and betrayed nothing. "I know his name. Where he was born. His height, his weight. I know everything now."

She swallowed as a strange kind of shame washed over her—when she should be *afraid* he could get all that information without her permission. She had nothing to be ashamed of. But knowing this didn't seem to change the course of her emotions.

"You could have asked," she pointed out. She might have kept Gio's existence a secret, but he could have had *some* understanding. He could have come to her with something other than all this controlled anger and self-important orders.

Or so she told herself to keep from crying. Or, worse, begging his forgiveness. When she refused to apologize for what she'd done, because it had been the *right* thing, even if the stories were wrong.

"You could have told me of his existence," Lorenzo replied evenly. "Even last night. You had ample opportunity. Yet you chose to keep him from me."

"Imagine that. That when I learned I was pregnant after being so coldly discarded, and decided I wanted to have this child, that discovering the man I'd shared my body and heart with had lied to me. Had hidden his true identity." But that wasn't why she'd kept Gio a secret, was it? Because she'd still been ready to tell Lorenzo, to hope for some kind of reconciliation no matter how hurt she was. Because love made a woman stupid.

But a child did not. "And still I would have told you," she said, though it was embarrassing to share the truth. But it was necessary he understand this wasn't about her.

It was never about *her*. "Until I learned you were engaged in some kind of business battle that would leave a child harmed. Now, whether this is true or not, does it matter? What I read was that a child was hurt. And I would not allow the same to happen to my child."

"You can be angry at the way things ended for us, Brianna, but you know I am not the sort of man to hurt my own."

"No. I *thought* I knew that. Then I learned everything I thought I knew about you was a lie. Why shouldn't your lack of violence be a lie too?"

His jaw was tight, and frustration flashed in those dark eyes. "Not a lie," he gritted out.

"What is it you said last night? Not a lie, but you kept something from me. Lots of somethings. You claim to prefer the truth, but you hid everything you were. So I couldn't trust anything I might have felt."

"A simple internet search when we were together would have told you everything. I was hardly engaging in back-alley machinations to keep you from discovering more about me."

"But I didn't search, Lorenzo. Because I trusted you." She looked away from him then because she hated reliving this pain in front of him. And it had been painful. More painful than she cared to admit to herself. Because she had loved him. Deeply. Immovably.

And he'd deserted her without a second glance. She had been that unimportant to him. "More the fool me, I know," she murmured, staring at the glittering building people were pouring into, glittering themselves like so many jewels.

She didn't belong here.

But she *was* here, and here was an opportunity. "I did

what I thought was best. I always will when it comes to Gio," she said, calm and detached, she liked to think. "You can be angry about it. You have every right to be. But it changes nothing. Not what happened, not how I feel."

Lorenzo's door opened. He didn't move right away. His gaze was on her, opaque and unreadable, for what felt like forever. Then he moved, sliding out of the car.

Brianna let out a long breath she had not been fully aware of holding. Holding her breath. Holding her own. She was managing and she had to keep managing, but it was a hard-won thing.

Her door opened, and Lorenzo stood there, still a figure that took her breath away. She knew what he would look like without the jacket, the tie. With the buttons unbuttoned, with his hands in her hair and his mouth hard and demanding. Or soft and exploratory. She knew what it would feel like to slide her hand into his as she now had to do.

With all that had happened in two years between them shooting barbs and reigniting old hurts. And still she knew the contact would spread through her like warmth and want.

She steeled herself and then took the hand he offered to help her out of the car. She looked up at Lorenzo and held that dark gaze, determined to be as strong and angry as he was. "I will do everything to protect my son. Right now, I'm trying to believe that you would too. The minute I don't—I don't care what billions you have, what power—I will do *everything and anything* to protect him from you if you or your business poses a threat. And I mean *anything.* So perhaps you should take a pause in hating me and blaming me and look inward and make sure nothing you've done will follow you and land on Gio's doorstep."

* * *

Lorenzo stood there, Brianna's hand in his, her blazing anger focused solely on him. She clearly had no idea how easily he could crush her. With his money. With his power. *He* had all the control.

And yet she stood up to him, all naive confidence that she could best him simply because she wanted to.

This was not the woman he remembered. How soft she'd been back then. Eager. There'd been passion in her, but it had been open. Enthusiastic. Not this sharp-edged force of nature determined to protect something at all costs.

Worse than this surprising new side to her, which did *nothing* to ease the lustful turn of thoughts that even now he was fighting off, was the fact that she was right. Regardless of his power or his money, there *was* the chance he was a threat to his own son.

There was a tiny, minuscule sense of rightness to her keeping his son from him. Protecting this boy he'd never met nor laid eyes on. Because even though he had not ordered the attack on Dante's son, Dante clearly thought he had.

And that made Dante dangerous. Just because he hadn't retaliated yet did not mean he wouldn't. Particularly if he found out that Lorenzo had a son of his own.

Brianna raised an eyebrow at him now. A silent look that said, *Are we going to go in or stand here and stare at each other all night?*

She'd rattled him with this idea that *he* was an inadvertent threat. When nothing in his adult life had been inadvertent.

*Except everything to do with* her.

He pushed all these whirling thoughts aside, tucked her

soft arm into his and moved them toward the building. A cocktail party was the last thing he wanted to deal with right now, but he knew how to compartmentalize. How to do that which he wanted for the greater good.

While *he* did not care about Brianna's dream or talent, their son no doubt would, as he grew. Lorenzo would never be the tool Brianna used to turn their son against him. He would ensure Brianna had *every* opportunity she desired. If he had to charm everyone at this party himself.

They entered, were greeted by the organizers, and Lorenzo didn't miss the speculative glances. The whispers in their wake. Perhaps he should not have had them arrive together, but he didn't trust her not to bolt.

He'd find her. No matter what. But this all worked better, would go smoother, if they did things his exact way.

His exact way was always best.

Or so he'd always thought. Until they moved into the buzzing room full of people and drinks and art and Lorenzo caught a glimpse of the last man he wanted to see here.

Dante. Over in a corner, laughing with a few other businessmen Lorenzo recognized as clients of Marino & Family Industries.

A dangerous temper swept through him. All those swirling feelings of anger, of indignation, of hate. This man was trying to ruin everything the Parisi name stood for, and it was worse now. Before it had just been him.

Now it was his son.

There was no reason Dante should be here. No reason at all. Except to bother Lorenzo in some way, and Lorenzo had a terrible feeling *this* was what his publicist had been chattering at him about that he'd been ignoring. Something about pictures in the paper. He'd been so focused on discovering he'd had a son that he hadn't paid any mind. There were *always* pictures of him splashed about after he attended an event.

Now he wondered if those pictures had included Brianna.

Brianna. Here and on his arm, while that pit viper turned his attention from his cronies to Lorenzo across the room.

No.

Lorenzo maneuvered Brianna into a corner. "You'll have to excuse me, *dusci*. I must talk to this odious businessman. Why don't you go make your necessary artist rounds?"

"I thought I wasn't to leave your side." She didn't say this in disappointment, but in suspicion. Her eyes narrowed as she studied his face.

He could not let her in on the danger Dante posed. It would complicate things. So he lifted her hand, brushed his mouth over the knuckles, making sure to keep eye contact. Holding her hand gently until a faint blush crept into her cheeks.

"Ah, but I trust you, my sweet Brianna."

The flush on her cheeks deepened so much that desire twined with satisfaction for having put her off guard.

He turned away from her, to head Dante off at the pass. He didn't look back at Brianna. It would give away too much to both his rival and the woman in question.

He met Dante halfway between the man's initial starting point and Brianna. "Hello, Dante," he greeted jovially, as it always set the man on edge when Lorenzo refused to deal in anger or veiled threats.

But tonight Dante only smiled. "Why have you sent off your companion? I wished to compliment the artist on her...alluring work."

Lorenzo did not outwardly react. Such sad little provocations didn't tend to work on him quite so effectively, but he would blame the roiling anger inside of him on the fact everything had changed this morning when his investigator had delivered the news.

"I did not know you were such a fan of the arts, Dante," Lorenzo offered with a smile that was likely sharper than it should be. "But I'm sure your compliments can be given by way of buying a piece."

"I was thinking more of funding the artist herself." Dante sipped his drink. "She's beautiful. American, a pity, but beautiful."

Lorenzo knew the emotions vying for purchase were more complicated than just hating this man. Something darker, with claws. Something far too close to *jealousy*. And a wave of old concerns that he would never, *ever* have again. Because no matter what he'd done or not done in his life, he would never allow himself to sink into the pain and suffering of his parents.

He was connected to Brianna now. He had a son. It left him too close to all the mistakes they'd made. But he was stronger.

Better.

"Perhaps you should better fund your staff, Dante. Last I heard there was quite the labor squabble in your offices in Rome. Best to focus your funding there, I should say."

Dante's self-satisfied expression flickered, but only for a moment. Which had Lorenzo bracing himself.

"There's quite a hubbub around you today," Dante continued, his eyes lingering on Brianna as she toured the room, led by her manager.

"Is there?" Lorenzo returned, thankful his voice could sound bored when his blood boiled and every effort right now was going to repressing old memories of his mother. What she had done. What she had lost. To men like Dante. All because his father had not been man enough to put his family first.

All because of *love*.

Lorenzo would correct these mistakes. Always.

"Last night you made quite the splash slobbering all over the American artist," Dante continued.

Lorenzo laughed, though he felt no mirth. Still, the little accusation made it easier to focus on the present. "Ah, Dante, your talent for exaggeration knows no bounds. Slobbering? Honestly. Even the paparazzi couldn't come up with such a story."

Dante shrugged philosophically. "I was certainly interested. Interested to go digging. You've met the artist before, have you? In Florence."

Lorenzo could not keep *all* emotion off his face. That shouldn't be easy-to-find knowledge, and who could confirm it? At Dante's grin of satisfaction Lorenzo knew his cold fury was echoing off him. A point for Dante, indeed, but a man could lose the battle and win the war.

Lorenzo would win this war.

"I'm deeply touched you would go through all the trouble to look into this for me, Dante. With so many labor disputes going on at Marino, you would think *that* would take up all your time and concern. How kind you would spare some for me."

Dante's expression didn't even flicker this time. He only smiled wider. "Gio is a nice name. Isn't it?"

For a moment, all Lorenzo heard was a faint buzzing in his ears. He could picture moving forward. Putting his hands on Dante's throat and squeezing.

But he did not do this. For two reasons. One, he had

the sinking suspicion Dante wanted him to. No doubt to aid in the rumors Lorenzo was a vicious monster.

Second, he saw Brianna. Watching him with a frown of faint puzzlement on her face. Her opinion of him didn't matter at all, but he had plans. A vision for the future.

Maybe she'd thrown him a curveball, but he'd already recalibrated. He knew what his life with a son looked like.

Now he just had to recalibrate again. Because Dante's curveball was nothing short of a threat.

"It seems congratulations are in order, Lorenzo. Though a confirming birth certificate seems to be missing. But that would suit you, wouldn't it?" Dante clapped him on the back and smiled. "Hurt my child. Ignore your own. The press will love it. They're probably halfway to New Jersey as we speak."

And then he walked away.

# CHAPTER FIVE

BRIANNA WATCHED AS Lorenzo spoke to a man. Older, shorter, his dark hair sprinkled with gray and his smile not warm or kind at all, but the fact he was smiling at all made the whole thing seem...worse.

The look of pure fury on Lorenzo's face was what held her attention though. She watched as Lorenzo's hand curled into a tight fist in reaction to whatever the man said.

Brianna was frozen in space, hearing none of the conversation going on around her. She was sure she was about to see all that violence Lorenzo had been accused of on public display, and then she'd have to escape somehow. Get back to New Jersey, get Gio, then erase her entire identity...somehow, and then what?

But Lorenzo never moved. Just stood very still as the man spoke once more, clapped him on the back and then strode away. Lorenzo did not watch him leave. He did nothing for a few ticking seconds. Then his gaze moved.

And found her.

He did not immediately cross the room, as she'd thought he might, based on the sheer force of his gaze. Instead, he moved in a circular kind of path. Talking to this person, taking a canapé from that tray, taking his time.

Always coming for her. No matter whom she talked

to, no matter how many sips of wine she took, she was far too aware he was headed for her.

Once he finally arrived, he slid his arm through hers as if they were still lovers instead of veritable strangers who basically hated one another.

She hated that she wished for the first.

He leaned close, his mouth at her ear. She would *not* shudder. She would *not* react. "We must leave at once."

Brianna might have argued, but she didn't particularly want to be here. She couldn't concentrate on any conversation with Lorenzo circling like a shark, and she liked even less the man he'd been talking to, whose eyes were on her everywhere she went.

She'd spoken to some people, made her rounds. Her manager wouldn't be too happy with an early exit, but a migraine was beginning to pound behind her eyes and she needed space. Time. To think.

"All right."

If he was surprised at her easy agreement, he didn't act it. He kept that pleasant fake smile on his face and maneuvered them toward the exit. When they reached her manager, Brianna didn't lie exactly. She explained she had a migraine and she needed some dark and some quiet to recover.

Once they were outside, everything about Lorenzo changed. His scowl was hard, his eyes harder. There was no mask, only fury.

His car and driver were already waiting for them right at the entrance. Worry began to displace her own discomfort.

"Lorenzo, what's going on?"

He didn't so much as look at her. Simply opened the

car door and gestured her inside. When she did not get in, he turned that ferocious scowl on her and leaned close.

"We must retrieve Gio at once."

Terror pierced her soul. "What's happened?"

He nudged her into the car and in her shocked state she had no fight in her. Gio. She had to get to Gio. That was all that mattered.

"The press knows," Lorenzo said quickly as he pulled the door closed behind him. The driver immediately pulled away from the curb.

"Knows what?"

He spared her a look, again like she was dim. "That I have a son. In New Jersey."

Brianna blinked, trying to find the terrible threat in those words. But they were only the truth. She frowned as she tried to calm her racing heart.

"We will collect him," Lorenzo was staying. "We will take him to my estate."

"Your *estate*? Here?"

"Outside Palermo, but yes, in Sicily. It is protected. No one will have access to him. I assume the same cannot be said of your home in America."

Brianna shook her head as if this would make the jumble of thoughts going on inside her coalesce into something rational. Something that made sense.

But the only thing that made sense was getting out of Sicily and far away from Lorenzo. She sucked in a breath and turned to face Lorenzo. When she spoke, she did so calmly and carefully. Much like she spoke to Gio when he was in the midst of a tantrum.

"Here's what we'll do, Lorenzo. I'll go home. You'll stay here. We'll make arrangements for you to meet Gio, of course. I'm not suggesting otherwise. But not when everything is so…up in the air." She didn't know why he was rattled by the press's knowledge, but she *did* want to keep whatever interest there was in Lorenzo away from her child. So it made no sense to bring Gio *here*. "I can't imagine why anyone would care all that much about a toddler, so we'll stay in New—"

"Dante will have planted a story to *make* people care." His gaze turned to hers, and she could not read it. It wasn't anger or even solely frustration. Something deeper and more complex sat there, making her ache for him when she should be angry with him. "I am afraid this changes things, Brianna. I cannot cave to your time line."

"Cave? My time line? Everything since you broke into my hotel room has been *your* idea, *your* time line."

He waved this away as if it was inconsequential, and she supposed it was. The current *consequences* were a business rival making an international story out of her son. Which didn't seem quite so serious as Lorenzo was making it out to be, not that she loved the idea. But Lorenzo was the expert on press and threats. Not her.

"Is he in danger?" Brianna forced herself to ask, even though she didn't know what recourse she had if he were. Just get home as fast as possible. "Are my parents?"

"I have dispatched every resource at my disposal to ensure everyone remains well protected. These reporters pose no direct threat to Gio or your parents, no. But I will be in charge of the public's access to my son so no threats can manifest."

*Manifest.* The idea of threats just *popping* up out of nowhere made her throat tight with fear. As if sensing this, something in his expression softened. In a move that shocked her, he took her hand in his.

"I will need you to trust me on this," he said earnestly.

"But I will make you this vow—no harm will come to our son on my watch. He is my top priority. Always."

She had known a different man two years ago. A charming, passionate man with a certain amount of intensity for *certain* tasks. But not this. Not this sharp-edged, severe, heavy-handed pushing forward like an invading army.

And it was for her son. Her son's *safety* and *privacy*. So two years ago hardly mattered. The man she'd known, the woman she'd been. Her clattering nerves and old feelings that should be long gone didn't matter. Only getting to Gio and keeping him safe did.

So, when the car pulled to a stop and Lorenzo got out, Brianna followed. All the way back home to New Jersey.

Lorenzo spent much of the flight across the Atlantic on his phone. He had men on the ground in America, so he knew that no one had descended on Brianna's family just yet, and that he had people in place to stop them if they tried.

Perhaps Dante had been bluffing. Lorenzo mulled this over between phone calls, not allowing himself to look over at Brianna.

Last time he had, she'd been watching the dark night outside the plane's window. Her expression had been soft and sad and had made something turn and twist inside of him. The kind of twist that had caused him to break things off with her all that time ago.

A twinge that reminded him of a childhood torn by too many terrible things, all cemented by love and duty.

So he didn't look at Brianna. And when the plane landed and they were ushered off the plane, he kept his gaze forward, though he had to offer an arm. It seemed the right thing to do.

His assistant led them to the awaiting car, and then they began a long drive through darkness that was slowly headed toward dawn.

Brianna hadn't really slept, and it seemed to be catching up with her. Lorenzo only felt wired. Desperate to get his son away from any place he might be a target. Once they were back in Sicily, safely ensconced at his estate, he could breathe.

Until then…

The car eventually pulled into a very suburban area, full of modest but neat homes that all had the same sort of air to them. Cleanly manicured lawns, leafless trees in a nod to the windy cold. Brick two-stories. Not the kind of money he was used to these days, but definitely not the poverty he'd grown up in. Something firmly in the middle.

Their car pulled up at one of the older-looking homes and his assistant nodded back at him from his position in the front seat. Lorenzo looked over at Brianna, who had finally succumbed to sleep, her head against the window, her coat wrapped protectively around her like a bubble.

She'd changed in the bathroom when they'd gotten on the plane. Out of the beautiful sparkling gown and into a gray ensemble of what looked like some kind of athletic gear.

Lorenzo still wore his suit. It only dawned on him now that these were the clothes he would meet his son in. Hold his son for the first time in. He didn't know what would be the appropriate attire, but a suit hardly seemed it.

There was no time to alter it. Somehow, they had beat

Dante's men here, or this had all been some kind of ploy. Either way, time was of the essence.

"Brianna."

She jerked awake, though he'd tried not to startle her. But she saw the house outside the window and was immediately shoving the door open. She sprinted through the yard and to the front door. Her purse dangled from her arm as she dug through it.

He arrived on the porch as she shoved keys into the door and turned the knob. She stepped inside the dimly lit entryway, and he followed.

He heard the sounds of people awake deeper in the house, though it was still well before 6 a.m. A woman who sounded a lot like Brianna said, "Mom's home!" and then the scrabble of little feet followed.

Lorenzo stood frozen by the door he'd closed behind him as a little boy bounded around the corner.

"Mama!" The boy shot across the floor and flung himself at Brianna as she crouched and caught him with ease. They held each other, just like that, for a very long time.

Lorenzo knew he should look at the two older people that had followed the boy into the room. Offer a handshake. A kind word. But he could only watch, mother and son wrapped up in each other. Love so evident he wished he didn't know. Wished he was blissfully ignorant of *this*.

"Baby, you shouldn't be up."

"I'm afraid he heard us making a bit of a racket trying to pack as instructed," the older woman said, fully dressed in slim slacks and a comfortable-looking sweatshirt.

Brianna stood, bringing Gio with her so the boy straddled her hip. Her blue eyes flickered with some emotion she hid well, although she was also clearly overjoyed at seeing her son again. "Gio. I want you to meet someone."

The boy turned his head to face Lorenzo. He had his short arms clutched around Brianna's neck, and when he looked at Lorenzo, tilted his head to lean it against Brianna's shoulder.

It was like being thrust back into time. Gio looked so much like his little brothers that Lorenzo felt as though he was that teenage boy once again, running herd on his younger siblings. With their dark shocks of hair and wild, expressive mouths. The only difference was the blue of Gio's eyes.

All Brianna.

"Gio," she said very softly. "This is your father."

The boy kept his head on Brianna's shoulder. He looked at Lorenzo with some speculation. Then he shook his head and turned away from Lorenzo, burying his face in the crook of Brianna's neck.

He mumbled something that sounded a lot like *scary*.

This seemed to amuse Brianna. "He is dressed a bit scary, isn't he?" she said with some humor and a nod at his dark suit. But her eyes were strangely wet. "But he isn't scary at all. I promise."

# CHAPTER SIX

BRIANNA HAD NEVER seen Lorenzo quite so off his game. He had an arrested look on his face, and his eyes never left Gio. Like he was seeing the secrets to the world unfurl to him all at once—awe-inspiring and terrifying.

She supposed that was parenthood in a nutshell. And it made her want to cry—for so many reasons. Time lost. What clearly hadn't been a terrible decision in the first place considering they now had to secrete Gio away at some Sicilian estate. And the ache in her heart she couldn't fully get rid of, no matter how right she'd been to keep them apart.

Gio held on to her neck for dear life as he often did these days around strangers. Brianna's first instinct was to protect him. To say he didn't have to look at or talk to Lorenzo if he didn't want to.

But that was not how she dealt with anyone else connected to Gio. And that didn't do Gio any good. Though Lorenzo was essentially a stranger to him, the boy had to learn to be comfortable around his father.

She stepped closer to Lorenzo so he could get a better look at his son even if Gio was burrowed into her as tight as he could get. She wouldn't *force* him, but she would give him the space to get comfortable with his father.

"Gio," she said, holding him close so he didn't feel abandoned. "We're going to go on a trip."

Gio didn't loosen his grip, but he moved his head a little. "Zoo?"

"Not the zoo, sweetheart. We're going to go to a whole different country. You, me, Grandma, Grandpa and… your father." She tried to smile encouragingly at literally anyone in this room but wasn't sure she succeeded.

And she didn't know how to make an impromptu trip to Sicily sound exciting to a child who was just over a year old. She didn't know how to make any of this palatable to him.

"There are zoos I can take you to in Sicily," Lorenzo said, his voice oddly…soft. Maybe it wasn't so odd since he was talking to a child, *his* child. She'd just assumed someone like Lorenzo would have no clear idea of how to talk to a child. The people she knew who were never around children tended to be stiff and formal, and Lorenzo was often that in the best of times.

This was obviously not the best of times.

"Sicily, where we're going, is my home," he continued. He did not reach out to touch Gio, though she got the sense he wanted to. "So there are many places I can take you."

Gio didn't loosen his grip, but his gaze moved somewhat suspiciously to Lorenzo. "Roars?"

"That's his word for tiger," Brianna explained.

Lorenzo held the boy's suspicious gaze and smiled. A smile Brianna hadn't seen out of him since Florence. She did not like what that did to her defenses.

"Of course tigers."

A silence stretched out as Lorenzo and Gio surveyed

each other, interrupted only when her father cleared his throat behind her.

Brianna turned to face him and tried to keep her smile in place. To treat her parents like she was treating Gio—timid toddlers who needed understanding and patience in a new situation.

"I'm sorry. Lorenzo, these are my parents. Scott and Helene. Mom, Dad, this is Lorenzo Parisi."

Lorenzo finally looked away from Gio and nodded at her parents, stepping forward and offering a hand. "It is good to meet you both."

Her parents each took a turn shaking the offered hand, and though they had polite smiles fixed on their faces, there was clear suspicion in both their expressions.

"I am delighted you will be accompanying us," Lorenzo said. "And apologize for the necessity of leaving on such short notice."

"We would do anything for our daughter and grandson," Mom said primly.

*"Anything,"* Dad said, with an attempt at menacing that might have worked on some football-playing boyfriend from high school, but hardly on this man.

Though Lorenzo nodded dutifully as if the threat had any weight against all his power and money.

"I've packed everything for Gio," Mom said. "We're almost done ourselves."

"Allow my staff to help you bring the bags to the car," Lorenzo said, gesturing for the door.

"We aren't ones for having people wait on us, Mr. Parisi."

"You must call me Lorenzo, and you must allow me to make this impromptu trip as easy on you and yours as possible."

Mom seemed to mull this over. "All right," she said eventually. "We'll finish packing." Her parents gave Brianna a look, but she could only smile overbrightly at them, hoping that at some point in the near future she'd be able to really talk with them.

But for now, it just… They had to go. She sucked in a breath as Lorenzo opened the door and gave instructions to his assistant and the driver who were to help with the bags.

"Do you have anything you need from here?" he asked, but his eyes were on Gio.

Brianna thought of her paints and embroidery supplies. It was the only thing of her own that she cared about. "I suppose not."

Lorenzo frowned. "There is no need to play martyr, Brianna."

She was too tired for her temper to flare. Mostly. "It's exhaustion, Lorenzo. Would I like my art supplies? Of course. Will my life look like something I can use art supplies in? How should I know? How could I possibly know what I need when I don't know what my life will look like in five minutes, let alone five days?"

She shifted Gio's weight, smoothed her hand over his flyaway dark hair. "But we'll have fun, baby," she said, forcing herself to sound cheerful. "An adventure!"

Gio didn't get excited about this, but he didn't voice his displeasure—which was a positive. He often voiced it and loudly.

But now there was only silence. The bustle of people going back and forth with bags. They were just waiting on her parents now, standing awkwardly in the entryway. Lorenzo never took his eyes off Gio, and Gio watched the man with careful wariness, never letting his grip on Brianna loosen.

"Would you like to hold him?" Brianna asked after a while. Because her back hurt, a migraine threatened, and if her parents didn't hurry up, she might actually go insane.

Lorenzo's smile was stiff and tight. Gio was practically strangling her—a clear sign he did not want to be held by a stranger. Brianna didn't *want* to hand him over to Lorenzo, but their first meeting should be more than this…surely.

"It is all right," Lorenzo said after a long while. "We will wait until he is ready. We have time."

*We have time.* It felt like a threat, even though it was only the truth. Who knew how long this would last? Who knew what lay ahead? All Brianna knew was she was doing this for Gio.

Everything was for Gio.

Safely on the plane, Lorenzo read the report from his head of security. They'd managed to waylay the small unit of journalists who'd been offered a tidy sum to get a picture of Brianna or her son, and they'd managed to make it back to the airport without detection.

A good start as they headed *back* across the ocean, this time with a toddler in tow. Lorenzo could not claim the flight was going *well*. Despite the attention of four adults determined to put every ounce of focus on Gio himself rather than dealing with each other, Gio did *not* enjoy the flight.

He screamed. He kicked. He ran about the cabin like some kind of wild, deranged beast. He hurled the remainder of his snack he didn't want and fought sleep like it was the very devil.

Lorenzo did not know why it filled him with a strange kind of pride.

*Yes, be wild and untamable, son. Scream your displeasure. Get what you want. Always.*

Brianna and her parents were clearly exhausted—both by the events of the day and Gio himself. The boy was tired and fighting it at every turn. The staff, used to children of all ages, were doing a pretty good job of keeping their feelings on the matter hidden behind stoic faces, but there were looks exchanged when the fever pitch of screams got especially high.

Like right now. Lorenzo got out of his seat and crossed to where Gio was huddled, ignoring his grandparents' attempts to calm him. Brianna sat in a seat like she'd given up. It was hard to blame her.

Lorenzo crouched in front of the boy, who immediately stopped screaming. His wide eyes studied Lorenzo in a mix of fear and uncertainty.

"Perhaps you'd like come with me to meet the pilot," Lorenzo offered pleasantly, holding out his hand though he didn't expect Gio to take it. It would take time for the child to trust him. "See how the plane is flown?"

On a whimper Gio scampered past him and to where Brianna sat, which was about what Lorenzo had expected. He didn't *want* his son to be afraid of him, but if he used that uneasiness to get Gio to sit still, the boy would no doubt drop.

Gio crawled up into the safety of Brianna's lap, shooting daggers out of his eyes at Lorenzo. But those eyes quickly began to droop now that he was forced to sit still. Just as Lorenzo had hoped.

Lorenzo crossed to the seat next to Brianna. Gio's eyes tracked him, blinking closed once, twice, and then finally staying there. His breathing evening out. His body relaxing in Brianna's arms.

Brianna relaxed, too, relief clear in her features. She even turned her head and smiled at him. "Good job," she whispered.

It should not fill him with warmth. That he'd succeeded. That Brianna had complimented him. Children at this age were easy enough to maneuver if you knew the tricks, and he'd had to learn them long ago.

It was a strange feeling, and one that made it easy not to be hurt by Gio's reticence, to be reminded of old responsibilities that had been thrust upon him too young. Responsibilities that had ripped his family into too many pieces. But he wasn't that powerless boy anymore.

He had *all* the power.

Which he was reminded of once again when they moved from plane to car, and then pulled up to his estate outside of Palermo. Saverina, his youngest sister, called it pretentious and over-the-top, while enjoying all its many amenities.

Lorenzo had been happy with both descriptors. The car pulled up the grand drive, around trees and fountains and marble fixtures that glittered in the sunlight. Brianna's parents practically had their noses pressed to the glass.

Lorenzo's staff stood waiting at the door. Everyone in the car filed outside and then the Andersen family simply stared, eyes wide and awed. No one seemed to know what to say. Even little Gio, who couldn't fully understand why this was impressive.

Lorenzo felt pride at this as well. Because *this* was the representation of his life's work. From hovel to *estate*.

From hunger to *excess*. Luck might have played a role in just how far he'd climbed, but luck could only take a person so far.

"Come," he said. "We'll get you settled in."

No one spoke, but they followed him up the stairs and into the grand entryway. Staff bustled by with bags and Lorenzo himself showed them to their quarters. An entire wing to themselves.

"I will leave you to rest. We will endeavor to begin a routine and stave off jet lag and serve dinner at seven. Should you need anything, there are phones in every room to contact staff. Feel free to explore in any ways you wish."

With that, he gave one last look at Gio...who was studying him intently. Lorenzo liked to believe there was less and less suspicion in the toddler's gaze, but it was hard to tell. Better he had some time with the family he knew in this unfamiliar place.

Lorenzo would be patient. Because they would never be separated again. He simply wouldn't allow it.

So he left Brianna and her family to settle in while he strode through the estate to the other wing. It would be in his best interest to rest, but he had to make certain there were no fires burning at Parisi Enterprises first. So he went to his office.

He lost track of time as he responded to emails and cleared his schedule for the next few days. There would be no leaving the estate until Gio began to look at him without fear, until he could figure out just what Dante was up to. So Lorenzo had to ensure all his seconds-in-command were ready to fill in for him.

He thought he heard something after getting off the

phone, and when he looked up, Brianna stood in the doorway. Still in her casual travel wear, looking exhausted.

"Is there something you needed?"

She stepped into the room, studying the walls of bookshelves, the crystal chandeliers, the big windows that overlooked the beautiful grounds. She shook her head faintly, like she couldn't quite believe what was right in front of her.

"My mother informed me that I needed to thank you. She wouldn't stop harping on it, so I came to do that."

"Well, please, go on then."

She rolled her eyes. "I feel like I *should* thank you. The flights. Plural. This place. It's a lot, though clearly nothing you can't afford. Still…this whole thing is all your fault to begin with, so why should I thank you for it?"

Lorenzo's mouth firmed at that—though he wanted to scowl. "*All* my fault?"

"Yes." She moved through the room, looking at the spines of books, dragging her fingers across the back of a leather armchair in front of the broad fireplace that dominated one wall.

He should not find the casual ensemble or messy hair or tired eyes alluring, but he couldn't stop his eyes from taking a tour of her form. He had once known her body as well as his own. Perhaps they had only been together two months, but she had become something like a part of him.

That was the problem with Brianna. Among so many other things.

"So there's absolutely no blame on your own shoulders? For not telling me my son existed, that is."

She let out a long sigh. "Do you remember what you said to me when I said I wasn't going to beg for an apology for the way you broke things off with me?"

*I'm not sorry.*

But he didn't answer, because unfortunately he understood her point.

"I'm not sorry either, Lorenzo. I can't be. We've both done…what we felt needed to be done at the time. Now we've come together once again and our sole purpose is to protect Gio, correct?"

"Correct," he returned stiffly, because if they could remain on that same page, nothing bad needed to happen. No angry fights. No painful betrayals. Just a business partnership.

"Then, that's what we'll do. As…partners of sorts," she said, as if reading his mind. Then she turned to face him with those heartbreaking blue eyes. The color of the seascape above his mantel.

The one he'd bought *after* he'd broken things off with her, convincing himself it wasn't because of that shade of blue and her eyes.

"I hope very much you and Gio can have a real relationship," she continued, with that natural warmth that was simply a part of her. "One that keeps him safe and allows him a father. I don't want him to grow up without one."

She said nothing about what that meant for them. Which was good because there was no *them*. Or shouldn't be.

But he was having a hard time thinking beyond the last time he'd seen her before these life-altering few days. Two years ago. Wrapped up in each other, pleasure and joy. A feeling so big, so dangerous, he'd slid out of bed the moment she'd fallen asleep. Packed his bags and left.

Because he would not love. He would not let such feelings tear him apart ever again. Not when he could help it.

And he could help it with her. Even if his body still ached for all they could bring out in each other. Lust and love got confused all the time. How well he knew this.

How well he kept them separate. And could. Always. Lust, he knew, gave him the upper hand, and didn't he need that now more than ever?

Something in the back of his mind whispered recriminations, arguments, warnings, but he could not heed them with his heart beating so loud. His body hard and wanting a taste.

Just a taste of what they'd once had. And why not? She was here. They were to keep *their* son safe. Together.

"There's just one problem," he said, moving from behind his desk to cross to her.

She watched him, wariness entering her expression the closer he got. But she did not back away. "What's that?" she asked, chin lifted. And it wasn't *all* wariness in those blue eyes.

She felt some echo of this as well. She had to.

He reached out and touched her cheek, just as he'd done the other night. Before he'd known. When he'd thought just another taste of her would solve the problem of Brianna. And maybe it was the sleep deprivation, but all he could think was he still hadn't had that taste.

Her breath caught, that flush creeping up her fair cheeks. So beautiful, his Brianna. *His.* He leaned close, and still she made no move to bolt, to stop him. He stopped when his lips were only a whisper away from hers. Then he met her gaze.

"You still want me."

# CHAPTER SEVEN

THE WORDS SHOT through Brianna like flame itself. He need only look at her and she throbbed with a yearning she'd forgotten existed. Or tried to. But he was so close. The words…incendiary.

*You still want me.*

And *how.* But she did not just give in to wants these days. She had a son to think of, and she was so very exhausted, and oh, she missed kissing this man. The way he made it feel like the entire universe was only them. Only heat. Only that explosion of what he could make her body feel.

No one before him had ever come remotely as close. She hadn't even attempted to find *close* since. Even if there hadn't been a pregnancy, a son, she was certain he would have ruined her for all men. Forever.

*You cannot be this weak.*

"You're very conceited," she managed to say. Not forcefully exactly, but not as breathless as she felt. He was so close. She could see that dark ring of near-black around the outside of his brown eyes. Each individual whisker that shadowed his jaw after all the flying back and forth they'd done.

Had he slept? Had she? Was this real life or a dream? If it was a dream…surely she could indulge in a taste?

She could lean forward, press her body to the strong wall of his. In a dream, she could relive everything she'd tried to forget.

His finger traced around her ear, then down her neck, and the sound she made was some embarrassingly desperate moaning sigh. Because his touch awakened every nerve ending, every foolish want she'd tried to tell herself not to have. He was going to crush her again. It was inevitable.

She didn't care. Not if he kissed her. She wouldn't care about anything.

Dimly, she knew this was stupid and ridiculous. A bad, bad move. But that throbbing inside of her had a mind of its own. Every millimeter of flesh felt sensitive. To air. To touch. To her clothes. Her breasts were heavy, and deep in the core of her she ached for something.

For him. Only him.

"You could walk away, Brianna. Leave this room. There is nothing holding you here, standing so close to me."

It felt like a lie. Like a million chains were holding her in place. Exhaustion, surely, allowing all that *want* to win. She knew better, and yet…

She did not leave. She did not put space between them. She could have and *should* have, just to prove to herself she could. But she didn't.

She swayed forward, this she knew. What she wasn't so sure about was who pressed their mouth to whose. Only that suddenly they were kissing—wild, hot, tinged with the pain they'd inflicted on each other, but this only made it a dark, potent emotion that took control.

Surely she had no control. Not when a fire like this could burn between two people. Simply by touching lips together. Lips then tongue, arms wrapped tight and bodies pressed together.

Two years seemed to vanish. *This* was everything she remembered. It didn't matter that her body had changed somewhat after pregnancy. Nothing between them had. His shoulders were still broad, his body hard, and the way he kissed her like she was a feast made just for him was every bit as intoxicating as it had been.

She arched against him, desperate for that friction that would bring her relief.

"Madness," he murmured, his mouth moving from her mouth to trail against her neck as his hand slid under the waistband of her pants. She might have thought to stop this if he hadn't said that. But if *he* thought it was madness, if *he* was too weak to fight it, then why should she be strong? Why shouldn't she embrace the madness?

Take it all the way.

His clever fingers found her core. She was nothing but sensation. But a desperate need to fall over that cliff he was running her toward. She moved with him as his mouth found her breast over her shirt. Nibbled until she stiffened as the pulsing culmination swept through her.

Then he was pulling off her shirt and she was fumbling with the buttons of his pants.

*Madness. Madness. Madness.*

And she wanted it all. Here. Now. Nothing else mattered but this wild, whipping desire that even climax hadn't eradicated. She couldn't think past wanting him naked, on top of her, inside her.

It was wild, desperate. Like two people who had thought of little else in their two-year separation. And she might have understood that if it was just her pathetic self. But he seemed just as lost. Just as found. Just as desperate.

This "dangerous" billionaire who understood how to be patient with a toddler and how to protect a son.

Whatever warnings existed in her head were drowned out by him. His kiss. His touch. The harsh, hoarse way he said her name into her neck. Until she fell apart. The tantalizing words whispered in her ear as he laid her out on the warm, plush rug of his office.

Naked now. Him naked. He took a moment and simply stared at her as if taking her in, and it should have been a wake-up call. A moment of clarity.

But it wasn't. It never was with them.

He ran his hand down the center of her, between her breasts, over her stomach. A possessive move when she wasn't his. When he didn't *want* her to be. Because she would have been *anything* to him two years ago and he'd walked away.

Left her. Without a *word*. And she would simply…give in to him now? Without an apology? Without even a conversation of why he'd left things the way he had, or what he planned to do about it now? Just because it *felt* good?

No. She couldn't be that immature, that reckless.

She called on every last shred of control and determination the past two years had built inside of her and rolled out from under him. She didn't scramble. Because this wasn't about panic. It was about making the *right* choice.

It was about being the adult.

So they sat naked, ridiculously, on his plush office rug with the distance and cool air between them, their breathing more like panting in the now quiet room.

He said nothing. Which gave her the opportunity to

take control of the situation and God knew she needed to be in control of *something*.

"I think we should chalk that up to some form of insanity brought about by lack of sleep," she said, even as she could barely catch her breath. Even as she wanted to give in to the heat in his gaze.

But she knew where that led. And it would be one thing to risk herself, her own heartbreak all over again. She thought if that was all there was, maybe she would have no choice but to follow this once more.

But she had Gio, and if she was heartbroken, she could hardly be strong enough to give him the father he deserved.

"I want you in my bed."

*God*, the way he growled that. She couldn't look at him or she'd be lost, so she calmly began to collect her clothes and worked on putting some censure in her tone. "Lorenzo."

"It is what you want too."

*And how.*

But she focused on the act of getting dressed. On the cold air around her now. On the truth of the situation.

The sex would be great. Life-altering—in more ways than one. But that was all it could be now. He'd had his chance for it to be more.

The chance was long gone.

"What I want? Physically? Sure. The sex would be good. It's always been good." Even that momentary lapse in her sanity had been *more* than good.

She didn't want to bare herself to him emotionally. Wanted to leave the nakedness and near miss of the situation as the only thing intimate between them.

But he had to understand. Maybe if he understood

he would keep his distance. He would… They could be *partners* in this. Parenting.

Not sex.

So she forced herself to meet his gaze and spoke her truth. "But you…left me. You crushed me. I can't be crushed again. I have a son to protect. A mother doesn't get to follow her wants every which way. And I don't get the sense what happened here is about…anything more than chemistry."

If only. If only she didn't remember the afternoons they'd spent in art galleries, hand in hand, arguing about different artists, the emotions different pieces should evoke. Elegant dinners where he'd spoken of the places he'd traveled, and she of the places she wanted to go. She had only realized in retrospect how cagey he had been about his own family, but she had told him everything about hers. And he'd asked questions. Remembered things.

He had been attentive. He had been *there*. And yes, there had been pockets of secrets. The kind of information he'd kept from her were the kinds of things that should have been a red flag, if she'd been more experienced, more worldly.

She should have known, yes. But in the moment she'd only been dazzled. That a man so handsome could find a not-so-special woman from New Jersey fascinating. That any man could listen, engage like he did. That they could be together as equals, *adults*.

He dressed carefully, saying nothing, until he stood there, a disheveled, gorgeous man with a frown on his face and the haze of lust in his eyes.

It hurt to look at him. To want him. Because one thing she knew for certain wouldn't change.

"What I want for myself is a real relationship," she said, forcing herself to maintain eye contact. "Built on love and respect and honesty. Not just for myself, but for Gio. I don't think you want that."

There was a strange beat of silence. He didn't look away. There was no guilt, no offense in his expression. Just a dark, unreadable intensity. "Love is a lie, *dusci*. A fairy tale. Love does not function in the real world."

She found it oddly comforting he thought so. Because he'd never said he'd loved her. So she'd never said it either, but she *had* loved him. So much it had scared her enough *not* to tell him.

But if he thought love was a lie, well, it was better than him just not loving *her*.

Maybe? God, she needed some rest. First she had to extricate herself from this without compounding a mistake. "I don't agree, but I don't need to. What I need is to make certain we're on the same page. We can co-parent. Hopefully as friends. What I cannot do is engage in this sort of behavior that threatens to put us at odds. We have to be on the same page for Gio, as much as possible. Having sex complicates things." She sucked in a fortifying breath. "We can't muddy the waters with a physical relationship. So we'll agree to work together to parent Gio, to determine how that works with our individual lives and his protection and safety. For our son. And everything from before…and this little blip… Well, we'll leave that behind. Do you agree to these terms?"

He was very still and very intently staring at her for a minute or so, then nodded. He even held out his hand, like they were shaking on some business partnership. She supposed, in a way, they were.

She moved forward, took his hand and shook it. Very

professionally, she liked to think. But as she moved to pull her hand back, he held tight.

"We will indeed parent Gio together, come to a mutually beneficial conclusion as to what a future looks like with us both in his life," he said.

Her heart was tripping over itself, though she couldn't say why. Just because he was holding her in place? Just because the brown of his eyes seemed dark and endless. Just because her body still throbbed and yearned for more—specifically *him*, deep inside her.

"And while we do that, you may remain as distant as you wish. I will not pursue you. I will not seduce you. But I will not pretend, Brianna. When I want you. When I'm thinking about how you feel under my hands, how you sound when I am deep within you."

She let out a shuddering breath. *Oh, dear.*

His grip on her hand tightened and he drew her near, his mouth dipping close to her ear. "And I will not say no should you come begging to finish what we've started," he said, his voice a low scrape close to a whisper but not quite.

Not quite.

Luckily the idea of begging gave her just a shred of backbone in the moment. She jerked her hand out of his. She tried to tell him it'd be a cold day in hell, but her mouth wouldn't form the words. Or her conscience wouldn't let her say them. All she managed was a very ineffective "Fine."

And then she scurried away like prey escaping a predator. Because that was *exactly* what she felt like.

# CHAPTER EIGHT

LORENZO WATCHED HER leave his office. She hurried. She looked back once over her shoulder. Much like when he'd first seen her again at the art gallery. But instead of fear this time, there was something else.

She wasn't running away from *him*. She was running away from what her body *wanted* from him.

He quite enjoyed that.

But once he turned back to his office and tried to remember what he'd been doing, what needed to be done, he was met only with his brain reliving that moment her mouth had touched his again.

Two years. It should have erased this grasping, painful thing inside of him. The kind of *thing* that tore people apart. That destroyed them…or worse, gave a person the tools to destroy themselves.

He could admit, now that he was alone and had a few moments to collect himself, that this had been…ill-advised. At best.

He did not relish having lost his control, or her being the one to find it first. It was an affront to acknowledge that his sharp mind had been lost to the taste of her and the feel of her and the noises she made as he made her fall apart in his arms.

*I think we should chalk that up to some form of insanity brought about by lack of sleep.*

He grunted irritably. She was not *wrong*, and this was why he'd said that last bit. He'd needed to get a shot in too. She could claim it was about Gio, but it was about *them*.

*You crushed me.*

Two years ago, he had given no thought to what she might feel. Not really. Oh, he'd known she'd be hurt. He knew she fancied herself in love with him and was just waiting for him to say it first.

He'd known all of that. But leaving had been an act of survival. Self-protection. He'd been more worried about getting *himself* out than what the aftermath might be for *her*.

Even now, he hesitated to put himself in her shoes. He could not be sorry for what he'd done. It was the only course of action he'd seen then. Now.

What might have happened if he'd stayed? If they'd found out about Gio's existence together?

*You would have been there from Gio's first breath.*

*You would have torn the world apart.*

He did not particularly care for that much clarity or insight into himself. Into the man he'd been two years ago. He would have handled it—Brianna, a child.

But he would have done it badly. Two years ago, Saverina had only just gone off to university in England—her dream, and with his youngest sibling out of his house, it had been the first time he'd had the time or space not to be the 24-7 father figure in his siblings' lives. A child would have been...

Why was he thinking about this? It did not matter. He *hadn't* known. Brianna had kept Gio from him. He didn't need to hold on to his anger over that—it was hard to when he understood her motivations were about protecting Gio. What he needed to do *now* was figure out how to move forward.

His people were still outmaneuvering Dante when it came to press coverage. So far, only a few piddly gossip sites had picked up the story and only the most die-hard of gossipmongers cared.

It would spread. You couldn't shove a story back into a bottle once it escaped, but he would have the time to craft *his* version of what that story would be. Dante wanted to paint him the villain. The deserter.

This wouldn't work for a wide variety of reasons. But Lorenzo had to have a good story in place as counterpoint. Irrefutable counterpoint.

He could marry Brianna. He ignored the spurt of something that went through him—an emotion that would do no one any good, so best not identified or labeled.

There was no good story to excuse away the two-year discrepancy between pregnancy and a union. Besides, this was a rather traditional way of thinking—marry the mother of your child. Dante and Marino Industries were traditional. Old money. Royal ties.

Lorenzo had always known he couldn't compete with that. So he'd fashioned himself a start-up. Sleek. Modern. The violence accusations had been a hit, but knowledge of a secret son would not be unless he pretended he was as traditional as Dante and this hidden son was a blight, a *bastard,* rather than a gift.

Instead, Lorenzo would create a modern story. He would use the truth and paint Dante and his unfounded accusations the villain that had kept him from his son. He and Brianna had parted amicably. And now, like so many others in his position, they would co-parent. Reasonable, responsible adults who had engaged in a short affair and were now fond of each other, but definitely not meant for something like marriage.

Though it wouldn't work if they both remained single. There would be too much room for a variety of gossip. No, he would need to get the ball rolling on finding someone else to marry. To create the perfect image of blended family.

Dante Marino's counterpoint. Always.

Lorenzo's potential wife would need to be someone who fit his vision for a modern billionaire. Definitely not an *American*. Ideally, someone with traditional ties he could use for Parisi Enterprises, but who knew how to work the press. Maybe someone in publicity. He would have his assistant create him a potential list.

He would not think of Brianna whispering his name while he'd touched her.

If he kept everything about business, love would never muddy the waters.

He sent a few missives off to staff and then, noting it was almost time for dinner, changed gears. He would find a way to win the press wars with Dante, but here at home, in private, he needed to win over his son.

He went to his wing. Stefano had two little ones, so Lorenzo had made sure the estate was outfitted for them whenever Stefano came to visit. It made Lorenzo an uncle, not a grandfather, and considering Stefano was only a few years younger than him it was hardly unorthodox. Still those two little hellions made Lorenzo feel *old*.

He bypassed this feeling by going to a bin of toys, fishing out the plastic creature he knew to be buried in there, and then returned downstairs. As he headed toward the dining room, he heard the soft sounds of voices—no doubt Brianna and her family.

He came around a corner, coming face-to-face with the quartet. Gio, who had been running forward, came to a skidding halt right at his feet. Slowly, the boy looked up and up, like he'd just run into a monster in a horror movie.

Lorenzo crouched and held the plastic tiger between them. "This was my brother's," he offered without pre-amble. "Perhaps you'd like to play with it during dinner."

Gio studied the tiger. He looked back at his mother, then at Lorenzo. He grabbed the tiger, then quickly re-treated behind Brianna's legs.

She reached down and stroked his dark hair. "Gio. What do you say?"

The boy peered at him from safety behind Brianna, but he was clutching the tiger. "Tank you," the little boy muttered, not making eye contact. Though he darted lit-tle glances Lorenzo's way as they headed into the din-ing room and then all throughout dinner, while he played with the tiger in between Brianna's urgings to him to eat.

This gave Lorenzo a deep satisfaction. As did slowly winning over Brianna's parents until they relaxed rather than looking around the opulent room suspiciously. Even Brianna looked somewhat relaxed.

"Brianna was telling us that one of the art shows she was meant to attend originally is tomorrow night. She's saying she's going to skip it, and we both think she should go," Brianna's father said, watching Lorenzo specula-tively. "What do you think?"

"Of course she should go." He turned his attention from Scott to Brianna. "You will all have a car at your disposal. If you need anything, you need only ask Maria. She will be your personal assistant while you're here. I'm afraid I must insist on a bit of a security detail to make certain the press won't become a problem, but there's no reason for you to miss it."

"I think we'd feel better if you went with her," Helene said earnestly.

Lorenzo hadn't expected *that*. He'd expected their continued distrust, figured this was some kind of a test. He cleared his throat. Going with Brianna would pose a problem with his current plans.

"I am right here," Brianna said, wiping Gio's messy mouth with a napkin. "And can make all these arrangements and decisions on my own."

"But you won't," her father grumbled, lifting his glass to take a sip.

"Lorenzo does not need to play chaperone. I've handled this before and can handle it again."

"But that was before…" Helene trailed off and glanced at Lorenzo. A clear look that said, *This is all your fault, so you should clean up the mess*. "Before the tabloids took an interest."

Lorenzo didn't say anything at first, and Brianna didn't look at him. She very carefully and purposefully kept all her attention focused on Gio.

"Done. Done!" The boy started shouting when Brianna tried to urge him to take another bite. He flung out his arms, and would have toppled his cup if Scott hadn't been quick to pluck it out of the way. As Lorenzo watched the three of them working as a team with such ease, something sharp and painful lodged in his chest.

"He's tired," Brianna said. "He needs a bath and a good night's sleep. You all stay and finish your dinners. Say good night, Gio."

Before the boy could say anything, Lorenzo stood. "I will come with you."

"You don't—"

"I would like to be a part of as many routines as possible. Both so he gets used to having me around, and so I understand what needs should be met."

Brianna opened her mouth, like she was going to argue, but in the end she only shut it and nodded. She lifted Gio onto her hip, encouraged him to give his grandparents a good-night hug, then they exited the dining room together.

"Roar bath?" the boy said, holding up the toy Lorenzo had given him before dinner.

"Yes, the tiger can come in the bath with you," Brianna said, following Lorenzo up the stairs to the wing he'd put her family in.

Lorenzo unlocked the built-in baby gate and opened it to let Brianna through.

"Was this left over from a previous owner? It's very helpful."

"No, I had it installed a few years ago for my niece."

"I guess that's a billionaire's prerogative, isn't it?" She moved down to their rooms and flipped on the light in the room he'd assigned her. It connected to the nursery, so she could either close the door and have privacy and use the monitors or leave the door open and feel as though they were in the same room together.

She moved for a suitcase, then turned to Lorenzo, who stood in the doorway. "What should he call you?"

"Call me?"

"Dad? Daddy? Father? A Sicilian word you'd prefer?"

Lorenzo blinked. In all of this, learning and accepting he had a son, meeting him, working to win him over, this was a strange thing not to have thought of. But it had not occurred to him that this little boy would have a word *for* him. His niece and nephew called him Zu. His brothers and sisters called him by name.

And it had been so many years since his father's death that he hadn't thought of how to address a father in so very long.

*Pá.*

No, he did not want to think of his father. Did not want that association. That bitterness when he heard his own son call out to him. He would never betray his son the way his own father had.

"Why don't we keep it simple?" Brianna said gently, as if she sensed that he was lost. At sea. "He calls me Mama, so we'll go with Dada. Gio, can you go to Dada for a second?"

Gio shook his head furiously and tightened his grip on Brianna. She sighed. "I need to put you down so I can get your clothes. Do you want to pick out your pajamas?"

This time he nodded. Brianna put him on the ground and he clutched her hand, sending those suspicious looks back at Lorenzo.

Lorenzo had been determined not to let it hurt. The child hadn't known of a father's existence all this time, and couldn't be expected to accept Lorenzo in a single day. Lorenzo understood that these were vulnerable years for children. Best that the boy be suspicious and careful. Much better than the alternative.

But Lorenzo already loved his son with a depth that threatened to split him open and no matter how rational it was for the boy to not trust him, it continued to shove a little shiv of pain under his heart.

Love was the enemy, yes, but he would always protect

his own. Never let love leave him weak and vulnerable again. When he took care, protected, it was okay. He did not allow anyone else to risk, to sacrifice. That was his job, and it always would be.

It was why Brianna and Gio were here. It was why he would send a security detail with Brianna to the art show. He would build a life for them here where they were all safe and taken care of. Part of a careful compartment of his life that did not...complicate things.

Gio picked out his pajamas and Lorenzo led Brianna to the bathroom well equipped for a child's bath. He gathered the necessities, including the little bath toy set his niece used. He ran the water, tested the temperature. When he turned to Brianna she was watching him with open-mouthed shock.

"*How*...do you know how to do all this?"

He didn't want to tell her. Not because it was some great secret, but because...he was very careful. Not to expose pieces of himself that she might use against him. Twist to make him something he couldn't be.

But perhaps if she understood, she would trust him alone with Gio sooner rather than later.

"I have brothers and sisters, and I am the oldest and had to help take care of them quite a bit."

"How many?"

A tricky question he also didn't want to answer. She could find the information out there on the internet, no doubt. Though not all of it. The depth of the horrible story that was Rocca. Only that he had once been the oldest of ten, and now he was the oldest of nine.

But he could never bring himself to lie, to pretend like Rocca did not exist. It felt too wrong. "There are eight now."

"Why *now*?" Brianna asked, carefully undressing the wriggling Gio who was clearly eager to play with the bath toys in the large bath.

*My twin sister died because love is poison.*

But he wasn't going to say *that*.

"Unfortunately, Rocca passed away a few years ago."

"Oh, Lorenzo." Brianna looked up at him, that easy warmth that radiated from her making the empathy seem less like the dreaded *pity*, and more like something akin to comfort. "I'm so sorry. I don't know what it's like to have siblings, but that must have been terrible. What happened?"

"It is of no matter. She is gone." A waste of a life all because their father was a spineless coward, and their mother was lost to love. Broken, so broken, and he had learned you could not put broken things back together.

Brianna did not press. She picked up Gio and placed him in the bath. She knelt next to it as she soothed his whining resistance at getting his hair shampooed.

When Lorenzo knelt next to her, she sent him a speculative look but offered no recriminations. She just handed him the washcloth so that he could help.

They washed the boy, let him play. It was very domestic and reminded him of days long gone. Those quiet moments with his brothers and sisters when he'd thought he and Rocca could protect them from everything. That they were better than their parents.

And then Rocca...

He would not go back to that place. Those feelings. He was in the present now. Money at his disposal. The remainder of his siblings safe and sound, with all they could ever want at their fingertips.

And he was kneeling here at the bath, hip to hip with Brianna. She was sunlight and warmth, and *that* was more dangerous than memories. She would be his end if he gave in to this feeling that was once again roiling about his chest, just as it had two years ago. As if he'd learned nothing.

Gio's hand slapping against the water sending a spray of water up and out of the tub was a welcome distraction from said feeling, and Lorenzo laughed at the boy's exuberance while Brianna gently scolded him.

But, sensing an ally, Gio splashed again, looking at Lorenzo for another laugh. Lorenzo gave it, because he would give anything to have his son look at him without suspicion.

Gio splashed with wild abandon now. And Brianna, droplets of water cascading down her hair and her face, glared at him. "If you're such an expert on children, you should know better than to laugh at such behavior."

"Ah, but my son should have all the fun he wants."

"He'll be spoiled in that case."

"I do not see anything wrong with that. I have worked hard. Why not allow my son everything that I did not have?"

Her eyes were so very blue and warm when she turned them on him. "What did you not have?"

He shrugged and looked back at Gio, who would no doubt have the tub well rid of water by the time he was done. "If you searched my name when you found out you were pregnant, you know I built myself and my empire from nothing. That is no exaggeration. We were very poor."

"With so many children," Brianna said, that same, soft empathy in her voice so that it didn't rankle as it did when other people spoke of it. "I can't say I grew up like this, but I never worried about money. I suppose as the only child I was spoiled after a fashion." She looked at Gio, and he could not begin to guess what she was thinking, as she said nothing else.

She informed Gio it was time to get out—which the boy *loudly* argued against—but they worked together to dry him off and get him dressed, both a little soaked themselves.

Brianna carried him back to the bedroom and Lorenzo followed. Since Brianna offered no objection, he walked through her room to the adjoining children's room. Watched as she laid Gio down, handed him a frayed-looking bear. She sang him a very short little song and his eyes drooped immediately.

She motioned Lorenzo to follow her, carefully and quietly back to the open doorway to the adjoining room.

"He's getting brave enough to try to climb out, so I'll leave the main door closed and the one between us open. No one will leave the gate open, will they?" she said in a low voice that wouldn't wake the child.

"Of course not. I'll have the toddler bed moved into this room tomorrow if that would make you more comfortable."

"A toddler bed. For your niece?"

"Yes."

"With so many brothers and sisters, are you overrun with nieces and nephews?"

"Not just yet. Many of my siblings are much younger. Saverina is only now twenty, but Stefano is only two years younger than I. He works for me at my offices in Rome, so sometimes business dictates he visit Palermo, and he likes to bring his family. As well he should."

They fell into a comfortable silence, standing there and watching the easy rise and fall of their son's chest in the dim light.

"I feel like I should apologize for my parents," she said quietly. "You don't have to go to the art show with me. I'm quite certain I can handle it."

"I would feel better having my eye on you, but it's best if we're not photographed together again until I can fully curate the story I wish to reveal. Perhaps this could work if I brought a date."

"A date?"

When he looked down at her, confused by the sharp note in her voice, he saw eyebrows furrowed and mouth curved in a frown.

"Yes. So there's no speculation about *us*. We'll make it clear we aren't together."

"We *just* had…" She dropped her already quiet voice to a complete whisper. "Practically had sex. Like a few hours ago. And you're going to go…date someone tomorrow night?"

"Practically doesn't count, Brianna. But yes. You made it quite clear you did not want to engage in any kind of relationship."

"No, Lorenzo, *you* made that clear."

It was his turn to frown at her. "This has nothing to do with…feelings."

"Maybe for you, but I still *have* feelings, Lorenzo. I don't have to like them for them to exist."

"What exactly are they?"

She seemed arrested by the question, and he should be arrested by it as well. He never should have asked it. He shouldn't be *here*. Gio was asleep. Nothing more was needed of him until morning.

"What do you remember about our time together?" she asked him. He didn't have the first clue why she'd ask him that in this conversation, but the answer was in his head even though he didn't want it.

*Everything.*

Walks under the stars where she'd told him about her

art, what inspired her, what she hoped to do. What the summer in Florence meant to her.

She had been so full of hope and light. Everything he knew of becoming successful was grit and hard work and sacrifice. The strangling balance between ensuring all his brothers and sisters had everything, while also building an empire that would see them always well looked after.

That trip to Florence had been the first thing he'd ever done for himself and only himself, and Brianna had been the fresh air he'd desperately needed. The idea that on the other side of this moment there could be such sparkling optimism.

And then she'd started to look at him with something deeper in her eyes than the dazzlement he'd seen when they first met. Like she knew him, though he never spoke of his past. Like she could offer him this brand-new world and he could be in it. They could be in it. Together.

And he had remembered. What it felt like to hope. What it felt like to think he'd finally arrived at a place where he could relax.

And Rocca's cold, lifeless body. A victim to all that hope.

"Lorenzo—"

But he did not wish to go back to Rocca's death. To his summer with Brianna. You could not go back. You could only go forward. "If you do not wish me to be there, I do not need to be."

She sighed and rolled her eyes, as if he was the biggest fool she'd ever met. "Good night, Lorenzo," she said, pointing him toward the door.

And though he was not one for obeying orders, he left. Because it was better than staying and risking everything.

# CHAPTER NINE

BRIANNA SLEPT LIKE the dead. Luckily, no amount of inner turmoil had been able to stop the complete and utter exhaustion that had claimed her. When she woke up, groggy and unsure of where she was, she still felt like she'd been hit by a truck, but at least like she could handle the damage of all that.

The truck that was Lorenzo and this place and her life upended. She could handle it because she had to. For Gio.

She didn't hear him making any noise in his crib, so she didn't get out of bed. But when she grabbed her phone, she saw a text from her parents.

Heard G babbling as we went down to breakfast. Took him with us.

At the mention of breakfast, Brianna realized she was starving. She should get dressed and head downstairs. Take Gio off her parents' hands. But the bed was so soft, the quiet so nice, and all her inner agitation from yesterday was still *right* there.

She'd almost had sex with Lorenzo. Just…right there in his office, like she had no will power whatsoever. She could blame it on fatigue or any number of things, but it didn't change the fact that she'd allowed far too much, even if not that final act.

Worse, enjoyed it.

She could not repeat it if she had any sense of self-preservation at all, even though a repeat seemed to be all she could consider.

*I will not say no should you come begging.*

She let out a shuddering breath, too many sensual memories assaulting her. Yesterday. Two years ago. She did not understand how two bodies could be so clearly made for one another, but their minds and hearts could be on such different planets.

Well, they agreed on Gio. They agreed on hard work and art. They had always had plenty to talk about *before*, so it wasn't like they weren't well suited.

But she believed in love.

And he thought it was a fairy tale.

A man who took care of his little brothers and sisters, and then their children. Who installed toddler gates and had beds and cribs and playrooms. Who knew how to bathe a child, how to be patient with them. How to accept them so easily, so wholly.

The two things did not compute for her. He loved his family deeply. Protected them, provided for them, clearly, if his brother with children worked for him. He was a *family* man.

And he did not believe in love. She couldn't work it out in her mind. Everything about her small family was centered in love.

She thought of the way he'd talked about his sister, the one who'd died. She'd thought if he really didn't want to discuss it, he wouldn't have mentioned her at all. But he'd gone completely blank when he'd said, *It is of no matter. She is gone.*

Gone.

Maybe there was more to that story. Or maybe there was another story. A lost love before her. Something that had soured him on the idea of *romantic* love, and so he threw all that he had inside of him into those he was related to.

Which she was still trying to wrap her mind around, since she hadn't known he was from such a large family. When she'd been searching for information about him after finding out about Gio, she hadn't seen much beyond business articles and the screaming stories about his violent tendencies and ruthless tactics that had left his rival's son in a hospital bed.

Nothing about *nine* siblings. Nothing about a sister who'd passed. Nothing about who he'd been before he'd become Parisi Enterprises.

Brianna contemplated the phone in her hand. She knew more now. Details that might allow her to find out about his family. It would be wrong to do an internet search on the sister he'd lost. Wrong to poke into his private life that way. An invasion of privacy. And who knew if the information would even be correct. She was quickly learning gossip columns didn't need a shred of truth or evidence to print whatever might get clicks or sell magazines.

But did she owe Lorenzo scruples when he had essentially put Gio in danger by allowing knowledge of him to be leaked to his rival?

*Or was that your own fault for coming to Palermo at all?*

Brianna blew out a breath. Maybe it wasn't about fault. Maybe it was just that…choices had consequences. Unforeseen ones. And a person had to deal with them without worrying about whose fault those consequences were.

And with that thought, she set her phone aside and got ready for the day. She wanted to spend it with Gio, because she'd be going to the art show tonight. She tried not to think about how much she hated the idea of Lorenzo attending with a date.

He could do whatever he wanted with whomever he wanted. He did not want any kind of serious relationship and she couldn't engage in anything else, not with Gio involved. It was all very mature and adult, really. He *should* date. Touch whomever he wanted. Have sex with a hundred women on his office floor.

She accidentally snapped the hair band in her hand by pulling it too hard. The sting of the snap was enough to remind her that what she'd said to him last night was true and perfectly acceptable.

She didn't have to *like* her feelings to have them. The truth was, no matter how pathetic, she hadn't fully gotten over Lorenzo in their two years apart. She'd been able to set aside her broken heart while focusing on becoming a mother, but it didn't change the fact that accepting he wasn't a violent threat to Gio meant...he was just the man she'd known.

Loved.

And how did she just get over that? Never had she felt such a connection to a man before, and maybe that was one-sided. Maybe his escape was simply growing tired of her and not wanting to deal with the fallout.

But if he didn't believe in *love*, maybe his sudden, unexplained exit two years ago had been less about her not mattering at *all*, and more about her mattering...a great deal.

She paused with the hairbrush halfway through a

stroke in her hair. If she hadn't mattered, he wouldn't have *escaped* like a scared man. Wouldn't he have just told her it was over? Wouldn't it have all happened at a normal hour? Not sneaking away in the middle of the night like a desperate man.

Brianna sat with this thought for a while, not knowing what to do with it. If she'd had it back home, before she'd reunited with him, she would have told herself she was a fanciful idiot.

But every way he'd behaved toward Gio, every new thing she learned about him in these short few days… did not speak to a man who ran away. Something had to *prompt* the escape.

Could it have been fear?

She rolled her eyes at herself. Now she was really grasping for straws. She finished getting ready and then went downstairs in search of her parents and son. They weren't in the dining room, but the staff insisted she sit and eat something, and since she was hungry, she didn't argue.

She ate and drank some coffee and texted her parents. They texted back they were in the playroom upstairs, so once she was done Brianna went to find them.

When she did, she realized it wasn't just her parents and Gio, it was Lorenzo as well. Gio had a little bin of brightly colored plastic balls in one corner, and Lorenzo was sprawled on the floor in the other. They were clearly engaging in some game. Gio never got too close, but he threw balls Lorenzo's way and squealed in delight every time Lorenzo made an exaggerated effort to catch the ball, and then dramatically bobbled it before catching it securely.

Her parents sat on a little couch, clutching mugs of tea, smiling indulgently at both of them. Brianna stood in the doorway, watching silently, her heart swelling painfully in her chest.

This was everything Gio deserved. And Lorenzo too. He was obviously a man born to be a father, or perhaps made to be one through circumstance. But clearly, any child was lucky to have Lorenzo in their corner.

She got a little choked up about it, but she didn't let herself cry. Just watched her son and his father engage in their little game and tried not to hope too hard for anything more than this perfect moment.

Lorenzo was playing with his son. He didn't let himself dwell on it too deeply. Later, in private, he would allow himself to feel the full joy of this moment, but for now he simply juggled another ball and watched Gio's face light up in delight.

He knew Brianna's parents were watching because they didn't fully trust him yet, but he could feel their approval. This would be important—Gio clearly loved them as much as they doted on their grandson.

Lorenzo didn't allow himself to think about introducing his siblings to his son, about bringing Gio into the Parisi fold. If he did… Well, all these emotions threatened to make him foolish. When he needed a clear head to ensure his son was protected.

He wasn't sure exactly what caught his attention—had she made a noise? Had that subtle scent reached across the room and teased him? Was there something elemental about them—a magnetism that meant he would always know when she was near?

But he glanced over and Brianna stood in the doorway. She was watching the game, her eyes shiny, though she wasn't crying. And it was not sadness on her face, but joy. A joy that echoed inside of him, bright and warm, like the time they'd been together before.

He was going to have to find a better way to navigate this. It was too dangerous. *She* was too dangerous.

Lorenzo must have looked too long in her direction, because Gio turned his attention to the door. He immediately forgot the balls and scrambled over to his mother, happily yelling, "Mama!" the whole way.

She knelt down to accept his eager hug and squeezed him tight. Just like when she'd greeted him at the house in New Jersey. As if they'd been parted for a long time when it couldn't have been more than twelve hours.

"Are you having fun?" Brianna asked, smiling as she brushed Gio's flyaway hair back.

Gio held up a red ball in Brianna's face. "Ball!" Then he flung it Lorenzo's way.

Lorenzo felt a bit foolish doing it in front of Brianna, God knew why, but he engaged in the same exaggerated bobbling before securing the ball.

Gio laughed hysterically as Brianna hitched him onto her hip. Before she could say anything, her parents stood.

"We're going to go take a walk around the gardens. It's supposed to be a lovely day and we could use some fresh air."

"We'll go with," Brianna said. "I'm sure Gio's ready to run around a bit."

But Brianna's mother stopped her before she could follow. "He's having fun here, Bri," she said gently. "Meet us there in a bit."

Brianna glanced back at Lorenzo, then nodded at her mother. Once her parents had left, Lorenzo and Brianna stood in the playroom in an uncomfortable silence.

"You have wonderful parents," Lorenzo said, hating

that his voice sounded gruff. But he appreciated everything the Andersens had been so far. Stability for their grandson. A rock for their daughter. Kind to him when they didn't have to be, even if he was housing them at the moment.

But this wasn't about debts. This was about giving Gio and Lorenzo the opportunity to be together as father and son. And not every parent would have been as gracious as hers.

"I do. I'm very lucky." Brianna brushed her hand over Gio's hair again. "You don't speak of your parents," she said keeping her gaze on their son.

Lorenzo found it difficult to say the words even though the wound was old now and shouldn't hurt quite so much. "Dead."

Brianna said nothing to that, but she nodded. She kept her gaze on Gio. "Can Dada hold you for a minute?"

Gio looked at Lorenzo. Lorenzo smiled, but he did not hold out his arms. He wouldn't pressure the child. But something about the game or the sleep must have softened little Gio's heart somewhat. He reached out a hand. Half-heartedly and a little uncertainly, without giving Brianna any verbal yes.

But it was enough. Lorenzo felt his heart clatter against his chest, like he was a young man making a business presentation for the first time, certain everyone in the room could read the *poor* on him.

But he'd succeeded then and he knew how to hold a child. He reached out and took Gio's willing form. Gio didn't wrap his arms around Lorenzo like he did when Brianna held him, but he sat there without reaching back for Brianna or giving Lorenzo a suspicious look. He paid attention to the ball in his hand.

Lorenzo felt frozen. He was holding his son. In his arms. The boy played with the ball, slapping it against Lorenzo's free hand. Lorenzo simply looked down at Gio for the longest time, trying to memorize the weight of him. The shape of his nose. Those blue eyes on the otherwise very *Parisi* face.

Lorenzo swallowed, trying to find his balance. Without thinking it through, he looked to Brianna, as if she could give to him that balance he so desperately needed. But she was watching with her hands clasped, a bright smile on her face even as a tear trickled down her cheek. She wiped it away before Gio saw.

Lorenzo wanted to reach out. Bring her into this perfect circle. So that they could be a family. So that this could be his life. These days, he got whatever he wanted, so why not this? Why not make *this* everything it could be?

But he did not move. Because he knew the dangerous feeling that swelled inside of him when Brianna was near. Then or now it did not matter. What he felt for her was too big, too complicated, and far too threatening.

Family only worked when one person was in charge. When one person was beholden only to the responsibilities of taking care of a family.

Being in love led to inequality. Weakness. It twisted things. Took the focus off the children and protecting them and put it on desperate needs that could only ever destroy everything.

So he held his son and did not reach out for Brianna. Did not attempt to bring her into this moment.

He focused on Gio. His son.

Not the woman who had stolen his heart long ago. Let her have it. Let her keep it. He had no need for it anyway.

# CHAPTER TEN

BRIANNA DID NOT let herself break down in front of Gio.
She waited. She got through the day until she could excuse herself to go get ready for the art show.

Then she let herself cry. Sob, really. Just let all the
swirling emotion out. It felt so wrong that Lorenzo and
Gio had lived without each other for over a year. All because of another man's lies and her own fears.

And the worst part was this overwhelming emotion
wasn't *just* about the time lost. The beauty of father and
son together. It was more than that.

How was she supposed to endure this and not feel all
those old, loving feelings? Lorenzo was the same man
she'd known. Little had changed. Except she was getting
more and more glimpses into what he'd come from, and
that only made him more understandable. More wonderful.

His parents were dead. His sister too. Lorenzo had
taken care of the rest of them, clearly, all while building
his own empire. She had no doubt he'd accomplished said
empire *because* of everything he'd had to take care of.

She wasn't sure how he'd accomplished it all. It was
awe-inspiring.

She supposed his siblings might have another view
of him, but if his brother visited with his children often

enough for Lorenzo to have outfitted his house for them, surely they were close.

And it would mean Gio had cousins. Aunts and uncles. A much larger family than the one he'd known. The kind of thing Brianna herself had always dreamed of but not been able to create for Gio herself.

She knew she should want to go back to her life in New Jersey once it was safe. Find normalcy once again. But she just…didn't. She wanted to stay here. With Lorenzo. With a whole big world and family to give to her son. She wanted Lorenzo holding Gio to become so normal it didn't make her want to sob alone in her room.

She wanted all of that for Gio, but she worried if that was because she also wanted it—and Lorenzo—for herself. She pondered that. Was this really selfish? Did she care more about her own wants and desires and what had happened in Lorenzo's office than what was best for her son? Was she just convincing herself it was all for Gio?

She sat with that worry for a moment, but she couldn't latch on to it. Gio deserved a good father and Lorenzo fit the bill. If Lorenzo's siblings were half as good with children as Lorenzo himself, that was more love and care for Gio than she had even imagined for him.

Maybe she yearned for those things too, but it wasn't at the expense of her son. So there was that. But there was also the lure of Lorenzo.

A headache threatened, so she focused on getting ready rather than the man causing it. She got dressed. Did her own hair and makeup though Lorenzo's staff had offered to bring someone in to help her. But she had come to Palermo originally prepared to handle these things on her own. It was pointless to change course now. She knew how to make herself look presentable. The colorful American artist—quite the oddity in these circles of sleek, sophisticated Europeans. And yet, she kind of liked it. Feeling different. Feeling special. She didn't mind the attention or the looks—maybe because she believed in her art. Believed in herself.

She *knew* what she created was good, interesting. The mix of paint and embroidery methods and the juxtaposition of whimsy and darkness, like all the fairy tales she'd grown up loving.

And even if no one else agreed with her, she created what she liked. What moved her. If it wasn't enough to support Gio, she'd simply go get a job.

*Except you have his billionaire father involved now.*

So there was that.

It was funny. She didn't feel like an oddity here in Lorenzo's gigantic, opulent house. She didn't have the same discomfort her parents did at the overt displays of wealth. It just felt…right. Like it reflected the man and his personality—and both those things were meant for her.

*Ugh.* They were very clearly not *meant* for each other, even if she could convince Lorenzo of the possibility of *meant for.* So…how did this go? After her art show, when she didn't have to be in Palermo anymore? Once Lorenzo dealt with the paparazzi and his rival and it was safe for her and Gio to return to America?

What happened once this was over? How did she move forward with Lorenzo as Gio's *involved* father? How did she move forward with her parents, who had stepped in and been everything she'd needed since they'd learned of Gio's existence?

What happened when Lorenzo brought *dates* to art shows or family Christmases and she was just supposed to accept it and think it was *great*?

She tried not to scowl as she fixed the rollers in her hair. The man wanted to bring a *date*. When clearly *something* still flashed between the two of them—even if it couldn't go anywhere.

No. That wasn't accurate. He wouldn't *let* it go anywhere. Because he viewed love as a fairy tale, and that fairy tales were bad.

Could that really be the whole story? Why did he care what she felt if he didn't believe in love? Why couldn't she love him and he just take it? Not that she'd told him or asked him for anything... No, she couldn't do that.

She looked at herself in the mirror. Dress on, makeup done. The only thing she was waiting on was her hair.

She knew he found her attractive. He certainly hadn't planned office floor seductions even if he wasn't opposed to them. He'd likely come to that initial art show to see if the spark still flamed between them.

But he had walked away once. *Something* had sent him away from all that very good and very available sex. Abruptly. In the middle of the night.

She sighed heavily. At some point, she had to stop having these circular thoughts. She had to stop being desperate and hoping for something to change. Lorenzo might find her attractive, might not be opposed to sex, but he didn't want a relationship. And she had to put Gio before her own wants, her own weaknesses.

*Or you could be honest with Lorenzo.*

The idea filled her with such dread and fear, and the certainty it would ruin *everything*, that she immediately shoved it away.

The next step after tonight was clear. She and Lorenzo would sit down and hammer out a parental agreement. Maybe she would find a way to stay in Palermo so such agreements didn't involve international travel. Maybe her parents would even be amenable to moving here. They'd always wanted to travel Europe and had never had the chance.

She and Lorenzo would work it out, figure it out. As *parents. Not* former lovers…no matter how recently they'd been grappling about on his office floor.

She unrolled the curlers and finished her hair, determined that she was a strong, capable woman who would do what was best for her son. Ill-advised *almost* sex in offices notwithstanding.

A knock sounded at her door before she could go through another cycle of self-recrimination. Before she could offer a "come in" the door opened and Lorenzo stepped inside.

She frowned at him, though she did not scold him for violating her privacy. It *was* his house after all.

He looked her up and down, something flaring in his eyes that had heat pooling in her belly. When his dark eyes met hers again, there was an intensity there that she felt burn through her.

*Not here. Not now. You cannot keep doing this, Brianna.* She told herself this, over and over again, but she knew…all it would take was a touch. That was how weak she was. If there was a way to fight that, she hadn't found it.

"I'll go with you."

He said it so…fiercely her heart tripped over itself. And worse, she felt that sensual haze threaten to invade her brain. But she was reminded of his plan to bring a *date*, and that was just enough figurative cold water to remind herself how to behave.

"Lorenzo, you made it very clear you do not wish us

to be seen together. I do not see why you would come with me when you've made other plans."

"You cannot wear that and..."

She raised an eyebrow when he didn't finish, standing in her doorway looking like a storm. "And what?" she asked, looking down at the deep red, one-shouldered dress that hugged her curves in a very flattering manner. She felt like a goddess in this dress.

His expression was hard, but his eyes glittered with that same *lust* they had almost acted on yesterday in his office.

*You cannot give in to that, Brianna. Not tonight. Not without him admitting some feelings. Not without him giving an inch or two.*

She considered that. Did he *have* feelings for her? *Could* he? It was the *could* that had her turning to face him fully. That had her asking the one thing she hadn't asked yet. "Can you answer me one thing? Truthfully?"

"I suppose that depends."

"Why did you leave me the way that you did two years ago? Snuck away in the middle of the night like a coward when I know you aren't one." His expression hardened even more at the word *coward*. "No word. No explanation."

His mouth got very stern. "Because the relationship had run its course."

"And that didn't warrant a discussion? Because that might have been *your* conclusion, but it wasn't mine. *I* was blindsided."

"I have no use for postmortems, Brianna. I am a busy man. I had business to attend to in Palermo and did not have time to deal with hysterical women in Florence."

She should not find that funny. It should be so arrogant and offensive, the way he said it with such complete authority. Like of course she'd be hysterical. "Do most women you break things off with rend garments, wailing at your feet and carrying on?"

His mouth curved, ever so slightly at the corner. All dark amusement. "You would be surprised, *dusci.*"

She tried not to scowl or smile and just remain neutral, but, oh, the man was arrogant. And probably right. Worse, she didn't know how she might have behaved if he'd broken things off to her face. She had been young and naive and desperately in love with him. She'd love to believe her pride would have seen her through, but… well, best not to dwell on it. What *would* have been did not matter in the here and now.

"You know, there was quite a lot of time to think when I was pregnant. To go over it in my head. I came up with all sorts of reasons for why you left."

"Do you not have an event to get to?" he returned coolly. But that arrogant quirk of the mouth was gone. Like she'd gotten to him. Like this conversation might make him *uncomfortable*.

The thought emboldened her. "You know, some men leave their partners because they are scared by the depth and breadth of their feelings."

If possible, his expression got even more remote. He voiced no admissions, no denials. Just cool disdain.

Brianna had to wonder if that was an answer in it of itself. Her heart twisted in a hope she knew was foolish but couldn't quash. So she continued on, wanting to find some chink in his armor of stoicism. "They can't handle how much they've come to care for and rely on the person, so they leave. Disappear." And of course *some* men were just assholes, but she wasn't trying to make that point in the moment.

Because she didn't think he was one, even when he wanted to be. Not to other people. The man might hide it, but he cared too much about *people*.

Still, she expected his response to be a laugh. A cruel joke. Something scathing enough that she'd stop talking about it. She expected him to put her very firmly in her place.

But he only turned and left, and Brianna…didn't have the first clue what to do with that.


Lorenzo didn't often attend events alone. He had a small group of women who were happy to accompany him anywhere at a moment's notice just to be seen on his arm or get into an exclusive event they might not have received an invite to. This group of women didn't get ideas, and he did not see "dates" with them as anything more than a business arrangement.

Neither did they.

These women never spoke of feelings. They never pressed for more. They were in it to boost their profiles and nothing more. He preferred these kinds of dates for business events, and this tonight was business. Maybe not in the traditional sense, but in the sense that he had to think of it like business.

Cold. Calculated. And nothing to do with the roiling, jagged things fighting for purchase inside of him after that little conversation with Brianna.

Which was why he'd obtained a date even though he'd decided against it earlier. When he'd walked into Brianna's room and seen her in that *dress*. That deep red. The way her body shimmered. Like sex itself.

The thought of her attending the event alone, a sheep to the wolves essentially, had torn him up inside. It wasn't jealousy, he told himself. Just…common sense. There would be men there and she was the mother of his child.

So he'd made the impulsive offer to go with her. Or maybe it was a demand. He didn't really remember past the punch of seeing her. The desire to touch her and forget *everything else*.

But then she'd started talking about ancient history. About feelings and leaving and… Well, it had reminded him where he got when he did things impulsively. Somewhere ridiculous.

So he'd gone back to the original plan. The calculated plan. A date. So he could protect her, and keep his distance.

Honestly, he deserved her gratitude, not her foolish questioning.

*That hit far too close to home.*

He scowled at himself as he strode up to his date's building. The doorman nodded him inside and when he knocked on her door, she opened it with her famous sultry smile.

"Natalia," he greeted, forcing his mouth to curve though it did not want to. "You look beautiful this evening."

She offered her hand and he brushed a perfunctory kiss against the knuckles. She wore a slinky black dress and smoky dark makeup. He should have been immediately distracted from the pop of color that Brianna had been.

But all he could think about was the way the red had made her skin glow. The way her blue eyes were dark and warm and full of so many things.

"I was surprised to hear from you," Natalia said, grabbing a handbag and a wrap. "This isn't our typical kind of event. I didn't know you had any interest in the arts."

They walked to his car, and he tried to focus on the dark, alluring promise that was Natalia. Not sunlight. Not warmth. Not the weight of Gio in his arms while a tear slid down Brianna's cheek.

This was growing harder and harder and he could not imagine why. He could not *accept* why. He was in charge of his mind. His thoughts, his choices. Feelings were of little consequence to a man of his superior control.

"I have an interest in many things," he said, trying to sound his charming self. But the words sounded brittle even to his own ears.

They rode to the art gallery where Brianna's artwork was the main event. She had made quite a splash at the first event, and her manager was eager to get her back into the studio. Lorenzo would need to create her an art studio on the property. She would need to get back to creating as she was going to be in high demand in short time.

*What's the plan there? Keep her and her parents at your estate forever?*

No, they would need their own place. But on the grounds. Close. So Gio was always within reach.

Well, why couldn't they all live in the same house? It would be easy. Best for Gio. Best for all of them. Maybe it wasn't the common thing to do in such a situation, but he wasn't trying to be common any more than he was trying to be traditional.

However, if he kept Brianna in his house, he would need to ensure that did not create too much interest or speculation. *Or temptation.* He'd need a wife. To convince everyone that it wasn't what it looked like. That they were very modern and accepting. A *blended* family.

He glanced at Natalia. She knew how to act, work angles. Maybe she wasn't exactly the perfect wife material, but she had a keen mind. If he could convince her this was in her best interest—if he could *make* a union in her best interest—he could have this settled soon.

*You know, some men leave their partners because they are scared by the depth and breadth of their feelings.*

Brianna's voice echoed in his mind. The image of her in that dress burnt into his mind no matter how he tried to erase it.

The sooner he had a wife in place, the better.

He helped Natalia out of the car and took her arm as he led her into the art gallery. He saw Brianna immediately in that brilliant red. And, as if she was keenly attuned to him, she looked over her shoulder and unerringly found him.

Their gazes met across the room. He watched the shock hit her. Convinced himself the dark thrill that wound through him was simply satisfaction of a plan well made. He would keep his eye on her, and no one would speculate. *That* was why his body reacted.

Not her beauty. Not the little flash of jealousy he saw there in her eyes before the person she'd been talking to regained her attention and she looked away.

Then snuck glances at his date as they made their way around the room.

Something like satisfaction swept through him. That she watched. That she cared. That she didn't like it.

Except, no. She had to like it. She had to agree. She had to understand if his plan was to work. He'd make her understand. Somehow. He would have a wife and Brianna could... She could certainly...

But even the thought of another man looking at her

twisted a deep, dangerous jealousy inside of him. He knew where these feelings led. He had to eradicate them.

"Lorenzo."

He was still looking at Brianna, but he got the sense Natalia had been trying to get his attention for some time. He managed to tear his gaze away from all that red and smiled at Natalia.

"She's lovely," Natalia said, gesturing toward Brianna. "I've seen the stories. Do you really have a child together?"

He found himself hesitant to bring Gio into this. "Does it matter?"

"Of course not. I'm only curious."

"Dante's trying to wage yet another war against me using my son and his mother. He won't win." And there was a war inside of himself that he had to fight. He forced his mouth to curve at his date. "How do you feel about marriage, Natalia?"

She laughed, low and throaty. "Oh, Lorenzo. You're such an idiot sometimes."

He frowned in utter shock. Natalia always spoke her mind but calling him an *idiot* was over-the-top. "I would make it worth your while."

"Of course you would. But what would make you think I'd whore myself out in such a fashion?"

That word left him utterly cold. "Never that."

She made a considering noise. "Regardless. I'm not interested in marrying you, darling. Maybe if I thought it *was* business and not just a powerful man's cowardice, we'd have something to talk about. But I won't be any coward's shield."

There was that word again. First Brianna, now Natalia. When he'd never had the *opportunity* to be a coward. For as long as he could remember, he'd had to be the brave one. *He'd* had to have the courage to do the hard things. Pay bills. Plan funerals. Build empires so nothing would ever touch his family again. "You have a lot of negative opinions of me this evening, *darling*," he managed to say without *too* much acid in his tone.

She shook her head. "No. I can just see through you this evening and you don't like it. I'm usually not the one men use for a distraction, and I'm trying not to be bitter about it because we've always gotten along well. But heed my advice, Lorenzo. You need to deal with her. Not me."

"I have dealt with her, thank you," he replied stiffly.

"Lorenzo," Natalia said quietly. Almost like a friend breaking bad news. "You're not even looking at me."

He managed to rip his gaze away from Brianna. Again. Focus on Natalia. "I need a business partner."

She shook her head. "You need a reality check." She reached up and patted his cheek. "And I am not part of that reality."

# CHAPTER ELEVEN

BRIANNA DID NOT care that he was here. She did not care about the gorgeous beauty on his arm. She didn't *care*. She was above Lorenzo and his dates and plans. She was here for *Brianna*.

She had people interested in her process. In her *motifs*. Her damn inspiration. She did not need Lorenzo's interest. His concern. His…whatever this was.

She hoped he had a wonderful time with his date. She hoped he fell in love with the woman.

*Love is a lie.*

If only *she* could believe that as vehemently as he did. If only anything she felt for him settled in her like a *lie*. Instead it was like some core tenet of everything she was. Loving him was in her blood and she couldn't get it out.

Worse, the way he'd walked out of her bedroom earlier, without refuting a single thing she'd said. Letting her think he loved her too was the worst kind of torture.

She tried to focus on the conversations around her, but her eyes wandered. Always veering straight for him. *Them*, because his date was always with him. And every single time she looked over, he wasn't gazing at said date. He wasn't cuddled together with the woman on his arm.

No, every time Brianna looked over, he was looking right back at her. And every *single* time a jolt went through her whole body. Every time she found herself fantasizing about him striding through the room and coming over to her and…

But he wasn't *with* her. He was with this…woman. Beautiful. *Tall.* Perfect. He didn't believe in love. Whatever he felt for her didn't matter to him because he was here with a date. They were a striking couple, really.

She hoped they both choked on their champagne.

She closed her eyes for a moment, trying to get a hold of her whirling feelings. She needed to find somewhere where she *couldn't* look at them. Because honestly, her feelings weren't the fault or responsibility of that woman, or even Lorenzo. Her feelings, her desire, her desperate wish he could believe in love were hers and hers alone.

Brianna made her way through the party, eyeing the balcony that looked out over the sparkling Palermo. Some fresh air, some distance, and she would find a way to get herself under control. She was strong. She'd had to be over the past two years. It couldn't dissolve just because Lorenzo was back in her life.

Maybe this would all be easier if he hated her. If he told her in no uncertain terms he would never love her. *Maybe.* But maybe it would just…all be hard, and she had to find some way to deal with it better than she had been.

There were people out here on the balcony, but not as many as inside. She wished she could escape the low buzz of conversation, but Brianna found a little shadowed area of the balcony where it at least felt like she was alone. The cool air against her hot cheeks. The stars above.

She had to find some inner strength out here. But it was hard. Because she did not understand him. There was a piece to his thought process she was clearly missing, and he wasn't about to share it with her.

No, he preferred to come into her bedroom, claiming he'd go with her. Refusing to answer questions about why he'd broken things off with her. Then showing up here with a date.

Was he trying to make her jealous? Was he stooping to something so childish? Or did he really think so little about her and what she might feel, that he couldn't fathom why this would hurt?

Worse, was it some combination of all those? Complicated and messy. Not so easily defined. Like everything swirling inside of her.

"Ms. Andersen, I am surprised to find you hiding in the dark. This is not quite the cheerful image of the artist we've been fed," a man's voice said.

Brianna looked over at the form that approached. She knew her manager had introduced her to this man at the cocktail party the other night, but that entire event was a blur and she didn't remember his name. Still, she smiled politely. "Art isn't always cheerful. Even mine."

"But I am fascinated by the cheer in it nevertheless."

"That's very kind." She tried to focus on the man, her art, this conversation. Forget everything else. "It's important to me that no matter how macabre the subject matter, the end result doesn't become bleak." Her core life belief. One it would do some good to remind herself of in the midst of this little pity party.

"I think that's what makes it so powerful. I particularly enjoyed the piece you had titled *Sunset Melancholy*. But someone has bought it out from under me."

It was the exact distraction she needed. Talk of her art. Talk of people *buying* her pieces. Lorenzo wasn't out here and this man had clearly inspected her work enough to really be able to talk about it, so she could get lost in discussion of craft. He was flirting with her, underneath all these compliments he showered on her as the conversation continued. She wasn't so naive she didn't understand that, but that too was a distraction.

Full minutes passed as she talked with the man. She didn't flirt back, but she didn't end the conversation either. It was a breath of fresh air that she didn't feel the need to search out Lorenzo. She could just stand here and talk.

So it figured that Lorenzo would then approach, bringing that small moment of respite to a crashing halt.

"Calo. How good to see you," Lorenzo said, without even excusing himself for interrupting the conversation. He thrust a hand toward the man as he came to stand next to Brianna.

The man in question turned his attention from Brianna and gave Lorenzo a vague kind of smile and shook the offered hand. "Ah, Mr. Parisi. It's been a while."

"Yes, it has." Lorenzo was every inch the smiling businessman, but Brianna definitely picked up on something less than friendly between the two. "Will you excuse us, Calo? I have something private I wish to discuss with Brianna."

"Of course," the man replied. He offered Brianna a smile and began to say something, but Lorenzo took her by the arm and led her away. Back into the main room of the party, then into a hallway. Away from people.

Brianna didn't jerk her arm out of his grasp. She wouldn't cause a scene, though she considered doing so. But what would that serve? They were trying to *avoid* too much paparazzi attention.

*So why is he anywhere near you?*

"Where's your date, Lorenzo?" she asked, trying to

keep the jealousy out of her tone as he drew her into a darkened room. Even if she felt jealous, she knew there was nothing productive about this feeling.

But if he had sex with that woman, she'd want to tear her hair out. That was just how she felt, whether she wanted to or not.

That all being true, she still understood the *whys* of him bringing a date. And those *whys* didn't make sense if he was going to drag her into darkened rooms.

"Never mind that," he said, turning to face her in the very dim light. He crossed his arms over his chest and looked down at her, expression thunderous. "You can thank me for saving you from that man."

For a moment, she could only stare up at him. Shock held her utterly mute. Could he truly be so out of touch with reality? "Saving me?" she finally managed, though her voice was strangled. "I was having a nice conversation with a man interested in buying one of my pieces."

"I am sure he was interested in *something*," Lorenzo returned acidly.

Acid. Anger. Because she'd…had an innocent conversation with a man? Fury erupted within her. "Let me get this straight. You get to bring a date to *my* art show, but I can't even have a conversation with a man? Lorenzo, you can't be serious."

"I know that man," he said, pointing back toward the event she could no longer see or hear. "I know what he's after."

"Oh. Do you? Perhaps you should be more worried about yourself, *dusci*," she said, trotting out that little term as if turnabout would somehow make this all fair play. But none of it was fair, and she was so…mad about that. At him. At the situation. At herself. "About what *you're* after. Because your actions are not matching your words."

"Three years ago I fired him, Brianna. Now he works for Dante Marino. The man bound and determined to make our son a target. I have kept that from happening, and will continue to do so, but you cannot be so…so…naive."

*Naive.*

"Oh, so flirting with me is his great revenge? Explain that to me, Lorenzo, when you don't even care about me. You brought a date. The whole idea is to make certain no one thinks there's anything remotely romantic going on between us. A man flirting with me—regardless of what he's after—suits your little narrative, does it not?"

His mouth firmed at that.

"You're, in fact, ruining your own plan by talking to me. By taking me off to this isolated room where no one can see us. If people noticed, don't you think they'll talk? Don't you think they'll wonder why you left your date to pull me away from a very *nice* man complimenting me about my art?"

"I don't care what people think."

She laughed, and she knew it was a tad high-pitched, maybe even borderline hysterical. But the man was driving her insane. On multiple levels. And still, in spite of all of that, she wanted to be right here. Talking to him—not…whatever the other man's name was. Not her manager. Not anyone but Lorenzo.

She wanted to know what Lorenzo thought of her latest piece. She wanted to hear him speak of his family, or she wanted to tell him a funny Gio story. She wanted to kiss him. To find a way back to Florence and those two blissful months she still looked back on as some of the best days of her life.

She still felt like that woman in a sense, but she wasn't. Because that had been before Gio. She was the same person in so many ways, but she'd grown. Matured.

Had Lorenzo? He hadn't known he had a son. He hadn't had a broken heart. He'd walked away scot-free and now some of the consequences were at his door. Was he exactly the same man he'd been? Would he change?

*Could* he change?

She studied him in the dim light. So full of restrained frustration. She *almost* felt sorry for him. He had taken Gio in with open arms. He was made to be a father after all, but that didn't mean he'd dealt with any of the emotional implications. No, he was too busy plotting and planning what the future would look like. Too busy thwarting Dante Marino's attempts to ruin his reputation.

He was trying to wrestle the world under his control, and he was very good at it. But there were things you could never fully control. Namely other people.

He thought he could though, didn't he? Control her. The woman he'd brought. The narrative of how people thought of him in regards to his *enterprises* and what he wished to do there.

The only reason Brianna was back in his orbit was because of their child, so he would mold her into the life *he* wanted…with no concern to her own wants. No concern to anything except his precious *plans* and *control.*

*He* dictated who she spoke to. *He* dictated what events they were allowed to be seen at together. *He* alone made the choices.

She could love him and still know that was no way to live.

"I am not some toy, some possession, Lorenzo. I never have been. Maybe that's why you left me the way you did. Because you could not control how I would react. You could not put a neat little bow on it if I had a chance to have a say in it." She preferred the dream world where he left because he simply loved her too much, but this one made a lot more sense.

He scoffed. "You are obsessed with the past."

Which was interesting because it was still not agreement or denial. Every time she brought up two years ago, he evaded. Would she ever understand what had happened or would he always leave her wondering?

It didn't matter. *She* knew she had no control over the world and most especially other people. That was a major lesson in motherhood.

"No, Lorenzo. Not obsessed. I'm working *through* the past. Working through the events that shaped me, that still affect me emotionally. It's healthy, actually. Necessary to adapt and grow. I'd suggest you do the same, but I know how you'll respond to that."

"The past is gone. We must prepare for the future."

"Ah, the future. Let me guess." She crossed her arms over her chest to mimic his pose. To meet his cold decisiveness with a frigid dismissiveness. "You know exactly how that's going to go."

"Yes, as a matter of fact. I have a plan."

He looked so...royal. Standing there tall and shoulders back. Expression remote, but with a confidence that never seemed to shake. She should not find it appealing. Should not be distracted by the shape of his mouth, the intensity in his eyes.

So she tried to focus on how she felt about his *plans*. "I'm eager to hear it. You'll have a hard time walking out in the middle of the night when I'm staying at your estate,

Lorenzo. What are you going to do? Escape to Florence this time when things get a little too real?"

He said nothing to that. Nor did he leave. Maybe he was not as in control as he liked to believe. Or she did.

"Go on then. Lay this plan on me. If not escape, what's next? How is our future going to go, oh, Wise One?"

"Now is not the time or the place."

She leaned forward, ignored the punch of the scent of his expensive cologne. The low twist in her belly that somehow seemed more potent and dangerous with all this anger whirling around inside of her. "Oh, it's exactly the time and place. Tell me, Lorenzo. What's the plan? What's my future?"

"Honestly, Brianna."

He made a move as if to leave. After dragging her here. After interrupting her conversation. All dismissive arrogance. Oh, no. She all but jumped in front of him, barring him from exit unless he bodily moved her.

He could, she knew, but he was being so very careful she got the feeling he did not want to touch her.

And what did *that* mean?

"Tell me, Lorenzo. What's my future?"

"Very well. It is simple. You will stay in Palermo, on my estate, as will your parents, should they be amenable. You will have your own space, an art studio, and whatever else you require. This way, Gio will never feel as if he's being shuttled back and forth between two different families." He recited these all as though they were facts. Set in stone. Already a foregone conclusion.

All that certainty that should make her volcanic, but Brianna had nothing smart to say to that. She *wanted* to be angry, but it was… It was everything she wanted. For Gio.

*For yourself.*

She blinked at that. Why did she want to stay and keep putting herself through this? The same estate? So close to this man when he couldn't admit anything about what he felt?

She couldn't believe love was a lie, because to her way of thinking, love was the only thing powerful enough to make an otherwise intelligent woman this stupid and willing to torture herself.

"It will go quite well. A modern solution. Then, to ensure it is seen as such, I will be married by the end of next year to an appropriate wife and stepmother to Gio."

Married. *Step*mother.

Because this *appropriate* wife would not be her.

The pain of the blow was truly astonishing. She should have been ready for it. But in one breath he was building her dream life—staying close for Gio's sake, an art studio for her. But in this dream life he was creating, he would be married to someone *else.*

She wanted to *weep.* Which she would decidedly not do in front of him. Not when he expected her to just… live on the same estate? Accept this as indisputable fact when the woman he was going to marry didn't even *exist.* Unless it was the woman out there…

Whom he'd paid very little attention to. He'd been looking at *Brianna* all night. Instead of engaging in conversation with his date, he was too busy dragging Brianna away from nice men making pleasant conversation.

So she didn't crumble at the idea of him marrying someone else and her just having to take it. Not yet. Because he wasn't claiming to *love* someone else. He was just building empires. Maybe it hurt. Maybe she thought him a complete and utter fool. But she could fight it if it wasn't about *love*.

She lifted her chin, still blocking his exit. "What about me?"

"What about *you*?" he returned coolly.

"Am I allowed to marry in this scenario?"

There was a long, stretched-out silence as a muscle ticked in his jaw. When he spoke, it sounded strangled. "As long as I approve of the groom."

*This* was enough to make her laugh, rather than cry. But before she could say anything, he continued.

"This is how it will be. You can argue with me. You can whine about it, but in the end, you will see, it is best and that's what will happen."

"You are an idiot, Lorenzo. Delusional or too arrogant to function, or both."

"I grow tired of this insult hurled at me this evening."

Brianna laughed. Again. Honestly, even with her heart cracking into a million pieces, the whole farce was hilarious. "Did it ever occur to you that everyone insulting you is *correct* if there's consensus?"

The expression on his face was such that it appeared he had *not* considered that. "I've had quite enough, Brianna. So move."

"But you brought me here. To shout at me about my naive choices in having conversations with men at an art show in which my *job* is to talk about my art. Tell me, Lorenzo, what did you expect to happen when you dragged me into this dim room, alone?"

"I expected to have a rational conversation. Clearly you're in no headspace for that, so I will leave you alone."

Her hand curled into a fist. She wanted to punch him. She really did. But that wouldn't get through to him. Nothing would. So why not be as *irrational* as she wanted? "Make me move then, Lorenzo."

He took her by the arm. But he did not move her. He didn't even pull. His hand just gripped her, branded her like an iron. Oh, how she wanted this infuriating, ridiculous idiot of a man. It would never make sense to her how easily he affected her.

*Never*, she thought, as his grip finally moved her. Not out of the way. Not away from him.

No, he jerked her to him in a move that had her crashing against the hard mountain of him. Before his mouth crashed to hers.

It was wild. Explosive. Rough and wonderful...and if she had even a shred of intelligence or self-preservation, she would push him away. She would end this ridiculous cycle of stupidity.

But she didn't. She held on. Clutched him like her life depended on it. Returned the furious kiss with one of her own. Because all that feeling climbed inside of her. It rushed through her like a drug. *Here* he admitted he loved her, even if he didn't believe in love. Even if he never said the words.

When he kissed her, when he touched her, when they came together as nothing but bodies seeking pleasure, she *felt* his love for her.

She *knew* she had to tell him to stop, because he'd never admit it or acknowledge that love. She knew kissing him back, wrapping herself around him was the kind of mindless lack of thought that had gotten her into this whole mess in the first place.

But his hands slid up the slit in her skirt, pushing the fabric up. It was dark in here, so she couldn't see him, but she knew him. His mouth, his hands, the shape of his body. She knew how to arch against him, how to nip at his jaw, how to curl her fingers into his hair.

His mouth streaked down her neck, bringing the strap down over her shoulder, cool air touching bared skin. She had to stop this before it went too far. Because… because…

"You have a date here. You brought someone else. She…" Brianna tried to find the words. To tell him it was wrong. To tell herself. She had stopped this once before. She had to be strong enough to stop it again.

"She knows what this is, Brianna." His eyes were dark blazes of fire. His words growled. He was intensity personified. Everything she wanted. "She has no designs on me."

"Lucky her." Because Brianna didn't have the first clue what this was. What to do about it.

Except succumb.

# CHAPTER TWELVE

THE THOUGHT OF another man putting his hands on Brianna had consumed Lorenzo from the moment he'd seen her in that dress. Being at this party, seeing other men look at her, it destroyed him. Whether it be that ineffectual weasel Calo Finetti or another man, Brianna was *his*, and anyone else so much as having a *thought* about her sent a fury through him he knew would destroy everything.

It wasn't that he didn't understand it was hypocritical to consider marrying another woman while hating the idea Brianna might marry someone else. Touch them. Be naked with them. He knew it was absolutely wrong and unfair.

He just didn't care. Not in this moment, when she was arguing with him looking like sunlight in a dim room. So that no matter what realities and truths existed, he only knew he needed her. He knew this dark ribbon of emotion inside of him was only cured if his mouth was on hers.

It made everything else disappear. Nothing mattered here with her mouth on his. Not tabloids. Certainly not Natalia and her refusals. Not Dante Marino or anyone else.

Brianna's mouth. Her arms around him. The sunshine sweetness of her even when she was angry with him.

She didn't push him away. Didn't refuse him. She kissed him back with the same wild desperation that had taken hold of every rational thought, every careful plan.

The plan was gone. Everything was gone except the velvet of her skin, the way she begged him.

Because she was begging him. For more. For all. He closed the door to the room, plunging them into darkness. He shoved the skirt of her dress up, found the soft, wet heat of her. Touched her there until her breath shuddered.

The scent of her filled the room. His body so hard he did not know if he would ever move again. Everything centered on Brianna. His sweet, beautiful Brianna, moving against his hand.

"Lorenzo. Please."

*Please.*

He freed himself. There was no time for finesse. He ached. Until there was nothing left but the ache. But her.

They both needed something more than gentleness. They needed the wild. To feed the desperation. So he drove himself home, as she wrapped herself around him. He used the wall for leverage, tried to calm the frantic panic inside of him with a demanding pace.

He was inside her. In this dark room. He couldn't see her, but he could feel her. Every breath. Every squeeze of her fingers against his shoulders. The arch of her back as she opened for him, took him deeper.

She shuddered out her first release, clutching him. He wished he could see her. He wished he could take his time. He wished…

For all those dangerous things. What they'd had before. The sweetness of it. The joy of it. When every time they'd come together felt like coming home.

*And you know where all that leads.*

In this moment he didn't care. He pulled down the strap of her dress until he freed her taut nipple. He bent his head and tasted. Licked, nipped. Until she was gasping, begging, writhing against him.

Wild. Wanton. His. His blood roared. His body throbbed for her and her alone. To the point of pain, and that pain was joy as long as he was inside of her. As long as her arms were around him and she panted his name.

*Mine. Mine. Mine.*

He wasn't sure if those chanted words were thoughts or something he verbalized but he didn't care because she could not be anyone else's. Ever.

So he made her his. Over and over again. With his hands, his mouth, his body. Until she was sobbing out his name. *His* name and only his.

Until he lost himself. Over that edge and into nothing but pleasure and release. His breath was ragged, and he held her there against the wall for long, pulsing seconds as they both tried to recover.

He didn't let his brain shift into gear. Then the thoughts would start. The recriminations. The reason. He couldn't go down that road just yet. Not with his blood still roaring in his ears. Not with a warm and sated Brianna limp in his arms.

He stayed in this moment, in this warmth. *In this love.*

The word love was always the antidote, and he began to extricate himself. There *was* a world outside this room. He smoothed down her dress, still in the dark, doing everything by feel alone. He tucked himself away, but he did not let her go. Did not step away.

Once he did…reality would come crashing down and—

"Lorenzo," she said in a pained whisper. She sounded

on the verge of tears and nothing could have pierced him more. "I cannot keep doing this with you."

It was strange. He'd meant to say those exact words once he had his faculties back. To gently put her in her place. To accept *some* responsibility, but certainly not all.

But her saying the exact words he'd been thinking, when she sounded so hurt, twisted something inside of him.

The words made him angry even though he agreed.

*She* should want to keep doing it. They were amazing at *it*, and that was all she should be thinking about.

"I need to go home," she continued, sounding no less devastated.

"I'll have my driver take you back at once," he said, angry at himself that his voice sounded so weak. That he *felt* weak. That he wanted to offer her a million reassuring words and, worse, feelings.

*Love is a lie. Love is destruction. Lorenzo, what have you done?*

"No, Lorenzo. I need to go *home*. Gio and I need to go back to New Jersey."

The words simply did not compute. He tried to look at her, read her expression, but it was still nothing but darkness in the room.

"I'm not saying the two of you shouldn't have a relationship," she continued. "I don't want to keep you from him. We'll have to work out some kind of custody agreement. You're a billionaire. You should be able to fly to the States as much as you want."

No words could have shocked him more, and he was still struggling to get his mind to return to reality. "Brianna." He was trying to sound stern. He had a bad feeling he was failing. When he never failed.

Couldn't allow himself to fail ever again.

"I can't do this. I can't watch you marry another woman. I can't keep…trying to resist you. Clearly, I can't do it for long. I do not know how to fight how much I want you, and before you say that's just fine, it isn't. If you don't want a relationship, it isn't *fine* for me. The only way I survive this is distance."

*Survive this.*

The brokenness in her voice, or maybe the dark, or maybe the way his heart felt bruised at the idea of her leaving had him reliving old moments he'd like to forget.

*I can't survive this, Lorenzo. I can't bear it.*

Rocca. His sweet sister who'd become so broken. So lost. The perfect image of his mother. They'd both paid the price for all that *love.*

He stepped away from Brianna, a cold ice trickling through him. It made his fingers feel thick and incapable of doing something as simple as opening the door.

*I can't bear it. I can't bear it.*

And then she hadn't. Because love broke things. It broke people. Crushed them into bits until they couldn't bear it. Until they made all the wrong choices. Wrung themselves out. It hurt until there was nothing left. Until they were gone.

He could tell himself it wasn't true, but his love for Brianna existed within him no matter how hard he denied it. No matter how many plans he could make to wed someone else. These horrible feelings would always be inside him. So she was right. Distance was the best option.

*I can't bear it.*

Distance was the only option to save Brianna.

"All right," he managed to say. "Give me a few days

to ensure you and Gio will be safe and then we'll make the arrangements for you to return to America."

"Thank you." Her inhale was so shaky he stepped away. He gave her the distance she needed. In the interim between now and when she could safely return to New Jersey, he would give her all the distance she asked.

He would not break her. He would not let his love break her, or hers break her. Perhaps she had the right of it with this…distance. He could accept this. He would.

He would make it right. Keep everyone safe. He would not fail again. He couldn't. For his son. For himself.

For Brianna.

What Brianna really wanted was to go back to Lorenzo's estate. Pack everyone up and head to the airport. Safety and all else be damned. She had to get away from him.

Or her feelings for him. Her weakness when it came to him. She didn't know what she was really running away from except maybe her own failures.

She did not understand her utter lack of control when it came to this man. It was one thing to love him when he didn't—or wouldn't—love her back. It was another thing to just…have sex with him. In the middle of a *party*? Knowing he wanted to marry someone else. Who did that? What kind of woman, what kind of mother did it make her?

Maybe it should have been some comfort that he seemed to have the same problem resisting when it came to her, but all she could think about was the way he'd left her before.

If she stayed, if she kept putting herself in a position to fall deeper and deeper in love with him, forever bending when it came to him—even when he came to *her* event with a *date*—she would break, and she couldn't.

She had a son who depended on her. Who loved her. She had to put him first. And herself.

She didn't have to worry about money anymore. Lorenzo would take care of Gio financially, probably to the point of spoiling. But she still needed a career. To support herself. To feel fulfilled.

So she forced herself to return to the party. She did not pay attention to what Lorenzo did. She was afraid she would start bawling in the middle of the art show, and that was enough to keep her will power intact.

Lucky her.

She spoke to a few more people who'd bought pieces. She smiled, hopefully. When she finally thought she'd stayed long enough, she went and found her manager to say her goodbyes.

"This has been such a success, Brianna," her manager said warmly, pumping her hands in a shake. "I hear you might be staying in Palermo longer. We could have another show next week. I could see about getting you some studio space and—"

"No. No, Juliette. As much as that sounds wonderful, I really need to get home. Spend some time there. In my home studio."

Juliette nodded, though her smile had dimmed. "Very well. We'll get the final numbers to you tomorrow, and the payments will be over the next few weeks."

Brianna thanked her, then collected her things and left. It was still a *little* early, but not unforgivably so. She happened to see Lorenzo out of the corner of her eye as she exited the main room, but she refused to turn her head and look to see what his expression was, who was on his arm.

Hopefully, he stayed. Hopefully, he and his date made whatever gossip story suited Lorenzo's plan and vision.

*I will be married by the end of next year to an appropriate wife.*

She would not torture herself by wondering why *she* couldn't be the perfect wife. It wouldn't matter to her in a few days. She'd be home in New Jersey, getting over him just as she had two years ago.

*But you didn't get over him.*

What a depressing thought. Brianna watched the city pass outside the car window. Over the past two years she'd pushed her heartbreak away by loving Gio. By putting those jagged feelings into her art.

So she'd do it again. Focus on being a mother. Put her pain into her art. Maybe it wouldn't solve the problem of being irrevocably in love with Lorenzo, but at least it was productive.

Except this time around, she would have to see him. She would have to co-parent with him. She couldn't even resist him when he brought another woman to *her* art show—did she really think she was going to be able to control herself in a co-parenting situation?

She was exhausted when she arrived at the estate. Emotionally wrung out from berating herself for the entire rest of the evening. From smiling when she wanted to cry. From knowing she needed to go home to New Jersey, for telling Lorenzo she did, and then for wishing he'd argue with her. Beg her to stay.

*You are pathetic*, she chastised herself silently as she was let into the house.

She'd go upstairs, check on Gio and her parents. Then shower, sleep, and hope clarity arrived by morning.

But before she could go upstairs, she heard voices. This in itself wouldn't have stopped her, but she heard what could only be Gio's excited squeal.

Brianna frowned. Well, at least that gave her something to shift her upset toward. Gio should have been asleep a good hour ago. She marched toward the living room, ready to lecture her parents, though they likely didn't deserve it.

They sat on the couch in the main living room, and Gio stood behind a curtain clearly playing a game of peeka-boo with... Not her parents, but a woman seated on the floor in the middle of the room.

The moment the woman turned her head to look at her, Brianna knew who she was. Not by name. Simply by looks. She *had* to be one of Lorenzo's sisters. Those dark eyes, that sharp nose. Something in the mouth. Oh, this woman was beautiful with her dark curly hair and expertly done makeup. There weren't just hints of Lorenzo on her face, but Gio as well.

The woman stood. She didn't smile Brianna's way. There was something speculative in her gaze even as Gio made a gurgling squeal and hurtled himself toward Brianna's frozen form.

One of Lorenzo's siblings. In the flesh. All the secrets this woman would know. Would she be able to explain him to Brianna? Tell Brianna what was wrong with her for being so desperately in love with a man who wanted nothing to do with it.

*Why does he think love is a lie? What can I do to change his mind?*

Brianna lifted Gio into her arms, knowing she couldn't

ask this woman any of the questions she wanted to. Knowing she should greet her in some way but finding herself mute.

The woman also didn't offer any pleasantries. But she wasn't looking at Brianna anymore. She was looking behind her.

"Saverina. What are you doing here?" Lorenzo's dark voice said from right behind Brianna.

The girl sauntered over to where Brianna stood, then moved past her. Brianna turned and watched as the woman marched right up to Lorenzo in the doorway.

"Meeting my nephew, of course," the young woman said with an insouciant shrug. "And before you start nagging, you should know it was Stefano's idea and the rest of the family will be descending tomorrow."

Then she wrapped her arms around Lorenzo and squeezed. "Come now, *frati*. Welcome me home."

# CHAPTER THIRTEEN

LIKE A PARENT, Lorenzo did not have favorites when it came to his siblings. But even he had to admit he had more of a soft spot for Saverina than the others. She had only been eight when their mother had died—and their mother had been less than helpful years before that. Saverina had just turned eleven when their father had also passed.

Lorenzo remembered holding her as an infant, more so than any of the others. Changing her diapers, feeding her meals. While most of his siblings were more like his children than his siblings, Saverina had never felt like anything other than his daughter.

His responsibility.

And here she was. Playing with Gio. Meeting Brianna. It was like two worlds clashing, and he wasn't ready for that. He hadn't planned or prepared. He hadn't found a way to erect all the necessary walls to make this…okay. That was why he had decidedly *not* invited his family to descend yet.

If he had wanted these worlds to mix already, he would have issued a family-wide invite. Hosted a dinner. He had planned to get to that point someday, but not until he was prepared.

But now Saverina was here with no warning, and he had to somehow juggle balls he wasn't ready to.

Worse, Brianna was standing there in her red dress, all sunshine and reminders of what happened when they were alone together. No control over themselves, over their emotions. At least at the party there'd been so much of their interaction in the dark. Now he was home and there were lights and her dark blue stare, full of pain, confusion and consideration.

She was looking at him like... He didn't know like what. He only knew it had his insides twisting into hard, painful knots. So that when he spoke, he was harsher with Saverina than he intended.

"Go upstairs."

Her eyebrows shot up, a clear sign his focus was split and he'd made a grave error. Saverina did not take well to being bossed around and he was almost always better at navigating and maneuvering her. She was the baby of the family. Spoiled in so many ways.

And the best and brightest of them. She remembered so little of the ugliness of the family, hoped for so much for her future, and had every opportunity to make a success of herself. Even without Lorenzo's help she would succeed, he knew, though he had given it and would continue to at every opportunity.

"I'll go," she said, with a raised eyebrow and narrow-eyed look of recrimination. "*If* you come with me."

Lorenzo did not see a way out of that, so he gave a sharp nod. They would talk privately. The walk up to her room would give him time...somehow, to put his thoughts in order. To refigure a plan.

Saverina turned and Lorenzo noted she didn't look at or acknowledge Brianna. Only the boy in her arms.

"And I'll see you tomorrow, *niputi*." She leaned in and gave Gio a smacking kiss on the cheek that had the boy squealing in delight. Clearly Saverina had worked her usual magic and already won Gio over far more quickly than Lorenzo had been able to.

Still, in this moment the boy smiled shyly his way too. He hadn't called him *Dada* yet, but he no longer hid. He no longer considered Lorenzo scary.

And Lorenzo did not have time to try and continue the work he'd done there. He had to deal with his sister.

She said nothing to Brianna. Just walked past, looking over her shoulder once to nod for Lorenzo to follow. He felt all the Andersens' eyes on him. Normally he would not behave in such a way that made it look like he was some sort of servant to his sister, but...

He needed distance from Brianna. Even if he'd followed her home. Even if looking away from her was torture. Standing here staring at her in front of her parents, his sister and their son made him...too vulnerable. Too exposed.

So he followed Saverina. Away from the Andersens, to the staircase and then up toward his wing and Saverina's room.

"So. This woman," Saverina said, making no attempt to whisper or keep her voice down, so her words likely echoed and carried behind them.

"The mother of my child, you mean?" Lorenzo returned at a much more reasonable decibel level.

"Yeah. Her. What's her deal?"

"She is an artist. She is here on business. We are working out an agreement on how to co-parent Gio. Then she is going back to New Jersey." The pain carved deep, but he saw no other way.

Protecting Gio had to come first, and they could not protect him with all these swirling feelings between them, that was for certain. This he knew from experience.

Saverina stopped abruptly on the top of the stairs, whirled to face him. "With Gio?"

"Yes, but we will have a custody arrangement in place. I will not be kept from my son again, nor does she wish to keep me from him. This is all very..." He didn't dare use the word *modern* with his young sister, who viewed him as anything but. "...civilized."

Saverina made a considering noise as she continued to walk down the ornate hall to her room. She had been sixteen when he'd finally amassed enough fortune to buy this estate, so she was the only sibling who'd still been living with him permanently when he did. She'd gotten the first choice of rooms.

"So, do we hate her?" Saverina asked conversationally.

"Why would we hate her? She is the mother of my son."

"She kept your son from you."

"She had her reasons. Unfortunate though they may be, they are more Marino's fault than her own."

Saverina rolled her eyes. "You blame that guy for everything."

"Oddly enough, Saverina, *that guy* being my rival and trying to ruin my business is to blame for many of my problems."

She pushed open the door that led to her room. Even though she was off at university, he left it just as she liked so that she could always have somewhere to come home to. So that she felt like she had a home with him always.

So she would never feel alone. So she would never think the answer to any of her problems could only be solved by ending it all. *He* would solve all her problems. Always.

Lorenzo would have liked to have made his excuses now, leaving her to settle in, but he needed to find a way to neutralize the damage Saverina could likely do with Brianna.

"Why have you come, Sav?"

"Well, I called Stefano about the story I saw on the gossip site. You didn't tell me." She settled herself onto her bed, then looked up at him, still all speculation. Looking like Rocca and their mother and a grown woman when she should still be a babe in his arms.

"You should have called *me*," he returned gruffly.

"Why? To get one of your famous Lorenzo talk-arounds? No thanks." She waved an expressive hand. "We're your family, Lorenzo. I don't know when you'll get it through your thick head that it isn't just you presiding over a kingdom with us your loyal subjects."

She'd lectured him over this before, so he merely grunted and crossed his arms over his chest as response.

"So I should be nice to this woman?" Saverina demanded. "She isn't an evil witch keeping your son from you?"

"No, she is not."

"Do *you* like her?"

The question seemed innocuous enough, but nothing was innocuous when it came to his baby sister. Still, ignoring the question or giving too much of an answer would encourage her. "Yes. She is a good mother. A kind woman. A fine artist." He stopped himself from saying more because she was watching him far too closely.

"Do you love her?" Saverina asked.

Like a knife to the heart. "*Bedda Matri*, Saverina. I am tired. Go to bed," he muttered, turning for the door.

"If you can't simply say *no*, that's a yes."

Lorenzo took a deep breath. Maybe it was, but he could only hear the pain in Brianna's voice. *I need to go home.* She needed to be away from him, and he needed to be away from her. Or they would only continue to hurt each other in ways that made no sense.

Because love was destruction. And if they didn't destroy each other, they would destroy Gio.

Just as his parents had destroyed Rocca.

"It does not matter how I feel about her, Saverina."

"Why? Is she married or something? I'm pretty sure if she was, I would have seen *that* on a gossip site."

Lorenzo stood at the door, staring at the knob. He couldn't explain it to her. She didn't understand. She didn't remember all he remembered. In her mind, their mother was a ghost. Their father a drunk, at best. Rocca... Well.

There was no doubt a sadness and a trauma there, but this was simply part of life. Saverina did not know who or what to blame the loss of Rocca on, but Lorenzo did.

"There is no *why*. We're simply being reasonable adults who are putting our son first. There is no reason to treat this as anything other than a business deal. We will come to an agreement about Gio, sign contracts if need be. Very luckily, we are on the same page about raising a child. And he will come first, always. That is what being a parent means."

Saverina was quiet for a few moments, but he heard her get off the bed and cross to him. When she spoke, it was with uncharacteristic gentleness.

"It seems to me, if you love her and agree with her

about how to raise your child, marrying her would be an option. Or at least keeping her here would be. Why would you let her go half a world away?"

Marry Brianna. He didn't let himself think of it. It didn't fit the plan. It was too dangerous. Perhaps if tonight hadn't happened, he'd be able to find some way to…make that okay.

But he'd hurt her. She'd been shaken, needing to leave and go home because *he* was too much. What they felt, far too much.

This would never make them happy. It would only tear them into pieces, leaving Gio with pieces he'd need to stitch together to survive.

Impossible.

"You can't let her take Gio back to America," Saverina said, squeezing his arm. "I know you have billions and all, but think of the sheer time commitment it'll take. Having had you as a father figure myself, I know he deserves you more in his life than that. You have to find another way, Lorenzo. One that makes *you* happy."

Happy. He wanted to laugh, but the feeling was so bitter it seemed to coat his mouth with thick ash and no sound came out. He cleared his throat.

"You do not understand, Saverina," he said very stiffly. "We have tried to make an arrangement here, but Brianna and I are too complicated."

Saverina was never so easily swayed. "You *do* love her. I can hear it in your voice. Lorenzo. You can't be so…*you* about it."

"What does that mean?"

"It means you can't plan, mold or control love so you want nothing to do with it."

It was hard to argue with that. Indeed, this was part

of what made love so dangerous. He didn't see this as a bad thing. He considered it a very realistic outlook. But saying *so* to Saverina would not get him anywhere.

"So you'll just send her away? Honestly, brother, do you ever make any sense?"

He pulled his arm out of her grasp, fixed her with an icy, authoritative look. "You do not understand, Saverina. You're a child. You know nothing of caring for others. Of sacrifice."

She did not waver. She didn't so much as flinch. But any warmth in her expression turned into icy disdain. "Let's say all that is true, Lorenzo," she said very coolly. "But all that means is *you* don't know what it means to care for yourself. You don't know how to do anything *but* sacrifice. And it would be in *your* best interest if you let me show you…what all else there is."

These words were little barbs. Not quite new. Maybe she'd never expressed it quite so bluntly, but he understood this was what Saverina saw. Though he might still breathe, he was as tragic a figure as Rocca was to her.

But she didn't understand. And he didn't know how to explain it to her. Anyone.

"We appreciate the sacrifices you've made, Lorenzo. All of your siblings. Even me. But that doesn't mean we want it. You want to call me a child, and fine. To you I am. But I'm also an adult when I go off and live on my own far away from you. We all are—every one of us— adults living our own lives. We don't need your sacrifice anymore, and Gio doesn't need it at all. He needs a *father*."

Gio. He would sacrifice everything for *Gio*, but he could admit, back at the party, he'd considered his son, of course. But not in terms of *himself.* He'd thought of saving Gio the pain of watching love destroy everything.

Not that he'd have to live without Gio in arm's reach. When he'd already missed so much.

Now that he knew Gio existed, held the boy and earned his smiles, it seemed unconscionable to let Brianna return home. Saverina was right about that.

Only because he hadn't had time to think. To plan. Saverina's surprise arrival had turned upheaval even more on its head.

But this was not Saverina's fight. He did not need to discuss it with her or have her tell him what to do. That was *his* job. And he had a long night of figuring out how to deal with his large, loud family if they were all descending tomorrow.

"I am glad you are here," he said, giving his sister a look that she should read as dismissal. "While I wish you all would have waited, I am eager for everyone to spend some time with Gio. To welcome him into the family. Brianna always wanted..." He trailed off, realizing Brianna telling him about wishing she was from a larger family, *wanting* a large family was something she'd told him back *then*, not recently in regard to Gio.

Still, he could picture her face as she'd said that. She'd been trying to get him to talk about his family without directly asking him about it at a little café in Florence. She'd been wearing a red top, not unlike the red of her dress tonight. She'd say something about large families, then look at him through her lashes.

He'd known what she'd been doing, and he'd mostly kept all details to himself out of self-preservation, but every time she'd look at him, searching his face for answers, he had not been strong enough to stop some little detail from emerging.

"Brianna always wanted what?" Saverina asked, her eyes too astute for his own good.

"A larger family for Gio. It is only her and her parents. She's eager for him to be part of a larger family unit."

"Well, we've certainly got that."

"Yes."

"But I don't understand how you can let him go back to America. How you can be in love with this woman— you, Lorenzo Parisi, billionaire, and I'm quite sure a man who's never accepted a *no* in his life—and simply give up."

"It isn't giving up. It is being sensible. Gio is our focus. Anything between Brianna and me is secondary to that, and if distance is… Distance will be cleaner. More careful. It will be best. He won't end up like…"

There was a heavy silence. She should not be able to read into him saying too much, but perhaps he gave her too little credit. Perhaps no matter what he'd done to cushion Saverina, she knew that Rocca had sacrificed herself. Because their parents' warped love had broken her. Irreparably.

"Nothing you do now with Gio brings Rocca back," Saverina said gently, when she was so very rarely gentle. Because he'd taught her to be strong and demanding. He'd taught her not to take no for an answer or be steamrolled by anyone. He had tried to give her every tool he'd failed to impart to Rocca.

Saverina bringing up Rocca while looking at him with soft, wet eyes was too much. He would have stepped into the hall and slammed the door behind him, but Saverina stopped him. Never one to leave well enough alone.

"I do not know what Rocca has to do with my son," he said, looking down at her as he tried to rein his fury in.

*Is it fury or hurt? Fury or love and grief?*

"You can't make it so he's never hurt. People die, Lorenzo. You can't protect him from…"

"From what?" he demanded because she did not know…she could not know…

"Well, the drugs that killed our mother, for starters. The mental illness that killed our sister. You can't control people. You can only love them."

*Love is a lie.* Only control could protect a person from it. And part of that control was Saverina not knowing… She wasn't supposed to be that aware of what had actually happened. This was not the story he'd fed her. To save her from the truth. "I do not know what you're talking about."

"You don't think I know what happened? That our mother killed herself with drugs just as Rocca killed herself with—"

"That isn't what happened."

"Yes, it is. Rocca told me about Mom. When she was having one of her…dark periods. And I know why they both had those dark periods."

"You were a child." And no one was supposed to know. It was Rocca's secret. Even he hadn't known right away, or he would have stopped it. Stopped their mother. Berated their father into being a man and not letting his wife whore herself out to put food on the table.

Then worse, so much worse, insisting his daughter do the same.

"I was *there*," Saverina said while Lorenzo reeled. "Not so much a child as you wanted me to be. I'll admit,

I didn't understand the prostitution stuff until I got older. It's only started to come together for me recently, but—"

"Stop."

"Stop what? Discussing the truth? We all know. Rocca, God rest her, did not possess the discretion about the situation that you did."

"You misunderstood her. She was…unwell and—"

"Are you calling her a liar, Lorenzo?"

It took his breath away, the accusation. The memory of his sister, so broken at the end. So desperate to stop the pain inside of her. All put there by parents who had used her.

And he hadn't been strong enough to see it. To stop it. To save her from it, or the end she'd chosen.

"How did we get on this subject?" Lorenzo demanded. This entire evening had been one moment after another where someone else was in control. Someone else was unraveling *everything*, and all without his consent. How had he arrived at this place where everyone could upend all his carefully structured walls and plans?

And still Saverina yammered *on*. As if this twenty-year-old knew more than him. Understood all while he floundered.

"I have watched you work yourself to the bone for years. And you were successful. It seemed to make you… content, if not happy. So I said very little about your choices. Oh, I know I made fun of you, but it was always a joke. This is no joke, Lorenzo. This is a son. A woman you love. And you're calling them *business*. Have you changed so much from the man who raised me so well?"

"I have not changed. I am who I have always been. My goal, my only goal, has been to protect and provide for my family. This is why you live the cushioned life you do."

"Yes. Yes, it is."

He didn't know what to say if she didn't argue with him. He didn't know what to do when it looked like she was about to cry rather than rage at him.

He was hurting every woman he cared for this evening and he didn't understand *how*. Distance. It was the only answer. Because this—discussing the past, being together, *love*—it only caused strife. Hurt.

"Without us to protect…is it all punishment for you now?" she asked, making no sense at all. "You've essentially been an empty nester for two years and I thought you might build your own life, but you haven't, have you? Rocca took her own life, so you cannot have anything for yourself?"

The words, the stark reality of them, stole his breath. Surely they couldn't be true, no matter how hard they landed. "You don't understand."

"She was my sister too. I know she was your twin, but that doesn't mean you get to own grieving her. Failing her. All that we couldn't do to save her."

He wanted none of that guilt or failure to touch Saverina. "She was my responsibility."

"She was our *sister*, Lorenzo. Not a task assigned to you by our parents. They *neglected* us, both of them. But you didn't. We weren't…bullet points on a company budget and a child isn't a business merger. I *know* you know this, so I cannot understand why you have decided to… pretend as though you are someone else."

But she didn't *understand*. Couldn't. Because he had ensured she had a life where his choices would ideally *never* make sense to her. "I am Lorenzo Parisi. I will take care of and protect my son the way I took care of and protected you and our siblings."

"You loved us too."

*Love*, that awful thing. Stabbing at him again and again tonight. "Why are we talking about this?"

"Because you're…messed up. Sacrificing the wrong things. And weirdly enough, when I realize I'm messing my life up, it tends to stem from some terrible thing that happened when we were kids."

The thought of her messing up, of knowing the terrible when he'd been so certain he'd shielded her from it…

"And when I realize that, and acknowledge that, deal with it—I know that's *your* influence, *frati*." She reached out to him then. Her eyes full of hurt that *he* had put there, whether he'd wanted to or not.

"*You* saved me from what could have been. Because you loved me, all of us, more than yourself. You put our needs above your own. When our father did not care, when he let everyone around him sacrifice so *he* didn't have to, you were our savior. That was…heroic, Lorenzo. You have always been my hero, no matter how I tease. But that cannot continue if on the other side of raising us, saving us, you push away any chance at love and happiness."

He was so tired of the word *love*. Saverina saying it. Him feeling it. Hating it. He pulled away from her. He was walking out the door, but that didn't stop her.

"If I was in your position, or Brianna's…what would you want for me?" she said as he walked away.

*Everything good.*

But not love. Because love was the root of all the bad. All the complex. All the *death*. When had love ever done anything *good* for the people in his family? It was duty, it was *sacrifice* that had saved them.

It was his mother's love for his father, and Rocca's love for both of them, that had been a curse.

But when Saverina put it *that* way, asking him to imagine her in his position, it haunted him. Because he wanted every joy for her, like he did for Gio, and he did not know how to protect either of them from all the pain that went along with it.

It didn't change his mind. Nothing would. Or so he told himself as he left Saverina and went to his office. To plan. Because feelings didn't matter. They only hurt. He would plan them away. Erect all the necessary defenses.

Saverina had said marrying Brianna should be an option, and she was right. It *would* be.

But he would put all the necessary walls in place to make certain it never broke him or her or their son.

# CHAPTER FOURTEEN

BRIANNA WOKE UP feeling bruised, body and soul. She had not slept well at all. Reliving fractured moments of the art show over and over.

Not just the sex, though she couldn't lie to herself. Reliving that had her body thrumming with need all over again because she couldn't seem to put it out of her mind. The way he touched her. The way he made her feel.

What was *wrong* with her?

But she was also stuck in that moment of pain at realizing... There was no cure for what she felt for him. If she would beg him the way she had in a *public* setting, two years after he'd left her so abruptly, there was no hope for her keeping her pride. No hope to be the strong, independent woman and good mother she needed to be.

So she had to get away. She knew this on an intellectual level. Even on an emotional level, as her heart twisted over the gruff way Lorenzo had spoken to her at the show. At the arrested look on his face when he'd seen his sister.

But deep down, no matter what, she didn't *want* to go home. There was still this part of her that wanted to ignore the complications and say *yes*. Living in an estate in Sicily with her child and the father of said child was just fine, regardless of the emotional turmoil of him marrying someone else.

"You need to go home," she said aloud to herself in the hopes that saying it out loud would get rid of her doubts.

She did not know how to not want Lorenzo. Even when he made her angry, she wanted his hands on her. And she cared about him too much as a person to believe they could burn through all that lust and be left with nothing. Take away wanting him, that ridiculous heat between them, and there were still other things. There was the whole of him.

The way he looked at Gio and his sister, with a kind of pride mixed with love that made her heart swell. The way he listened—not just to her, but to her parents. Then there were the glimpses of hurt she saw underneath all that control that she wanted to soothe. Memories of *before*, when he'd listened to her prattle on about her art and made her feel special. Important.

She loved the man he was, even if she could somehow get rid of all this physical chemistry she felt for him. But they were two parts of the same coin. Something about this man—body and soul—called to her.

And he wanted to *marry* someone else, while she was tucked away in a corner of his estate. She just…couldn't.

Could she?

She heard quiet voices and realized her mother must have entered Gio's room. She went through the adjoining door to find Mom lifting Gio out of his crib.

"Oh, you're up," Mom greeted with a smile. "I heard this one babbling and I couldn't resist."

Brianna took in Gio's sleepy eyes and the way he leaned his head on her mother's shoulder and wondered if Mom just didn't like exploring the estate without Gio as a buffer.

She smiled at her mother. Soon, Mom could be home.

They could go back to the way things were. They wouldn't need to be uncomfortable in this strange world that wasn't theirs.

*Except Lorenzo will be in your life, not something you can pretend doesn't exist.*

She shook that gloomy thought away. "Well, we'll be heading home soon. Get back to a normal routine for you and Dad."

Helene's eyebrows drew together. "I thought you might want to…stay."

Brianna cleared her throat and expressly did not meet her mother's gaze. Instead she stared out the window in Gio's room, taking in the beautiful and expansive gardens. It would be such a treat for Gio to grow up here.

And he would. Part of the year. It would kill her to be apart from him for any swath of time, but how could she stay here? She would become pathetic in no time. She needed to be strong, like her parents had taught her to be. Never codependent.

"I think it's best if Lorenzo and I have some distance between us. I don't plan on having a custody fight, of course. Gio and Lorenzo should have a relationship and will. We'll find ways so that Lorenzo will be very involved in Gio's life."

"From half a world away?" Mom asked, not with accusation but with genuine concern.

Brianna ignored the twinge of pain and guilt. "He's a billionaire. He can fly anywhere he wants whenever he wants. He could even buy a place in New Jersey to spend some time at if he'd like. Whatever he decides, we'll come up with an acceptable custody agreement so that we each have a role in our son's life."

She sounded like him, she realized. Plans and agreements. Not the pain in her heart, or the weakness there. Maybe she should confess it all to her mother, but the idea made her feel far too vulnerable.

"You know I hesitate to tell you what to do, Bri. It's your life. Your choices. It's none of my business how you and Lorenzo decide to raise Gio."

Brianna nodded. Her parents had been lifesavers. Rocks. But they had always been very careful when it came to advice. They had been raised by difficult and overinvolved parents and had endeavored to be the opposite for Brianna.

But Brianna could *feel* her mother's disapproval. In a way she never really had before. Even when Brianna had announced she was pregnant and the father wouldn't be involved, her parents had just given her quiet support.

Never disapproval.

Until now.

Brianna turned to face her mother, determined to be strong. "But you have something to say about this decision?"

Mom took a deep breath, slowly let it out as she brushed a hand over Gio's hair. "Lorenzo is a generous man, a good father to Gio, kind to you. It's very clear you both have feelings for one another, so I'm failing to understand this insistence that you remain apart."

It felt like an unexpected betrayal. Even though her mother didn't know everything, and would likely change her mind if she did, Brianna had not expected this. She had expected what she'd always gotten from her parents. Unconditional support.

"The problem is…complicated. Lorenzo and I are complicated."

"Life is complicated. I think it's very clear he has feelings for you, Bri. The way he looks at you. *Anyone* can see it."

"A look doesn't mean much, Mother."

"Maybe not, but don't you owe it to Gio to try? To stay here and see what you and Lorenzo might be able to build. As a family. Lorenzo clearly has a very good idea of what family means. Saverina was telling us about all the brothers and sisters he raised. He's a good man, Brianna."

"I'm very well aware."

"Then why would you go home? Why put Gio through custody arrangements? Why put yourself through that? I want to support you, Bri. I always want to support you, but I'm just lost here. Help me understand."

Understand. What was there to understand? She supposed last night was the best example of why she couldn't stay. He couldn't fathom marrying *her*. He didn't understand...anything.

*Then shouldn't you want to stay and teach him?*

But how did you protect yourself and teach a brick wall?

"He wants to marry someone else," Brianna said, turning back to the window and staring at one of the trees outside sway in the wind. "He took a *date* to that art show." She tried not to let that hurt throb in her voice. "He... I know he has feelings for me. I do *know* that, but he doesn't believe in love. He thinks it's a lie. A fairy tale. I don't know why, when he has so much love to give, but I have not been able to get through to him, and I have made some bad decisions in the process. It's best for me and Gio if there's more...separation. If I'm not throwing myself against a brick wall." Did sex count as throwing herself against a brick wall? It sure felt like it.

"So you told him you love him?" Mom asked.

Brianna thought back to every interaction. She chewed on her bottom lip. "Not in so many words, but he knows."

Helene pressed her lips together. More uncharacteristic disapproval. "Perhaps you should tell him."

"You don't understand."

"No, I'm sure I don't. And I don't need to. Your relationship gets to be your own, but you've always been a very…self-contained type of person."

Brianna looked at her mother, surprised this was the corner more hurt was coming from. "What does that mean?"

"It's not a criticism, Bri. It's just… I could see where there might be some room for confusion. Have you told him, bluntly, how you feel? What you want?"

Brianna felt a somewhat hysterical laugh bubble up inside of her. Didn't sex at a party say enough? "He knows," she repeated. She had told him she wanted a relationship built on love. Wasn't that clear enough?

"Are you *sure*?"

Brianna was sure. *Almost* sure anyway. Maybe she hadn't told him she wanted *him* to be the loving relationship, but why would he tell her love was a lie if he didn't know she loved him?

Unless… Unless he was worried about *his* love for her, not hers for him. Unless all of his thoughts and fears when it came to love had very little to do with *her* love… and everything to do with his.

Maybe…maybe if he knew, maybe if she assured him that she loved him, it might help him get over his reticence.

*Don't be an idiot, Brianna.*

"Men are not always the most adept at understanding

emotions and feelings," Mom continued. "Sometimes you think you've been very clear, but they're still in the dark. The things I've had to explain to your father over the years." She rolled her eyes. "Lorenzo is quite adept in many areas, but perhaps he needs some help and some more directness in interpersonal relationships."

It sounded so…rational. So correct. She *knew* she was letting herself get her hopes up when she shouldn't, but this was her mother. Helene Andersen was a model of clear thinking and good decision-making. Shouldn't that mean Brianna should listen to her? She turned from the window and looked at her mother.

It made her feel so vulnerable it hurt. To believe any of this could be true. But her mother held Gio and looked so…in control. Like she knew what she was doing.

"Do you… Do you really think so?" Brianna managed to ask.

Helene took a long moment to answer. "Bri. I can't promise you that he will behave in the way you might want. I can't promise you his feelings. But I can promise you it's better to try than not. It's not…quite the same. Family love. Romantic love. But when I made the decision to cut things off with my family, it was because I knew I had tried *every* avenue. Any pain I feel over that loss is…grief, not guilt. Because *I* gave it my all. At the end of the day, you can't control Lorenzo, make him think or feel what you want, but it's better to give it your all and fail and grieve that, than spend your life wondering and feel guilt or regret."

Brianna wasn't sure she believed that. Wondering left…avenues. Mental gymnastics. Baring everything could be the definitive end, and wouldn't that hurt worse than the possibility?

But her mother was looking at her expectantly, holding a little boy who looked so much like his father, who *deserved* a father—*his* father in his life. Maybe... Maybe she was too scared to do it for herself, but she should do it for Gio. For Lorenzo.

"I guess... I guess I should go talk to him."

Mom smiled broadly and Brianna used that as courage. She went back to her room and got dressed and practiced what she would say.

*Lorenzo, I know you think love is a lie, but I love you. I have since the beginning. I think we should try to make something work. Can't you at least try?*

Well, that made her want to throw up. It sounded so much like...begging. And she wouldn't beg. She had to have *some* pride, didn't she?

*Does pride matter to your son?*

Someday it would. Someday he would be old enough to look at his parents and understand the complicated world around them. Brianna wanted Gio to grow up thinking she was a good person, a good example. She wanted Gio to feel the same way about her that she felt about her parents.

Could she be that if she kept throwing herself at his father...and failing?

She looked at herself in the mirror. She couldn't hide the effects of her lack of sleep. She couldn't hide anything if she was going to go tell him she *loved him* and wanted a chance. She would be the pathetic character in the situation if he kicked her to the curb. The sad little girl begging for crumbs where there were none to be had.

But she...she *did* believe he loved her. Or cared for her at least. He wouldn't behave the way he did if he didn't have *some* feelings for her. Was it really so pathetic to be up-front and honest with him and demand the same?

No, it didn't have to be pathetic. Not if she kept her wits about her.

*And when have you done that when it came to Lorenzo?*

Wasn't there some saying about insanity being behaving the same way over and over again and expecting different results?

But if she could get through to him... Wasn't it possible that she got through his walls, his plans, his *love is a lie*, and get to the heart of the matter? Even if it wasn't love on his part, if they could be honest with one another, maybe that was the actual answer. Maybe that would take away their inability to resist a physical relationship.

She moved out into the hallway because spending any more time getting ready was just going to continue her roundabout thoughts. She needed to take action. Decisive action.

She shouldn't get her hopes up. With her luck she'd end up saying nothing and having sex with him in a closet or something. Then he'd tell her he had a plane ready for her to return to New Jersey.

She huffed out a bitter little laugh. Why was she doing this?

But as she stepped into his office, she knew *why*.

She loved him.

Lorenzo was holding a young girl who didn't look any older than Gio and speaking to a man who could have been his twin. He had a broad smile on his face. This was the man she'd fallen in love with. This was the man she wanted.

But when he noticed her there, everything changed. Stiffened. But he acknowledged her, bidding her forward.

"Brianna, this is my brother Stefano."

Stefano held out a hand and she shook it. His smile was wide and easy. "My wife had to take the baby up for a diaper change, but she's eager to meet you and Gio."

"We're eager to meet you all as well," Brianna managed with a smile. It wasn't a lie. She wanted Gio to have all this. To look around and see people who looked like him, who shared his blood, who loved him because they were connected by bonds that could only be broken if you chose to break them. Aunts, uncles, cousins. She wanted it *all* for her son.

"Well, I'll apologize in advance. You get us all together and it can be overwhelming, but I can assure you my wife and I have done a lot of work to train everyone not to inundate the children with attention if they aren't having it." He took the girl from Lorenzo as if to demonstrate. "Which is why this one needs a little nap before the rest of the troops arrive. I'll be back down for the eleven o'clock conference call, Lorenzo."

Lorenzo nodded and said nothing as Stefano took the shy little girl out of the room. And closed the door behind him.

Which was for the best. This was a very private conversation and it looked like privacy might be on the premium once the rest of the family arrived. But Stefano had also mentioned a conference call. It *was* a workday, she supposed. She just wasn't sure how much that mattered to a billionaire. "Do you have a few moments to talk?"

Lorenzo pointed to a chair in front of this desk. "Yes, I was actually going to request your presence once I was done with Stefano."

He spoke very carefully, but he didn't look like himself. He looked…tired. Like perhaps he too had struggled to sleep. Had he thought of what they'd said?

Or what they'd done?

Brianna tried to think of neither, but the dark room at the party loomed large in her head. She had begged him last night. *Begged.* Her cheeks had to be red as tomatoes at this point because it all replayed in her head like an erotic movie.

But he did not smile charmingly. He did not point it out. He stood there. Stiffly. Businessman Lorenzo Parisi, nothing else.

"I have come up with an alternative plan to you returning to New Jersey," he said, clasping his hands behind his back and moving to stand behind his desk. Like they were in a business meeting. Or she was an employee and he was about to fire her.

She was here, trying to spell her feelings out for him— for the first time—and he was…planning. Plotting. Controlling. She wanted to roll her eyes, but she tried to hold on to some patience. He didn't know what she wanted to say.

"I think we should talk before you offer any…plans." Like he just got to make the plan and she'd jump to it.

He shook his head. "No. I've made the plans. This is what we'll do."

The man could be such a tyrant. "Lorenzo, my God." She was about to get up, whirl away, march off, pack a bag and *never* look back.

*Except he's the father of your child and you don't get to just run away like he did before.*

She took a deep, settling breath and focused on what she'd come here to say. "I want to discuss—"

"We will marry."

She thought maybe she blacked out for a minute and hallucinated those words. Just yesterday he had talked about marrying someone else. Just last night he'd been on the same page about her going home. "Excuse me?"

"As much as I would like to grant you your space, after calming down and giving it some thought, I realized I simply cannot live with Gio so far away. I have missed too much already. I know you won't leave him, nor should you. He should have both mother and father within reach at all times."

"What does this have to do with getting *married*?" Brianna asked, pinching the inside of her arm to make certain she wasn't having some kind of bizarre fever dream.

But he stood behind his desk, looking remote and determined, even with the exhaustion evident on his gorgeous face. "You did not care for the idea of me marrying someone else, so *we* will marry. We will find a way to very carefully divide our lives, but we will both live on this property so we both might be in our son's life."

It was what she wanted. Sort of. But she thought of last night. Even if he didn't marry someone else, they weren't on the same page. The only thing they agreed on was Gio. And she could live like that, but not on his property. Not *married*.

"We will be married in name only," he said, fully driving that point home. "We will live separate lives on the same piece of property. We will not engage in relationships with anyone else, so there will be no jealousy. We will not be alone with one another so there will be no...temptation. Your parents and my siblings will act as buffers."

It wasn't that it sounded so terrible, it was just that she didn't understand where this was coming from. She didn't understand how he thought he could just make pronouncements like that. "And we have to marry for this ridiculous plan?"

"I will need to be married at some point in the next few years for optics' sake. If it bothers you that it might be someone else, it might as well be you."

*It might as well be you.*

Ouch.

Brianna scrubbed her hands over her face, trying to make some sense of this man. Some sense of her feelings for him when he was clearly…delusional. At best.

"How can you stand there with a straight face and say we will be separate, have no relationships, and there will be no jealousy?"

"Because it is what I've decided. Because it is the best course of action."

"Great. We're *people*, Lorenzo. People grow, change, *feel*. They don't always choose the best course of action, as we've demonstrated the past week. Because making the right choice always is…hard. Because *always* choosing the best course of action is a little bit soulless."

He waved a hand, as if dismissing it all. "People should make a conscious effort to be better than all that."

For a moment she simply sat in the chair and stared up at him. He was serious. He truly believed all it took was an *effort*. As if last night could have been avoided if they had better *effort*.

She got to her feet, needing to do something or she might simply explode. So she began to pace. "I cannot fathom why I am so desperately in love with you when you are the densest man alive." That wasn't exactly how she'd meant to tell him, to say the words. He had to know, but this was the directness her mother had spoken of.

"Love is a—"

"Yes, you think it's a lie. A fairy tale. I get it." She waved a hand in a broad gesture as she turned and paced toward him. "Well, no, I don't. Because you love your son, and so quickly. You love your sister, your brother, your niece and so obviously that it's there on your face when you're in the same room with them. I suppose you had some bad experience with romantic love. Funny enough, so did I. I wish you leaving me the way you did had cured me of the fantasy of it all like your experience did, but alas."

He stood there, very still, but there was something in his eyes. That flash of pain. Whatever it was he kept well hidden and buried. Whatever it was that made love a lie in his mind.

She had never asked, she realized. Her mother had urged her to be direct and Brianna hadn't been cognizant of just how indirect she'd been. She had tried to know him before, but it had not been direct questions. It had been careful, roundabout conversations.

Little had changed since he'd been back in her life. The one direct question she'd asked him, about why he'd broken up with her, had gone unanswered. She'd let it.

Now she realized that she needed to know what he held back. And that meant she had to be brave enough to ask rather than live in fear. Fear of how he'd react to her poking her nose in it. Of what it might be. Of how it might hurt *her*.

Was this love if she didn't have the courage or strength to ask? To continue asking until she got true answers?

"You will stay," he said, again. His plans, always the answer. "We will marry. We can wait a year or two if you'd rather, but we *will* marry. And we will keep our distance. I do not believe introducing the idea of 'love' into our marriage will do anything except hurt Gio."

She crossed to him, trying to be brave enough and sure enough to face down whatever this was. She put her hands on his chest and looked up at him. "*Why* do you think that?"

He looked down at her, icy and remote. But underneath that was *something*. If only she had the strength, the determination to reach it. So far they both had been very good at running away from those sore spots.

Something had to change. She looked up at him, at that cool, remote facade he worked so hard at. She had to be the one brave enough to challenge him. To work on herself to get through to him.

If she wanted *more*, if she wanted *love*, she couldn't change *him*. But she could try to deal with *herself* in order to get through to him.

"Tell me, Lorenzo. What hurt you? What made it so impossible for you to believe in love when it comes to *me*. Because I know you love Gio. I know you love your sister. Your brother. Your niece. It's evident in everything you do, every second you're with them. And I know…" For a moment, her voice faltered, but she thought of their son. Everything he deserved. A father who worked through his demons was one of them. A mother strong enough to face down uncomfortable truths was another. "I know you care for me in *some* way. So what is the lie?"

She expected *something* from him, and she supposed that was her first mistake. Thinking she could get past whatever walls he'd built.

"This is not open for discussion, Brianna. I have made the plan. We will marry. We will lead separate lives.

That's final." He stepped away from her. Like she was *dismissed*.

She wanted to keep being strong. She wanted to believe her mother was right and she just hadn't found the words. But this was almost as demoralizing as last night. It didn't matter if he loved her if he refused to acknowledge it. She couldn't *change* him, she knew this.

So why was she trying?

"You won't bend, even a little? Even for your son?"

"Everything I do is for my son."

"Well, me too, Lorenzo. So my answer is no. No. I won't do it."

He scowled at her. "I do not understand how you could refuse me. This will solve all our problems."

"No, it won't. You can't seem to grasp *my* problem. It isn't that I love you. I don't mind loving you. Maybe if I thought you didn't love me back, that would be more uncomfortable. I don't know. But it's impossible because you do love me."

"Love, love, love!" he muttered. "Why is this all anyone speaks of?"

"Because it's important? It makes life meaningful? You love so many. Why do you refuse to accept that you love me? What is so wrong with who I am? What I am?"

For a moment, there was something in his expression. A softness and a pain that she thought meant she'd gotten through to him. But he didn't speak.

He also didn't leave.

So she pressed on no matter how much it hurt. Because she loved him. She wanted him to accept that love as much for herself as she did for him. She could make him happy. They could *be* a happy family if he'd just let her in. "I don't understand what you're afraid of. But I understand you're afraid. Tell me—"

"I am not afraid of anything. Every challenge in my life I have met head-on and will continue to do so. You have no choice in this matter, Brianna. I am in charge."

In charge? No, she didn't think so. She'd had enough. "Why?"

For a moment, his mouth opened and no sound at all came out. Like he couldn't *fathom* the question, let alone an answer to it. "What…do you mean?"

"What exactly are you threatening me with to keep me in line, to assert you're in charge? Because you aren't the president of me. Or the CEO. You can't just make decrees and expect me to follow them. We're just two random people in the world. So why are you in charge? How are you going to assert this? Are you going to fire me? Well, I'm not your employee. Are you threatening me for custody? I don't think you are. Maybe you want to kill me off? That would be the simplest way."

His jaw clenched. "Brianna." So disapprovingly.

"You're so used to everyone jumping to do your bidding, but I cannot go against my best interests. I *love* you. I will do a lot of things to put Gio first. I would sacrifice almost anything for him. But I can't sacrifice myself— every happiness. If I did, he would feel it."

"He will have us both. Every privilege and opportunity afforded to him. He will have family. That is what matters."

"Those things *do* matter. But so do I. And so do you. Being parents doesn't mean we have to be robots, sacrificing every emotion for our child. We get to be human." Maybe it wasn't romantic love that had made him bitter. His parents were dead, so she hadn't given much thought to them, but maybe they were responsible for what he thought of love. "What did your parents do that hurt you so much? Perhaps I should ask your sister. Maybe she'd be more forthcoming."

*That* certainly got through to him, but he didn't warn her off. Didn't divulge any family secrets. He just stood there, looking like a sailor lost at sea in a storm. She wished she could reach out and be his anchor.

But he'd have to choose it first.

"You may ask Saverina whatever you wish. You may find out every dirty family secret. Be my guest, Brianna," he said, so coldly she shivered. "But I will not change my mind, and if you wish that to be a threat, so be it."

Then he stormed out of the office, leaving her no better than she'd been when she entered. Just more hurt.

But she had tried. Her mother was right. If she had left without trying, there would have been guilt. She would have had regrets.

Now she could return to New Jersey free of all that.

If only she could be free of loving him and hurting for him.

# CHAPTER FIFTEEN

LORENZO SAT AT the long dining room table surrounded by his family. His *entire* family. Somehow they had managed to all come this weekend despite the fact that every Christmas was a circus act trying to get everyone home at the same time.

Suspicious.

But nothing was more suspicious than Brianna interacting with his siblings. Smiling and laughing along with them, like she hadn't come to his office earlier and dropped all sorts of bombs.

Like she was *enjoying* herself.

And why shouldn't she be? He'd taken care of everything, hadn't he? He'd spent his afternoon neutralizing another round of stories about Brianna and Gio planted by Dante. He'd moved forward with his plans to renovate the north end of the estate to outfit Brianna and her parents and build an art studio.

She remained safe and taken care of because of *him*. She would not enjoy the same back in New Jersey.

She should be thanking him. She should be following all his plans to the letter with nothing but gratitude. Because that would be best. For *everyone*. He always did what was best for everyone. Because if he didn't…

Brianna wasn't Rocca. He'd never let her be put in a position where she had to sacrifice so much.

*Rocca should be here.*

It was his failure she wasn't.

But he hadn't failed again. He was surrounded by evidence of all he'd done. The way every step from that mistake, that loss, had been exactly the right one.

He looked around the table. So many voices. Laughter, little arguments, children's meltdowns. It was the sound of a job well done. There weren't loud, angry fights. No one here had to worry about money. No one had to sell themselves for a scrap of bread. No one here had to lose themselves in a haze of drugs in order to deal with the weight of the things they'd done to survive, to earn a dollop of praise.

Because *Lorenzo* had stepped in. Unlike their useless father. *He* would have let them starve. *He* would have let them all be ruined.

Lorenzo refused.

So he should be able to enjoy it, his success, but he couldn't, because Brianna sat shoulder to shoulder with Saverina and Isa, Stefano's wife, discussing *something*. Meanwhile, Gio had voluntarily climbed into Lorenzo's lap and was playing a kind of peekaboo game with Karl, Valentine's partner, the two of them the last to arrive, coming all the way from Germany.

Why had Saverina done this to him? The whole evening was interminable. And he struggled to stick with any conversation because his gaze kept traveling to Brianna. Thinking over what she'd said in his office. What she'd said last night.

Watching the way she fit right in. Her and Gio, even

her parents. They didn't feel like a little American island, out of place in the midst of his loud, opinionated family.

It all fit.

And Brianna loved him.

He had known she cared for him. He had been afraid she loved him—well, no. Not afraid. That wasn't the right word. *Concerned*. But her saying the words this morning… It shouldn't change anything. The words weren't a surprise.

So why did he feel rocked to his core?

*"I love you. I will do a lot of things to put Gio first. I would sacrifice almost anything for him. But I can't sacrifice myself—every happiness. If I did, he would feel it."*

Those words haunted him. On a constant loop.

*If I did, he would feel it.*

As if sacrifice, as if control and plans would *hurt* Gio, when everything he was putting in place was to protect Gio. Just as he'd done for all his siblings over the years he'd finally been in control.

Brianna came over to him, and she didn't meet his gaze. She looked at their son.

"I better put this one to B-E-D," Brianna said, holding her arms out to Gio. The boy went easily, but he smiled at Lorenzo as he did. He was warming up. Step by step. And Lorenzo knew that time would only strengthen their bond. Gio would never remember Lorenzo had missed out on him as an infant.

Gio would only know his constant presence. Because it *would* be constant. No matter what Brianna said *no* to.

"Say good night to Dada," Brianna said to Gio.

"Night, Da."

It was the first time Gio had actually said *Da*. The boy clearly didn't feel the weight of that first, but Lorenzo did. And when he lifted his gaze to Brianna, he knew she did as well. It would be a moment that would stick in his memory for all time.

Gio in his mother's arms. Lorenzo's family chattering around them. And one simple word. *Da.*

Brianna turned away quickly, Gio in her arms, her parents trailing after her. Leaving him to face down his family. The exit of the Americans seeming to put everyone's attention squarely on *him*.

"Saverina says you're in love with her," Valentine offered, rather loudly, considering the Andersens had only *just* left the room.

Lorenzo skewered him with a look.

"I heard that she loves him right back," Stefano offered.

"Then why is she still planning to leave?" Saverina demanded. "What is *wrong* with you?"

"As lovely as this little family reunion is, without the excuse of Christmas, I can't imagine why I'd put up with it." He tried to get up, but Accursia, who sat on his other side, put her hand over his.

"Because we're your family and we care about you, Lorenzo."

"You're desperately in love with her," Isa said, holding her dozing baby in one arm and the glass of wine she sipped from in the other hand. "It's obvious to anyone with eyes."

He had missed that baby stage with Gio. It hurt, even knowing he would never let Gio out of his life again. That year without the boy would always hurt.

Because that was what love did. Crawled into all your weak spots and *hurt*. It worked when it was your family, people in your care, because you could stop all that hurt with sacrifice. With careful planning and important walls for distance.

"I am never desperate, I assure you. Everyone speaks of love as if it is some great thing, but the only thing love does is destroy. That is all *I* have ever seen. A good marriage is not based on *love*, it is based on mutual understanding."

"Are you insinuating my husband doesn't love me?" his sister-in-law asked, with such an open, innocent expression on her face only experience told him she was needling him.

He spared her a quelling glance, but she was clearly unmoved. He moved his gaze to Stefano, but Stefano had put an arm around Isa and looked as disapproving as his wife did.

"This is *my* life," Lorenzo reminded his family.

"But you're mucking it up," Saverina insisted with a certainty Lorenzo could only chalk up to youth and a lack of experience. She continued on as if *she* knew all. "And every time we've just about mucked up our own lives, you've stepped in to correct course. So, guess what? We're all stepping in to correct *your* course."

"It's kind of comforting," Valentine said, studying the wine in his glass. "That you *can* need correction. You aren't *so* perfect."

Lorenzo scowled even deeper at his brother. "All right. If I am not perfect, and you are all so old and wise now, what should I do?"

"I know what you shouldn't do," Stefano offered. "Demand a loveless marriage. Declare plans like a general giving orders to a soldier."

Isa and Saverina's eyes widened as they stared at him. "Is that what he did?"

Stefano nodded as Lorenzo fumed. "How do you know anything of what I've done?"

Stefano shrugged, wholly unconcerned. "I eavesdropped."

This time Lorenzo did stand, pulling his hand out from Accursia's. "You have crossed a line, brother." To think all that Brianna had said might have been listened to. That they might all know...

"Yes. I wonder where I might have learned to do that."

Lorenzo shook his head. "I have raised all of you. Protected you. Afforded you every opportunity. And this is how you repay me? Come here without warning, criticize my every choice, eavesdrop and gang up on me? Very well. Clearly I have failed."

"Oh, don't be such a martyr," Saverina said. Then, when he glared at her, she rolled her eyes and even faked a yawn.

He made a move for the exit, but Saverina stepped in front of it. Valentine blocked the other exit.

"No running away today because you didn't get to control the situation," Stefano said. As if he had any right. "Time to face up to some very important facts."

"We're all grown up," Saverina said, working in tandem with Stefano from the opposite end of the room. "It doesn't mean we might never need you, but not the way we once did. Now you're free. Do you really want to spend that freedom like some kind of robot monk when you have a nice, smart woman with a backbone, far as I can see, who shares a son with you and *loves* you?"

"None of you remember what love does?" He looked at Stefano and Valentine, because though he'd tried to shelter them, they were the closest in age and likely knew as much as he did. Then there was Saverina, who'd known more than he wanted her to. Maybe they all did.

But Stefano and Valentine were standing there, both with partners. Stefano with children. A family. Love.

How could they bear it?

"I don't blame *love* for what happened to Mother, Lorenzo," Stefano said, all of his nonchalant defiance gone. In its place was a calm if sad reverence. "Real love does not demand sacrifice. Real love is not what we witnessed—the desperate need to please someone else."

Lorenzo watched as Isa put her free hand on Stefano's arm. A simple, silent comfort. "Some relationships are toxic, Lorenzo," she said, with something warm in her eyes that felt too much like pity. "Some people make choices because they aren't mature enough to handle their consequences, or because they were traumatized and haven't dealt with it, or any number of other reasons. From everything Stefano told me—"

"You told her?"

"She is my wife. I've told her everything about our childhood. It is how I work through those traumas."

"Have you told Brianna anything of Mother? Of Rocca?" Saverina asked gently.

"Why would I?"

"So she could understand. So you could deal with it. You can put us all in our little boxes. You can put your memories in some sort of lockbox under eighteen kilometers of denial, but it's still *there*. And no amount of planning or control changes the past."

"That is why we focus on the future."

"Yes," Stefano agreed. "But *your* future. Not plotting out Brianna's or Gio's, but actually thinking about what *you* want."

"I am a *billionaire*. Everyone in my care is well taken care of. What more could I want?"

"That's a question only you can answer," Stefano said. Very quietly.

But it echoed like thunder inside of Lorenzo. Especially as everyone began to get up. His siblings walked by, brushed kisses across his cheek, patted him on the back, but they all filed out and left him alone. The last thing said: *That's a question only you can answer.*

He wasn't sure how long he stood in the dining room. Alone. When he finally convinced himself to leave, he knew he should go to his office. Check on the moves Dante was making. Get to work on the renovations, the studio building—because Brianna wasn't leaving. He refused to let her.

*So why are you in charge? How are you going to assert this?*

He didn't know yet, but he'd find a way.

Still, when he walked by his office he didn't stop. He walked out the back of the house and into the gardens. He hadn't known she'd be here.

Had he?

But she was sitting on a little bench he'd had installed that he sometimes sat on when he needed air and solitude. The trees weren't in bloom this time of year and it was too chilly for her to be out here.

But somehow he'd known she would need air after all that, just as he did.

She must have heard him, because she turned. He watched her as she straightened her shoulders, lifted her chin. As she braced herself for dealing with him.

Why had he come? He knew he would not get through to her yet. He had no plan. No threats or entreaties. Only this black, roiling thing inside of him that threatened to have him begging at her feet.

Because that was the kind of behavior love brought out in a person. Desperation. Pathetic, destructive needs. Hers or his, it did not matter.

"Your family is lovely."

"That is not the word I would use in this moment."

Her mouth curved ever so slightly. Then she sighed. "Well, I'm very tired. I should get to bed." She stood, but he stopped her.

He wanted to ask her what he should want. He wanted her to lead him. It was unacceptable, but he couldn't let her arm go. He could only stand here, blocking her exit, holding on to her. Her soft, chilled skin under his fingers. He couldn't resist drawing his hand up her arm, pulling her closer.

She even went, without censure or resistance. Until he'd pulled her to his chest. Where she belonged.

She looked at him. He'd expected a flash of anger or something, but all he saw was a grim kind of exhaustion. "We can do this again, Lorenzo. God knows we'll enjoy it." Tears shone in her eyes. "But it won't change anything. Is that what you want?"

Why was everyone suddenly so concerned with what he wanted? "You want to know what I want?" He dropped her arm and staggered away from her, everything inside of him threatening to erupt. He strode away, then back and pointed at her. "I want you to listen to reason. To do as I say."

"To think as you think? To feel as you feel?" she returned, again sounding more tired than frustrated.

*He* was frustrated. "Yes!"

"I wish I could. It would make things so easy, wouldn't it? If I could be your little lap dog, but I am not."

Lap dog. It brought up all those unpleasant memories. What his mother had twisted herself into. All for love. Because his father had never been moved. By his mother's pleas. By her sacrifices. He'd never thanked her. He'd only found more blame.

*That* was love.

"You think you understand, but you do not. You should trust me on this. I only seek to do what is right for all of us. You cannot defy me on this. I cannot let you."

"Why did you come out here, Lorenzo? To say the same things? To have sex again?" She shook her head, but she didn't move away. "Something has to give. If it cannot be you, if you cannot love me, if you cannot give me a *chance* for something real, then it will be me. Leaving. It is the only way *I* know how to sustain this. I love you, but—"

"You think… You think you love me. That I love you. You think this can lead somewhere, but I know what love does."

She looked up at him, those tears swimming in her eyes. The same from this morning. The same entreaty. She even reached out and clutched him. And he had his sisters' and brothers' words ringing in his ears. About love and trauma and responsibility. About wants. About life—lives they'd all gone out and built…while he'd built an empire. For them.

"Lorenzo, tell me. Tell me what you think love does."

"It breaks everything!" It was a shout, tinged with all the pain and then it was as if some dam broke. The dam he'd built up himself, with every piece of responsibility, control and grim determination.

Now it was in pieces and the words rushed out. "My mother loved my father. She was desperate to please him. She would have done anything for him, and it never mattered. You cannot love away destruction. You will get there eventually, or I will, and the hurt we will cause in our wake will be...catastrophic. If you or I give in to it, we will destroy everything."

"What did your mother do, Lorenzo?"

He stood there, breath coming in short pants, but somehow Brianna maneuvered him back to the bench, into a sitting position. She even slid next to him, taking his hand into hers and settling it on her lap while her other arm came around his shoulders.

"Tell me, Lorenzo. Tell me everything."

He shouldn't. Knew there was no point, no outcome that changed the things he'd seen, the things he'd survived. But the dam was gone, and so the story poured out. "We were very poor. I don't remember anything else. Every time another child came along, food on the table got more scarce. Arguments about work, money. My father couldn't keep a job. He could never stand anyone telling him what to do."

Brianna nodded, sitting there next to him. Warmth on a cool night as her hand rubbed up and down his arm.

"I'm not sure when it started. She didn't want to do it. I know she didn't. But my mother would have done anything to make my father happy. Yes, to put food on the table for us, but she could have demanded *he* do something. She wouldn't though. He was her world, and she wanted to serve him. She loved him so much. I can't count the times I heard her crying over how much she loved this worthless man. She didn't want to, and he shouldn't have let her."

"What did she do?" Brianna asked gently.

"She got a job where she worked at night. I believed this for a very long time. That she was off being a waitress somewhere. That it was all on the up-and-up. Even as she…became less and less herself. But I suppose we all believed it because we wanted to. Because it brought money in. We were scraping by. Rocca and I acted as parents. Father drank. Mother became more…erratic. Then she got pregnant with Saverina and had to stop working her mysterious night job."

Lorenzo knew he should stop there. It was enough. Surely she understood now, but the words continued. "Father said Rocca could take Mother's place at her job until Mother was back on her feet. Rocca was only fourteen. I insisted I should do it, but Father said it was only women's work. So I kept my job at the butcher shop during the day. Watched the children at night. Rocca helped with the children at day and worked at night. While my mother loved our father and he did *nothing*."

"You must be so proud, Lorenzo," Brianna said. "So many sacrifices, and those children you raised are in your home. Responsible adults. Good people. Who love you."

"Not Rocca." Was that his voice? So ragged. So weak? But these were words he'd never spoken. A story he'd never stitched together for anyone but himself. And it was something about that, about Rocca's memory, that seemed to insist he finish it.

"She was my twin sister. We were more parents to everyone than our own, but… She began to act like Mother. More erratic. Depressive episodes. Mother went back to work and I suggested Rocca not work there anymore, but Father insisted. Still… I didn't know."

"What didn't you know?"

He sucked in a breath. It shook all the way out. "They were prostitutes."

Brianna's grip on him tightened, but she said nothing. Only held him there. As though he weren't to be blamed for all this. She didn't speak. Not to argue, not to offer platitudes. Not to be so shocked and horrified he felt the need to hide it all away again.

She simply sat there. Holding his hand. Waiting. As if… As if, as Isa and Stefano said, talking about these secrets, these horrors could help a person *work through them*. Understand them.

And it was that dinner tonight, and this woman here, who finally dragged the words out of him. Just by being here. Just by loving.

"I began to find out things…later. A client introduced Mother to drugs at some point, and the…price for her went down. Eventually it was the drugs. She died of an accidental overdose, but I still did not know. I should have. Rocca continued on. She never told me a thing. But like Mother, she became more erratic. I told her she needed to quit this job. I would scrape together more money. I would find a way to get her another that didn't affect her so. At first, she refused, but then… After Father died, it was as if something lifted and she finally explained everything to me."

"Poor girl," Brianna murmured.

"I was so stupid. So blind. I should have seen it. I got her out of there once I understood. I tried to get her help, but she was…"

Everything in him felt ragged. He was a million jagged edges. Pain. So much pain. Because Rocca should still be here. If he'd known, if he'd had a chance to step in, she would.

Brianna stroked his hair. "Their sacrifices weren't your fault, Lorenzo. You were a boy."

"I should have said something. Stood up for her. For them both. If I was only a boy, Rocca was only a girl." Because how could he absolve himself when they had been a team? And only one of them had suffered so?

But it was as if Brianna did not see this as his weight to bear alone. Because she didn't leave him. She didn't accuse him. She just kept speaking and holding on to him.

"Here is one thing I know about you, and I think all of your family knows too. You would have. If you'd known, if you'd had the opportunity, you would have sacrificed everything for them. Your father is to blame here. *He* knew. If she told you after *he* died, he had some hold over her."

It had never occurred to Lorenzo. Maybe he'd never let it occur to him. Blame felt so much more controllable. So much stronger.

But Brianna was right, and he could no longer deny that as much as he wished he had known, could have done something, the adult in the situation had made it impossible.

"Just because you couldn't sacrifice instead of Rocca doesn't mean... My love, this is a terrible story full of tragedy, but you have done everything you could in the shadow of that tragedy. Sacrificed for your siblings. Gave them everything."

"Not Rocca."

"No. But that is on your father. You took on the role of adult because the adults would not. But why does it mean we can't love each other? We aren't your parents. Our love does not need to be like your mother's. For one, we both love each other. And you are so clearly nothing like your father."

"But I hurt you. At the party. When I brought Natalia. When I suggested I marry someone else. In that room, you cried and said you had to go home. That is my fault. That is what love does. It hurts."

"Yes," she agreed. So easily.

He looked at her because she made no sense.

"I'm still standing, Lorenzo," she said, calmly. Accepting every word as a truth when… When it wasn't. "People hurt each other. It's that whole human condition you seem to think you can escape. By making yourself everyone's…boss, father, ruler, whatever. But you can't be any of those things to me, so you have to keep me away?"

"You don't understand."

"No. I'll never understand what you went through. I won't ever pretend to. But I love you regardless. I don't need to understand to love you."

"I will ruin you. The way my father ruined my mother. If you'd just… If we make a plan, if we stay apart, if we treat it like business, we can make it okay." He knew how desperate he sounded. How afraid. All those things he'd convinced himself he wasn't. But those feelings were there in his voice. In his heart.

She shook her head. "No, Lorenzo. I can't do that. I wasn't there. I didn't know your parents. I don't know what either of them went through, what they were thinking when they did the things they did. Maybe I'd do the same thing in their position, but I am not in their position. Neither are you. We have the power to make our own choices. Some of them will be mistakes. But loving you, even when it hurt, even when you walked away, has never been a mistake. It has given us Gio."

*Gio.* The boy he'd only known a handful of days, who already owned his heart. That Parisi face with blue eyes. A shyness that warmed into love so easily. His heart. His soul. Just as this woman who'd listened to all he'd said and...loved him through it. Saw him in the middle of all that hurt.

She had not walked away. She had not laid blame. She still spoke of love as if... As if his mother's behavior was her own choice, her own feelings. As if his father's indifference and blame weren't stamped into Lorenzo's bones.

As if the hurt he'd caused her was the "human condition," to be dealt with and forgiven. Not a poison that would ruin them all.

"I know you would give Gio everything," Brianna continued. "Just as you've given your siblings everything. You are not your father and never have been. You have always put the people you love first. But it must be a balance, Lorenzo. You must give yourself the space to also have *your* wants and needs met. Giving yourself over to your sacrifices and your business doesn't make you any different than your mother if you do not take care of yourself along with it."

This hurt. *The human condition.* But again, Brianna did not leave. She did not drop the accusation and withdraw. She loved him through it.

Stefano had told him only he could decide what he wanted. And it wasn't that he didn't know. Of course he wanted Brianna. And not just because it would keep Gio close, but because she had always been the sunshine in his dark. Ever since he'd first laid eyes on her.

But he was so *afraid.* Not concerned, no. Terrified. Of what love had done to his mother. Of the utter destruction wrought, not just on his parents, but on Rocca.

Destruction. That had come from two damaged people. A love that had blotted out responsibility and the love his mother should have had for her children. Because there had been none of the balance Brianna spoke of. Only a kind of selfishness.

One neither he nor Brianna possessed. No matter how scared he was, he believed Brianna. Standing here in his garden, pouring her light into him.

"I've never been poor," she continued. "So I won't trivialize how important money can be, but our son deserves a father who isn't afraid of love. Couldn't you at least try to give him that?"

It was a million moments coalescing. Hurtful ones and healing ones. Saverina's voice asking him, *"If I was in your position, or Brianna's...what would you want for me?"*

The same as he wanted for Gio. For Brianna. For everyone...

*That's a question only you can answer.*

What did he want out of this life? The courage to give his son everything. Brianna had said that she could not sacrifice her happiness because Gio would be touched by that. She was right. Giving Gio *everything* meant also... allowing himself balance. Love. Light.

"I fell in love with you the moment I saw you, Brianna. More every moment we spent together. Nothing has ever terrified me more."

She reached out, cupped his cheek with her chilled hand. "You dazzled me. And underneath all that dazzle was a man I could not help but love. It never went away, Lorenzo. Even when I wanted it to. This doesn't have to destroy us."

"But what if—"

"We can't what-if ourselves out of this. There are too many. Those first days as a mother, my entire head was what-ifs. So many things could have gone wrong, but my mother gave me advice I have held on to ever since. Any person can only do their best with what they are given, and that best is cushioned by love."

Lorenzo didn't want it to make sense. Didn't want to believe it was enough, but why... Why was he so bound and determined to make things harder on himself?

*Rocca took her own life, so you cannot have anything for yourself?*

Saverina had said that to him, and he had spent the past day trying to deny it. Desperate to ignore it. But it was true. His entire life since he'd lost his sister had been punishment. Because he'd loved her, but he hadn't been able to save her.

If he looked back with an adult's maturity and experience on everything that had happened when he'd barely been an adult, he knew Brianna was right. He had done all he could.

It hurt, but it was true. Love had not been enough, but that didn't mean it was poison. Still... "I could not stand to lose you."

Her thumb brushed back and forth across his cheek. "Loss is inevitable. But I'd rather lose knowing I'd held everything I loved close, than that I'd pushed it away and never enjoyed it."

He had already missed time with Gio. Missed these two years with Brianna. If he had not, perhaps he could not have accepted her words. But the past two years had taught him that if he could dig under his fear, holding on was better than hiding.

"I love you, Brianna. I want to do that perfectly, so that you never hurt."

"I wish that were possible. But loving is enough, Lorenzo. I promise you. We can love each other *and* ourselves. Love our son so brightly that even those hurts will be cushioned by all we've given him. I'll show you. If you'll let me."

He covered her hand with his. He held her gaze. And he made a promise to her, and to himself. "I will. We will marry and—"

She shook her head, even though she didn't pull her hand from his grasp or lean away from him. "I can't marry you, Lorenzo."

Confusion swept through him. "But—"

"Not yet. But I'll stay. And we will work through… everything. Our pasts. Our hurts. Your trauma. We will build a foundation. And once the foundation is strong, we'll discuss marriage again."

Lorenzo did not argue. Perhaps she was right. Perhaps building and foundations and *working through* were the things missing when love failed so spectacularly. He would not fail at this. Not now. For Gio. For Brianna, and also, strangest of all, for himself.

Because as his siblings had tried to get through his head earlier, as Brianna had stated this morning when she'd confessed her love to him, he deserved some of his own wants as well.

"You will at least share my bedroom, Brianna."

She laughed. A bright, beautiful laugh like sunshine. She would always be his sun. She leaned into him, and they wrapped their arms around each other. "Naturally."

She made it seem like love could be an answer instead

of a fear. A hope instead of destruction. Maybe he was a fool to believe in it, but how could he not believe in her?

He would believe in her, and he would prove to her that he could do love as well as anyone. He would not be afraid. Not anymore.

And they would be married within the year. End of story.

# EPILOGUE

THE WEDDING WAS one for the ages. With a family the size of Lorenzo's it was hard not to be. Brianna and Lorenzo had agreed to let the press be involved in the reception, but the ceremony was to be all theirs.

Dante had tried over the course of the past year to plant more stories besmirching Lorenzo's reputation, but the more Lorenzo didn't care, the more it did not matter. The press got tired of trying to paint him the villain when all he ever seemed to do was work, dote on his wife and son, and refuse to ever retaliate against Dante.

Sometimes living well really was the best revenge.

And they had lived well. They had learned each other all over again. They had let their families mesh and meld and they had worked to parent Gio together. It had not always been easy, they did not always see eye to eye, but when Gio had turned two with a party full to the brim with aunts, uncles, cousins and his grandparents—just as Brianna had always wished for—Brianna had realized it was time to make things official.

Since Lorenzo proposed almost every week since that night when he'd finally confessed himself to her, she only had to wait two days, then finally surprise him with a yes.

He'd gone into wedding planning mode immediately.

Well, not *immediately*.

Now here she was in an ancient church, while Saverina and Accursia and her mother fussed over her. Right before she was to join her father and walk down the aisle, Saverina pulled her aside.

"I was wondering if you would put this on your bouquet." She held a tiny picture frame on a pin in the palm of her hand. In the frame was the picture of a teenage girl, smiling, looking so much like Lorenzo Brianna immediately knew who it was.

She blinked desperately so as not to cry and ruin her makeup. She gave Saverina a nod and Saverina attached it to the ribbon around her bouquet. They hugged, both doing their best to keep the tears at bay.

Then it was time.

She stood, her mother on one arm and her father on the other, as the doors opened. Gio stood at the end of the aisle next to his father, wearing a matching suit.

"Mama!" he called out, doing an excited little dance that had the entire church laughing, including Brianna. She walked down the aisle, and her father and mother handed her over to Lorenzo. Gio wrapped his arms around her leg before being gently coaxed by Stefano and Valentine to stand next to Lorenzo.

Brianna looked up at Lorenzo with a bright smile. His gaze swept over her, stopping once at the little picture frame in her bouquet. He took a deep, steadying breath, then lifted her hand to his mouth.

He brushed a kiss across her knuckles, reminding her of a night long ago in Florence. That had changed the entire course of her life. And had given her everything she could have ever dreamed of.

So when they said their vows, she had no doubts. Love was not the enemy.

It was the answer. Always.

* * * * *

# COMING SOON!

We really hope you enjoyed reading this book. If you're looking for more romance be sure to head to the shops when new books are available on

## Thursday 14th September

MILLS & BOON

# MILLS & BOON®

## Coming next month

### REDEEMED BY MY
### FORBIDDEN HOUSEKEEPER
Heidi Rice

My taste buds were already dancing a jig as Jessie uncovered the feast she had prepared for me.

But as my gaze devoured her lean frame disguised in the baggy T-shirt and scuffed jeans she always wore, and I noticed the flushed dewy skin of her face devoid of makeup as she straightened and grinned at me, the swell of something hot and fluid blossomed in my groin. *Again*.

The irritation twisted into resentment in my gut.

Somehow, the housekeeper I didn't even like had begun to captivate me. I was actually beginning to look forward to seeing her each day, anticipating her arrival like a lovesick teenager.

"I'm sick of always eating vegetables," I added, knowing that my anger had nothing to do with her choice of menu and everything to do with the fact I could not act on my attraction to her, even if I had wanted to.

I did not sleep with my employees. Even ones that fascinated and—*damn it*—excited me.

*Continue reading*
REDEEMED BY MY
FORBIDDEN HOUSEKEEPER
Heidi Rice

*Available next month*
www.millsandboon.co.uk

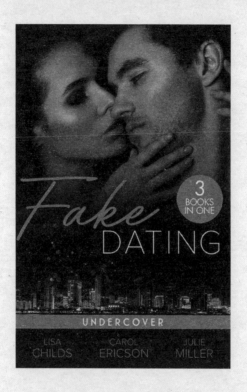

# OUT NOW!

Available at
millsandboon.co.uk

MILLS & BOON

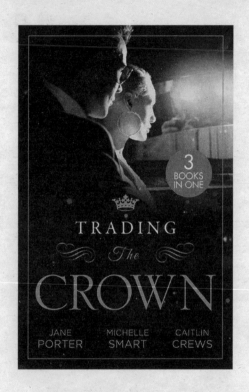

# MILLS & BOON

## THE HEART OF ROMANCE

---

## A ROMANCE FOR EVERY READER

---

**MODERN**

Prepare to be swept off your feet by sophisticated, sexy and seductive heroes, in some of the world's most glamourous and romantic locations, where power and passion collide.

**HISTORICAL**

Escape with historical heroes from time gone by. Whether your passion is for wicked Regency Rakes, muscled Vikings or rugged Highlanders, awaken the romance of the past.

**MEDICAL**

Set your pulse racing with dedicated, delectable doctors in the high-pressure world of medicine, where emotions run high and passion, comfort and love are the best medicine.

*True Love*

Celebrate true love with tender stories of heartfelt romance, from the rush of falling in love to the joy a new baby can bring, and a focus on the emotional heart of a relationship.

*Desire*

Indulge in secrets and scandal, intense drama and sizzling hot action with heroes who have it all: wealth, status, good looks…everything but the right woman.

**HEROES**

The excitement of a gripping thriller, with intense romance at its heart. Resourceful, true-to-life women and strong, fearless men face danger and desire - a killer combination!

To see which titles are coming soon, please visit

## millsandboon.co.uk/nextmonth